A RISK WORTH TAKING

As they went up on deck Anna's glossy curls caught the moonlight with a glow Phillip remembered all too well. He tried to concentrate on the star-filled heavens and the sparkling water rather than on her loveliness but the softness of her voice was every bit as seductive as her remarkable beauty.

"I envy you your freedom, Captain," she said softly. "Had I been born a man I would have chosen to go to sea. I would not have been forced to accept a future I dreaded."

The sorrow in her gaze pierced Phillip's heart with a pain so real he reached out to dispel her anguish in the only way he knew. His mouth captured hers easily, drinking deeply of her kiss as if he meant never to let her go.

"Perhaps we should avoid any further strolls in the moonlight for they are obviously too dangerous for us both," Anna whispered.

"There is no life worth living that is without risk, Anna."

His eyes held a taunting fire. She knew exactly what risk he meant and suddenly she realized whatever price she'd have to pay to know his love would be worthwhile. . . .

MORE CAPTIVATING ROMANCE FROM ZEBRA

FORBIDDEN FIRES (1295, $3.50)
by Bobbi Smith

When Ellyn Douglas rescued the handsome Union officer from the raging river, she had no choice but to surrender to the sensuous stranger as he pulled her against his hard muscular body. Forgetting they were enemies in a senseless war, they were destined to share a life of unbridled ecstasy and glorious love!

WANTON SPLENDOR (1461, $3.50)
by Bobbi Smith

Kathleen had every intention of keeping her distance from Christopher Fletcher. But in the midst of a devastating hurricane, she crept into his arms. As she felt the heat of his lean body pressed against hers, she wondered breathlessly what it would be like to kiss those cynical lips—to turn that cool arrogance to fiery passion!

LOVE'S ELUSIVE FLAME (1267, $3.75)
by Phoebe Conn

Enraptured by his ardent kisses and tantalizing caresses, golden-haired Flame had found the man of her dreams in the handsome rogue Joaquin. But if he wanted her completely she would have to be his only woman—and he had always been taken women whenever he wanted, and not one had ever refused him or pretended to try!

ECSTASY'S PARADISE (1460, $3.75)
by Phoebe Conn

Meeting the woman he was to escort to her future husband, sea captain Phillip Bradford was astounded. The Swedish beauty was the woman of his dreams, his fantasy come true. But how could he deliver her to another man's bed when he wanted her to warm his own?

Available wherever paperbacks are sold, or order direct from the Publisher. Send cover price plus 50¢ per copy for mailing and handling to Zebra Books, 475 Park Avenue South, New York, N.Y. 10016. DO NOT SEND CASH.

PHOEBE CONN
ECSTASY'S PARADISE

ZEBRA BOOKS
KENSINGTON PUBLISHING CORP.

ZEBRA BOOKS

are published by

Kensington Publishing Corp.
475 Park Avenue South
New York, N.Y. 10016

First printing: October 1984

Printed in the United States of America

Prologue

Capt. Phillip Bradford had no love for Southampton. Indeed, he had not the slightest bit of regard for any European port the *Angelina* visited but his cabin had grown oppressively confining. Leaving it hastily he strode down the gangplank eager to find some diversion to pass his last night in the British city. A dense fog had descended upon the waterfront, bringing visibility to zero and giving his footsteps a hollow ring as he made his way along the docks toward the tavern where upon occasion he'd found passably amusing companions. For a price, he thought bitterly; it was amazing how enchanting a wench could become when she knew a man was able to pay well for her favors and that he could most certainly do.

Phillip's mood was as dismal as the night but he did not slacken his brisk pace as he continued through the mist toward the faint glimmer of light which shone in the tavern's windows in the distance. Without warning two figures came out of the fog so suddenly he had no time to step aside and collided soundly with the man who was not nearly so tall and well-built as he. He was no merchant seaman, Phillip saw instantly, but a gentlemen dressed in formal attire and reeling unsteadily. He grabbed for the man's shoulders, breaking his impending fall and setting him again upon his feet. His companion came forward so swiftly the hood of her black velvet cape fell back revealing a thick tangle of curls of golden blond, surrounding her sweet features with a halo of brilliant sheen. Her long dark lashes swept her delicate brows framing an exquisite pair of light brown eyes shot through with flecks of gold, her gaze widened in alarm but she relaxed visibly when she realized the handsome stranger had offered help, and willingly. She slipped her arms around her escort's waist and whispered no more than a breathless, *"Merci."* As quickly as the remarkable couple had appeared they were gone; turning down a side street, they disappeared into the night.

Phillip stood staring blindly where nothing could be seen, the astonishment plain on his finely chiseled features. The man had obviously been wealthy, but why would he have drunk himself into a stupor when he had a beauty so exquisite as that little French blonde to share his night? She had been more than merely beautiful: her fair hair and creamy complexion had glowed with an inner radiance not even the dreariness of the night could diminish. Yet it was her golden eyes that shined in his memory with a persistence he could not forget. She had been so very young, no more than sixteen at the most, Phillip thought with the painful realization of the scandalous type of life she must lead. Stunned by the brief encounter, he cursed the longing which filled his loins with a dull ache for he knew it was

6

pointless to seek the company of any other woman when he wanted that sweet French child so badly.

He had just turned when a bobbie's whistle pierced the chill night air with an ear-splitting wail and Phillip braced himself as he heard the sound of running feet approaching. He stepped to the edge of the walk, this time prepared to avoid a collision.

The breathless men paused only an instant, gasping for air before one managed to ask hurriedly, "Did you see a finely dressed couple pass this way? The man may have been injured. There was an argument over a game of cards."

Phillip laced his hands behind his back and shrugged. "Can you describe them more fully? Perhaps I did see them."

Encouraged, the bobbies explained excitedly, "Yes, they are from Sweden, the man in is forties, fair, quite handsome, his daughter a great beauty. They are wanted for questioning only, but cheating at the gaming tables is outright theft."

"I see." Phillip took a deep breath, stalling for time before he pointed in the direction in which he'd come and reported calmly, "I did see a pair who might possibly fit that description about twenty yards back. If you hurry you might still overtake them."

"Thank you, Captain." Once more making use of their shrill whistles the two raced off in the wrong direction while Phillip watched them vanish into the mist.

An amused smile curved the corner of his well-shaped mouth but once alone he laughed out loud. What an astonishing pair of thieves! The man had not been drunk at all, but hurt, perhaps badly, and his

7

charming daughter was most certainly not French but had merely spoken in that language to confuse those in pursuit. Well, he'd given them a good head start and he chuckled to himself as he returned to his ship. The men on watch met him with surprised glances but he offered no explanation for his swift return or his jovial mood. His cabin was warm and he hummed softly to himself as he stretched out upon his bunk, "Wrap me in your loving arms, *Angelina*, for I am yours again tonight." The lovely child had looked every inch an angel he realized, moaning sadly as his loneliness overwhelmed him anew for she was an angel he'd be unlikely to ever meet again. Why had he not followed her when he'd had the chance, for the love of a young women so beautiful and brave as that one would be worth the risk of the most perilous journey.

While Phillip dreamed of her, Anna gave him no more than a second thought. Still badly frightened, she closed the door of the rented room quietly then helped her father to his bed before lighting the lamp at his bedside. "Papa, we must return home immediately, we simply must, another inch and Lord Ramsey's knife would have pierced your heart!" She watched anxiously as he peeled off his coat and waistcoat. His shirt was drenched with blood and she was horrified by the sight of the long slash on his chest.

"It is nothing, Anna, but I will not argue. At first light you must book passage for Gothenburg on whatever vessel you can find. I care not if it is not a fine one."

"Yes, Papa." Anna smoothed back his blond curls and kissed him lightly upon the cheek. "The wound is a clean one, not deep. Perhaps a physician's care will not be required."

"No, we dare not summon a doctor who might inform the authorities of my whereabouts. No one will take my side against Ramsey's but the bastard lied, Anna, I did not cheat him!"

"I know, Papa, I know you would never stoop to such treachery." Anna worked swiftly to tear a piece of clean linen into strips to bind his wound. "We used to come to England so Mother might visit her cousins and the card games you love to play were all friendly ones then, but now . . ."

Eric Thorson looked up, pained by his daughter's words. "I am not proud of my vices, Anna, but I find life without your mother nearly unbearable. I know gambling is a poor substitute for her love and most assuredly I should not have brought you along with me this time. Should I ever leave home again I will go alone; this life is too dangerous for someone so lovely as you to lead."

"Papa," Anna reproached her father gently, "it is obviously too dangerous for you as well!"

Eric lay back upon his pillows, wincing as he felt a surge of pain course down his side. "What I must do is find you a husband, Anna, some fine gentleman who can provide well for your future, see that your life is a carefree one."

Disagreeing with his requirements, Anna replied with a lilting giggle, "What I truly need is simply a young man, a strong and willing worker who will help you to return our estate to the prosperity we have always enjoyed. Our wealth is in the land, you've always said that."

For a long moment Eric stared up at his lovely

daughter then he nodded thoughtfully. "Yes, I have neglected my duties shamefully, I'll admit it and promise things will be better as soon as we reach home." He closed his eyes, tired beyond endurance by the evening's unexpected strife. "I promise, Anna, I promise."

"Go to sleep, Papa, do not worry so. I know our luck will change soon." Anna picked up his torn and blood-stained shirt as she prepared to leave his room to enter her own. If she hurried she could rinse out the stain before it set and mend the tear in the morning. She was far more frightened than she'd let her father see. Pausing at his door, she looked back at the man she loved so dearly. How could Lord Ramsey, or for that matter any man accuse him of cheating at cards when he so frequently lost all he had to wager?

Chapter One

Anna sat with her hands clasped tightly in her lap as Sophia attempted to brush the tangles from her long golden curls. Her hair was thick. Grooming it was not an easy task but Anna barely felt the pain the clumsy maid inflicted upon her tender scalp. She had had no warning her uncle was coming to call and it would be a miracle if she were able to appear presentable after she'd spent the morning supervising the work in the fields.

"Forgive me, Lady Anna, but I am so anxious over the count's visit I cannot seem to make my hands stop shaking. What can he want with you now? There's nothing left. He's taken everything you owned, down to the last jewel your dear mother left for you."

"Hush, Sophia, there's plenty left, are you forgetting there's our home? We still have a roof above our heads and the land, there's that much."

"Lady Anna, he'd not take your home! What would become of you, of us, if he were to do that?" The petite woman broke off in a terrified wail, tears flooding down her flushed cheeks in huge drops.

"I'll be fortunate indeed if the villain does not decide to sell me. Now stop crying, Sophia, your tears will not change a thing." Anna's voice was bitterly sarcastic but she was certain it would come to that soon. Her father's untimely death had left debts it would take her a lifetime to repay and her uncle held all the notes.

Gustav Thorson did not rise as Anna entered the sparsely furnished hall, he only nodded stiffly, as if the mere hint of courtesy pained him greatly. Try as she might, Anna could not even imagine her uncle as having once been young; she was certain he must have been born at an advanced age, born wrinkled and mean. Her father had been the younger son, born of his father's second marriage and Gustav's exact opposite. A lively and charming companion, he'd been the dearest of fathers and she missed him more each day. "Would you care for more tea, Uncle?" Anna brushed a piece of straw from her brown woolen skirt as she swept into her chair and hoped the last of her mother's perfume had effectively disguised the aroma of the barnyard since she'd had no time to bathe.

"No thank you, this is no social call, Anna. I've come on a matter of the gravest importance." Gustav inclined his head and squinted for a better look at his only niece. "How old were you last week. Was it seventeen or eighteen?"

"I am eighteen, Uncle." Anna straightened her shoulders proudly. Whatever errand had brought the man to her home, she was certain it couldn't possibly be pleasant. He had brought no present so it wasn't to celebrate, not that she had expected a gift from a man so miserly as he.

12

"Eighteen is it? Good, then it is time."

"Time for what, Uncle?" Anna raised her hand gracefully to sweep back a stray curl. Sophia was the worst of hairdressers but that was a slight problem in their household.

"The sale of the crops did not cover the taxes again this year, girl. I told you what would happen if they didn't."

Anna's tawny eyes widened in alarm. "We discussed several options; selling a few acres was the least painful alternative as I recall."

"That would be no solution!" the gray-haired man exploded angrily. "I'll not allow my brother's estate to be chopped up piecemeal to feed the king's vulturous tax collectors! I want it kept whole, to remain in our family as it has for generations."

"Then how am I to make up the difference between what the poor harvest brought and the taxes which are coming due?" Anna leaned forward, knowing he would have no easy answer to her dilemma. The winters in Sweden were always harsh but the previous one had arrived with no warning, the freezing rain ruining the wheat as it stood in the fields. She'd been fortunate to feed her staff all winter; there had been no surplus to sell for income.

"It was a mistake for me to allow you to continue to reside here after your father's death." Seeing her expression grow defiant Gustav lifted his hand in warning. "I am your guardian, Anna, I must consider what is best for you and I have decided to hire an overseer who is an experienced man to manage this estate more profitably so your father's debts may be paid in full in the shortest time possible. He and his family will arrive on the first but by that time you will be gone."

"The first? But that is not ten days hence. I am to be put out of my home and have but ten days to pack and leave?" Anna was astounded by what he'd done without the courtesy of consulting her first. She had known he had such power but was nonetheless shocked he'd used it.

"A simple task, Anna. There is nothing to pack save your wardrobe." The old man wrinkled his nose in disgust. "Which should probably just be burned."

Anna was too hurt to cry at his insult. She was past tears; she'd shed far too many when her beloved father had died and had no more to expend upon her own misfortune. "My wardrobe is pitiful, that is true, but it is all I possess." She swallowed with difficulty, her next question a most distasteful one. "Am I to come live with you and Aunt Lillia? Is that your plan?" Her heart plummeted even lower at the thought of that possibility for his home was a dreary place, enormous in size but devoid of laughter and love.

Gustav frowned, then shook his head. "Did your father ever mention the name Lord Clairbourne to you? I believe he met the man on his final trip to London."

"My father traveled frequently, Uncle, you know that. He was too restless to remain at home after mother died but he seldom mentioned his acquaintances. If this Lord Clairbourne was a friend of my father's then I shall be happy to meet him."

"Your father was extremely proud of you, Anna, with good reason. You are an exceptionally beautiful young woman. I am happy to say that my brother at least took advantage of your assets to the fullest. Before his death he arranged for your marriage but Lord Clairbourne wished to wait until you were eighteen before he took you as his bride."

"His what?" Anna leapt to her feet. "My father would never have done such a thing without telling me. How can you suggest it?"

"Sit down, child, I have no time to waste on your hysterics. That the man is British should please you. That he has a title makes the match even more attractive. Your mother was from Great Britain so you speak his tongue fluently and at least in part share his heritage. Clairbourne is an earl, the equivalent of our count. He is quite wealthy, makes his home at Briarcliff, his estate in Devon, but his business interests in the Caribbean are extensive. He made your father's aquaintance in London as I said and will make the perfect husband for you from what Eric told me."

"You would accept my father's word for the man's character? I thought you considered his opinions worthless in all matters!"

"Silence! I will tolerate no more of your impertinence!" Gustav commanded harshly. "I know Eric permitted you to express yourself freely but I do not believe in spoiling children by such leniency."

Anna again perched upon the edge of her chair; she knew all her uncle's tirades by heart. He considered looking after her a bothersome nuisance and said so frequently. She was too willful, too much like her father for them to ever get along, but to be forced to leave her native Sweden to take up residence in England as the wife of a man she'd never met was more than she could endure in silence.

"I will begin again. You will be a countess before the

15

summer is over. The man is a widower, he has two small sons. From my experience I'd say he will expect you to be more of a governess than a wife. This is an excellent match for you and I expect your grateful compliance. Few men will accept a wife with no dowry but I believe Clairbourne and your mother were distant cousins, so he undoubtedly was impressed by your bloodlines as well as your father's description of your beauty. I am certain he will be kind to you and provide you with a comfortable home."

"Uncle, I am not some pathetic old hunting dog who would be grateful for a warm place by the fire for the rest of her days!" Anna forced back her temper unsuccessfully. "Am I to have no choice? Are we not to meet before the wedding?"

"Be reasonable, Anna. Do you honestly believe Lord Clairbourne has the time to travel here so you might give your approval? That your father met the man in London was a great stroke of good fortune, his last gift to you and you should not abuse it!" Gustav paused a long moment for the force of his words to register fully. "Clairbourne has arranged for your passage to his home, he is sending someone before the end of the month to escort you to Gothenburg where you will board a ship for the voyage. It will be better that way so you need not meet the man I've hired to take charge. You realize, of course, that were I not willing to assume responsibility for Eric's estate it would have to be sold at public auction. Your home is therefore mine and the deed will be changed accordingly. Your signature is not required since I am your guardian. This marriage is a godsend for you, Anna, and you should thank your father for it every night in your prayers."

Anna shook her head in disbelief. "I can not comprehend why he did not tell me something so important as this."

Gustav shrugged, unconcerned about his brother's motives. "As you will recall, he was quite ill when he returned home for the last time. Undoubtedly he wished to wait until he recovered his health to discuss this matter but death overtook him first. You were only sixteen then, Anna, perhaps he felt you were too young to fully appreciate what he'd done to insure that your future would be an easy one."

Anna squared her shoulders, forcing herself to be practical. If her father had chosen Lord Clairbourne for her then she would go to him without further argument. "Sophia has been with me all my life, Uncle, may I take her with me?"

"That woman is worthless; you may keep her to attend you since she would doubtless be fired immediately in any other household. As for the others, I have told the overseer they are diligent workers and are to be treated well."

"Thank you, Uncle." Anna looked around the room as she gathered her thoughts. She still missed the paintings; the walls were so bare without them but Gustav had gotten a good price for them. Another of his shrewd business deals, she thought bitterly. "I have no suitable clothes, Uncle, not for travel, nor to meet Lord Clairbourne."

"I thought of that. Lillia had several garments she no longer wanted. I know she is not exactly your size but you are a clever girl and can alter the clothes to fit you."

"Please thank Aunt Lillia for me, but I am much

17

taller than she is, far more slender. I doubt any seam-stress, no matter how skilled or talented she might be, could alter her dresses to fit me. Is there no money at all left in my father's estate so I might have one nice dress made to wear when first I meet Lord Clair-bourne?"

Gustav pulled himself up to his feet. "The garments are in the small trunk by the front door. I'll provide no others. Now good day."

Anna did not show her uncle out. She sat alone as the room grew cold, shivering in angry silence. But when Sophia came to find her she could barely control her rage as she recounted the man's visit. "See if cook can use my aunt's clothing. She might like her things and they would fit her. If not, then we'll send them to church for the poor although there's no one more poor than we."

"Lady Anna, don't fret so, surely this Lord Clair-bourne will be a fine gentleman. Maybe he will be like your father, so handsome and fun."

"Please stop, Sophia. He can't be all that young if what he really requires is a governess. No, my only hope is that he will prove to be as kind a man as my uncle promised." Yet Anna continued to sit silently in the poorly furnished hall, knowing she had lost every-thing, two loving parents, the beautiful estate which had been her only home, and now even the hope of a happy marriage had been taken from her. Why would her father have gone to his grave with such a secret, why?

The following week passed swiftly. Anna was busy brushing one of her few remaining horses, currying the mare's glossy chestnut coat on the morning the expected carriage came down the overgrown entrance way to stop at her front door. She left the beautifully groomed animal tethered by the stables and ran toward the fancy black coach. She had seldom seen so magnificent a conveyance; the four matched bays were spirited thoroughbreds and she tried to hide her dirty hands under her tattered apron for it was too late for her to escape into the house unseen. The footman had already climbed down to lower the step and open the door for his finely dressed passenger. Anna found herself staring openly as the tall man stepped out of the carriage. His hair was such a deep shade of brown, the soft curls glistened with copper highlights and his skin was tanned to a rich bronze making his even features all the more handsome. His eyes were a bright clear blue which swept over her quickly with a disapproving glance before he reached into the pocket of his well-tailored coat and tossed her a gold coin.

"Run, lass, fetch your mistress for me. I am in a great hurry to return to my ship. Well, go, run!" The man gestured emphatically, certain if she didn't understand English she would still comprehend his meaning.

Anna glanced at the gold piece lying at her feet then again at the arrogant stranger. She scooped up the coin and slapped it back in his hand as she replied in softly accented English as fluid as his, "I am the mistress here, sir, and I do not accept tips!" As if to emphasize her position she tore off her scarf revealing a bright mass of lustrous golden curls which fell about her shoulders in glistening profusion.

The stranger gasped in dismay, shocked as he instantly recognized the exquisitely beautiful young woman who had so often appeared in his dreams, the erotic nature of which brought a bright blush to his cheeks which he prayed his deep tan would cover. "You can not possibly be Lady Thorson!"

Anna struck a defiant pose and answered proudly, "And why not? Surely Lord Clairbourne was informed my circumstances are minimal. I have only a small staff here and must work as hard as anyone else simply to insure our survival! Do not look so stricken. I shall be far more presentable than this by the time I reach his home."

"You shall have to be!" The handsome man laughed heartily at his own joke then continued in the same taunting tone. "Show me inside yourself then and be quick about it. I want to leave within the hour."

"Today, you mean we must leave immediately? I was expecting some word of your arrival. I am not prepared to depart this very day!" Anna protested heatedly.

The dark-haired man put his hands on his slim hips and scowled, his blue eyes darkening in hue as he responded fiercely, "Lord Clairbourne is not a patient man and neither am I, Lady Thorson. If your circumstances are indeed as you describe, minimal, then why should it take you more than one hour to pack?"

Sophia came running to her mistress's side, brandishing a broom. "You'll not speak so rudely to Anna. She is a fine lady even if you are no gentleman!"

Anna hugged her maid to her side. "It is all right, Sophia, I am not offended, pride is a characteristic I can ill afford. Please come inside. I will see you and your men are given refreshments while I pack what little there is to bring."

The hostile man watched closely as Anna moved toward the door, her posture proud, her step light, as graceful as a fawn. As she glided through the entrance, he called after her. "Wait, I was too brusque, forgive me. I am Phillip Bradford, captain of the *Angelina*, and I am not accustomed to running errands such as this. I did not mean to insult you so rudely."

Anna was astonished by the man's unexpected apology and turned to give him a warm smile. "I will not tell Lord Clairbourne how rude you were to me if you will not tell him you found me grooming horses. Is that a bargain?"

"Yes, we will both be silent on the circumstances of our first meeting, it is agreed."

Pleased by his change of tone Anna gestured graciously. "Please come in, Captain Bradford." She led him into the main hall and taking a place on the small love seat waited while he made himself comfortable in the adjacent wing chair. The sorry state of her once-elegant home embarrassed her dreadfully but she hoped if she did not mention anything was amiss perhaps he would not notice how sparsely the room was furnished. She was ashamed of her dress as well; the bodice was too snug, as it was on all her clothes. In two years time she had grown slimmer in all but one place it seemed but she could afford no new apparel. She hoped Captain Bradford would not take note of her appearance but when she looked up he was observing her closely with an amused stare which brought a blush to her lightly tanned cheeks. "I wonder, did Lord Clairbourne send anything for me?"

"Presents you mean? If you were hoping for extravagant gifts, I'm sorry to disappoint you but it is the woman who is supposed to bring the dowry not the other way around." Phillip appeared to be thoroughly disgusted by her question and gave his full attention to scanning the large room rather than to her.

Horrified by his harsh insult Anna rushed to explain, "No, you misunderstood me, Captain Bradford. I meant only to inquire if he might not have sent me some message, a letter perhaps to tell me something about himself and his sons. I was not expecting any gifts." She was aghast he'd thought her so mercenary. She was obviously existing under greatly reduced circumstances but that did not mean she had no pride and the deep gold of her eyes grew bright with indignation.

The captain shrugged. "My mistake then, but Lord Clairbourne gave me no such letter for you. My instructions were quite brief in fact. I am merely to escort you to his estate in Devon with all possible haste and I intend to fulfill my contract to the letter."

Sophia brought in a tray of tea and sandwiches Anna hesitated to leave until her guest had been served. Then she decided she'd enjoy a cup of the soothing beverage herself before she began to gather her belongings. Her maid had been thoughtful enough to provide moist towels so they might clean their hands and she took one eagerly. "Is a ship's captain not an unusual person to send upon such a mission?" She sat back, sipping the hot tea, grateful for its refreshing sweetness.

Phillip's blue eyes narrowed slightly. Offended by her question, he opened his mouth to respond in kind then saw the innocence of her expression and replied calmly. "As captain of the *Angelina* I am responsible for your safety and comfort on your trip to his home.

22

He did not feel any further escort was required and frankly neither do I. My business is ferrying cargo, not passengers, Lady Thorson, I simply do not have accommodations for others to accompany you."

Worried, Anna asked quickly, "There will be room for my maid, won't there? Surely I wasn't expected to travel alone."

"Of course not. She will share your quarters on board."

"I see." Phillip Bradford was unlike any man Anna had ever met. He seemed totally committed to viewing her passage as a business matter, not that she had expected him to flirt with her. That would have been most unseemly since he'd come to escort her to her future husband's home. Accepting his dedication to his assignment as commendable, she searched for some further question upon the same theme. "The ship is yours then, not Clairbourne's?"

Phillip Bradford laughed briefly, showing a smile of the most charming sort, but that pleasant expression vanished swiftly. "She will be completely mine after this voyage, Lady Thorson. I will be able to pay off the last of the loan I received to buy her once I deliver you safely to Clairbourne at Briarcliff. Now it would please me greatly if you would tend to your packing. I do not need to be entertained any further."

"Of course." Anna replaced her cup upon the wooden tray and turned to go. She found the captain's company as disagreeable as he seemed to find hers and had no wish to prolong their conversation either.

When her luggage had been secured in the compartment at the rear of the carriage Anna turned to bid her loyal servants farewell. All were as miserable as she at their hurried parting and she hugged and kissed each of them, then climbed quickly into the waiting coach followed by Sophia and Captain Bradford. As the elegant vehicle rolled down the unkempt path Sophia leaned out to wave goodbye to her friends but Anna sat silently looking down at her hands. They were chapped, the skin bright red from all the scrubbing she'd done to get her nails clean. She hoped by the time she reached Briarcliff they would look presentable once more, soft and white as a lady's hands should, as her mother's always had.

When they reached the main road, Anna asked the driver to stop a moment and quickly got out of the carriage. "This spot provides the best view of my home, Captain. I want to remember it always as it looks from here." Nestled among bright green linden trees, atop a small rise, the spacious home was surrounded by rolling fields of growing wheat and presented an idyllic scene of pastoral contentment.

"Yes, from this vantage point the shameful neglect and lack of repair can't be seen. Frankly, I was appalled by the interior, it looks as though it has been stripped by vandals."

Anna turned to stare at the tactless man by her side. He was easily the best looking man she'd ever met but she did not like his caustic personality one bit. "My uncle sold most of the furnishings last year to pay off the back taxes." Seeing by his expression the captain had no interest in hearing her problems, Anna returned to the carriage, her memories of the beauty of her home undiminished by his disparaging remarks.

The sun was warm that afternoon and the rocking motion of the carriage soon lulled Sophia to sleep.

Anna sat gazing out at the bright wild flowers which each spring decorated the country roadsides with a splendid array of color. Her serene expression belied the turmoil within her heart; she brushed her curls off her face time and again but they would not stay put. Finally in exasperation she began pulling the pins from her hair and simply let it cascade about her shoulders in casual disarray. "Forgive me, I am not in the mood to fuss with my hair."

"We are quite alone, what does it matter?" Phillip replied softly. "Your hair is very beautiful but that was a most unusual style. I don't believe I've ever seen anything quite so, well, extraordinary. Did your maid arrange it for you?"

"You are not usually so diplomatic, Captain Bradford. Sophia is a very poor hairdresser; my hair was simply a mess, was it not?"

"Frankly, yes. You will have to employ a more accomplished maid once you become Lady Clairbourne."

Anna smiled as she glanced over at the sleeping Sophia. "Perhaps I will have to employ a hairdresser, but Sophia will always have a home with me. I shall never replace her."

"Despite her obvious lack of talent?" Phillip inquired incredulously.

"She is the best friend I shall ever have, and I would never hurt her by replacing her with another no matter how accomplished that other woman might be. I have taken care of myself too long to rely that much upon a maid's attentions anyway."

"Let us hope Lord Clairbourne is not offended by your independence."

25

At the mention of that man's name Anna sighed wistfully. "Do you know Lord Clairbourne well, Captain?"

"Extremely well, why?" Phillip stretched out in the seat opposite hers, the length of his legs making a comfortable position difficult to achieve.

"Would you please tell me something about him? I am so very curious as to what sort of man he must be."

"He is an enormously wealthy one, what more do you need to know?" Phillip flecked a speck of lint from his breeches and said no more.

"And you are a very cynical one, aren't you?" Anna observed perceptively.

"With good reason, Lady Thorson."

"I am sorry to hear that, but surely you can not believe the size of a man's purse is a fair measure of his character."

"It isn't? You have so much experience with men, with human nature itself to allow you to make any sort of wise judgments?" His deep voice dripped with sarcasm as his light eyes filled with disdain.

"I have not known so many people as you have surely, but I do know the ones who have impressed me the most were kind, loving people who cared more for their fellow man than for a profit on their investments."

"Astonishing. Can you give me an example of such a person?"

"Yes, my father was a wonderful man, a loving husband and devoted father. I am sorry you were unable to visit our home when my mother was alive, it was so very beautiful then."

Phillip's expression softened as he inquired, "What

happened to her?"

"She loved to ride. One afternoon she was thrown while taking a jump and died instantly of a broken neck. That was five years ago. She and my father were so much in love, he missed her terribly. He simply died of a broken heart for he no longer had the will to live."

"It does not occur to you that no truly 'devoted' father would have left his only daughter in such a sorry state?"

Ignoring his taunt, Anna replied, calmly. "He could not have predicted the harshness of the winter which ruined the crops last year. The estate always carried itself before then."

Phillip continued his insults. "Wasn't there also a matter of gambling debts to be repaid?"

"Yes, I won't deny that he left many outstanding debts." Anna straightened her shoulders proudly, shocked he would have heard such gossip. "My uncle was able to make good on all my father's notes however."

"Then he simply sold off your inheritance to pay himself back?" Phillip asked pointedly, his disdain clear.

"Yes, but there were other debts as well, taxes my father had neglected to pay as I mentioned before," Anna admitted softly, convinced the man would persist until she had revealed the complete story.

Phillip scowled impatiently. "Yet you regard this man who nearly landed you in debtors' prison as the best of fathers?"

"Why yes! He was wonderful to me." Anna took a deep breath and let it out slowly. "Captain Bradford, I know he was weak, you needn't point out the obvious, but I loved him dearly. All his problems began after he lost my mother and not before. He adored her and life without her was simply not worth living."

"It is plain to me you loved your father, completely without reason I might add."

"Love needs no reason, Captain, none at all, it simply exists on its own, that is its beauty."

"Ah, so you are also an expert on love, Lady Thorson?" Phillip's bright blue eyes held a teasing sparkle which was new.

Anna blushed; she knew nothing about the kind of love to which he was obviously referring and quickly changed the subject. "What sort of father is Lord Clairbourne. Does he devote a lot of his time to his sons?"

"No, the man neglects them shamefully. I believe their welfare is his primary motivation for this marriage."

"My uncle thought that might be true, but still—"

"But what? You have some objection to playing the part of mother to another woman's children? Were you hoping instead to have children of your own?"

Anna tried not to be embarrassed but she felt her cheeks redden as she replied, "Naturally I hope Lord Clairbourne will come to love me in time, that we might have children someday."

Phillip shook his head in a gentle reproach. "I won't encourage you to entertain such romantic delusions, Lady Thorson. It is doubtful the man will ever grow fond of you."

"Oh." Anna's creamy complexion paled noticeably at his unpleasant prediction.

"Don't look so downcast, you will have the consola

28

tion of his considerable fortune if not his affection to brighten your days."

"Captain Bradford, really! It has been so long since I had any money I would not even know how to spend it should the man be so generous as to give me some."

"A trip to London for some gowns which fit would be a good place to begin." Phillip nodded toward the hooks straining at her bodice and grinned.

"Oh you . . ." Anna folded her arms across the soft swell of her breast but that did little to end her embarrassment. The man seemed to delight in tormenting her but she stopped short of calling him a vile name although she was sorely tempted.

"Yes?" Phillip continued to chuckle at her show of righteous indignation. "Do you have a gown for your wedding, some suitable garment for the bride of Lord Clairbourne to wear?"

Anna refused to look at the hateful man while he was taunting her so rudely. "No, but I hope there will be time to have something made at Briarcliff."

"I see, you expect Lord Clairbourne to provide your trousseau?"

"I only hope he does not share your preoccupation with my lack of resources! If he wants me enough to offer marriage, won't he feel I am worth the expense to clothe?"

Phillip shrugged. "That will be for him to decide, but I don't believe there will be time for a seamstress to create a suitable gown. Perhaps one of his first wife's dresses will do."

"What? You expect me to marry the man in his deceased wife's clothes? That is ghoulish, Captain Bradford, and I'll not even consider it!"

"I believe you told me pride was something you could ill afford, but no matter, do as you wish." Phillip leaned back and closed his eyes, his interest in their conversation clearly over.

Anna watched, fascinated as the man slept. How could he have such an attractive facade and such a tasteless nature? He had made her feel worse than ever; she'd have wealth and position apparently if not love but how could she survive in such a sterile environment? How could she bear to call a man husband if all he gave her was money? Finally she leaned forward and tapped Phillip's knee lightly, awakening him in an instant. "Captain Bradford, I was only informed of this marriage proposal last week; I've really had no opportunity to consider it fully. Won't there be some time for Lord Clairbourne and me to get to know each other and decide if we really want to marry? Why did you say there would be no time for a dress to be made?"

"Your uncle did not explain? This is not a proposal you may consider. From what Lord Clairbourne told me, your father gave his word two years ago. You will wed the man within an hour of your arrival at Briarcliff. Now do not annoy me again with your trivial concerns while I am resting!" He shut his eyes and, shifting to get more comfortable, went back to sleep.

Anna shut her eyes too, but not to rest. She was terrified by his words, how could she possibly marry a complete stranger? She searched her mind frantically for someone to whom she could turn for help. Her uncle cared nothing for her happiness. Her father's passion for gambling had cost him all his friends, but was there not someone among her mother's friends who would come to her rescue? She waited a moment longer and certain the captain was sound asleep gave their driver new directions. It would not delay them greatly to stop at Catherine's home. She remembered the woman as a beauty, a countess who was a favorite of the court; if she could provide no way to escape a forced marriage she would at least be able to give her a dress or two to make her arrival at Briarcliff less of the disaster it would surely be. Smiling happily for the first time in over a week, Anna relaxed and watched the miles of deep green forest roll by with a lush panorama which soothed her aching heart. She was her father's daughter, but also her mother's and she prayed Catherine would remember her fondly and come to her aid.

Chapter Two

Catherine greeted Anna with a warm hug and effusive kisses but her eyes never left Phillip Bradford's lean physique. A woman in her late thirties, she was a raven-haired beauty with the dark flashing eyes of a gypsy, who missed no opportunity to meet a handsome man. She turned her most enchanting smile upon him.

"Captain Bradford, do not despair. Anna's dear mother can offer her no advice on her forthcoming marriage so it is only natural that she would seek mine." She smiled seductively, her knowledge of the secrets of the marriage bed obviously extensive.

"You are most gracious to offer us lodgings for the night, Countess, but you must appreciate my surprise at finding myself here when Gothenburg was our destination!" Phillip could scarcely contain the fierce temper which blazed within him. When he gave orders he expected them to be obeyed, not countermanded if he closed his eyes for an hour or two.

The countess moved forward to take his arm, pressing her soft curves against his side. "Since this is your first visit to Sweden, Captain, I will forgive you for not realizing you are no more than a half day's journey from Gothenburg still. That you should arrive this afternoon is most fortunate for we are hosting a weekend of entertainment and our guests have just begun to arrive. Our parties are lavish, and I am certain you will enjoy yourselves immensely."

"I did not mean to intrude, Catherine." Anna swallowed nervously as she looked down at her faded dress. "My wardrobe is very limited and prohibits my accepting your invitation. I had hoped only to stop here to speak with you. I can't possibly meet your friends."

"Nonsense, Anna, there are few coming tonight who did not know your parents and they will be delighted to see you again. Have you formal dress with you, Captain? If not my husband can loan you something. And as for you, my little kitten, you may choose whatever you like from among my gowns." Catherine smiled brightly, certain she could entice her unexpected guests to accept her invitation.

As Phillip stood looking down at the attractive brunette he was suddenly seized with the desire to teach the young woman who'd so quickly disregarded his wishes a lesson. It was clear Anna did not wish to be presented at the party as some poor waif in a borrowed dress but perhaps that experience would take the edge off her willfulness and make her more agreeable for the rest of their journey. He'd not known what to expect of her home and had indeed brought his formal clothes on the chance he might have to dress for dinner had they been unable to leave her house as quickly as he'd hoped they could. He also recognized the unspoken invitation in the countess's eyes for exactly what it was;

the evening might prove far more amusing than he'd first thought. "Since we are already here I see no reason why we should not remain to enjoy your hospitality. The fiancée of Lord Clairbourne will be welcome in the finest homes of England so I see no reason why she should be ashamed to be presented anywhere in her native land." He smiled broadly, but the expression in his eyes did not change, his glance was murderous and he dared Anna to dispute him without speaking a single threat.

Anna clenched her fists at her sides yet responded sweetly. "Why, Captain, how thoughtful of you to consider my happiness. Since it is doubtful I will ever return to Sweden this will be my last opportunity to see many of those who were my parents' friends. I will be happy to wear one of your gowns, Catherine, but I insist you choose it for me."

Phillip nodded slightly, hiding his surprise at her sudden change of mood. Who could predict the whims of a woman? "Perhaps we should go to our rooms then so we will have ample time to dress before your other guests arrive."

"As you wish, Captain." Catherine was elated by his decision to remain and directed him to the room which adjoined hers while she placed Anna and her maid at the far end of the hall.

As Anna bathed in the large copper tub Catherine sat close by watching with undisguised admiration. "You are as lovely as your mother was, Anna. The men will be enchanted with you tonight. A new face always provides excitement and yours is exceptionally pretty."

"Thank you, you are kind to say so." Anna relaxed in the warm, fragrant water, Catherine's perfumed

34

soap filling her senses with the delicious aroma of rose petals. She could barely imagine what a frivolous life the woman must lead but kept that thought to herself. "I was hoping you might be able to help me, Catherine. Apparently my father agreed to give me to Lord Clairbourne. Is there no honorable way I can break such an engagement?"

"Why would you wish to, Anna?" Catherine waited a moment then continued in a conspiratorial tone. "You have not even met the man, my dear. He may be delightful or a buffoon but what difference does that make? The English are not so liberal as we, but I'll wager the noblewomen still have their lovers when their husbands do not please them."

"Catherine!" Anna was shocked by the woman's words. The countess was very attractive but Anna had never imagined she might share her favors with more than her husband.

"My dear, I can see you need far more advice than I can provide in one brief afternoon. Your parents were the exception, child, not the rule. A woman enters marriage for the security it offers her. If she finds love so much the better, but if she does not, well then there are always handsome young men such as Captain Bradford to brighten the afternoons."

Anna's long lashes nearly swept her delicate brows as she turned to stare. "Is he merely an example or do you actually plan to, well to—"

"To invite him to my bedchamber? You needn't be so shy with me, Anna, you can say what you think without fear of offending me. My husband is twenty years my senior. He loves giving parties but he frequently drinks more than he should. He will sleep

35

soundly tonight from the moment his head touches his pillow and I may take whatever pleasures I care to without fear he will discover the deed or be upset if he did. He is a practical man, a realist, not a dreamer who expects fidelity in one so young as I."

Anna could scarcely believe her ears. That she was naive about the relationship between a man and his wife she had known, but to be advised to marry one man and seek love in the arms of another appalled her. "Is it not possible for a woman to marry a man she loves?"

"Of course it is, and it happens to some I'm sure. But what would you do if you could break your engagement? Is there another man waiting to marry you, Anna? Perhaps one to whom your Uncle Gustav objects?"

"No." Anna shook her head thoughtfully. "All know my financial situation is a dismal one and it does not inspire any suitors." Nor would she inspire much attention that night, she thought sadly, no matter how elegantly she was clothed. Catherine had only complimented her to be kind.

The dark-eyed woman held the towel as Anna rose from the tub. "Then this marriage is a rare one. Perhaps Clairbourne is a young and dashing man you will love at first sight. Hope for that, Anna, and do not worry needlessly over your fate. Now come, let us look over my wardrobe. I have many pretty things I will give you to make your journey more pleasant; your arrival at Briarcliff will be a more confident one with fine clothes."

Anna hated to ask for such charity, no matter how close Catherine and her mother had been. "If you

36

would give me one nice dress I will be most grateful, one will be all I'll need."

Catherine laughed as she hugged the attractive blonde. "Nonsense, you can not have just one dress, you will need lingerie, will you not, and clothes for travel? That your uncle is so parsimonious is unfortunate, but I will help you to create the illusion your family is a proud one. We do not want your future husband to think he can mistreat you and receive no punishment from your relatives."

"Yes. I understand your point. I can not arrive on his doorstep in rags and expect much respect, can I? Thank you for your generosity, Catherine, for it is greatly appreciated."

"It is merely repayment for the kindness your dear parents always showed to me." Catherine smiled sweetly knowing her husband would be touched by her gesture and provide her with a generous allowance to replace whatever she gave away with new silks, satins and the finest brocades, the thought of which inspired her to be more generous in her gifts.

Phillip waited anxiously at the foot of the stairs. The countess had knocked upon his door, startling him from his bath as she came to inquire as to his comfort. She was attractive in a rather predatory fashion, but something in her manner warned him an hour spent in her embrace would not be worth the price and he had been abrupt to the point of rudeness as he'd sent her away. He continued pacing, his long stride carrying him up and down the long hall with the cool even step of a palace guard. He turned when at last he heard someone approaching, then could only stare in wonder as Anna slowly descended the curving staircase.

Catherine had provided a gown of a rich emerald green and the fine silk rustled softly with each step Anna took. The deep color of the brilliant fabric made her light brown eyes dance with a sparkling gleam and her lightly tanned skin glow radiantly. Her golden hair was coiled stylishly atop her head, showing off the graceful curve of her throat and bare shoulders to every advantage. The ill-clothed young woman who'd entered the stately home a scant two hours prior now appeared to possess the elegance of a princess and Phillip could not find his voice to greet her.

Catherine recognized the handsome man's mystified gaze for the admiration it was and laughed softly as she followed her pretty guest down the stairs. "Captain, you look splendid. My husband will join us in a moment, but tell me something more of yourself while we wait. Did you serve in the Royal Navy before you took command of your own vessel?"

Tearing his eyes from Anna's, Phillip hastened to explain his heritage. "I am not British, Countess, but from America and my only memories of the Royal Navy are of when I served as a cabin boy during the War of Independence and we had British vessels within the sights of our cannon."

"How exciting that must have been. You must describe your adventures to me, Captain. Ah, here is my Alex now." Catherine introduced her husband quickly then swept across the hall on Phillip's arm, leaving Anna for the count to escort, a duty he did not mind in the least.

The spring days are long in Sweden, the twilight hanging on for hours, and the elegant home was flooded with light without the need for candles as the guests began to arrive. Finding herself alone with Phillip while Catherine and Alex were greeting their friends, Anna remarked shyly, "I did not realize you were from the Colonies. I do not speak English so often that I could place your accent with any accuracy."

"It strikes me as odd you would remark upon my accent when yours is so unusual." Phillip found it difficult to look directly at the young woman, her beauty was too compelling, exactly as it had been the night he'd first seen her. He tried to recall how many years it had been, three he thought; she would have been only fifteen and so lovely her memory had lit many a dark night. Angered by his own foolish sentimentality he had responded curtly, caring little that his tactlessness had hurt her.

"Unfortunately my accent seems to be strange in all the languages I speak, Captain. Most people are too polite to point out that flaw however, for it is comprehension that is foremost, not accent surely."

Phillip nodded absently, his gaze traveling about the entrance way as he noted the others present. The opulence of the large home did not surprise him for he could readily imagine Anna's had once been as grand, but the finely dressed men who surrounded him seemed a foppish lot, feminine in their pastel brocades. He preferred a far more simple mode of dress. The gold braid and brass buttons upon his dark blue coat clearly identified his profession, his buff-colored waistcoat and breeches were immaculate and his high black boots were polished to a brilliant sheen. He was an imposing figure, tall and dark, his glance so menacing only a fool would have dared to provoke him. The silence between them had grown awkward before he thought to ask, "Why is that, Anna? Surely your Swedish must be perfect."

"My mother usually spoke to me in English, but she had learned Swedish from a tutor after she married my father. As he had learned English from a tutor himself, his pronunciation differed from hers. I suppose with the way he spoke English and she spoke Swedish it is remarkable I can converse in either tongue. Do you think you might help me so Lord Clairbourne will not think my speech too foreign?"

"I am no fit tutor on any subject, Lady Thorson, and doubtless he will not expect you to possess flawless speech. In fact, I doubt he will hear anything you say when you are so very pretty."

Anna blushed deeply, astonished by his unexpected compliment. "Why, Captain, I had no idea you had noticed." She was very pleased, for he seemed to dispense compliments only rarely so she knew he must be sincere. "I think you are quite handsome," she murmured shyly then turned away as Catherine drew her aside to share a bit of gossip. The evening was turning out far better than she had dared hope and her smile was genuine as she responded to those from people standing nearby.

When everyone had arrived a small orchestra began to play and Catherine had insisted Phillip dance with her as her husband swept Anna across the parquet floor of the ballroom. But with each note the musical group played he regretted his haste to attend the party more. Dancing was not something he'd been taught, but a skill he had learned by watching others when it had proved unavoidable. He had a natural grace which made him a fine partner but dancing was not an activity he enjoyed. He preferred to hold beautiful women in his arms for an entirely different purpose and thought moving to music a ridiculous waste of time. Catherine's endless stream of charming friends seemed not to notice he spoke no Swedish as they batted their eyelashes coyly and chatted on without realizing he did no more than nod occasionally and smile politely. Surprisingly, he saw Anna more frequently alone than dancing and when the musicians paused for a break he made his way to her side.

"You do not enjoy dancing, Lady Thorson?" He inclined his head slightly so only she might hear.

Confused by his question, Anna had no idea how to respond. "Why do you ask, Captain?"

"I thought perhaps you did not enjoy it since you seem to find the evening as tedious as I do."

"Tedious, Captain?" Anna's tawny eyes swept his taunting expression coldly. "The extent of my popularity, or should I say lack thereof is hardly a concern of yours!" She turned and gracefully lifting her long skirt made her way out to the terrace then sped on down the steps to the gardens and disappeared into the gathering darkness.

Catherine saw only Anna's pained expression as she'd fled the crowded room. Leaving her circle of friends, she rushed to Phillip's side. "Anna should not wander the grounds alone, Captain. Whatever did you say to upset her so badly?"

Phillip was at a loss to explain the young beauty's haste to flee his company. "I have no idea, but perhaps it is still light enough for me to find her." He crossed the room swiftly with his long stride but it was not until he reached the terrace that he realized the countess had

41

followed him. Exasperated, he chose to ignore her presence until he realized the gardens were not going to be the orderly pathways he'd anticipated but a complete wilderness instead.

"Let us go to the right, Captain, come, I will show you the way."

Phillip had no desire for the woman's company but did not see how he could refuse it. They had not gone far when they came to a large circular fountain, carved of marble; the voluptuous female figures in the center represented the three graces and the bubbling water filled the night air with a fine spray.

"Let us stop for a moment, Captain, there are several paths she might have chosen, but if we wait here a moment she may reappear."

Phillip stood in the center of the path, hands on his hips, a furious frown creasing his brow. "Blast, where is the girl?"

Catherine circled him slowly, her manner openly flirtatious. "She is naive, a very sweet child but as everyone knows a penniless one. I did my best to see she was not ignored but unfortunately—"

"What?" Phillip looked down at the brown-eyed beauty. "What has her financial situation to do with any of this?"

"Come now, Captain, you are a man of experience surely, are customs so very different in your country? Are not the wealthy girls the most popular?" She ran her fingertips slowly up his lapels, bringing her lips as close to his as possible but he did not respond as she'd expected.

Phillip took Catherine's wrists firmly in his hands and backed her toward the fountain. "Madame, perhaps you would find a cool bath more refreshing than my company as I have no time for your games. I am responsible for Anna and I intend to see she is not insulted any further."

"Captain Bradford!" Catherine looked back over her shoulder; she was dangerously close to the water's edge. She realized she'd made a grave error in believing so handsome a man would also be a vain one who'd respond to her flattery with affection. When he released her and strode off down the path she made no move to follow him but returned to her now brightly lit home where she knew the company would be far more amusing.

Anna sat alone on a wooden bench, dreamily hoping she'd never have to face another such wretched evening. Her father had taught her to dance, but she'd had no opportunity to practice since his death and was embarrassed she'd been such a clumsy partner for the few men who had been gracious enough to invite her. She spread out her skirt, enjoying the richness of the fabric and wondered if Lord Clairbourne enjoyed dancing. She spoke his name in a throaty whisper as if it were a secret too precious to share. She would soon be Lady Clairbourne, accepted as the wife of a wealthy nobleman rather than shunned for being the orphan of Count Gustav Thorson's younger brother, little better than a pauper in the eyes of Catherine's many fine guests. When she heard someone approaching on the path she sat up straight, gathering her dignity for whatever confrontation might ensue.

"Lady Thorson!" Phillip called impatiently. He was delighted to have found her so rapidly and obviously unharmed but he'd shouted angrily, none of his relief apparent in his harsh tone. "Surely it is not deemed proper for young ladies to roam this forest alone!"

"Probably not, but I am used to my own company and prefer it."

Phillip was taken aback by the honesty of her response and did not question it. He sat down by her side and attempted to be more reasonable. "I should not have left you without an escort, forgive me, I did not realize you were not enjoying yourself as the other guests were."

Anna turned to look up at him, her unusual golden-flecked eyes bright even in the darkness. "It has been too long since I enjoyed any amusement, Captain, but I was glad to see you were so readily accepted."

"Just what do you mean by that?" Phillip demanded promptly.

"Nothing sinister I assure you." Sound carried easily on the crisp night air and hearing the orchestra begin a new tune Anna grew curious. "What is Clairbourne's first name?"

"His name is Charles. Does that make him seem more human to you?" Phillip leaned back, making himself more comfortable upon the sturdy bench.

"Yes, it does. Charles is a pleasant name. Do you know if he enjoys dancing?"

"Good lord, no! I can not even imagine him attempting such a frivolous thing." Phillip chuckled at the absurdity of that idea. "He is not a man given to such inconsequential pursuits." And neither am I, he thought to himself with a sullen frown.

"He does not entertain?" Anna inquired softly, more uncertain than ever of the man's personality.

"He has many friends but they are all as serious as he I'm afraid." The whole group behaved with the same arrogant stiffness he recalled with a sudden chuckle he could not suppress.

Anna laid her hand upon his sleeve, not wishing to allow him to continue his mocking laughter when she could not understand the joke. "Well just what do these men do, hunt or play cards or—"

"They enjoy investing their considerable fortunes and counting their profits to the exclusion of all else from what I've seen."

Depressed by his gloomy comments Anna rose to her feet and waited for him to join her. "Shall we return to the party? They should be ready to serve a light supper soon. I'm really rather tired and would like to return to my room after we eat. But you needn't leave the party until you wish to surely."

"Anna." Phillip called her name softly, startled by the gruffness of his own voice. But she was so very lovely he could not bear to think she'd not been treated politely. "I will stay with you for the rest of the evening, for as long as you wish to remain, I will not leave your side." When Anna turned to look up at him, a sad sweet smile gracing her pretty mouth, it seemed most natural to him to take her into his arms, to draw her into a close embrace. Without a word his lips found hers, his mouth was warm, his touch gentle and when she did not resist he held her even more tightly, his hand sifting her soft, shining curls as his mouth dominated hers with a slow, lingering kiss.

When Anna suddenly came to her senses she pushed him away abruptly. She was breathless, her heart pounding violently in her ears from no more than the sensuous caress of Phillip's now-smiling lips. He had a very charming smile, she realized, an expression she'd never seen. "Please, you must not kiss me ever again."

Phillip pulled her back into his arms and whispered softly, "Hush, do not argue with me now, not now." He trailed light kisses slowly down her slender throat, enjoying the smoothness of her silken skin before returning to her pink-tinged lips once more. Although he found her innocence charming, he wanted so much more. "Open your mouth, Anna, like this."

Raising her hands to his broad shoulders Anna obeyed him without realizing why. She simply clung to him, lost in the delicious sensation of his kiss. It seemed to last forever, sweeping away her fear on a tide of rising passion too strong to resist. His affection was so unexpected, yet so sweet she returned it readily, relaxing against him to accept the warmth of his lean body with a small shudder of surrender. When at last he drew away she was confused, uncertain as to what had happened between them but she knew instinctively it had been wrong.

"Perhaps it is only the spirit of this romantic setting which has made us forget ourselves so completely, Captain, but I dare not remain here with you when my absence has undoubtedly already caused considerable comment." Her voice was breathless as she turned away but she was unused to receiving such flattering attentions from young men and did not know how she should respond. Perhaps he thought her as vain and easily seduced as Catherine but he'd no right to kiss her when she was engaged to Charles which was something he knew quite well but had apparently not considered important since it stood in the way of his own pleasure. Furious with his conceit she raced up the path, intent upon returning to the security offered by the crowded party.

Amused by her haste to escape what he'd considered a most pleasant interlude Phillip lengthened his stride to overtake her and offered his arm as they reached the bottom of the stairs leading up to the terrace. "Be careful, these marble steps are slippery."

Unable to control her temper Anna responded as though she'd been deeply insulted. "Do I seem so clumsy as that, Captain, so lacking in grace that I would fall on my face climbing a simple flight of stairs?" Anna made a concerted effort to ascend the stairs as gracefully as possible but the dampness in the night air had made the way treacherous and she was grateful for Phillip's steady hand. When he lowered his arm to encircle her waist she did not draw away. But as soon as they reached the terrace he stepped away to put a more discreet distance between them before they re-entered the ballroom.

The evening did not go well in Phillip's opinion. The festivities had been as elegant as promised, the food delicious, the wine plentiful, but the pain which had filled Anna's eyes as she had stood on the edge of the dance floor watching the finely dressed couples swirl by had not been worth it. He'd kept his promise and not left her side, but could think of little to discuss during supper; he had no talent for small talk. He knew he was a poor companion for so beautiful a young woman but could not seem to help that. It had been a long and tiring day, one which he wished to end alone but Catherine's suggestive glance as she bid him good night held hopes of far more. When he went up to his room he locked both doors securely before undressing and getting into bed. He'd not considered that in her own home the countess would have a complete set of keys.

Phillip was on the edge of sleep when the exotic beauty entered his room. She was scantily clad in a filmy gown of pale yellow silk, her long flowing curls nearly reaching her waist, her heavy perfume filling the air with the heady scent of seduction. She perched on the edge of his bed and leaned down to kiss his cheek lightly before she called his name softly in an inviting whisper. "Phillip?"

Phillip reached up to wind his fingers in her long curls and pulled her mouth down to his, bruising her lips badly with a savage kiss he quickly brought to an end. "That is a fair sample of my affection, madame. I do not believe you'd care to see more."

Catherine leapt to her feet, backing away as she brought her hand to her ravaged mouth. "You beast, how dare you treat me so brutally? I am not some whore you picked up on the docks!"

Phillip laughed at her outrage. "No, such a woman would have more manners than you possess, Countess. Now get out of my room unless you've decided to take your chances with me but I can't promise your husband won't see the bruises in the morning."

With a strangled shriek Catherine fled from the room and slammed the door, locking it this time from her side then blocking the entrance to her room further with a heavy chair before she felt she'd be safe in her bed.

Now fully awake, Phillip stretched out upon the comfortable bed and propped his head on his hands.

The count did not seem like such a bad fellow, but Phillip had had his fill of women like the countess who relied upon their beauty to fill their beds with a different man each night. Spiders searching for victims to ensnarl in their webs, he thought with an evil sneer. Well, he'd certainly spoiled her fun that night. His conscience pained him not at all until he began to consider what Anna might become as the wife of a man like Lord Clairbourne. Would she turn to lovers as so many young women forced into loveless marriages soon did? He saw Clairbourne frequently: would he be able to ignore the type of invitation he'd received that night if it came from Anna? The question tore at his emotions, filling him with dread for he already knew what his answer would be and the folly of it as well. When the sun rose he'd slept little. He assembled his small entourage with all possible haste to continue their trip to Gothenburg without further delay.

Chapter Three

The spring morning grew oppressively warm, the close confines of the carriage stifling. Sophia again napped and Anna found herself alone when Phillip also dozed. She tried to distract herself by focusing upon the scenery but the captain was simply too handsome to ignore. She could not seem to stop staring in his direction. His dark eyelashes were as long and thick as her own, yet not in the least bit feminine against his finely chiseled features. There had been no finer looking man at the party the previous evening. But she knew Americans scorned titles of any sort so doubtless he was heir to none. That he'd fallen asleep so readily was not surprising she considered; as Catherine could barely cover her constant yawns at breakfast she could well imagine where Phillip had spent the night. For some reason that knowledge pained her. He was free, of course, even if she were not, but still she wished he had not found the lovely countess quite so enchanting. He'd been surprisingly aloof with the woman that morning though, perhaps in deference to her husband's feelings, but she could tell something had happened between them and was very curious as to what it might have been. She was not nearly so naive as most young women her age; she knew men and women enjoyed being together. Her father had revealed that much to her if not the specifics of what they actually did. Her imagination was a vivid one, however, and seated opposite the handsome young man she found her thoughts returning again and again to the same sensuous theme.

Gazing dreamily at the dashing captain took Anna's mind off the dreariness of her future for the moment, but offered no possible way for her to avoid the inevitable. When she noticed the road had curved near a stream she quickly asked the driver to stop for a while, welcoming any excuse for a delay. Her fellow passengers did not awaken as she slipped off her shoes and stockings and climbed out of the elegant coach to wade in the swiftly running water. She held her skirt above her knees to enjoy the brook's refreshing coolness, taking in the beauty of the spring day as she forced away all thought save the joy of life until she heard Phillip's disapproving shout.

"Lady Thorson, that you will become Lord Clairbourne's bride so shortly is appalling! Do you plan to become more circumspect in your behavior then? Or is that simply an impossibility?"

Anna thought better of pointing out his behavior was far from exemplary. Instead she smiled invitingly as she called to him. He could not reach her without coming into the stream and she doubted he'd do so. "Please come and join me, the water is very pleasant and the coach was unbearably warm."

Phillip shook his head, then sat down at the water's edge, leaning his elbows across his knees. "Go ahead and play if you must, you'll have little enough opportunity for such foolishness once you reach Briarcliff."

Her brief happiness vanished with that depressing thought. Anna came out of the stream and after shaking out her skirt knelt in front of him. Awake he was even more delightful to look at. Suddenly she was seized with curiosity about the attractive young man. "I don't want to hear another word about Briarcliff, Captain Bradford. Tell me something about yourself instead."

Phillip's deep blue eyes narrowed in response to her request, clearly displeased by her interest. "I am of no consequence to you, Lady Thorson, and my life is certainly no fit subject for your contemplation."

"I can not place people in categories so easily as you seem to do. We will spend considerable time together. You know all there is to know about me it seems, my past as well as what my future will be, and yet I know so little about you. That is unfair, now tell me something about yourself, anything at all. Were you a happy child, did you have as loving a home as I did?"

"I was orphaned at an early age, Anna. You may draw whatever conclusions you care to from that fact."

Anna's beautiful light eyes reflected the lush green hillside where they rested. Perhaps without realizing it Phillip had used her first name; rather than being discouraged by his curt rebuff she was undaunted and continued in a soft, enticing voice. "I know you are American at least, and that you served as a cabin boy in the War for Independence. That you have risen to the rank of captain of your own ship so rapidly must

52

mean you are both industrious and resourceful. I think you must be very clever to have become so respected a friend of Lord Clairbourne that he has entrusted you with my well-being for this journey. You are bright as well as pleasant to behold but I do not understand why you are continually so angry."

"Angry!" Phillip ignored her compliments to scoff at her final observation. "I have every reason to be livid, Lady Thorson. I find this trip as tiresome as you must and while I am not despondent over having to make it I do not understand why we could not have gone straight to Gothenburg yesterday as I had planned. First it was a detour of considerable distance to visit your mother's friend and now we have halted our progress so you might frolic in this brook like some wood nymph! Is it not obvious to you why I find it impossible to hold my temper?"

Yet even as he yelled at her Anna could not help but feel he was hiding something far more serious and dared to say so. "Since you are the captain, surely your vessel will not sail without you. I think there is an entirely different cause for your perpetual rage. A woman perhaps, someone you love and long to see?"

"Is it your custom to discuss such personal topics with men you barely know? Is this how you entertained your suitors?" Phillip was astonished as much by her perceptiveness as by the intimate nature of her questions.

Anna licked her lips thoughtfully before she replied, completely unaware of the sensual image she created. "I have had no suitors, sir. Had my mother lived she would have taken me to the Swedish court as well as to London for the season to meet suitable men as young women of my similar breeding usually are. But it was as if time stopped when she died, I can not imagine how my father convinced Lord Clairbourne to accept me for I have no more to recommend me than my good name. You seem far too serious a gentleman to enjoy talking of inconsequential matters but if I have offended you by my boldness please forgive me for it was unintentional."

Phillip forced himself to turn away. Longing for the company of a beautiful young woman in a dream was one thing he'd found, speaking to her in the flesh quite another. He was not in the least bit disappointed in her, however; he had never imagined she would be either so bright and inquisitive or so continually perplexing. "You must have been thirteen when your mother died. Had she not taught you to be a lady, was she not one herself?" he asked caustically, pushing his mind again into a logical channel and away from the surge of desire her mere presence sent through every inch of his powerful frame.

"Yes, she was a great beauty in both her manners and appearance. She taught me many useful skills and encouraged me to be myself, not to flirt and be pretentious. I can not believe men truly like that sort of thing in a woman." That was her own opinion, she realized, one obviously not shared by the lovely countess with whom he'd spent the night.

"Oh, but they most certainly do, Lady Thorson, it makes them feel more like men you see."

Anna sighed impatiently, exasperated by his patronizing tone. She could not understand why he would not be as honest with her as she had been with him. "Now we are back where we began, Captain. Is Lord Clairbourne such a dolt as that?"

"You have found the limit of my patience once more, Anna. Now get back into that carriage and don't speak to me again before sunset!"

"Aye, aye, Captain!" Anna smiled triumphantly, at once defying him and complying with his demand. She watched his face fill with rage. Laughing, she ran swiftly back to the black coach where she made him wait outside until she donned her stockings and shoes once again.

Phillip was soon sorry he'd issued an edict of silence. He was now awake. His distractingly attractive companion giving all her concentration to the passing scene as if he did not exist made him feel more frustrated than ever. He did not speak, however, until they reached the outskirts of the port city of Gothenburg and a large boulder at the side of the road caught his attention. He called to their driver to stop, then offered Anna his hand to help her down the steps of their carriage. "I have seen several of these rocks here in Sweden and am most curious as to their origin and purpose. Can you explain this one to me?" Phillip smiled smugly, daring her to do so as though he truly believed she'd be ignorant of the landmark.

"Of course, Captain." Anna reached out to touch the faint carvings with her fingertips. "This is a Runestone. These lines incised in the stone are letters, rune-staves, but the runic alphabet itself is called the Futhorc for the first six letters, f, u, th, o, r, c. The Norse word, *run*, meant something secret or magical. This is a monument erected to commemorate some event, a victory in battle, a birth, or perhaps a death."

"You can read these?" Phillip asked incredulously,

astonished by the depth of her knowledge.

"No, Captain," Anna replied softly. "The carving is too faint to allow me to do it without considerable study and I know you are in a hurry." With a soft smile she returned to the carriage and continued to look out the window at her side, giving her attention to the medieval city's wide canals and well-tended parks for a long while before she spoke. "Do they have cities so wonderful as this one in America, Captain?"

"No, indeed we do not, but you must realize our history is quite brief compared to that of Sweden."

Intrigued, Anna pursued the subject. "I know very little of your country. Where do you make your home?"

"The *Angelina* is my home, Lady Thorson, I have no other." Phillip was not ashamed to admit the truth, yet suddenly it saddened him to think there was no one anywhere on earth eagerly awaiting his return.

"That is the name of your ship, the *Angelina*?" Encouraged by his openness, Anna had promptly forgotten her earlier disappointment with her attempts to draw him into worthwhile conversation.

"Yes, I have been at sea most of my life and have no desire for a permanent home in any port. I hope you are not disappointed in your accommodations. The *Angelina* is a cargo ship. I seldom carry passengers but asked my mate to bunk with the crew so you might have his cabin."

"Was that really necessary, Captain? Sophia and I are accustomed to making do with what we have. I hate to take the man's cabin if there is any other possible alternative."

"You might sleep in the hold, I suppose, or share my

56

cabin. Which would you prefer?" Phillip raised an eyebrow quizzically, waiting for her reply while he viewed her rising discomfort with a wicked grin.

"Really, Captain, why is it you find it so difficult to be civil with me? When I am trying to be reasonable, why couldn't you reply in kind?"

"Oh, but I am being reasonable, Lady Thorson. Shall I assume you've decided to stay where I wished to put you in the first place?"

Anna forced herself not to scream. He was unspeakably rude and she was sick of his high-handed manner. "Please thank your first mate for me, I shall be delighted to use his cabin rather than share the hold with the rats or your quarters with you!"

Sophia sat staring wide-eyed at her mistress, not fully comprehending what was happening. Although her English was adequate for conversation she was certain she was missing most of what was passing between Anna and the captain for not all the messages seemed to be in words but in the flashing light in their eyes.

Phillip threw back his head and howled with laughter, greatly amused by her words. "Why, Lady Thorson, you make a rat-filled hold sound more attractive than my cabin."

"Believe me, it is!" Anna responded readily, unable to hold her tongue. "I am not like Catherine you see, and have no wish to share my bed with strangers."

Instantly Phillip's jovial mood vanished. "Shall we leave the countess out of this, Lady Thorson. As I told you, I doubt you need worry Lord Clairbourne will disturb your solitude."

Anna clutched her hands tightly in her lap and rode in miserable silence to the docks, again sorry she'd tried to converse with the arrogant man and wondering how she could avoid his distasteful company on what would seem to be an interminable voyage.

The lines of *Angelina*'s gleaming black hull were sleek, proof that for a merchant ship the schooner was very swift. Her three tall masts were fore and aft rigged, permitting her to carry the same tonnage as a square rigger with only one third the crew. Her decks were alive with activity and Phillip Bradford rushed up the gangplank ahead of his two charges eager to speak with Jamie Jenkins, his first officer.

Anna waited by the carriage until her recently augmented luggage could be unloaded, then she and Sophia preceded the driver and footman on board and waited for Phillip's directions. When he turned it was with surprise, as if he'd forgotten them completely. But after a moment's hesitation he walked to Anna's side, accompanied by the mate.

"Lady Thorson, Sophia, this is Jamie Jenkins. By some stroke of good fortune he was able to secure a cargo of furs for us to carry to England but they've only just started loading this afternoon so our departure will have to be delayed until the morning."

Anna could not understand the captain's apologetic tone. "I see. Then if we'd arrived last night and sailed on the morning tide you would not have been carrying any cargo, Captain?"

"Only you, my dear," Phillip replied sarcastically, but he saw her point was well-taken. "Thanks to your detour my men and I stand to make a considerable sum we'd have otherwise missed. I am in your debt therefore." He gave a mock bow then went on to explain, "You would be far more comfortable tonight in

58

n inn than in Jamie's cabin. There is one in the next
block which appears to be a fine establishment so I'll
ell the men to reload on the carriage whatever belong-
ngs you'll need for the night."

Anna glanced at Sophia and realized her maid saw
no reason not to go. Jamie Jenkins was smiling widely;
a nice-looking young man with thick black curls and
lashing brown eyes, he reached down to pick up a
small trunk the driver had just placed on deck. "No,
please wait, if it is not too much trouble I'd really pre-
er to remain on board for the night. I know our presence is an inconvenience to you, Mr. Jenkins, but I'm
sure we'll be comfortable in your cabin tonight."

Phillip counted backwards from ten to one, thinking
hat might help his temper but it did not. "Lady Thor-
on, must you disagree with me on every issue? I
vould like for you to go to the inn and I mean to see
hat is where you go. Is that understood?"

Anna looked out over the docks where about a dozen
men had been working busily to load provisions and
bales of furs but had now stopped to look up at their
captain and her with keen interest. "Captain, I want
o remain here, I find travel extremely tiring and have
no wish to go any further tonight."

"The inn is no more than one block away, hardly a
great addition to your travels. Come, let us go." Phillip
moved forward to take Anna's arm but she pulled
away angrily.

"Captain Bradford, I must speak with you privately
or a moment." Anna turned away and crossed to the
opposite side of the deck where she stood waiting impatiently by the rail.

Phillip looked at Jamie for help, but seeing the

young man's ready grin he frowned in exasperatio
and followed Anna. "Jamie is in command of th
Angelina in my absence; there may be many a tim
you'll need to speak to him rather than disturb me
And I can't imagine why you'd not wish to speak i
front of Sophia. Don't most women confide in thei
personal maids?"

Anna licked her lips lightly as she turned to look u
at the man who seemed to relish tormenting her mor
than performing any of his other duties. "I would pre
fer that my lack of resources were not widely known
Captain, but there is no way I can afford to pay fo
lodgings in an inn. I have no money at all in fact."

She had spoken proudly, without a trace of embar
rassment at her predicament and Phillip was appalle
that he had not understood her concern in the firs
place when she'd made no secret of her lack of wealth
Lying convincingly he reassured her in a comfortin
whisper, "Lord Clairbourne provided well for all you
travel expenses, Anna. I did not realize you though
you would have to pay your bill. I will see that every
thing is taken care of for you." When he offered his arm
this time she placed her fingertips lightly upon hi
sleeve and went to the inn without further argument.

"I will take the room next to yours, Lady Thorson
then I will escort you to the *Angelina* in the morning.
After ordering their suppers to be served in their room
Phillip bid the two women a terse good evening an
returned to his ship to supervise the rest of the prepara
tions to sail.

The thick fish stew was tasty but Anna had little ap
petite. She picked at her portion, moving the bits o
fish and vegetables about her plate but conveying fe

to her mouth. Sophia, however, ate her meal with enthusiasm, happy to have a full stomach for the second night in a row.

"Captain Bradford is a very thoughtful man, isn't he, Lady Anna? Imagine him taking the time to think of your comfort when he has so many other responsibilities."

Anna threw down her fork in frustration. "I find him exasperating in the extreme, Sophia, far too demanding in his manner. If Lord Clairbourne is anything like Phillip Bradford I shall refuse to marry him. I do not care what my father promised the man!"

"He is a handsome devil, though, isn't he?" Sophia offered shyly, her admiration for the young man plain.

"Yes, he is that," Anna admitted hesitantly. "But what good is such a pleasant facade when he has no heart?"

"Has he not done whatever you wished? He may complain loudly, but still he complies with your requests. He has a heart, but perhaps he has been abused and does not reveal his feelings easily."

"Abused?" Anna's golden eyes filled with sorrow, her pretty features suddenly taking on a mask of despair. "Oh, do you really think that could be true? Could that be why he is so terribly pessimistic? No matter what I say he seems to take the opposite view just to spite me. He makes me feel so helpless, Sophia, but I can not bear to think he has been hurt so badly his whole outlook on life has become cynical."

Sophia hastened to caution her mistress. "Lady Anna, you must be more careful with your sympathies. You are to become Lady Clairbourne, not Mrs. Phillip Bradford."

Anna's reaction to that bit of unwanted advice was immediate. She left her chair and made haste to prepare for bed. "That is undoubtedly the most absurd thing you have ever said to me, Sophia, as if I'd ever consider marrying such an arrogant and obnoxious man." She scoffed at the thought with a laugh which was a bit too forced to fool the older woman.

The small, dark-haired servant leapt to her feet and rushed about the room trying to catch Anna's discarded apparel before it landed upon the floor. "Please, Lady Anna, this isn't like you to be so careless with your things!"

Anna stopped pacing so abruptly Sophia nearly slammed into her back. "Yes, you are right, I am behaving like a child. Just because Captain Bradford is impossible is no reason why I should be the same. Please find my nightgown and I will try to compose myself in an adult fashion and retire for the evening." Truly, she was exhausted and was soon sound asleep only to be awakened shortly before midnight by raucous laughter and loud voices coming from the next room. She sat up in bed and listened. Clearly there was a man speaking and a woman's answering giggles. The couple continued their conversation, becoming increasingly boisterous until finally they awakened Sophia as well.

"Well, there is your thoughtful Captain Bradford again. What do you think of his manners now? Is he being considerate or merely trying to make my night as miserable as the day?" Anna asked pointedly.

Sophia climbed out of the high bed and put her ear to the wall. She blushed deeply, then dared not repeat what she'd overheard as she returned to the bed.

"Well, he is obviously not discussing the rates he charges for carrying cargo, is he?" Outraged that the man would have so little regard for her rest, Anna left her room swiftly and pounded angrily upon the door of the room from where all the merriment could be heard.

After a moment's delay, a stocky man with a full red beard appeared at the door. He stood bare-chested, clutching a tankard of ale and glared angrily at having been interrupted until he saw his visitor was an exquisitely beautiful young blonde. "Well, lass, what is it? Do you want to join our party?" Before the astonished Anna could reply, he reached out to grab her wrist and yanked her into the room, tossing her upon the unmade bed where a buxom brunette of indeterminate age and nationality lay nude, her ample figure only partially covered by the tangle of sheets.

Anna rolled off the bed as the man grabbed for her again, eluding his grasp by inches. But he caught the hem of her nightgown in one hand, spinning her around as he threw the contents of his tankard with the other, drenching the filmy silk of her gown so it clung to her form, revealing her high, firm breasts to his full view.

"Look at this, sweetheart, ain't she a beauty? I don't mind sharing my bed with the two of you!" The red-bearded man was clearly elated by his sudden good fortune and laughed loudly at Anna's attempts to get free. His female companion cackled in response, apparently eager for such sport too.

Anna struggled to get free, fighting with all her strength. But the wet floor was slippery and she fell to her knees where the man caught her again, lifting her into the air, his hands rudely grabbing for the tender swell of her bosom. She began to scream in terror then, shrieking hysterically, but the brute clamped his hand over her mouth then turned to kick the still-open door shut. Anna bit down on his fingers until she tasted blood and her attacker dropped her, cuffing her soundly with the back of his hand as he began to swear vile oaths, cursing her loudly for injuring his hand.

Before she could rise, the door flew open with a resounding crash, the old wood splintering as Phillip hit the iron handle with a brutal kick. He crossed the room at a run and struck the offensive man with a sharp jab to the chin, followed by a stunning punch to the midsection. The redhead was strong, however, and did not fall. He came back at the captain with a wild swinging left which Phillip easily avoided before landing several more punishing blows to the man's face and body. The woman on the bed cried out in fright, her coarse features contoured in anguish. When her companion glanced in her direction Phillip seized the opportunity to deliver another crushing blow to his adversary's chin sending him sprawling against the far wall before sliding to the floor in an unconscious heap.

Satisfied the red-bearded oaf would no longer trouble him, Phillip scooped up Anna and carried her back into her own room. "Sophia was clever enough to realize I was in the room on the opposite side when she saw you were in trouble. I've been in the inn for no more than five minutes; had this happened earlier you would have been on your own. What did you think you'd accomplish by going to that man's room?" Phillip took a seat in the nearest straight-backed chair without relaxing his grip upon the lovely blonde's waist. He continued to scold her, "Well, what explanation can you offer? Out with it!"

Anna was horrified by what had happened to her. It had occurred so swiftly she'd had no time to react sensibly. She relaxed against the handsome man's chest hoping he would not notice the transparent state of her gown or the fact she reeked of ale while she tried to think of some coherent reply to his question.

"Anna? Answer me this instant! Are you injured? I swear I'll go back and kill that swine if he hurt you!" Phillip was frantic; Anna seemed so small and frail as she lay in his arms. He realized suddenly she might have been seriously injured. He'd not seen her fall and had paid no attention to her condition as he'd fought off her assailant. "Anna, answer me!"

Anna sat up primly, as a child might perch on her grandfather's knee. "I will be all right in a moment, Captain. I meant only to ask the man to be more quiet as he disturbed our sleep. I would not have bothered him at all but I remembered your saying you would be in the room next door."

Phillip found it difficult to believe his ears. "Oh, I see, you thought I'd decided to invite some whore to my room and throw a wild party which you could not help but overhear?" Clearly he found her excuse ridiculous.

Anna's cheeks colored with a bright blush as she spoke. "You have not always treated me kindly, Captain. That you would wish to entertain a woman within my hearing did not seem so difficult to imagine."

"Oh, Anna." Phillip sighed sadly as he gave her a warm hug, contrite she'd again misunderstood him so completely. "Let me tell you something, my dear. This is the second time I've rescued you from an unfortunate situation. In Southampton three years ago you bumped into me in the fog as you and your father were attempting to elude the police. Men I promptly sent off in the wrong direction. I hope you accomplished your escape from that predicament in better fashion than you evaded that man's attentions tonight."

Anna's unusual tawny eyes took on an admiring sparkle as she glanced up shyly. "Why Phillip, was that you? I remember only that the man was tall and most kind. That it was you who helped us did not occur to me. I am sorry I have no way to reward you for saving me from disaster, not once but twice." As he began to smile, his expression was so wonderfully charming she found it irresistible and lifted her lips to his, kissing him with a sweetness which broke his heart.

At that moment she seemed more child than woman to Phillip, a tantalizing contradiction, a being with the effervescent charm of a young girl alive within the amply endowed body of the most alluring temptress. She was so much more complex than any woman he'd ever known and he felt himself being drawn into her kiss with a response so passionate he was shocked by the need she'd created within him. His hand left her waist to move slowly up her shapely figure, gently caressing the soft fullness of her breast until the flushed tip strained against the wet fabric of her gown. As her breathing quickened to match his own, he knew if it were a reward she was offering now he was seizing it far too hungrily. Disgusted by his own weakness, he drew away angrily, then got to his feet and carried her over to the bed where he dropped her in a startled heap.

"As Lord Clairbourne's fiancée, such a display of affection is totally inappropriate! I don't care if there is a riot which destroys the entire inn, you are not to leave this room again tonight!" With that firmly worded command he left, slamming the door soundly in his haste to flee her perpetually maddening company. But he could not escape the torment of his own growing desire.

Chapter Four

Sophia answered Phillip's knock when first he rapped at the door but he glanced impatiently over her head at the blond beauty who still lay sleeping soundly upon the bed. Anna's hand was drawn up to her slightly open mouth. She looked so sweet he could not recall why he'd been so angry when he'd come to her room. Seeing his expression change but not comprehending why, Sophia pushed the captain back out into the hall and closed the door softly.

"Is it time to be leaving, sir? I did not want to awaken Lady Anna until I had to as she spent a most miserable night and needs her rest. Yell at me for not waking her if you must, but do not be angry with her again, I beg of you."

Phillip could not help but smile at the diminutive servant's eager defense since he had not even spoken, let alone raised his voice in rebuke. "You are very loyal to your mistress, aren't you, Sophia?"

Sophia was puzzled by his question. "Of course. I have been with her all her life, sir. She never speaks harshly to me or complains about my work although I know I am often more trouble than help to her. She has always considered the welfare of her staff before her own; she would never sit down to eat if any of the rest of us were hungry and you can see for yourself my dress is far newer than most of hers. Had her dear mother's friend not been so generous with her wardrobe I don't know what we would have done to see Lady Anna properly dressed. But truly there is no finer mistress in all the world."

"That she is a young woman of such patience and virtue astounds me, Sophia, but I believe your description is sincere. I will have the innkeeper bring you some breakfast but you must hurry for I can allow you little time to prepare before we must return to my ship. The tide will not wait for Lady Anna, no matter how wonderful a mistress she might be, so I suggest you wake her immediately."

"Yes, sir, I will." Sophia turned to re-enter their room but hesitated at the doorway and watched the tall, broad-shouldered man walk down the hall. She hoped with all her heart Lord Clairbourne would be as good-looking and bright as Phillip Bradford for her dear Anna deserved no less.

Less than an hour later Anna stood on the deck of the *Angelina*, the sea breeze tossing her fair curls gently for she'd given no thought to confining them beneath a scarf or hat. She leaned against the rail enjoying the sunshine's bright gleam upon the water as she watched the port of Gothenburg fade into the distance. She'd sailed to England so frequently with her parents she tried to make believe this voyage would be like all the others rather than the one-way trip to doom she

69

was dreadfully afraid it was.

Phillip kept an eye on Anna as his men followed his orders to unfurl the sails for maximum speed in the light wind. She was not in the way where she stood, but still she was distracting for he could not recall ever having so lovely a young woman on board. His men seemed to be giving far more effort to watching her than they did to their own safety as they climbed the rigging that morning. They would be damn lucky if no one fell and finally he decided it was irresponsible of him to permit her on deck when the lives of his crew were at risk.

He approached her with long, sure steps and spoke confidently. "Lady Thorson, as I have mentioned on numerous occasions, my business is ferrying cargo, not passengers. I would prefer that you spent your time in your cabin as your presence on deck is far too distracting for my men and I'll not risk an accident which could easily claim a life."

"Surely you are not serious!" Anna responded hotly, aghast at his command. "I'll not be shut up in a room that's no more than a closet for the entire voyage!"

Phillip swore under his breath for indeed she did make his demand seem unreasonable. "I did not mean you were confined to your quarters for the duration of the voyage, Lady Thorson, only that I would prefer you to limit your time on deck to short periods. A few minutes per hour during daylight hours, there will be no harm in your strolling the decks after sunset."

"When I can't be seen?" Anna inquired snidely.

"Precisely." Phillip grinned broadly, pleased she'd understood his reasoning so rapidly.

"Then if I am the one to suffer an accident in the dark, to trip over a length of rope and break my neck the fault will be all mine?"

"I will provide an escort for your safety so you and Sophia will not encounter any unexpected danger," Phillip offered in a softer tone, hoping she'd see the wisdom in his words.

"I can't agree with you, Captain. Surely that will only make my presence here all the more distracting if your crew can look forward to seeing me so seldom. If I am out on deck frequently my presence will become so routine your men will no longer be distracted, I'm certain of it."

"Oh, really, and what is the source of your knowledge? Did the men who work your estate not dare glance up from their labors as you rode by?" Phillip put his hands on his hips, his pose as defiant as his words. "My crew are free men and not nearly so docile as the servants you have known."

Anna straightened her shoulders proudly. "Our estate is not staffed by slaves but by tenant farmers with a share in our production. Unfortunately, none of us did well last year as you know, but the men were not afraid to speak with me, nor were they so awed by my presence that they tripped over their plows when they did."

"Be that as it may—" Phillip began impatiently.

"Sailors are no strangers to women, Captain. I'll wager they become accustomed to my presence in a day or two and none will suffer any harm."

"And if any do?" Phillip inquired belligerently.

"Then they'd probably be such poor seamen they should just be flung overboard and be done with!"

Anna turned back toward the rail, her delicate brows creased by a furious frown. She had no intention of giving in to the overbearing man. Her mother and father had always enjoyed strolling on deck with her between them. Now she was the only one left alive and she'd be damned if she'd remain in her cabin like a prisoner!

"I hope there are no serious injuries to weigh heavily upon your conscience, Lady Thorson. You may stand there until you are sunburned to the shade of mahogany for all I care!" But as Phillip turned to go Anna called out to him in the low, seductive voice of a siren.

"Thank you, Captain, but I have one question."

"Yes? Be quick about it, I haven't all day to stand here and chat with you."

"I could not help but notice the row of gun ports below deck. Since this is a merchant vessel, why is she so heavily armed?" Anna turned to face him, the seriousness of her question surprising him once more.

"You are very observant, Anna. While I do not expect to be boarded by pirates in the North Sea, their numbers are many in the Caribbean. The *Angelina* is exceedingly fast, and she is well armed, both for a good purpose I assure you." With a brief nod, Phillip walked off to see to his other duties and did not look her way again.

Anna smiled to herself. Pirates indeed! She returned her gaze to the sparkling sea and did not go below to her cabin for more than an hour at which point she found Sophia had unpacked their belongings and folded them neatly upon the two bunks.

"I shan't need the clothes Catherine gave me until we arrive at Briarcliff, Sophia. You may put those away and just keep my own things out. They will do for the time being."

"Doesn't the captain expect you to dine with him, Lady Anna? You'll need these pretty garments to wear for him."

Anna stared at her maid for a long moment, then began to laugh. "Are you the same woman who warned me only last night to be more careful of my feelings? Is it not plain to you by now that the man does not even like me? It will matter little what I wear to meals; I will not go to any great lengths to dress in order to please Phillip Bradford."

"Still, you are soon to be a countess and you should behave accordingly," Sophia pointed out with a disapproving frown.

"As the captain is fond of saying, this is not a passenger ship. He undoubtedly dines with the mate and my presence would be most awkward as I am sure they usually discuss business matters. I think it would be best if I asked to have my meals served here and avoided his table altogether."

"But you can not eat here with me as though you were a servant too!" Sophia protested tearfully.

Anna hugged her maid warmly. "Hush, the matter is settled. I will go and tell Captain Bradford of my decision now for surely he will be pleased."

Phillip, however, was not pleased. "It is only common courtesy that the captain of a vessel share his table with his passengers, Lady Thorson. It is the custom and one I will not change for this voyage. No matter how distasteful you may find my company, I insist you will share it."

Anna looked up, her long-lashed eyes wide, surprised by the man's hostile attitude. "I have tried to be friendly, Captain. It is you who does not like me, not the other way around. I will not accept the blame for our continual lack of accord. I meant only to spare you the ordeal of my company, it is not that I would not enjoy yours."

Taken aback, Phillip could think of no reply, nothing at all to say to the striking young woman who stood watching him closely as if he were some strange curiosity on display for her amusement. "I am not used to such flattery and consideration, Lady Thorson. I did not mean to seem less than a gracious host. I will look forward to your company tonight and trust we can pass a pleasant meal together."

Anna smiled readily, pleased that for once he had given in to her without arguing until she realized it was she who had agreed to his wishes. What a perplexing man! Embarrassed that she'd not been able to recall why she'd come to see him in the first place, she blushed deeply as she turned to leave. "Until later then, Captain."

Phillip glanced around his cabin after Anna had gone. Like all ships' quarters there were ingeniously placed shelves and drawers so all gear could be neatly stowed away, but he had to admit the room lacked any sort of tidiness. He spent the next half hour refolding his clothing so the drawers would shut properly, then gave his attention to his desk and charts which hadn't been straightened in recent memory. He and Jamie knew where everything was kept but they'd both become lax; he restored the intricate maps to their proper order. With any luck, they'd make the journey rapidly and he would be able to hand the lovely Anna over to Lord Clairbourne and sail away, at last the sole owner of the *Angelina*. That thought brought no joy, however, for no matter how well he was being paid for the task, delivering the gorgeous Anna Thorson to Lord Clairbourne would not be worth the price to his conscience.

After careful consideration, Anna chose a soft gray cashmere dress to wear to dinner. It was one Catherine had provided for travel. With a high neck and long, close-fitting sleeves it was extremely modest and provided precisely the image she wished to project. She was going to be polite, a perfect lady in all respects. She secured her gleaming curls in a tight coil at her nape to complete her preparations. "There, what do you think, Sophia?" She turned slowly, showing off her efforts proudly.

"You look as though you were in mourning, Lady Anna, but why?"

"I want only to appear to be a grown woman, and a most serious one too. I have failed to earn the captain's respect, for a reason I do not pretend to comprehend, and I want to remedy that sorry situation tonight."

Sophia opened the door slowly. "Perhaps he respects you too much, rather than too little, Lady Anna. Do not try and be too clever."

Ignoring her maid's advice, Anna swept through the door with a brisk, determined step and met Jamie Jenkins as she approached Phillip's cabin. The mate was handsomely dressed in a brown velvet coat and beige breeches and smiled widely as he greeted her.

"I have been looking forward to this all day, Lady Thorson. It is not often that I have the honor of dining with a countess."

"I am not a countess as yet, Mr. Jenkins, so I am

afraid your enthusiasm is premature."

As Jamie began to laugh Phillip opened his door and stood aside to allow them to enter. He'd gone to as much trouble to dress properly as Jamie had. He lifted an eyebrow quizzically, puzzled by his guests' jovial mood.

"Lady Thorson was explaining her title, for as you know I have had little opportunity to dine with royalty." Jamie found flirting with the pretty blonde far easier than he'd expected; it was a pastime he enjoyed immensely and practiced often.

"Please, Mr. Jenkins, I am not one of the royal family. While my family is among the Swedish aristocracy, we're not considered to be royalty. My father was the younger son and had no title, his elder brother is the count. I am called Lady but it is as a courtesy, for I have no title of my own. In fact, I did not use the name Thorson at home. Our custom is different than that of the British and a child takes his father's first name for his last. My Father was Eric Thorson because my grandfather's name was Thor. Had I had brothers, their name would be Ericson; I was known as Anna Ericdotter. Since we went to England so frequently, my mother preferred I use Thorson so our names would all be the same and no confusion would be caused. So while I would like to be called Lady Thorson, you need not treat me as though I were a princess."

Jamie helped Anna to her chair, entranced by the lovely young woman's easy manner and delightful smile. Phillip took his seat in a far more somber mood. That Anna had chosen so modest a gown confused him for he had expected something in silk, low cut and elaborately trimmed with lace, not a garment so subtle in both texture and hue. Yet as his glance swept down her slender figure he found the form-fitting dress impossibly distracting, for it accented her fair beauty with a subtle perfection he could not ignore. When she looked his way and smiled he could barely find his voice. "Would you care for some wine, Lady Thorson?"

"Yes, please." Anna was surprised by the elegance of the table. The white linen cloth was spotless, the utensils were heavy silver as were the goblets. "No wonder pirates stalk the *Angelina*, Captain. You have a fortune in silver right here."

Phillip leaned forward and whispered slyly, "There are some who say I am a pirate, Lady Thorson. Perhaps this is part of some unfortunate ship's booty."

"Now you are teasing me, Captain, and that is unfair," Anna replied demurely, astonished by his comment, for it was so unlike him to be playful.

"No, he is not teasing you, Lady Thorson. There are few among the crew of the *Angelina* who have not sailed on ships with questionable missions and cargo." Jamie readily joined in the fun, giving her a sly wink.

"Do you expect me to believe Lord Clairbourne sent a ship full of pirates to fetch me? He will be fortunate then if you do not hold me for ransom I suppose."

Jamie groaned loudly. "Clairbourne would blow us out of the water before he'd pay a ransom on his own mother; you need have no worry we'd consider asking for one for you."

"Jamie, let us allow Lady Thorson to form her own opinion of her future husband. We are being well paid for escorting her safely to his side and we should be satisfied with that show of generosity on his part," Phillip interjected abruptly, ending their game with a solemn command.

Jamie frowned, then shrugged and fell silent as a young man brought in the silver tray laden with covered dishes. First he served a sumptuous fish chowder, then a savory roast chicken before he left them to dine alone.

Anna was sorry she'd spoiled their playful mood by mentioning Clairbourne's name for she'd known Phillip would have few good words to say about the man and should have known better. Hoping to make amends she offered a sincere compliment. "This chicken is delicious, Captain. Your chef is obviously a fine one." She had found the tender fowl finely seasoned and well prepared, but as she glanced up the two young men were smiling sheepishly and she could not understand why. "Did I say something wrong, gentlemen?"

"Michael is our ship's cook, but he is certainly no chef. He spent the entire day trying to decide what to serve for your dinner tonight," Jamie confided with a charming grin. "I will tell him you were pleased."

Anna laid her fork on the side of her plate and frowned unhappily. "Captain Bradford, really, I did not mean to cause so much trouble for your crew. Please tell your men not to go to any special lengths on my account. It simply isn't necessary."

Phillip shot Jamie a knowing glance then grew stern as he replied, "Since you delight in spending so much of your time on deck, I can not demand they ignore you, Lady Thorson, so why does it shock you to learn our cook, or any of the other men, would try and im-

78

press you favorably? Surely you are not so naive that you can not appreciate the effect a beautiful young woman has upon a man."

Anna was mortified by his taunting insult. She knew little about pleasing men but she knew all she cared to know of Phillip Bradford. "I have enjoyed your company, Mr. Jenkins. Please forgive me but I believe I've just been sent to my cabin. Goodnight, Captain." Anna left their presence so swiftly neither man had time to rise. She ran the short distance to her quarters and slammed the door soundly.

Sophia sat at the small desk eating her meal from a tray, startled by her mistress's sudden return. "What is it, Lady Anna, what has happened?" she asked in dismay.

Anna folded her arms across the fullness of her breast and leaned back against the door. "I know I am not an unreasonable woman, Sophia, I am sure of that, but Captain Bradford twists every word I speak until it is no longer recognizable. He seems to believe I go up on deck simply to tease his crew."

"He would not dare say such a thing to you!" Sophia protested heatedly.

"Oh, yes, he would, he just did in fact and I said goodnight. I'll not dine with that beast ever again, even if I have to toss a line off the stern and catch fish for my supper!" Anna vowed as she tore the pins from her hair. Hot tears of anger burned her eyes but she would not shed a single one over that monster's nasty insults. "Compared to Phillip Bradford, Lord Clairbourne will seem a prince, no matter how great a fool he might prove to be!"

Sophia wiped off her hands and pushed her half-eaten meal aside. "Whatever are we going to do now, Lady Anna? You can not pass the entire voyage without speaking to the captain!"

"And why not? The sea gulls which follow in the ship's wake hoping for scraps of garbage are better company than he is! I swear I will take up fishing on the morrow!"

Sophia rushed to find her mistress's hairbrush, hoping to groom her long tresses before she prepared for bed. "Please sit down and compose yourself, Lady Anna. Tomorrow I am certain things will look brighter."

Anna sat down, but composure eluded her grasp. "How long have we known that man, Sophia, has it been no more than three days? It seems like a lifetime, our encounters are so incessantly disagreeable. I have done nothing to deserve such dislike as that impossible man shows me."

"Well, for one thing, he did not like your surprising him with a stop at Lady Catherine's, nor did you exercise good judgment in going to that stranger's room last night, Lady Anna. Captain Bradford provokes easily it seems and you must admit you have given him cause for his anger. Perhaps now that we are on board his ship he will feel more confident about trusting your behavior but you must give him a few days to adjust to your presence."

"No! I'll give him nothing!" Anna declared vehemently, her hands held in tightly clenched fists in her lap. "Not one single thing!"

A sharp knock rattled the door and both women turned, yet neither cared to answer the noisy summons. After a moment's pause Sophia laid the brush down and moved to see who had come to call. When Jamie Jenkins asked politely to speak with Anna, the young lady rose and came to the door.

"If Captain Bradford sent you to apologize to me, you may tell him he must come himself but I still won't forgive his rudeness!"

Jamie laughed at her show of temper and shook his head. "No, the captain would never come here nor would he send me on such an errand. The night is too lovely to waste in quarreling. Won't you come walk with me for a while?"

"Well, I . . ." Anna was astonished by the invitation. The view of the stars would be spectacular from up on deck, the air so fresh and clean, but the company appeared to be far too forward for her tastes. "I must regretfully decline your invitation, Mr. Jenkins. I am really very tired and have already begun my preparations to retire."

Unwilling to give in so easily, Jamie persisted. "You ate little at supper. Might I bring you something more?"

"No, thank you, I've quite lost my appetite. Now I really must bid you a good night." But as Anna moved to close the door Jamie stepped forward to block her way.

"I will see you in the morning then, Lady Thorson, and I am truly sorry, even if the captain is not, that you two had a misunderstanding. He is one of the finest men I've ever known. As a captain he has no equal for he knows more about the sea than the fishes do, but he has had scant experience entertaining elegant young ladies of the Swedish court and—"

"Mr. Jenkins, please, if Captain Bradford only had

the manners of the most ignorant peasant I would be pleased but unfortunately he has none! Now goodnight!" Anna closed the door so abruptly Jamie had to leap out of her way, but he walked away whistling happily, for if Anna disliked Phillip so greatly, surely she would come to enjoy his far more eager company, and soon.

Chapter Five

The *Angelina*'s sleek, black hull sliced through the gleaming waters of the North Sea with flashing precision; in full sail she raced the moon with her tall, proud captain at the wheel. He was determined to better the record time between Gothenburg and Southampton. His ship was swift, but he made her swifter, pushing her along her course until she nearly flew over the waves. Never had he looked forward to a voyage's end with such eager anticipation as he did this one. His blood still boiled in his veins, his anger undiminished by the hours which had passed since Anna had pranced out of his cabin during supper. The woman seemed to have been placed on earth merely to torment him and he could tolerate no more of her high-handed antics.

Jamie was no help at all, he thought bitterly. The man was positively drooling over Anna like all the rest of his idiotic crew. Imbeciles every one of them, so taken by their aristocratic passenger's fair hair and slender figure they saw none of her proud disdain.

"Lady Thorson!" he snarled to himself. Her very name annoyed him immensely for she was no lady but a willful girl out to drive him to the limits of his endurance for the mere sport of it! Clairbourne deserved such a wife. Surely if any man did it was that bastard and he'd see Charles wasn't kept waiting a minute longer than was necessary either.

Anna lay upon her bunk no more content than Phillip, her fingers nervously pleating the soft woolen blanket as she tried vainly to fall asleep. She was too anxious to rest, far too restless to find solace in slumber and stared up into the darkness waiting for the dawn of the new day to flood the cabin with sunlight. Gradually her mind turned to her last memories of her father. He had returned home in the summer of 1801, tired and thin. He'd said little of his lengthy journey and had immediately taken to his bed with a fever which consumed his energy quickly, burning away what was left of his life in a few days' time. There had been no opportunity to bid him farewell let alone discuss how she should spend the rest of her life without him, but Anna still could not understand why he'd not mentioned his meeting with Lord Clairbourne. They had been so close, each so dear to the other after her mother's tragic death that she'd never suspected him of keeping any secret from her. Yet secret seemed to be too insignificant a term to describe his silence over her engagement for it was treachery of the grandest sort. Had he expected her to argue? Had he feared she'd refuse to leave him to take up residence in England? What could his reasoning have been that he would have confided the news of her forthcoming marriage in his brother whom he'd never even liked and not told her

84

whom he adored?

Pained by that unanswerable question, Anna sat up and threw back the covers. She'd not go up on deck after the remarks the captain had made, but she felt as though she were suffocating in the small airless cabin. The room was only slightly larger than a cell. It contained two bunks, a desk, minimal storage, not even enough floor space to pace successfully so she sat dejectedly, dangling her long legs over the side of the bed while she tried to sort out the muddle her life had become. Captain Bradford was merely a nuisance, a bothersome distraction when she should be concentrating all her efforts on her preparations to meet Lord Clairbourne. Why had the man not contacted her after her father had died? Shouldn't he have been concerned about her welfare if they were to be wed? Surely her uncle would have written to the man, if only to make certain the arrangements her father had made would be honored, whatever they might have been. None of it made any sense to her; she was on her way to marry a stranger about whom she knew very little. Phillip had never described the man's appearance so she had no idea what to expect. Perhaps he would be bald and fat, or very tall and spare with a dour mood to match. Her father's constant worry had been money, so apparently he'd found her a rich husband and considered his duty done, but finances were such a small part of marriage, and she could not believe they were all that important.

Had her mother still been alive Anna knew she would never have been treated so badly. Her mother would have insisted upon a younger man, a bright and happy individual who would have made her daughter's marriage the paradise her own had been. As Anna heard the bells tolling the half hours of the watch, it seemed as though her very life were slipping through her fingers, the hours like grains of sand she could not catch and hold. Sophia was always optimistic, thinking Clairbourne might be a fine man, but she had no such high hopes herself. Catherine had said it mattered little what sort of man a woman's husband might be when there were so many others willing to provide affection. "No!" Anna exclaimed angrily to herself, "I will not wed one man and share my bed with others!" Such an existence was unthinkable to her; she'd not make a mockery of her wedding vows by becoming a whore who'd provide pleasure for whomever cared to partake of her favors.

Anna felt trapped. She knew she had rebelled against the only person she could reach, only now realizing none of her problems were of Phillip Bradford's making. She was angry with her father for his secrecy, furious with her uncaring uncle, suspicious of the stranger who would become her husband, but she'd have to do better to see the captain didn't suffer because of her problems with the other men in her life. "I am sorry, Phillip, truly I am." With that small promise she lay back down on the narrow bunk and closed her eyes, exhaustion providing the needed reason for sleep at last.

When Anna next awoke it was midday, the weather had turned foul and Sophia lay moaning upon her bunk too seasick to rise. A breakfast tray sat untouched on the desk, the only evidence a new day had begun. "Oh Lady Anna, I am so dreadfully ill I cannot even stand. Can you do without me today?"

"Of course, you just rest quietly. Perhaps the storm

86

won't last much longer and then we can go up on deck. Fresh air is the best cure for your ailment but I'll not take you out now and risk your catching pneumonia."

Anna had a difficult time dressing as the ship sped through the high swells of the sea, creating a rolling motion which gave her no firm footing as she attempted to pull on her numerous layers of clothing. "It looks as though I won't be able to fish today after all. It is fortunate this weather is not conducive to building a hearty appetite."

"Oh, please, I beg of you, Lady Anna, do not mention food to me again!" Sophia pleaded softly as she raised her arm to cover her eyes.

Anna smiled sympathetically at her maid's discomfort but wondered what she could do with herself all day. She'd brought along a few books but the sharp roll of the *Angelina* made reading nearly impossible and she soon gave up the effort and curled up again upon her bunk. She could not recall the last time she'd had absolutely nothing which needed to be done but she did not enjoy her enforced leisure one bit. She wanted to speak to Phillip, to accept whatever conditions he wished to impose upon her activities in the interest of restoring harmony to his ship. By evening the storm had still not abated and her dinner was brought to her cabin along with Sophia's.

Anna recognized the young man who had served their meal the previous evening and greeted him warmly. "Thank you. I'm sorry, but I don't know your name."

"It is John, Lady Thorson," the startled boy replied with a stutter. "I am the cook's helper and he apologizes for the meager nature of this supper but the storm is too fierce to permit him to prepare more than soup and bread tonight." Drawing a deep breath he continued as if he were afraid he'd forget all he'd been told to say. "Neither Captain Bradford nor Mr. Jenkins can spare the time to eat and beg you to forgive them."

"I understand. This is fine. Please thank Michael for us. Does the captain think the storm is nearly over?"

"No, ma'am, it seems to be moving right along with us."

"How dreadful. Well, thank you again for bringing our supper. Goodnight." Anna waited until John had left then turned toward her maid. "Would you like to try and eat something? I'm certain it will make you feel better."

Sophia only moaned and turned on her side, preferring to face the wall rather than the steaming tureen of soup. She pulled the covers up to her chin and went back to sleep, certain she had died sometime during the afternoon and Anna had been too polite to tell her.

Anna ate the tasty vegetable soup slowly, trying not to spill as much as she consumed. How unfortunate that the weather had deteriorated so badly when it had been so lovely in Sweden for the past few weeks. Perhaps the gods themselves did not want her to travel to England, she thought bitterly, but they needn't have made everyone's life miserable if they'd wanted only to make her turn back.

The weather the next day was no better, the sky overcast and gray. A freezing rain swept the deck repeatedly keeping Anna again confined to her cabin and Sophia confined to her bunk while Phillip was too busy maintaining the ship's course to worry over his passengers' comfort. He kept Jamie too occupied for the mate to have time for Anna; he had no men to spare for one young lady's entertainment. He felt a grim satisfaction as the driving rain soaked through his clothing and ran down his back, for at least the deck was again free of the exasperating Lady Thorson. Without realizing it his eyes continued to sweep the rail where she'd stood as they left Gothenburg; not that he'd thought she'd appear again as a phantom from the mist but she was such a contrary female he half expected her to brave the rain simply to spite him.

When he was relieved at the end of the watch, Phillip made his way to his cabin, peeling off his coat, then pulling his sweater over his head as he came through the door. When Anna spoke he wheeled around to face her, shocked by the intimate tone of her voice as much as by her unexpected presence in his quarters.

"I have seen men without their shirts before, Captain, but before you disrobe any further I'd like a word with you." Anna could not help but smile as she noticed a blush fill his cheeks with color. Drenched by the rain, his thick, dark curls lay flat against his head giving him a boyish quality she'd never expected him to have. His deep golden tan extended to his waist, evidence he seldom wore a shirt on deck in good weather, and a tangle of coarse, dark hair covered his broad chest narrowing to a thin line as it grew across the taut muscles of his flat stomach. He was a handsome sight, well muscled and sleek, but she was surprised he'd be so embarrassed by her presence and attempted to reassure him. "You are a very handsome man, Captain, as I'm sure you know but I didn't come here to pay you compliments."

Phillip groaned with real pain. "Lady Thorson, you may have five minutes of my time then I'm going to strip off the rest of my clothing and crawl into my bunk. Now what is it? Surely this is not purely a social call?"

Anna laughed, hoping he was teasing her again. "No, of course not. Why don't you sit down here with me? John just brought a pot of hot tea, or would you rather have some rum or ale?"

"This is my cabin, not yours!" Phillip pointed out angrily. "I'll serve myself whatever I want." Then with sudden insight he asked, "Don't tell me you've decided your cabin is too small and you want mine instead?"

Anna shook her head and gestured toward the chair at her side. "Won't you please sit down and talk to me for a moment? I'm sure you can do it without shouting if you'll only try."

Phillip glared fiercely, but was too tired to argue. Sighing unhappily he sat down beside her, placed his arms upon the table, then laid his head upon them and, getting comfortable, closed his eyes. "Hurry up, you've no more than four minutes left and I'm already falling asleep."

"Would you like me to rub your back? I'm very good at it." Before he could refuse Anna rose from her chair, stepped behind him and placed her slender fingers upon the back of his neck in a gentle caress. "See, doesn't that feel good?" she purred softly, already knowing what his answer would be.

It felt heavenly but Phillip was too astonished to admit the truth. Whatever was the young woman doing to him? Her fingertips moved in small, even circles, massaging away the tension which made his whole back throb with a dull ache. His cool, wet skin was soon flooded with a delicious warmth which brought a satisfied smile to his lips. "Where did you learn how to do that, Anna?"

"I told you my mother taught me many things." Anna leaned down slightly to watch his expression and was pleased by his widening grin. "Ah, that's much better. I see your mood has improved. I wanted to apologize to you, Captain. I've been on my own for a long while, since my mother's death five years ago really, although losing my father too made my independence complete. Until two weeks ago I'd never even heard Lord Clairbourne's name let alone considered marriage to the man. The world I've known has disintegrated around me, left me with nothing I can truly call my own but I shouldn't have given you such a difficult time. I can't believe I suggested you toss overboard any men who might fall while they were looking at me. I'm not usually so vicious but you had every right to be cross with me. Will you forgive me?"

Phillip could barely summon his voice to reply. Her touch was exquisite, tantalizingly sensuous, and he could neither tell her to stop nor beg her to continue for a long moment. He wanted simply to pull her into his arms and insist she share his bed, for the desire she aroused within him was too strong to deny. Yet deny it he must for she was to become Clairbourne's bride and not his. Finally by a great force of will power he was able to whisper hoarsely, "Yes, you're forgiven."

Jamie Jenkins knocked on the door as he came through it, then halted abruptly, his mouth agape as he took in what appeared to be the lovely Anna Thorson caressing Phillip's half-clothed body. "Oh, my God, excuse me, I mean I never even thought. I'm sorry Captain."

Anna remained where she stood, her hands resting lightly upon Phillip's broad shoulders and he made n move to escape her touch as he sat up to respond to th mate's embarrassed greeting. "What is it, Jamie Can't you see we're busy?"

"It was only a minor problem, Captain, I'll tend t it myself." Jamie turned, nearly stumbling as he ran from the cabin, his haste was so great to leave their in timate scene.

Anna laughed impishly as she dropped her hands t her sides and turned toward the door. "Goodbye, Cap tain, we seem to have shocked Mr. Jenkins rathe badly and I'm certain my four minutes must be up b now."

"Wait!" Phillip reached out to catch her hand the released it quickly, surprised by the warmth of her fin gertips as well as his own boldness. "I am far more vi cious than you will ever be, Anna. All that I ask is tha you stop to consider your actions more fully before yo take them. Then neither of us will have to suffer an further."

There was a softness in his glance she'd never befor seen, the light in his deep blue eyes as tender as a ca ress. Her breath caught in her throat as she tried t speak. "I must go, Captain, please send for me whe next we might have supper together." She left his cabi as swiftly as Jamie had, shocked by the remarkabl change that had come over the handsome man. He ha been so nice, his deep voice gentle, why, he'd seeme not to have been the same person. He had responded t her touch not as she'd expected him to but as a love might and she could not believe what she had done. Whatever must he think of her now? He'd seemed so tired, simply worn out and she'd meant only to ease his fatigue, but her effect upon him had obviously been a far more erotic one. She was clearly as naive as he'd accused her of being but he'd shown her a side to his personality she'd not even imagined existed, and even more amazing, she had truly liked him!

By the time the inclement weather finally cleared, several days had passed and Anna was uncertain just what had really transpired between them the afternoon she'd gone to Phillip's cabin. Perhaps the entire incident had been an innocent one, as she'd intended it to be, and yet she could not help but feel her original impression had been the correct one and that something unique had passed between them, a delicious tension she could not name but had felt as strongly as he had. When she awoke at dawn to find the sun shining brightly again she hesitated to go up on deck for fear she would incur the man's wrath all over again. But Sophia would listen to none of her pathetic excuses for not spending their time enjoying the morning's unexpected beauty.

"Let us go for a stroll, Lady Anna. You've grown so pale cooped up in here with me that Lord Clairbourne is likely to receive the impression you are sickly when nothing could be further from the truth."

"I do not want to be in the way again, Sophia. The crew will be hard at work and Captain Bradford has enough to do without worrying about my presence on deck." Anna remained seated at the desk, pretending to read a novel she'd begun three times but could not seem to finish.

Sophia stared at her pretty mistress, her expression filled with surprise. "I did not expect to ever hear you say you were concerned about what he would think of you. Why I thought that—"

Anna slammed her book closed, again giving up the effort to read as futile. "Yes, I know what I said and it would be better if we did not dwell upon it. Let's go up on deck and see if we can find a spot where we will not be in anyone's way." But as soon as they left the seclusion of their cabin they could hear Phillip shouting orders and the sound of running feet as his men rushed to obey. Anna was torn by indecision. She wanted to spend all her time out in the open for the sea provided an endlessly changing panorama she greatly enjoyed but her freedom was not worth risking another bitter argument with Phillip. Anxious for a breath of fresh air, Sophia simply pushed her reluctant mistress out into the sunshine, the tiny maid too impatient to wait any longer for what she considered much-needed exercise. Anna moved quickly to the rail and hoped their presence would not be noted for some time but Jamie Jenkins was at her side in less than a minute.

"Good morning, Lady Thorson, how pleasant it is to see you again." He bowed slightly, then turned so he might lean back against the rail and folded his arms across his chest. "Let us hope that is the last of the bad weather between here and Britain. Captain Bradford is making every effort to increase our speed, although why he is in such a tremendous hurry I do not pretend to understand. There is no need to rush a load of furs to their destination with such haste as he is making nor is there any reason to want to escape your delightful company so shortly either."

94

Anna was amazed the mate did not seem to understand what he was saying but clearly he did not. "You mean the captain is making better time than you'd anticipated for no apparent reason?"

"Oh, he has a reason I've no doubt for that man does nothing without cause, but he explains little to me. Close-mouthed he is, perhaps the Swedes have some similar expression to describe a man of few words."

"Yes, I understand what you mean. I'm just beginning to appreciate the fact my father was more that type of man than I'd realized." Anna's knuckles grew white as she clutched the mahogany rail with all her strength. She'd been wrong obviously, nothing had changed between them. Phillip wanted only to be rid of her and with all possible haste! Why had she been so foolish as to consider his feelings that morning when he clearly had no regard for hers?

"Lady Thorson?" Jamie spoke again, attempting to penetrate her veiled glance.

"I'm sorry, did you say something to me?" Anna turned her golden gaze upon the young man. He was quite nice looking, using all his charm to win her attention, but she cared little what he might have said.

"Yes, I asked if you've found my cabin satisfactory. I know it cannot be nearly so elegant as your bedchamber must have been in your own home."

Anna frowned slightly. Surely it couldn't be considered proper for a man to inquire about a lady's room. Jamie's eagerness to converse with her was unsettling. She was unskilled in flirting as Phillip had discovered, but she knew the mate of a Yankee schooner should not treat her with such a shocking lack of respect and was most insulted. "Your quarters are adequate, Mr.

Jenkins, I appreciate your loaning them to us. Now, please don't let me keep you from your other duties this morning." Anna turned away, giving her attention to the distant horizon and hoped the young man would have sense enough to leave her before she was forced to reject his attentions even more rudely.

Jamie touched his cap lightly in a mock salute. "I will look forward to this evening then." He moved across the deck with a jaunty swagger, whistling to himself as he went about his work.

Sophia waited until they could not be overheard, then whispered softly, "He seems very taken with you, Lady Anna. I do hope Lord Clairbourne is not the jealous sort."

"Why should he be? I'll give him no reason to criticize my behavior, none whatsoever!" Anna was shocked by her faithful servant's remark, appalled that Sophia could even think such a thing. Hurt, she turned away so abruptly she would have collided soundly with Phillip Bradford had he not reached out to catch her shoulders in a firm grasp.

"Lady Thorson, the day is such a fine one, are you returning to your cabin so quickly?" Phillip chided her with a sly smile. "I expected you to spend the entire day with us."

Anna tried to pull free but Phillip only tightened his hold so she could not escape him without replying. Furious, her eyes filled with a murderous gleam as she looked up at him. "I know you find my presence on board your ship most distasteful, Captain, but unfortunately it cannot be avoided for the time being. Now if you will be good enough to stand aside I will leave you to enjoy the sunshine alone."

With a puzzled nod, Phillip dropped his hands to his sides and stepped back. "I will blame your insufferable mood on your enforced confinement of the last few days, Countess, and assume your parents taught you better manners than you usually display."

"I am not yet a countess!" Anna walked swiftly back to her cabin, her step light despite the roll of the deck beneath her feet. She wanted to scream, to shriek at everyone to leave her alone but Sophia followed rapidly on her heels.

"Lady Anna! Must you continually insult that man without the slightest provocation? He said no more than good day and your response could not have been more argumentative!" Sophia wrung her hands nervously. "I do not understand why you have become such a shrew when you have always been the dearest of young women!"

Anna sat down at the desk and put her head in her hands. "Please, Sophia, don't you turn against me too." The fair-haired beauty could barely control her rage. She was being pushed, no shoved, into the arms of a man she had no desire to even meet, let alone wed. A true gentleman would have come himself to claim her or at least sent some close friend or relative to escort her to his home, not simply dispatched some Yankee captain to fetch his bride. Was this a fair sample of how she could expect to be treated by Lord Clairbourne?

Sophia had never seen her mistress so distressed and had no idea of the cause for her mood. She waited only a moment then returned to the deck to seek the captain's advice. He was a reasonable man in her opinion and she prayed he would be able to lift Anna's spirits from the depths of depression to which they had so obviously sunk.

Phillip clasped his hands behind his back and made an effort to listen attentively as Sophia wept openly over her lovely young mistress's plight. The Anna the little woman clearly adored was so far removed from the high-spirited girl he knew he could not believe they were discussing the same individual. "I will send John with a pot of tea, Sophia. I can do no more to soothe Lady Thorson's volatile temper. Personally I think she is a spoiled brat who should simply be spanked but I will allow Lord Clairbourne to have that pleasure himself!"

Sophia's dark eyes widened in terror. She reached out to clutch at the tall captain's sleeve in a frantic grasp. "Surely the man would not beat her! You must put us ashore elsewhere, tell the man Anna drowned, but I will not let that sweet child go to a man who would mistreat her!"

Phillip chuckled at her panic. "Sophia, you completely misunderstood me. I cannot predict what Clairbourne's reaction to your mistress will be, I only know my own and she gives me not a moment's peace. I will expect her to join me in my cabin for supper tonight. If she is too depressed to speak then so much the better as perhaps it will save us an argument for a change!" Phillip summoned John to serve tea as he'd promised, then forgot Anna completely until he went below to dress for the evening meal.

Anna had chosen a blue gown which set off her exquisite coloring to every advantage but she was so subdued during supper Phillip began to lose patience with her again. Jamie kept up a steady stream of conversation, seemingly unaware of their guest's lack of response as he described one of their more adventurous voyages in colorful detail. Phillip had great difficulty believing he had shared the same experience when finally Jamie drew to the end of the long but amusing tale. Anna did not even glance in the mate's direction, let alone acknowledge the young man's efforts to entertain her. When Jamie looked to him for some help Phillip did no more than shake his head, but he was not pleased when the mate made an excuse to leave them alone at his first opportunity.

"Lady Thorson, is it impossible for you to be pleasant even for so brief a time as it requires to share one meal? Jamie did everything but stand on his head this evening and you did not even smile at him. The man has feelings even if you are unaware of them. You seem to go out of your way to ignore his best efforts to please you." Phillip was clearly angry, the muscles along his jaw tense, the set of his lips firm.

"What? I beg your pardon?" Anna took a sip of her wine then placed her goblet carefully upon the table before she turned to look at her host, giving him her full attention for the first time that evening.

Startled by the innocence of her glance, Phillip attempted to be more courteous in his complaint. "Mr. Jenkins was only trying to amuse you tonight. It would not have cost you anything to smile even if you did not listen to his story with rapt attention." Which she obviously hadn't, he didn't bother to add.

"I am sorry, Captain, perhaps your customs are different from mine, but would it not be unseemly for me to encourage the man when I am engaged to another? That he flirts with me so openly does not please me but

99

I had hoped I would not have to tell him so to his face. I thought he would soon realize I did not enjoy his attentions and desist. Have I been unforgivably rude? I assure you I did not mean to be."

Phillip was unable to respond for a long moment, but once he understood her concern he had to agree her point was well taken. "Jamie is behaving no differently than he usually does. He loves women immensely and any pretty young thing appeals to him greatly. Since our voyages are usually devoid of such an enticing diversion as you present he undoubtedly did not consider your station in life far exceeds his own and that—"

Anna reached out and touched Phillip's sleeve lightly. "Please, Captain, you have seen my home even if Mr. Jenkins has not. My nobility is merely an illusion, a deception my father managed to maintain with Lord Clairbourne but not one to which I cling. I am a penniless young woman on my way to marry a man I do not love. I have terrible misgivings, a feeling of foreboding that the marriage will be a most regrettable mistake for us both and yet I can think of no way to avoid it other than throwing myself into the sea. If I do not find Mr. Jenkins's superficial charm appealing, can you not understand why?"

Her serious tone left no room for doubt. Her fair beauty was always astonishing, but now at last he understood her miserable mood had just cause. "I cannot help but believe I am partly to blame for your unhappiness, Anna. My remarks about Lord Clairbourne were most inappropriate ones to make to his future wife. I know him as a business man only, not as a friend. He will treat you far differently than he treats me, I am certain of it and I am truly sorry if I've added to your worries by my thoughtlessness." Phillip spoke in the most reassuring manner he could affect, but still the sorrow was so deep in Anna's golden eyes he was disgusted with himself for having caused her such needless pain. "Let us go up on deck. The night is a fine one and the fresh air will help you sleep."

"How did you know I have had difficulty sleeping, Captain?" Anna rose gracefully from her chair and placed her fingertips upon his outstretched arm.

"Your mood is far from tranquil, Lady Thorson. It is not surprising that you would be too tense to rest, even on board the *Angelina* which rocks as gently as a cradle on most nights."

Anna smiled with genuine delight for the first time in days. "You truly love this ship, don't you, Captain?"

"Yes, she is all I've ever loved," he replied confidently, but his conscience pained him considerably. A ship was unlike a real woman, he thought bitterly, for it could never respond to his tender emotions in kind. As they went up on deck Anna's glossy curls caught the moonlight with a glow he remembered all too well and he tried to concentrate on the star-filled heavens and the sparkling water rather than on her loveliness. But the softness of her voice was every bit as seductive as her remarkable beauty.

"I envy you your freedom, Captain. Had I been born a man I would have chosen to go to sea. It is an ancient tradition among Swedes, an exciting life and I think a richly rewarding one as well."

"It can be, but the sea also has a cruelty second to none. It is an unforgiving mistress, Lady Thorson."

"Won't you please call me Anna? You have seen me

101

at my worst and I do not think we need any further formality between us. I was angry when first I realized how much you wanted this voyage to pass swiftly, but now I think perhaps it is best not to prolong it, for Lord Clairbourne cannot possibly be the monster I've made of him in my mind."

Phillip opened his mouth to argue, then thought better of it. But he could not think of a single virtue that would reassure his lovely passenger of her future husband's character. "You told me you had no suitors, yet I find that impossible to believe, Lady . . . Anna. Were you to return to Sweden, would there not be many who—"

"Please, Captain, how can I return?" Anna interrupted. "You are being well paid to see me safely to Briarcliff, are you not? There is no way I can go back to Sweden and none there who would rejoice to see me if I did. No, my future awaits me in England, but it is one that I dread."

The sorrow in her gaze pierced Phillip's heart with a pain so real he reached out to dispel her anguish in the only way he knew. She had not forgotten how he liked to be kissed and opened her lips readily to accept his affection. He was in no hurry, but relaxed and gentle, as if there were no more to making love than this single gesture which he could extend through all eternity if she would but allow him to hold her in his arms.

When at last he drew away her voice was hoarse with desire as her golden eyes swept his enchanting grin. "Captain, I—"

"Phillip. You must call me Phillip now, my dearest Anna."

"Phillip, then, you have been so quick to remind me

102

I am promised to Lord Clairbourne. Do you wish me to break that promise now?"

"He is a titled gentleman with an enormous estate in Devon and a profitable plantation on Jamaica while I am a sailor with no more to my name than the ship upon whose deck we stand." His lips teased hers playfully before he continued. "It would not be to your advantage to consider that question seriously, Anna."

"Then why did you kiss me?" Anna held her breath. She wanted only for him to kiss her again. She couldn't understand how he could have shown her such delicious affection if truly he felt none in his heart. There was the softness in his gaze she'd seen before and she hoped with all her heart his feelings for hee were sincere.

Phillip traced her high cheekbone lightly with his fingertips. "There is a vast difference between kisses stolen in the moonlight and a proposal of marriage, Anna. Didn't that wonderful father of yours ever explain that to you?"

Anna recoiled from his touch as if he'd struck her. "No, but he did teach me to play with another's emotions is unspeakably cruel!" She backed away, ashamed she'd responded so eagerly to his kiss when it had been no more than a brief amusement to him. "You are no better than Jenkins, are you? The only difference between you is that you don't bother to flirt, you simply grab for what you want!"

Phillip would tolerate such verbal abuse from no woman and quickly reached out to again imprison the nearly hysterical young beauty in his arms. She was no match for his strength and his mouth captured hers easily, drinking deeply of her wine-flavored kiss as if he meant never to let her go. Her image had filled his dreams for three lonely years and he longed to take his passion for her to its limit, crushing her slender body against his own until she ceased to fight him. But his joy at her surrender was brief for she had simply fainted; had he not caught her swiftly she would have slipped to the deck in an unconscious heap.

Phillip scooped the limp beauty into his arms and hastily scanned the deck to make certain they had not been observed before he carried her back to his cabin and laid her gently upon his bunk. She was tall but weighed little and he had had no trouble carrying her, but waking her was a far more difficult problem. He could not simply throw cold water on her face as he would to arouse a drunken sailor. He had to see she returned to her cabin in the same well-groomed state she'd left it. He'd been an idiot to kiss her so passionately she could not even draw a breath and he cursed himself for having been so lost in his own pleasure he'd not realized he'd given none to her. He knelt down beside her and kissed her pale cheeks softly but still she did not stir and he grew frantic with worry and shook her. "Anna, Anna, wake up, you cannot spend the entire night in here!"

Slowly Anna opened her eyes, their amber hue bright as she studied Phillip's troubled expression without speaking. When a single tear escaped her thick lashes he bent down to kiss it away, his touch again sweet as his lips brushed her cheek lightly. She reached out shyly to touch his dark, shining curls. His hair was as soft as silk to her fingertips and he caught her hand in his, bringing it to his lips for a tender kiss. "I will go now, Phillip. I know I can't stay here with you." But as she sat up and swung her legs over the side of his bunk he sat down beside her, pulling her back into his arms, making leaving impossible.

Relieved she was not screaming hysterically about his brutish behavior, Phillip gave Anna a warm hug. He could think of no gentlemanly way to beg her forgiveness but to his amazement her glance held no trace of anger, only a gleam of curiosity as she looked up at him.

"Do most women faint when you kiss them, Captain?"

"No! Of course not!" Phillip's cheeks flooded with color. Anna was actually laughing at him and it was all he could do to take it without responding in kind. He held his temper by the barest of margins but his clenched fists showed his outrage clearly.

"Maybe it was only the wine then." Anna put her hands over his as she reached up to brush his lips with a light kiss. "Well, perhaps we should avoid any further strolls in the moonlight for they are obviously too dangerous for us both."

"There is no life worth living that is without risk, Anna."

His sparkling blue eyes held a taunting fire she could not resist. She knew exactly what risk he meant and suddenly she knew whatever price she'd have to pay to know his love would be worth it and she lifted her mouth to his, softly inviting him to take her into his arms once again. When he opened his mouth eagerly to accept her deep kiss she found his taste delicious, impossible to resist and relaxed in his embrace as he pulled her down upon his bunk. His warmth flooded her veins with desire and when he slipped his hand beneath her bodice to unfasten the tiny hooks which barred his way she found his intimate touch far too enjoyable to make any objection. She wanted only to know the secrets he'd hidden in his heart, to feel his strength and this new tenderness to the depths of her being. She leaned into his embrace, delighting in the sweet kisses he trailed down her throat. Winding her fingers in his thick curls, she pressed his face close as his lips found the tip of her breast; flushed with passion the rosy peak grew firm under the touch of his playful tongue.

Shifting his weight, Phillip drew Anna closer still so he might run his hand up her silk stocking to the creamy expanse of thigh. Feeling her shiver, he was not content to stop and moved his hand higher still, gentle, deliberate; he knew exactly how to please a woman and with lazy precision he let the motion of his fingertips match that of his tongue, circling, teasing, tempting, but always magical in its effect. When he slipped her silken undergarments aside no barrier remained to inhibit the pleasure of his slow sensuous caress. He wanted to learn all the secrets of her soft, tender body, ready if need be to devote the entire night to his cause. Far from immune to the romantic spell he was creating, Phillip attempted without success to ignore the longing which filled his loins with a dull, throbbing ache. He forced the thought of his own pleasure away, deepening his concentration as he sought only to give Anna the greatest of earthly joys before he took his own.

Anna knew no name for what Phillip was doing, only that the sensations he gave were exquisite, pleasure so rich she wanted him to plunge deeper and deeper into her very essence to capture whatever she had to give if it would end the longing which grew within her to an unbearable yearning. She pressed against his hand then relaxed, enticing him to continue the slow, loving caress she could no longer endure without calling his name in a low, throaty moan. Knowing such abundant pleasure was meant to be shared, Anna unfastened Phillip's belt buckle with a deft flip of her wrist then slid her hand beneath his belt, intent upon exploring the secrets of his masculine body with the same tantalizing touch which had driven her past all reason. Surely it was possible for him to feel the same delicious ecstasy he was lavishing upon her. In the next instant she cried out in pain as Phillip's hand closed around her wrist with the strength of a steel trap ending her lazy caress with an unspoken rebuke.

Phillip had never been so shocked. He sat up abruptly, his mind clearing all too rapidly as he rebuckled his belt. Anna was an irresistibly appealing young woman, but also a most innocent one who had been entrusted to his care. He'd not meant to take his passion for her so far. That she would not only invite further intimacy, but demand it with a touch as expert as the most highly skilled courtesan was a shock so deep he could scarcely find his voice to speak. How could he have spoken to her of taking risks when he had no intention of flaunting his responsibility for her in so outrageous a fashion? What had possessed him to take such outrageous liberties? Had he taken leave of his senses completely?

Anna sat up slowly and wiggled back into her wrinkled garments, embarrassed she'd apparently com-

107

mitted some unpardonable breach of etiquette she did not wish to ever risk repeating. "Is there some reason women are not supposed to do that, Captain Bradford?"

The innocence of her question amused Phillip so greatly he threw back his head and howled with laughter for her humor was so unintentional he could not help himself and he completely forgot his own distress. "I distinctly remember insisting earlier this evening that you call me Phillip. Don't you think you know me well enough now to call me by my first name?"

Anna found his deep chuckle revolting in the extreme and slid off his bunk hurriedly. "How dare you laugh at me, how dare you? You are the one who is afraid to take risks obviously. Do you think me so empty-headed I'd give myself to you and then tell Charles about it? How did you describe the way Jamie sees me, as 'an enticing diversion'? Well I'll not be a diversion for any man, Captain, most certainly not you!"

Incensed by her insults Phillip leapt to his feet, crossing the short distance between them to slam the door shut just as Anna drew it open. He held her captive between his outstretched arms, his blue eyes glowing with a furious luster as he snarled, "I have treated you as a gentleman should and you call me a coward for it? No man would dare insult me so vilely and I'll be damned if I'll take it from you!"

Anna's long-lashed eyes widened as he shouted angrily at her but she was past caring how rude she might have been and had no intention of apologizing no matter how loudly he yelled at her. When he paused to take a breath she leaned back against his door to put more space between them before she spoke. "I know I do not please you, not ever, but I did not imagine you would find my touch so repugnant."

Phillip frowned, caught off guard by her calm response to his heated taunt. She was so terribly wrong he could not bear to let her believe he found her so unappealing, but no words of reassurance came to his mind. He could think only of her loveliness. The sight of an unshed tear glistening upon her thick lashes filled him with such a longing to console her he leaned down to silence her complaint, dropping his hand to caress her throat gently as his mouth met hers.

Anna lifted her hands to his broad shoulders, leaning against him now as she accepted his unexpected affection. He had hurt her badly by refusing her loving response to his tantalizing caresses and she opened her mouth hesitantly to return his kiss, hardly daring to hope she could again lure him to the point where his need for her would drown his reason in the same torrent of desire which still flooded her veins.

After no more than a brief moment Phillip pulled Anna into an eager embrace, no longer even recalling why she'd left his bed or why he'd been so angry. He knew only that he'd never wanted another woman as desperately as he wanted her and the many barriers which prevented them from ever having any future faded from his mind. He understood that for the moment she was his and he meant to see he did not waste that precious opportunity in arguing when they could be making love instead. He swept her up into his arms and carried her back to his bunk, covering her flushed cheeks with kisses as he hurriedly peeled away the layers of her lace-trimmed clothing and tossed them aside.

He made no protest this time as she reached out to help him undress for he was too lost in his own desire to now consider her boldness shocking.

Joining her in the narrow bunk Phillip whispered softly, "I am pleased with you, Anna, so very pleased." He dared not admit even to himself how much he wanted her love. At last she was no longer the elusive beauty who had haunted his dreams but a real flesh and blood woman who responded joyously to his touch. His kiss grew hungry, deep and demanding as he slid his hand over her hip and down between her velvet smooth thighs. She was so easy to love, so giving with a sweet, liquid warmth which lured his touch ever deeper until he could no longer restrain the force of his desire with such gentle affection. He moved then, sparing her the burden of his weight as he slid slowly upon her, caressing her whole body with his, drawing her into his passion until her breath came in hoarse gasps. He knew she would feel only pleasure as he put an end to her innocence with one smooth, swift thrust which carried him deep within her slender body where he remained motionless as he continued to savor her marvelous kiss. He wanted her to respond, to feel the rising ecstasy as it flowed through him to her and he waited for what seemed like an eternity before he began with a strong, sure rhythm to finish what he'd begun.

Anna clung to him, hugging him tightly as the pain which had pierced her loins with his first deep thrust began to subside and she felt instead a rapture so perfect she could not lie still but moved her body slowly in time with his. The pleasure continued to swell within her, filling her heart as well as her soul with the sheer joy of being his. He was so dear, so tender a lover she wanted to remain in his arms forever, to stay on the *Angelina* and be his with no thought of where the graceful ship might take them. But he had still given her no hope that he loved her, no promises of any kind and that realization filled her with such deep sorrow she could not stop the tears which escaped her long, dark lashes to roll down her face in salty streaks.

Phillip raised his hand to her cheek to wipe away her tears but he completely misunderstood the cause of her sadness. "You have no reason to weep, my pet, and do not tell me now that I did not please you as greatly as you pleased me for I know that I did." He brushed her lips lightly with a gentle kiss, but did not move away. She lay pinned beneath him still for he planned to take her again and again and saw no reason to waste a moment of the joy they could share in needless exercise. "I do not know why a woman is so poorly made that her first knowledge of a man's love causes her pain and tears but you must not blame me for the way nature has designed the female body."

Blushing deeply, Anna let him think her pain was no more than physical. "When you are always so coolly logical, why should the obvious escape you so completely? How else would a man know his bride was a virgin if our bodies bore as little trace of our pasts as a man's?"

Phillip kissed her soundly as he saw her point was well taken. She was delightfully bright; that was only one of the many things he liked about her. "Life is filled with many ironies, Anna. That most men are such fools is only one of them but you are so clever I'm certain you'll be able to fool Charles should the need ever arise." An occasion he seriously doubted would

111

ever occur and he nuzzled her throat playfully, biting her ear lobe before he drew away, grinning happily still, for his delight in her surrender was so very great. He had expected her to be shy if not awkward but making love to her had been a pure joy from beginning to end. She had a grace to all her actions which continually amazed him but he could think of no proper way to pay her compliments and so kept still, content for the moment to simply hold her in his arms. There was so much he wanted to teach her and yet lessons were superfluous where she was concerned for she seemed to have been made for loving. He drew closer, wishing silently she had been created solely for his pleasure but he dared not reveal so selfish a desire when they both knew her future lay with another man. That bitter knowledge tore at his conscience but he wanted nothing to ruin the perfection of that moment and closed his mind to such distracting and irrelevant thoughts.

"You are so very lovely, Anna, no princess was ever more precious." His lips moved down the curve of her shoulder, brushed the tip of her breast softly then returned to her mouth which trembled slightly beneath his own for no more than a second before she wrapped her arms around him again, holding him with a desperation he sought to end with the most passionate reassurance he could provide. He was soon lost in the rapture she gave so lavishly, making love to her again with the same splendid tenderness he had shown before until at last, filled with the deep contentment of her generous affection, he drifted on the edge of sleep, his dreams and reality at last merging as one. When Anna rose to leave his bed he was so startled he grabbed for her wrist to pull her back into his arms but she slipped from his grasp and moved away.

"Captain, please, I must return to my own cabin now. If Sophia is still awake she must be very worried about me and I do not want to arouse her suspicions as to why I've been with you for so very long." Anna pulled on her clothing as she spoke, hoping he would not notice how badly she was shaking as she attempted to fasten the hooks on her dress.

Phillip groaned in frustration. She was right of course, neither of them could afford the gossip her lengthy stay in his cabin might already have caused but he'd given little thought to the quality of her reputation when first he'd taken her into his arms and now it was far too late to worry over his lack of discretion. "Once you are Lady Clairbourne your life will be far easier to live for Charles is so involved in his own life he will take little notice of how and with whom you spend your afternoons."

"It is not the afternoons which worry me, Captain, goodnight." The bright gleam in Anna's golden eyes flashed over him angrily before she slammed his door, for indeed if he could speak of Charles after what they'd just shared she did not want to hear anything more.

Chapter Six

The first light of dawn found Anna up, dressed in a light muslin blouse, flowing wool skirt and knit shawl. She made her way up on deck before Sophia had even awakened. She remembered the sea often had a calm in the early morning hours which she longed to see again and was not disappointed. The water was smooth as a looking glass, the *Angelina*'s motion steady upon her southeasterly course. With the chill breeze bringing a bright blush to her cheeks and a gentle disarray to her fair curls, Anna leaned against the starboard rail, trying to decide how she should behave when she saw Phillip that morning. She was not sorry for what had happened between them, not in the least bit ashamed either. Her feelings for him were sincere and expressing them had seemed far too natural to regret now. In fact, she could scarcely suppress a mischievous grin when she thought of the handsome man. It was obvious he did not care as much for her as she cared for him, but that did not diminish the depth of her emotions or make them any less real. She had so

114

little time before she reached Briarcliff and became Lady Clairbourne, but she now planned to use each second more wisely. It mattered little that Phillip was more often angry with her than not. There was far more to the man than he usually let her see, but she was determined to unravel the puzzle of his perplexing personality, to know him better than he knew himself before they parted company. He simply fascinated her, and not solely because his appearance was so pleasing either, but because there was a depth to his character which made him well worth the effort to get to know. She recognized the distinctive sound of his boots as he crossed the deck. An impish smile lighting her delicate features, she bid him a good day. She would simply be discreet and not mention the way they'd spent the previous evening but she could not hide her delight at seeing him again.

Phillip stopped to stare, expecting at the very least a hate-filled glance. He could not accept Anna's warm greeting graciously. "What are you after now, Lady Thorson?"

"No more than a polite good morning, Captain. Is that too much to ask?" Anna's light eyes swept his lean frame with a seductive glance before focusing upon his well-shaped mouth, which she observed held not even the hint of the charming smile he'd shown her when they'd made love. "Apparently it is. If you have bothered to note my presence on board in your log, please describe my mood as a good one today." Anna turned away before she was tempted to become even more teasing but she was disappointed to find the man so sullen when she felt so deliciously happy to see him for a change.

"Your moods are not of sufficient interest to navigation to record, Lady Thorson. I suggest you keep a diary yourself if they are of such fascination to you," Phillip offered calmly, his deep voice mellow despite the rejection in his words.

The idea was not without merit, Anna thought suddenly. Perhaps recording the routine of her days in detail would help her to pass the time at Briarcliff more swiftly. In her mind's eye she saw an entire bookshelf filled with dusty, leather-bound volumes, her whole life reduced to a few feet of space. Perhaps someday someone would chance to read them and wonder why she'd led such a tormented life but that person would not be her descendant from Phillip's gloomy predictions.

As Phillip watched with growing wonder, Anna's whole appearance seemed to change. The wool of her skirt was a pale gray, her shawl a light blue and her figure blended so readily with the surrounding sky and sea he blinked his eyes to be certain she truly stood before him. The pride in her bearing relaxed, until she seemed to be smaller and so very vulnerable he was tempted to reach out and touch her shoulder with a reassuring pat, as he would touch an attractive child while passing by. But he caught himself quickly, knowing he dared not be so bold when the men of his crew were undoubtedly looking their way. He moved to her side and stood silently observing the sea, searching the horizon for sign of another craft, the comfort of his presence all he'd offer that day.

After a long moment, Anna turned to inquire, "How old are Clairbourne's sons? I neglected to ask and really should know their ages."

"Thomas is five and William seven if they've not

116

had a birthday since I last saw them. They are—" Obnoxious little brats, he'd almost said, but caught himself before he made another unfortunate blunder. "They are very young still."

"Yes, they do need a mother then." Anna found herself morbidly curious and since Phillip was in an obliging mood, if not a warm one, she asked, "Do you know how the first Lady Clairbourne died?"

"Yes," Phillip admitted grudgingly for it was not a pretty tale. "She and a cousin were killed when their carriage overturned on the road to Briarcliff. It had been flooded by spring rains and it isn't known whether they were crushed or drowned."

Anna shuddered with revulsion. "Oh, how horrible! When did the accident occur? Was it several years ago?"

"Almost four now, it happened about this time of year. Fortunately, Lady Clairbourne's sons were with their father at the time of the tragedy."

"That was a blessing indeed, but still Charles must be dreadfully lonely. I know how impossible it was to console my father after my mother's untimely death. He never truly recovered from that loss."

Phillip shook his head knowingly. "Wealthy men are never lonely for long, Lady Thorson, and Charles is no exception."

"Anyone can be lonely, sir, it is a matter of having caring friends, of having love and affection, not material wealth," Anna declared firmly, confident of the truth in her words.

"Of course, I had forgotten you are an expert on such matters." He laughed ruefully, dismissing her comments as rapidly as usual.

The light in Anna's golden eyes grew fierce as she responded angrily, "You are an expert on something else entirely, aren't you, Phillip?" She snarled his first name as she lifted her chin proudly, daring him to argue with her but he did not. In a surprising change of tone he stepped near.

His mouth was set in a stern sneer as he began to speak in a hoarse whisper so none of his crew would be able to overhear. "If it is my expert opinion you want, Anna, perhaps it would be more valuable if I told you what it was like to have been a child who lost his mother. To have been passed from one uncaring relative to the next until I was sent to sea when I was no more than eight years old and made to work as hard as a grown man or beaten senseless and sent to a flea-ridden bunk with no supper! Clairbourne will have no need for your sympathy and neither do I but you might be able to raise his boys to be decent men if you aren't too late to instill some sense of hope in their hearts." As he turned his back on her, Anna reached out to catch his arm.

"Sophia told me you might have been abused but I did not even imagine how cruelly you had been treated or how greatly you must have suffered. I am so sorry you grew up surrounded by neglect rather than the love you deserved."

Phillip simply stared at the beautiful young woman, for she had never seemed so desirable. Yet he knew there was no possible way he could continue to take what he wanted from her without destroying her very soul and he shook his head sadly, leaving her alone by the rail to contemplate the complexities of her future without his taunting bitterness to distract her from her task.

Anna continued to watch the tall man as he moved about the deck that morning. Though her gaze appeared to be on the distant horizon, she found him a far more exciting subject to view. He laughed frequently, joking easily with his men, yet when he gave an order it was promptly obeyed by a crew which clearly respected him highly. Soon she began to recognize each of the men on board the *Angelina* as a distinct individual and found them to be a diverse lot, yet all were as young or younger than their captain and she could not help but note the admiring glances they sent her way. She blushed deeply with embarrassment, for she was not used to such attention from men and, not knowing how she should respond, tried to ignore it with a demure nonchalance.

When Sophia finally joined her in the sunshine, Anna pretended an interest in the little woman's conversation but she heard only a few of the words the maid uttered as her eyes followed the handsome captain's motions about the deck.

"Do you suppose Michael has to work on deck too, Lady Anna? I imagined him to be an older man but perhaps he is as young as these other men all seem to be." Sophia frowned with concentration as she scanned the deeply sun-tanned faces, trying to discern which might be the cook who prepared such delicious meals. With the return of the fair weather, her appetite had returned also and she was most anxious to learn the cook's secrets.

"What?" Anna was surprised by Sophia's interest in the man. "I do not care what his age is as long as he continues to prepare such tasty meals."

119

Sophia laughed at her mistress's confusion. "I want only to learn how he prepares such savory fowl, Lady Anna. I am not interested in meeting the man for any other reason at my age!"

"Why, Sophia, there is no age limit on love surely!" Anna laughed too, for she had never considered Sophia's age at all. She knew the woman to be older than her mother, but would not be so rude as to inquire in what year she had been born. Sophia was simply Sophia and she'd never thought of her as having any existence other than the one provided by her occupation. "Sophia, tell me something, have you ever been in love, perhaps been married? I hope you would not think I would forbid you to marry no matter what your age should you find a man you can love."

Tears came to the spritely maid's eyes but she quickly brushed them away. "I have had my share of love, Lady Anna, and husbands too, but that was long ago, when I was younger than you, but not nearly so pretty."

"Husbands! Why, Sophia, you were married more than once? You must tell me all about these men at once!" Anna reached out to hug her maid joyfully, suddenly filled with hope the little woman's knowledge might have more practical value than she'd realized.

Phillip lifted his hand to shade his eyes. The sun's glare was bright but he saw Anna still standing where he'd left her earlier that morning. He could not imagine what topic she'd found to discuss with her maid with such animation but she had so graceful a manner she seemed to belong upon deck. Her golden curls were swept back from her face as she leaned into the wind, giving her the same elegant pose as the carved figurehead which decorated the *Angelina*'s prow. Far from being wooden, however, she was so full of life he had to turn away, forcing himself to concentrate his attention upon his navigation rather than upon the perplexing young woman whose existence he was so hard pressed to ignore. Whatever had possessed him to relate that pathetic tale of his childhood? He'd never confided his past in any woman, never shared even the smallest bit of himself with any of his feminine companions and yet Anna seemed to continually involve him in topics of conversation he'd much rather avoid. It was not that she lacked charm, quite the contrary, there had been times when she'd turned her amber eyes upon him and spoken with such sincerity it broke his heart, but as he looked to their journey's end his emotional turmoil continued to mount with each passing hour. No matter how desperately he wanted her gone, he knew he'd never be able to forget the sweetness of her lithe, young body or the wistful light which filled her lovely eyes when she looked up at him.

After a splendid morning spent enjoying the open air and a refreshing afternoon nap, Anna made a firm vow to try and respond to Jamie's attempts to amuse her. But the mate was uncharacteristically silent during the evening meal and rather than encouraging his attentions when truly she did not want them, she turned to Phillip with a question. "How much longer will this voyage last, Captain? We seemed to be making very swift progress today."

Phillip eyed the enchanting blonde with a steady glance. "We should dock at Southampton around noon tomorrow if the wind holds."

"Which it most certainly will," Jamie interjected

confidently.

"Tomorrow?" Anna gasped sharply. "Noon tomorrow?" She felt her throat tighten until she had difficulty drawing a breath. She reached quickly for her wine goblet and drained it in one long swallow.

"My goodness, Lady Thorson, you need not become so alarmed. I will have to see the port authorities and arrange for transfer of the cargo to a warehouse. It will be several days before we'll be able to continue on up the coast to Briarcliff." A slight reprieve from her fate, he thought bitterly, but remained silent on that point.

"Will Lord Clairbourne not come to Southampton to meet me?" Anna inquired softly, curiosity outweighing her fear now.

"No, he will not expect us for several days as I was uncertain how long the voyage from Gothenburg would take. We'll sail on to Exmouth and from there I'll rent a carriage as I did in Sweden. You needn't worry I'll make you walk the distance to your new home."

Anna tried to smile at his attempt at humor but found it difficult. "Do you have a map I might see? I'd like some better idea of where the estate is located."

Jamie laid his napkin beside his plate and after asking to be excused rose to his feet. "If you will allow me to miss the geography lesson, Captain, I will check on our progress."

"Of course." Phillip nodded curtly but he was not pleased to again be left alone with Anna. He cleared a space on the table then brought out a tattered map. "While I use Bowditch's Practical Navigator to chart our course, this particular map will provide a far better illustration of the coast near Briarcliff." He pointed

122

out Southampton, then traced the British coastline. "It is faster to sail through the channel than travel overland. Briarcliff extends to the sea, right here on Lyme Bay, east of Exmouth."

Anna studied the map thoughtfully before she inquired, "Why couldn't we just go ashore there on the bay? You have lifeboats and I have so few possessions they would not fill even one."

Phillip sighed impatiently. "I hardly think Charles would expect you to hike from the bay to his home for it is a considerable distance, all at an incline, and I'll not ask my men to carry your luggage so far either."

Anna looked up slowly, startled by the harshness of his tone. "Forgive me, Captain, it is difficult to judge the distance accurately from this map. I meant only to save you the trouble of sailing into port and the expense of renting another carriage."

Phillip rolled up the old map hurriedly. "The cost is slight, Lady Thorson, as is the struggle of weighing anchor. Neither is beyond my capabilities, I assure you."

Exasperated by the hostility of his mood, Anna prepared to take her leave, then hesitated. "I want to tell you how much I appreciate what you told me about yourself this morning."

Swearing too softly for her to hear, Phillip shoved the map among his others before he turned back to face the pretty young woman. "I meant only to point out the need Charles's sons have for a mother's love, not to draw attention to myself, Anna."

"Yes, I understood your purpose, Captain. I know you value your privacy and I will not violate your confidence."

Phillip lifted an eyebrow in a disbelieving glance.

123

"All women love to gossip; I've no hope you'll refrain from that practice. Is that not what you and Sophia were doing all morning with such rapt interest?"

Shocked that he'd been observing her so closely, Anna replied indignantly, "We were not gossiping, for that is talking about others and we were discussing our own lives!" She rose swiftly and walked with a purposeful stride toward the door before she turned to add another thought. "I know I have concentrated solely on my own misfortune which is unforgivable when there is the welfare of two young boys to consider as well. You merely used your own experience to illustrate what should have been obvious to me. I thought it was a secret meant for me alone as no one else would have need of such knowledge and I've no intention of sharing it." She slipped through the door and was gone before Phillip could stop her with any more insults. But she'd meant what she'd said, she'd never tell a soul what he'd told her. His past was clearly precious to him, and although he didn't realize it, it was therefore precious to her as well.

When the *Angelina* docked at Southampton, Anna remained in her cabin. Her last visit in that city had been fraught with such peril she had no wish to be seen there ever again, but as usual Phillip had other ideas.

"The weather is mild, the city not uninteresting, Lady Thorson, I have no objection to your traveling about while we are here in port." Phillip extended his hand in a sweeping gesture. "Perhaps you'd care to visit the shops or—"

"Captain Bradford, really." Anna gave him a withering glance. He knew full well she could not afford to go shopping though that was not her only reason for

124

avoiding the city. The disagreement with Lord Ramsey had never been settled as far as she knew and she'd no desire to be arrested. "I am content to rest here on board your ship today. Do not trouble yourself worrying over my happiness."

Phillip frowned, perplexed by her indifference, for he had thought she'd be eager to step upon land once again. "There is the matter of your lodgings also. The men will have free time the next few days to—" He hesitated, suddenly realizing she probably knew exactly what type of recreation sailors preferred when they were in port, but her gaze was so innocent he wondered if it were possible she did not. "To relax, and other than those standing watch the ship will be unoccupied, not a safe or a comfortable place for a young lady and her maid to reside."

Anna sighed unhappily, not pleased he understood so little. "Must I go, Captain? Sophia and I can prepare our own meals, we don't mind staying on board the *Angelina*. It will be no great inconvenience for us and I'm sure we'll be safe."

Phillip decided he'd waste no more time on the matter as any argument with Anna seemed only to lead in circles. "I will be gone all day. Should you become bored, there is a livery stable run by a Mr. Joshua Coombes in the next block. Simply walk down the gangplank, go to your left and you'll see it on the corner. Rent a carriage and driver for the afternoon and give my name as they know I am good for the fee. There will be enough time later to discuss where you'll spend the night but I certainly won't allow you in Michael's galley and neither will he! Now good day!"

Anna watched Phillip stride down the gangplank

and disappear into the crowds milling about the docks and forced back the bitter insult she was sorely tempted to scream. The cargo had been unloaded the previous afternoon but Phillip seemed to be in no hurry to take her to Briarcliff and she found the wait excruciating in the extreme. Recalling his map she made her way hurriedly to his cabin and finding it unlocked slipped through the door. His maps and charts were neatly organized but she had to scan more than a dozen before she came across the one he'd shown her. Briarcliff appeared to be no more than sixty miles from Southampton. Why should she wait several more days to leave the city when the morning was fresh and with a fine team she would be able to reach Lord Clairbourne's estate before Phillip was ready to weigh anchor? Excited by the cleverness of her plan she rolled up the map and carried it with her as she ran to tell Sophia to pack up their luggage while she went to hire the carriage.

Chapter Seven

Phillip spent the entire day haggling with shipping agents over possible cargos. It was sailing he loved with an all-consuming passion, not the endless bargaining to assure a fair profit on his ventures. But he felt no sense of urgency and left more than one office rather than accept cargos which he could have loaded immediately but at what he considered to be too low a margin of profit. He kept telling himself he owed such perseverance to his crew since they shared in a percentage of his profits, but his conscience pained him over that bit of self-deception. He felt uneasy, apprehensive, barely able to concentrate on business matters when what he truly longed to do was spend the day with Anna. He'd told himself that was not an acceptable option however, as she'd be Lady Clairbourne so shortly. But the more difficulty he had arranging for a suitable cargo, the more time he'd have to spend at least part of his days with her. That prospect teased his senses until he could no longer bear it, yet he forced himself to remember he had no right to her affections and that he had once sampled them so liberally was not an occurrence he could risk repeating.

Torn between the desires which flooded his muscular frame each time he thought of the delectable Anna and the discreet distance and proper respect he knew he would be wise to maintain, Phillip grew more morose with each passing hour. He stopped at one tavern and then another before forcing himself to begin walking back toward the *Angelina* where he knew he'd undoubtedly have to face another bitter argument with the pretty blonde, but he didn't want her to be alone on the ship when she'd be far more comfortable elsewhere. He laughed at his own lack of logic then, for he was the one who'd be more comfortable without her enticing presence on board. She was so very lovely, he could not bear to think of how quickly the time would pass before he'd be forced to escort her to Briarcliff and bid her farewell. He'd certainly not remain for the wedding ceremony though. He already knew he'd be unable to witness that travesty and still keep his sanity. Furious again with the fate which had given him such a brief chance to cherish the woman of his dreams, a young woman he could never call his own, he turned into the tavern at the next corner, sat down at a secluded table and, after giving the barmaid his order, proceeded to simply sit and ignore the scene in front of him while his mind returned to the night three years past when first he'd seen the fair Anna appear from the mist as though she were an enchanted princess in desperate need of a brave knight to protect her. What a fool he'd been to let her go, if only he'd pursued her, and . . . He sat up abruptly, realizing there was no point in daydreaming over a night long past and a choice not made. What could he have offered the blond beauty that night? A vagabond existence of endless travel or the wretched loneliness shared by all captains' wives who remained in port to make a home and raise children single-handedly for the most of the year? What could he have said to win her love? Come with me to where the warm Caribbean wind whispers melodies only the heart can hear. Come with me to where the moonlight turns the sea into a ribbon of golden magic where all dreams come true. Come with me and be my bride, share my life so I will no longer have to be so dreadfully alone.

Angered by his own ridiculously adolescent self-indulgence he slammed his now-empty tankard down upon the table top and left the tavern determined to return to the *Angelina* prepared to escort Anna to a respectable inn where he'd bid her a good night and force her distracting image from his tormented mind as well as his aching heart. In all his life he'd never made such a fool of himself over a woman. His only consolation was that Anna was completely unaware of the depth of his feeling for her. It was pathetic, he told himself, for a grown man to let a female, no matter how delightfully young and pretty she might be, fill his thoughts to the exclusion of all else as he'd allowed Anna to do. Frowning unhappily, he had to step aside quickly to avoid running right over John as he crossed the deck, intent upon going straight to Anna's cabin to send her away before his temper cooled.

"Captain Bradford, sir?" John stuttered nervously as he saw the murderous gleam in Phillip's eyes, for he had no wish to provoke him.

"What is it, John? Out with it. I'm in a hurry to find

suitable lodgings for the night for Lady Thorson and have little time to lose before darkness falls."

"She has taken care of the matter herself, she told me to tell you that, sir. She rented a carriage from the stable you told her about and she said you'd know where she'd gone."

Puzzled, Phillip drew himself up to his full height, towering above the trembling teen-ager. "What exactly did she say, John? You needn't be so worried. It is Lady Anna who'll have to bear my wrath, not you, no matter what her message was."

John swallowed with difficulty, trying to dislodge the lump of anxiety which made speech nearly impossible to produce. "She, that is she rented the carriage just after you left this morning. She said you had suggested she'd be more comfortable elsewhere so she was leaving."

"Splendid. That is one less worry at any rate. Now just where did she say she planned to go? This city is full of fine inns. Did she not tell you the name of the one where I might find her?"

John's pale blue eyes widened in alarm. "I did not even think to ask as she seemed so certain you'd know where she'd be, sir. I did not think it my place to question her actions." He was horribly embarrassed, certain he had bungled an awesome responsibility and would suffer the most dire of consequences because of it.

"No, that would have been pointless anyway with that woman." Phillip reached out to give the lad a friendly slap on the shoulder, cuffing him playfully, for he could see John was mortified by his error. He did not want him to suffer any further for Anna's continual willfulness. "The livery stable is nearby; they will surely recall where they took her. Had it occurred to me she might wish to leave before I returned I would have directed you to accompany her to be certain she had a proper escort."

John blushed deeply at that comment. "I am not a proper escort for such a fine lady, sir, I am not fit to—"

"Oh, John, you are man enough to carry a valise or two and that was all that was required."

"But she took everything she owned with her, sir, the small trunk, all her luggage, she took it all."

"For a night or two?" Phillip inquired incredulously, then his heart leapt to his throat as he realized where she had gone. With no more than a strangled cry of anguish, he bolted from his ship, shoving aside those strolling the walks as he ran the short distance to Joshua Coombes's stable.

A boy of ten stood at the entrance of the large barn, currying a handsome black gelding. He greeted Phillip politely. "Good afternoon, sir, if it's a horse you'd like, Fritz here is a beauty."

Phillip drew in several deep breaths in an attempt to appear far calmer than he felt. "That he is, but it is not a mount I need but simply information. Is your father about? I must speak with him concerning a most urgent matter."

The lad shrugged. "My elder brother is here, sir, but our father is away, driving a carriage to Lyme Bay for the most beautiful lady I ever saw. Her voice was like a song, the melody of her words foreign but very nice to hear." Phillip swore the vile oath he could no longer suppress, but the young boy had grown up along the docks so thought nothing of it and continued to groom

131

Fritz, preferring to give his attention to the lively animal rather than to his irritable customer.

Phillip regarded the horse with renewed interest, but knew that even if he were to rent the swiftest mount in the stable he would not be able to overtake Anna's carriage when she'd had a full day's head start. To add to his problems, he did not know the roads along the route to Briarcliff and would undoubtedly lose his way when darkness fell. He might arrive first if the *Angelina* were to sail immediately but his crew was scattered all along the waterfront, probably full of ale and sound asleep in obliging wenches' eager arms. "Damn the woman!" He turned to go, then had to ask, "How many hours does such a journey require? Do you have any idea?"

"No, sir, but the lady was in a most dreadful hurry and said she'd reward my father well if he made good time. He knows all the short cuts, little-known paths which would speed their way. But he will not return for several days. Is it him you're after or the lady?"

Appalled that a mere child could see his purpose so plainly, Phillip strode off without replying. In an hour's time he'd gathered the majority of his startled crew and was under sail, promising the men another liberty in Southampton in a few days time. But they were not fooled and laughed amongst themselves as to their captain's motives for their unscheduled departure.

Jamie Jenkins was too clever a young man to tease Phillip over his desire for haste. "The wind is a strong one; our time will be swift."

Phillip's unpleasant scowl deepened as he glanced down at the mate. "Not swift enough, I fear, and I

132

must reach Briarcliff in time to escort Lady Thorson through the gate or Charles will say I've not kept my half of our bargain."

"Oh, it is the money which worries you, is it?" Jamie clasped his hands behind his back and rocked back on his heels, unmoved by Phillip's totally implausible explanation.

"Of course! The wench is no end of trouble but I'll not let that man cheat us out of the sum we've rightfully earned by going to fetch her!"

Jamie nodded thoughtfully. "Why are you so certain she's not simply run away? I do not recall ever receiving the impression she was eager for this marriage."

"Lady Thorson will honor her father's promise, I've no doubt of it," Phillip replied impatiently, the strength of her character not the issue. "She'd not turn tail like some frightened rabbit and bolt for parts unknown. She's gone to Briarcliff, I've no doubt of it." Yet as Phillip considered the mate's words he grew worried. Anna had mentioned relatives of some sort in England, as he recalled, what if indeed she had gone to seek their advice? He pounded his fist into his palm with an anxious rhythm. If Anna were not at Briarcliff he had no idea where he might find her and then what would he be able to tell Charles, or for that matter, himself?

Jamie wasn't fooled by his captain's ridiculous protests, merely surprised the man would lie when admitting a fondness for the pretty blonde would have surely been closer to the truth. "Get a good night's sleep, sir, we will reach Exmouth by dawn. She'll never arrive at Briarcliff before you overtake her as they undoubtedly stopped somewhere along the way to pass the night at an inn."

Having no such hopes, Phillip shook his head sadly. "No, she would not have tarried en route, she'll go directly to Briarcliff." How could she stop when she had no money for lodgings? Had she wanted to go shopping he would have been generous, lied again by telling her it was Charles's money rather than his own, but she'd seemed so uninterested in visiting the shops he'd not pursued the matter.

"She might have at that." Jamie continued to observe Phillip with a skeptical eye. It was not that the taller man disliked women; on the contrary, he'd known exactly where to find his men that afternoon because he knew which establishments catered to sailors from personal experience. He had the normal appetites of any virile, young man but he had no favorites in any port, never mentioned any wench by name and Jamie doubted he'd ever bothered to ask. Any attractive female would please him apparently. Then recalling several erotic excursions they'd made together Jamie realized the captain favored blondes, was partial to them for some reason. That thought shook him to the marrow; he was sorely afraid the reason Phillip wanted so badly to overtake Lady Thorson was neither a monetary nor an honorable one. He'd seen them together on one occasion. Was it possible there had been many times she'd been alone with Phillip in his cabin? Forcing himself to risk a possible rebuke he spoke up clearly, "Lady Thorson is very attractive, both her face and figure are perfection but surely you do not want to, well, to—" He found it impossible to continue as Phillip turned to face him. Clearly he was offended, and severely.

134

"I am well aware of that young woman's physical assets, Jamie. I am also well aware she is engaged to Lord Clairbourne who expressed a desire to marry her at his first opportunity. If we do not make all possible speed that bastard will say she arrived at his home alone and pay her the sum due us! Now see that we make sufficient speed so that travesty doesn't occur!" Phillip crossed the deck rapidly, his long stride sure in spite of the ship's roll as he made his way to his cabin. His dark mood did not lift as he ate a light supper and stretched out upon his bunk. Rather than being soothing, the gentle creaking of the wooden ship provided a constant annoying distraction, making sleep impossible. When had he last slept the night through, he wondered caustically. Not in weeks, not since, not since, he'd tossed that blasted coin at Anna's feet! Seeing no point in wasting the night in such miserable torment he rose, dressed warmly, then went up on deck where he'd have enough room to walk off his anxiety and plenty of fresh air to clear his mind. When finally he returned to his cabin, he fell asleep promptly, too exhausted to dream of the fair beauty who gave his waking hours no peace.

Anna yawned sleepily, lifting her hands to cover her mouth as she struggled to sit up. She'd convinced the helpful livery stable owner to continue traveling long past sundown since the lanterns upon the front of the carriage illuminated the narrow roadway adequately. But finally the team had grown weary and they'd had to stop. She could hear the man talking quietly to his horses as the first light of dawn gave the eastern sky a soft pink glow. Tapping Sophia lightly on the knee to wake her, Anna coaxed her to leave the dusty vehicle. Standing beside it, they stretched vigorously to restore the circulation to their cramped limbs.

"How much longer must we travel, Mr. Coombes?" Anna smiled prettily as she shook the tangles from her long curls. They'd spent the night near a stream so she knew she'd at least be able to wash in fresh water, even though she would have much preferred the luxury of a hot bath before she faced Lord Clairbourne for the first time.

"No more than a few hours, my lady." He grinned happily; his wife was a nasty shrew whose company he never missed an opportunity to avoid. He'd agreed readily to the request for a carriage and driver, volunteering his own services rather than sending his twenty-year-old son along with such a beauty. "I am sorry if I woke you. There is no need to rush."

"Do not apologize. The sooner we arrive at Briarcliff the better. We'll hurry with our preparations and be ready to leave when you are."

Having spent the previous afternoon discussing her wardrobe in order to select an appropriately modest but stunning gown, Anna directed Sophia to unpack the beige silk gown they'd chosen. The maid shook it out promptly, then gathered up her mistress's toilet articles. "That you should have to dress beside a stream is unfortunate but Lord Clairbourne will never know if you do not tell him." She held the elegant gown carefully as they followed the winding path Mr. Coombes had told them led to a brook where they might refresh themselves, the thick forest growth providing all the privacy they'd require.

136

Anna could barely conceal her excitement as she skipped down the narrow trail with tiny, dancing steps. "I care little where I've had to dress, Sophia, I simply want the morning to pass quickly so that I may finally meet the mysterious Lord Clairbourne without further delay. This suspense has been unbearable to me."

Sophia pursed her lips thoughtfully as she hastened to agree. "I imagine the man is as anxious to meet you, Lady Anna, as you are to make his acquaintance. Surely Captain Bradford must have given him some idea of when we'd arrive so he has no doubt been making special preparations for your wedding."

"One thing at a time please, Sophia. I want first to meet Lord Clairbourne before I allow the thought of marriage to enter my mind," Anna vowed emphatically, for truly the thought of marriage terrified her still. She slipped off her dress and folded it nearby upon the rocks at the edge of the clear brook. The water was far too cold for bathing and she went about her ablutions hurriedly, not enjoying either the chill of the icy water or the crisp tingle of the morning air upon her bare skin. The noise of the stream was rivaled by that of the birds which screeched as they flew about the treetops gathering their morning's share of insects and wild berries. The beauty of the surrounding woods gave Anna's spirits a boost. She refused to believe Clairbourne would not come to love her. She knew she was attractive, surely the man would be pleased with her appearance even if he were not impressed by her independence. His home would be ample in size; they'd not need to be together if neither wished to be, but she could not believe he'd choose a solitary existence if she offered him true friendship. She forced herself to think only of ways to charm him so she'd at least have the hope of finding happiness. Surely she did not deserve to spend the rest of her life without love as Phillip had so frequently predicted she would. At the memory of the handsome captain her thoughts grew confused again and her cheeks filled with color for she knew how angry he'd be when he discovered she'd left his ship to complete her journey on her own. But all had gone well so he could not argue that her decision had been the wrong one. Finished with her preparations, she adjusted her lingerie as she stood, ready to step into the silk gown. She turned expecting to find Sophia waiting to assist her but to her horror found she was surrounded by a group of strangers. Her cry of alarm was silenced by a burly man's ready hand as he pulled her into a rude embrace, lifting her off her feet so she had no leverage to fight him.

Sophia was nowhere in sight and Anna readily understood the five men who stood nearby were ruffians of the worst sort. Highwaymen who'd undoubtedly come upon her carriage and seized the unexpected opportunity to further their aims of easy wealth. That she had none only increased her terror for she had no means to purchase her freedom and feared they would not take happily to that bit of news. She gagged as the man tightened his hold; his breath held the foul stench of stale ale when he spoke, nauseating her further.

"It is gold we're after, my beauty. Tell me where you've hidden your jewels and valuables and we'll bid you a pleasant good day and send you on your way."

When he lowered his hand, Anna replied angrily, "I've nothing to steal, you swine! Now unhand me and be gone!"

The leader of the bandits scoffed at her outrage but he was not truly amused and shook her soundly, his fingers cutting into her bare shoulders cruelly. "You're pretty now, lass. I don't want to see you lose your beauty as well as your purse. Now where is it?"

Anna tried to focus her eyes so she could identify her assailants later but was so dizzy she could make out little other than the leader's narrow brown eyes and yellow teeth. His hair was covered by a worn hat and his haggard features were obscured by a thick black beard. The others were an equally unimpressive lot, one tall and slim, the next two stocky of build, the last no more than a half-grown boy. They stood back, apparently content to let their hostile leader threaten her, leaving her no hope they would step forward to help her should he grow even more mean. When she found her voice its hollow sound rang false even to her own ears. "I have no purse. You're wasting your time for I've neither gold nor jewels to steal."

The aggressive man again laughed rudely in her face. "You have gowns of the finest silk, a carriage and driver, an attentive maid and you have nothing to steal?" Clearly he thought her denials blatant lies as did his companions.

"It is the truth! My clothes are another woman's castoffs, my carriage only rented, and what have you done with my maid? She will tell you just how poor I am!" Anna protested heatedly but she was frightened they might have hurt Sophia and scanned the small clearing for some sign of the little woman.

The felon did no more than draw back his hand and slap Anna soundly as he snarled, "Stop your foolish lies or you'll force me to be brutal!"

139

Dazed, Anna would have fallen to her knees had the man not yanked her to her feet. She'd found her pleas rejected rudely but had no idea what would satisfy the greedy thieves. Neither the horses nor carriage were rightfully hers so she could not offer those. When she did not respond, the black-bearded man doubled up his fist and drew back his arm, ready to strike her a vicious blow. But she ducked at the last second, avoiding his punch by a hair's breadth. When the roar of a pistol shot exploded in her ears with a frightening blast, she was certain she'd been shot but the bright red blood which splattered her lace-trimmed lingerie was not her own. The bearded man cried out in agony as he slumped to his knees, clutching his pierced thigh in a desperate attempt to stem the flow of crimson liquid. Despite his efforts, it continued to ooze through his fingers.

Phillip Bradford stood at the edge of the clearing, a smoking pistol in his right hand while another weapon in his left was leveled at the fallen man's head. "You villains need a lesson in manners as well as strategy, for the lady is indeed penniless." Gesturing with the empty weapon he pointed to Anna. "Bring your shoes and clothing. We'll leave these fools to contemplate the error of their ways alone. Where is Sophia?"

"I don't know!" Anna cried out hoarsely. She clutched the dress she'd been wearing to her breast, then grabbed up the silk garment before bending down to retrieve her slippers and stockings from the grass. "They must have taken her someplace."

Hearing that accusation the four able-bodied thieves sprinted off in separate directions, disappearing into the forest before Phillip could fire. He approached the leader, pale with his attempt to tend his own wound, and placed the loaded pistol against his temple. "Where is the maid? You'll answer truthfully or I'll blow your head right off your filthy neck!"

"There, to your left in the bushes. I did no more than give her a slight blow to silence her. She is unharmed!"

Anna rushed past them, tossing down her elegant clothing as she pushed the underbrush aside in a frantic search for her servant. "Sophia! Sophia!" When she could not readily arouse her, she called to Phillip for help.

The captain did not move for several seconds, his thoughts easy to read in his stern expression. "If that dear little woman has so much as one scratch I'll be back to send you to hell!" With that dire threat he shoved the pistols under his belt and followed Anna to where she'd found Sophia whimpering softly, huge tears rolling down her pale cheeks. Still dazed, she tried to sit up but could not. When Phillip put his arms around her to lift her, she cried out in pain.

"It is my back, Captain. I must have hit a sharp rock when I fell."

"You did not fall, Sophia." Phillip let her rest where she lay for a moment. "Put on your dress, Anna, then get a cup from Mr. Coombes and bring Sophia some water. Perhaps she is only badly bruised and needs a moment more in which to recover." Yet the worried look in his eyes sent a far more chilling message Anna readily understood.

"Yes, I'll go. Just help me with the buttons please." Anna stepped out of the blood-soaked petticoat, then slipped her dress on over her pantaloons and camisole.

141

"Forgive me, Captain, but I'll not arrive at Briarcliff drenched with some madman's blood!"

Phillip was fascinated by the delicious, creamy smoothness of her bare shoulders, the soft fullness of her breasts above her narrow waist, her gently rounded hips which led to a superb pair of long, slender legs. He completely forgot what she'd asked him to do until she held her glossy hair out of his way and looked back over her shoulder to see what was causing the delay. He stepped up behind her then and fastened the buttons with trembling fingers he was afraid she could feel through the sheer silk dress. "There now, run, bring us some water." When she returned he held the battered cup to Sophia's lips and prayed she would be able to rise on her own but she still could not.

"You'll have to carry me, sir. I am sorry to be so much trouble." Sophia looked up at the powerfully built man, certain he could do it but she feared it would be painful and it was.

Phillip carried the injured maid carefully to the carriage and laid her inside upon one of the seats. Joshua Coombes hovered about anxiously, fearing the worst. "This is entirely my fault, sir. I know the roads are often unsafe but I didn't think to stand guard while Lady Thorson bathed. If she'd been killed—"

"Mr. Coombes!" Anna interrupted sharply. "The fault is mine alone for insisting upon the trip. Now let us hurry to Briarcliff before any more adversity strikes!"

"Wait one moment, please." As Phillip turned back toward the path, Anna rushed to follow. "Stay with Sophia, Anna, I'll not be more than a minute."

Horrified by the deed she knew he'd carry out, she

grabbed his arm and hung on tightly. "No, the man is already badly wounded; you can't shoot him again!"

"I do not make idle threats!" Phillip responded hotly and brushing her aside started off down the path, but Anna ran after him so closely she nearly tripped on his heels.

"Let's take him with us, we can turn him over to the sheriff. You need not execute him yourself!"

Phillip's blue eyes blazed down at her with a menacing fury. "You'd save the man for the gallows? How charitable of you!"

"He'd hang?" Anna gasped, filled with dread. The man's fate was decided no matter what she did.

Stopping abruptly, Phillip turned and put his hands gently upon Anna's shoulders as he softened his tone. "Please go back. You needn't witness this; it won't be a pretty sight. But the villain hurt Sophia badly and would have done far worse to you. The man deserves no better than a swift taste of justice and I'll not allow you to interfere!"

Anna bit her lip savagely to force back the hot tears of frustration which burned her eyes. "I wanted only to meet Charles, not to cause this tragedy. But Sophia's back is broken, isn't it? And the bandit who did it will die?"

"What did you expect would happen to you when you left the *Angelina* all alone?" Phillip was ready to shake her as soundly as the highwayman had and was able to restrain himself only by a great force of will. "You're a little fool who always lands in trouble because you've far more beauty than brains!" Yet as he glared down at her his rage fused with his desire until he could no longer bear to suppress the wildness of his passion. He saw a tiny drop of blood appear as Anna's lower lip trembled and he leaned down to kiss it away. His mouth was gentle for no more than an instant then he pulled her into a demanding embrace that molded her supple form to his powerful frame with a strength she could not resist until at last he had savored her delicious kiss to the fullest. Satisfied he'd finally subdued her defiant spirit, he drew away.

Terrified as much by the lust he'd made no effort to hide as she was by his thirst for revenge, Anna turned and fled back up the path to the carriage. She put her hands over her ears to block the hateful sound she knew would come but as the minutes lengthened she heard only the sounds of the forest, making the dreadful nature of the wait all the more painful. When Phillip finally returned he took her arm and helped her up into the carriage before he answered the unspoken question in her fearful gaze.

"Cease to worry, Anna. The man was nowhere to be found. His friends had not deserted him after all." With that bitter announcement he slammed the carriage door and, after nodding to Joshua Coombes, mounted the horse he'd ridden from Exmouth. Taking up a position ahead of the vehicle, he kept a sharp lookout for further signs of trouble but thankfully saw none.

Chapter Eight

Anna held Sophia's hand tightly and tried to smile bravely for the maid's sake, but she knew she couldn't fool her. She was trembling badly despite her attempts to display a reassuring serenity. That Sophia was so terribly injured was dreadful, but that Phillip had used her so badly was disgusting! Did the man think she had no feelings? He seemed to believe his kisses meant nothing while they shook her to her very soul. She'd no idea a man could present such a confusing pattern of behavior, rejecting her coldly one minute then nearly ravaging her brutally the next. He seemed to have forgotten the night they'd made love while she would cherish that precious memory to the last of her days. Whatever did he want from her, what was she supposed to do or say to make him behave in a gentlemanly fashion toward her? One thing was certain, she'd say nothing about him to Charles, for she did not want him to even suspect how deep their friendship had been. The suddenness of that decision came as a further surprise; he was not even her husband as yet and she was planning quite calmly to intentionally deceive him. The fault was all Phillip's, she knew, but that made the lie no less real.

Anna was soon distracted from that painful bout with her conscience as the gatehouse of Briarcliff came into view. She moved closer to the window so she might catch a glimpse of her new home. She tried to describe it as best she could to Sophia as the road curved past the gatehouse to continue up a gentle incline. Briarcliff was centuries old. Set upon a hill, it had a commanding view of the surrounding terrain and for as far as the eye could see the land belonged to Lord Clairbourne. Lush and green, the estate was a prosperous one but Anna thought only of the man she was soon to meet and did not let the magnificence of his holdings impress her. The mansion itself had been rebuilt in modern times from the stone of the original castle; stately and elegant, the Palladian architecture beckoned invitingly but she felt a sudden chill and sat back in her seat, frightened to think what Clairbourne's reaction to her morning's adventures would be.

Phillip dismounted swiftly and handed his reins to the groom who'd rushed out to meet him. He then walked back to the carriage, opened the door and spoke sharply to Anna. "Wait here, there will be no way to avoid telling Charles what's happened but I'll do it as diplomatically as possible and send for a physician to attend Sophia." Turning to the little woman, he smiled warmly and reached out to give her knee a reassuring pat. "I will be gone no more than a moment. I want to summon help so that we may carry you more comfortably." With that promise, he entered the magnificent manor. Although more than a dozen servants

146

poured out into the courtyard, Phillip did not return for a long while. He was then accompanied by a small, gray-haired man who appeared to be the butler and several younger men whom he directed to lift Sophia gently from the carriage before he reached in to help Anna himself. Taking her hands in his, he drew her aside and whispered, "Charles isn't here. I'll explain later but first let's tend to Sophia's care. The servants' quarters are on the third floor and—"

"No!" Anna disagreed sharply, "I insist she be taken to my room. I want her to occupy the finest room available."

"I should have known!" Frowning angrily Phillip hurried after the group carrying the injured servant to direct them to Lady Thorson's bedchamber. Those instructions were met with curious stares, but the startled men complied. None cared to argue with the captain as he obviously expected his command to be obeyed.

As they reached the second-floor landing they were overtaken by a slender woman dressed in somber tones of gray. Her age was impossible to discern as her complexion was unlined, but her lively brown eyes held a most skeptical gleam as if she had seen more than her share of adversity. Her hair was covered by a lace-trimmed cap but that touch of delicate beauty seemed misplaced above the severity of expression which graced her sharply defined features. She was not unattractive, but her manner was a forbidding one, inspiring neither confidence nor trust.

"What is the meaning of this, Captain Bradford? Surely you do not plan to place the injured maid on this floor?" the haughty woman inquired sarcastically.

Phillip failed to hide his smile as he glanced back toward Anna. "Lady Thorson, this is Lydia Shepard, Charles's housekeeper. Perhaps you would care to speak with her yourself since the efficient running of this house is her responsibility."

Anna smiled graciously, knowing full well Phillip had led her into a dangerous situation in which she'd already given an order the housekeeper was clearly loath to obey. She extended her hand then pulled Mrs. Shepard with her down the wide richly carpeted hall. "Mrs. Shepard, please forgive me for arriving without giving you the proper time to prepare."

"Briarcliff is always prepared to receive visitors, Lady Thorson," Lydia Shepard replied coldly, insulted by the young woman's attempt at an apology.

"Yes, of course you would be but we are not visitors. This will be my home and Sophia's as well. I wish to place her in my room so I may supervise her care. She has been with me since I was an infant and deserves no less." Anna's amber eyes sent a clear, determined message; she was no timid stranger who'd cower before the stern housekeeper. She intended to assume the role of mistress of Briarcliff immediately.

"Such devotion is commendable of course," Lydia responded curtly. "There is a sitting room adjoining your bedchamber. I will have a cot brought in so that your maid may occupy that room for the time being."

"Thank you," Anna murmured softly but told the men to place Sophia upon the four-poster bed meant for her. "I will use the cot myself, Mrs. Shepard. Now, has someone already left to summon the physician?" Anna leaned down to kiss Sophia's pale cheek lightly before she turned to again confront the hostile woman.

"Yes, Frederick left for Exmouth at Captain Bradford's insistence," Lydia explained through clenched teeth, furious the young woman would disregard her suggestion so completely.

"Good." Anna smiled warmly at the men crowded around the bed. "Thank you so much for your help. Please leave us now so my maid may rest until the physician arrives." Although she had not included Phillip in her glance, he left also and she did not call him back. Left alone with Sophia, Anna allowed herself to relax sufficiently to notice her surroundings. The spacious room was decorated in shades of pale green, the walls covered in the finest silk while the draperies and small cherry wood chairs were upholstered in a matching brocade. It was a lady's room of the most elegant design but its attractiveness failed to raise her spirits.

Noticing her glance, Sophia spoke softly. "This room is so lovely, Lady Anna, perfect for you. The whole house must be this fine."

"Yes, no doubt it is, but it will be difficult to think of it as home right away. Now, you must rest. Does your back give much pain?"

"It feels as though I've been tied in a knot. It all happened so suddenly. I was watching the sunlight's sparkle upon the stream, then that horrid man plucked me from my feet and tossed me into the bushes. Why did this have to happen, Lady Anna? Who will take care of you if I cannot?" Huge tears filled Sophia's blue eyes and Anna hurried to her bedside and gave her hand a warm squeeze.

"I can manage for a day or two, Sophia, you must not fret so. Close your eyes and rest until help arrives. I'm sure you'll feel better if you do." Anna paced the room slowly. Nothing had gone as she'd hoped it would but perhaps it was a blessing Charles was away as she had too much to worry about with Sophia to try and impress him favorably that day.

Two hours passed before Dr. Beckwith arrived. He was clearly a competent man, tall and spare, and he gave Sophia a thorough examination before he made his diagnosis. "You have been badly bruised, my dear, and appear to have received a sprain in your back so I must insist you remain in bed until the pain has vanished entirely. Then you may resume your duties on a limited schedule but do not overdo, be careful until you have recovered your health completely. Do not exert yourself serving your mistress for there are many here to attend her."

Anna knew the man meant well but Sophia's expression was filled with distress. "Thank you, Dr. Beckwith, but I will need no other servants. Frankly, I am so pleased to hear Sophia has suffered no broken bones I will be happy to attend to my own needs for a few weeks. I appreciate your arriving so promptly. Now as to the matter of your fee—"

"Captain Bradford has seen to that, Lady Thorson. I will return in two days' time to see how you are doing, Sophia, but if I find you have left your bed I will be most displeased." The physician frowned sternly, but was clearly teasing her in a playful fashion.

"You will find me right here, sir, I promise." Sophia smiled wanly.

Anna was encouraged by the doctor's soothing words and listened carefully to his instructions. There was little he could advise other than bed rest it seemed, but she was pleased he had so gracious a manner. That

Phillip had paid for his services surprised her though. Why hadn't the doctor planned to present his bill to Charles for payment? After seeing him to the door she sat down to rest at the window seat while Sophia napped. She wondered where her luggage had been taken as she wanted to bathe and dress before her future husband returned home but she had no desire to summon the disagreeable housekeeper to inquire. As she glanced out over the gardens she was surprised to see Phillip strolling slowly along a distant path. He held his hands behind his back, apparently lost in thought as he walked aimlessly through the well-tended lanes, his mind obviously occupied with some difficult question. Knowing he would be able to tell her when Charles would be home, Anna first moved to the bed to be certain Sophia was resting peacefully, then she left the room. She made her way down the staircase unobserved but found the first floor of the impressive home a hopeless maze, the endless succession of rooms confounding her sense of direction time and again as she attempted to find a passage to the terrace which overlooked the gardens. She'd seen no one to ask until she rounded a corner and came face to face with Lydia Shepard. She tried to smile although she was frustrated to the point of tears.

"Lady Thorson? Whatever are you doing wandering the house alone? There is a bellpull beside the bed in your room. Did you not see it?"

Anna had no time for verbal sparring and ignored the woman's taunt. "I wish to go out to the gardens. Would you please show me the way?"

"Of course." The housekeeper turned abruptly and led the way with a brisk pace, not speaking once until she came to a small library. "The French doors lead to the gardens, but be careful you do not lose your way there also."

After thanking the woman sweetly, as if she were the most helpful of servants, Anna went on outside. Phillip was some distance from the house and rather than approach him sedately she lifted her skirt and ran across the lawn. The thick, green grass absorbed the sound of her flying feet and when she called his name he wheeled around to face her, his surprise apparent in his startled expression. He'd turned so quickly they nearly collided. He reached out to grab Anna's shoulders to avoid such an accident then dropped his hands abruptly to his sides and stepped back.

"How is Sophia? What did the doctor have to report?"

"He believes her to have suffered no more than a bad sprain. I was certain her back was broken in a dozen places but it seems there were no fractures after all." Anna smiled with relief, pleased by his genuine concern for her maid. "Her injury is still my fault, however, and I should be the one to cover the doctor's fee, not you."

Phillip waved away her objection with an impatient gesture. "It was a small matter, but what of you? Did he not examine you also?"

Anna's eyes widened in surprise. "I was not harmed, there was no need—"

Phillip reached out to touch her bruised cheek lightly. "That you were hurt is plain, that you did not suffer a far more serious injury is due to the fact I arrived in time to prevent it."

Anna pushed his hand away angrily. "I seem to be

constantly in your debt, Captain, and it is not that I am not grateful for your assistance but—"

Phillip laughed out loud at her comment. "Assistance? Don't you think that's too subtle a term? I wounded a man severely and would have gladly sent him to his reward and you refer to that as only rendering assistance, as if I'd done no more than pluck a lace handkerchief from the grass."

Anna blushed deeply, embarrassed by his teasing words as well as his wicked grin. "I have spoken little English since my mother's death. If my meaning is not clear, please inform me but my speech should not be a cause for such ridicule!"

Sighing deeply, Phillip placed his hands on his hips, his pose as threatening as his tone. "I am not ridiculing your English, I am trying only to make you see how desperate your situation truly was! Had I not arrived when I did, a savage beating would have been the least of the humiliations you'd have suffered. I trust the word rape is in your vocabulary?" Phillip's stern expression darkened to a menacing scowl. "If you think Charles would have been pleased to see either of us had you been raped then you're sorely mistaken!"

Anna swallowed with difficulty, thoroughly sickened by his perpetual foul-tempered insults. "All you care about is your fee, isn't it? Just that you're paid in full for delivering me to Lord Clairbourne, you don't care one bit about what happens to me!" Anna lifted her skirt as she turned, then ran back up to the stone pathway toward the house, her fury too great to contain. She dared not remain in his presence and risk prolonging an embarrassing scene by further argument but Phillip overtook her swiftly, ending her flight by lifting her completely off the ground in an embrace she could not escape.

Phillip set the lovely blonde gently upon her feet then reached for her hands. "Come with me. There is a bench nearby and we will talk for as long as it takes us to decide what must be done now. I've no time to waste watching your tantrums. You are constantly running off in the midst of our conversations and nothing is ever settled!"

Struggling to pull free, Anna continued to argue. "Let me go, I've no wish to discuss any subject with you!"

Undaunted, Phillip simply swept her up into his arms again and carried her over to the small wooden bench where he sat down holding her captive upon his lap. "You're behaving more like a spoiled brat than a fine lady so that's how you shall be treated!"

Appalled to find herself again perched upon his knee, Anna cried out in frustration, "Captain, please! Wasn't one attack sufficient for the day? Must I be mauled again?"

"Again?" Phillip laughed at her complaint and gave her a warm hug, his mood suddenly turning playful. "Surely you do not consider this an attack for I am merely attempting to help you regain your composure."

"I would not have lost it were it not for your continual insults!" Anna folded her hands in her lap and lifted her chin proudly. "What will Clairbourne say should he return to find us in so intimate a pose?"

"There is no fear of that," Phillip offered smugly. "The man is not expected to return to Briarcliff for some time, which is why we must confer immediately."

Anna turned to look at him more closely, her face mere inches from his. He'd managed to bathe, shave and change his clothes in the time she'd spent with Sophia and she was captivated as always by the attractiveness of his appearance, mesmerized by the depth and sparkle of his azure gaze. Forcing herself finally to pay more attention to his words than his features, she decided he was far too pleased with himself and while he might have every reason to be, she'd not forgive him for it. "What do you mean he won't return for some time? Where has he gone?"

Phillip reached up to brush a stray curl from her cheek and flashed his most disarming grin. "Are you curious about his whereabouts or merely disappointed this will not be your wedding night after all?"

Anna's cheeks flooded with color, filling her delicate features with a crimson blush. But as she drew back her hand to slap the smirk from Phillip's face, he caught her wrist in a firm grasp and she gasped in pain. "How dare you!"

"You are obviously distraught over having to wait, but unfortunately it is unavoidable, for Charles has left England and will not become your husband for some weeks yet. You will just have to bide your time here and try to stay out of mischief as best you can until he returns."

Mystified by his words, Anna yanked her hand away. "Enough of your incessant teasing, Captain. Just where has the man gone and when is he expected to return?" Without realizing it, the relief Anna felt showed in her pose. She relaxed against Phillip's chest, her supple form molding gently to his as she lifted her arm to encircle his neck, content to rest in his arms if

155

he'd answer her questions.

A hostile young woman was one challenge, this enticing creature quite another and Phillip cleared his throat with a forced cough as he plucked Anna from his lap and placed her upon the bench at his side. He rose then and began to pace up and down along the path in front of her. "I have none of the details, unfortunately, and I am no more pleased about this than you must be. You are wrong, however, if you believe me to be devoid of feelings, Lady Thorson, for I—"

"Captain, this is my marriage we are discussing. Can't you bring yourself to call me by my first name?" Anna asked softly. Would the man never admit that he knew her?

"Ah, yes, Lady Anna then." Phillip frowned, she'd distracted him from his purpose and he had to begin anew. "As captain of the *Angelina*, I am responsible for the health and safety of my crew and naturally if I have passengers I do not wish to see them come to any harm either. I agreed to bring you here, and in spite of your continual disregard for what any sane person would regard as common sense . . ."

Anna ceased to listen as the young man exhausted every uncomplimentary term he could summon to mind. She let her imagination wander as her gaze swept over him, caressing the contours of his powerful build with her golden gaze. It was foolish she knew and yet she enjoyed the sight of him so greatly. When he stopped moving abruptly and turned to face her, she realized he was waiting for the answer to a question she'd not heard. "I beg your pardon. Did you just ask me something?"

Phillip glanced up at the heavens in a silent plea for

aid in an impossible task. "All I want is your promise you will not cause havoc here for it may be several months before Charles is able to return home."

"I see. Knowing full well I was on my way to Briarcliff to marry him, he decided there was somewhere else he needed to be? Just where has he gone. Is it some secret?"

"No, the message he left was brief. There was an uprising of some sort among the slaves who work his plantation in Jamaica. His overseer was slain and Charles went to hire a replacement and to help quell whatever elements oppose order on the island."

Anna leapt to her feet, appalled by that revelation. "The man owns slaves, traffics in human beings?"

Phillip nodded, surprised she'd not understood so basic a point about the Caribbean economy. "Yes, he has dozens, men and women who staff his residence and work in the sugar cane fields. All the plantations are worked by African slaves."

Anna shuddered as if with a sudden chill. "Oh, Phillip, you don't ever carry slaves aboard the *Angelina*, do you? That's not how you met Charles is it?"

"No, of course not. I'd no more captain a slave ship than I'd—" Give you to Charles, his agile mind supplied the end to that sentence, but he dared not speak it. Somehow he wanted to win her admiration more desperately than he'd wanted anything in his life and forced himself to continue. "I'd send the *Angelina* to the bottom before I'd ever carry human cargo."

Relieved, Anna stepped forward, a pretty smile lighting her sweet features. "If Charles left a message for you, was there none for me?"

Phillip shrugged helplessly. "I really don't know.

Perhaps he did but Mrs Shepard would not have given it to me."

Anna glanced toward the terrace, not eager to search out the haughty housekeeper. "She should have given it to me immediately then, not made me seek her out to ask for it."

Phillip found Anna's disappointment most natural and agreed. "Yes, I had barely stepped through the door when she thrust Charles's letter into my hand. It is possible he had no time to leave more than the message he left for me but if you will wait here for a moment I will go and inquire."

Anna licked her lips thoughtfully as she considered his offer, her gesture an irresistibly appealing one of which she was totally unaware. "Yes, would you please? She is not the most hospitable person and I'm certain she would be more receptive to your queries than to mine."

"As you wish." With a curt nod Phillip strode into the sumptuous manor, deciding as he went that if no message had been left for Anna he'd pen one himself with all possible haste. He could not bear to think how badly she would be hurt should she have been ignored. She deserved to be treated more sweetly than he believed Charles could possibly manage.

Anna wandered aimlessly, too nervous to remain sedately seated when her life seemed to be continually taking such unexpected turns. She had blocked the prospect of her impending marriage from her mind until Phillip had teased her about her wedding night but his remark had brought back the reality of her situation all too graphically. How could Lord Clairbourne have left England when he knew she was on her way to

158

marry him? Was he not as anxious to meet her as she was to meet him? Was the arrival of his future bride of such slight consequence to him he could postpone their meeting indefinitely? She was bursting with curiosity, so anxious to make the acquaintance of her future husband she'd risked making the trip to his home unescorted with most disastrous results and the man was not even in residence! His home was as fine as many a palace but held not the slightest bit of attraction for her. She would have been satisfied with a far less magnificent dwelling, if only its owner had been there to greet her. Depressed that her future was more uncertain than ever, Anna continued to walk down the path, unmindful of her lovely surroundings.

Phillip scanned the expansive gardens impatiently. Where had Anna gone now? Could she not even follow so simple a direction as to remain within sight? The heavy perfume of the nearby roses assailed his senses with a taunting fragrance, for the day was warm and, the bushes laden with bright blossoms. Briarcliff was as splendid as he had remembered it. Well-tended and prosperous, it served as indisputable evidence of its owner's wealth and proud heritage, attributes Phillip dismissed with a disdainful sneer. He tapped the parchment envelope against his palm and, tired of waiting, took the central path hoping to catch sight of the elusive Lady Thorson. His efforts were soon rewarded, for Anna had not strayed far, but merely strolled alongside a tall hedge which had screened her graceful figure from his view. When she heard Phillip calling her name she ran to meet him.

Smiling as she saw the letter in his hand, Anna called out breathlessly, "Is that for me? Did Charles truly leave a note for me?"

The hope in her amber gaze pierced Phillip's heart with a sharp stab of guilt yet he lied again with a confidence which gave her no cause for suspicion. "Yes, I knew you would be pleased."

Anna took the envelope and turned it over to break the seal, her slender fingers trembling with excitement as she withdrew the single sheet. She read the brief message quickly then looked up at the handsome captain. "He begs me to forgive him for not being here to welcome me to his home and promises to return at his first opportunity." Again scanning the few sentences she smiled. "Well, he did not say much but his penmanship is very attractive, quite masculine but neat and very easy to read."

Startled, Phillip looked down at the writing. He'd not thought to disguise his own hand but he'd not considered Anna would analyze the letter so thoroughly. "Surely you do not believe a man's character can be read in his hand, Lady Anna. That is no better than witchcraft!" He laughed at her efforts as if they were truly ridiculous.

Insulted, Anna replied indignantly. "Are you calling me a witch now, Captain?"

Still chuckling, Phillip shook his head. "Of course not, you are far too lovely to be mistaken for a witch, even on the darkest of nights."

Blushing at his unexpected compliment, Anna chose to ignore it. "He doesn't mention his sons. Do you know where they might be?"

"Yes, he had taken them to Jamaica with him, undoubtedly to emphasize the point he is unafraid to live there himself or to bring his family there."

"Then I should be there too!" Anna insisted instantly, her only option suddenly clear in her mind.

"What?" Phillip gasped in astonishment. "That's absurd, and utterly impossible as well!"

"Why? What is your next port of call? Is the *Angelina* not bound for Jamaica? You have said repeatedly you were paid to escort me safely to Lord Clairbourne's side and your job will not be completed until you've done so!"

Phillip drew in a deep breath and exhaled with deliberate slowness in a vain attempt to quench the fiery temper which threatened to explode from his lips in language he knew to be far too vile for a lady's ears. "Lady Thorson, will you please stop for a moment to consider what you are suggesting?"

Anna replied calmly, "I have done little else since my uncle informed me of my forthcoming marriage. Perhaps it is your turn to consider what is best for me. Come sit down with me and we will discuss this issue as fully as you wish."

When she turned, Phillip followed, his fists clenched tightly at his sides. Only this morning he'd thought this would be the last day he'd ever have to spend with the bewitching Anna Thorson and he could not lift his gaze from the slow, undulating roll of her hips as she preceded him up the path. Tall and lithe, she was a woman so desirable he wanted only to reach out to encircle her narrow waist, to make her turn back toward him and come into his embrace. Yet he made no such foolhardy move. He sat down beside her and leaned forward to rest his arms across his knees. "What would be best for you is simply to wait here as Charles expects you to. I know Mrs. Shepard is neither warm nor gracious, but you'd not want to spend your time in her company regardless of what her personality might be."

Anna listened attentively as Phillip continued to extoll the virtues of Briarcliff and the easy life which he was sure she'd enjoy if she'd only accept it. "Phillip, I am not a woman who enjoys enforced leisure. Let us contemplate for a moment what would happen to me should Charles meet with some misfortune while he is in Jamaica. If there has been a slave rebellion, the possibility of violence exists still, does it not?"

"Undoubtedly, but—"

"If he were killed," Anna interrupted swiftly. "I would find myself in a most awkward situation here. Neither wife nor relative, I would have no choice but to leave. My uncle would be no more pleased to have me return to Sweden than I'd be to again suffer his domination and while my mother has family here in England I'll not accept their charity either. There's no point in my remaining in this country if Charles is unable to return. Would America not be a better place for a young woman to try and make her own way?"

Phillip was so astonished he could not respond for several seconds. "Your imagination seems to know no bounds, Lady Thorson, and Charles would be astounded to hear you expect his imminent demise!"

"Will you please be serious, Captain! What would you suggest I do should Charles not return? Should I take a few of his paintings to sell, or perhaps take a silver candelabrum or two? Just what would you suggest I do to support myself if I am not to become Lady Clairbourne?"

Phillip gestured helplessly as he spoke. "One thing at a time, Anna. For the present Charles is very much alive and there's no reason for you to anticipate such dire circumstances. All you need do is wait here and he and his sons will return in due time."

Angered that he'd consider her very legitimate concerns trivial, Anna eyed him coldly. "I'll not stay here, Captain. If you won't take me to Jamaica then I'll just have to find someone else who will for I've really no other choice."

Phillip leaned back, stunned by her determination, and forced himself to logically explain the reason behind his decision. "Anna, the *Angelina* is as you well know a cargo vessel and Britain does not permit other countries to do business with the colonies she guards so jealously. The United States received no special concessions for trade although we sought them after we won our independence. Now I must have a cargo to sell or I cannot pay what I owe on my ship in a timely manner. I am not bound for the Caribbean, but Philadelphia and I'll not change my plans when taking you to Jamaica would mean I'd have not only pirates with whom to contend, but the Royal Navy as well! Should we be boarded, which would be a most likely possibility, they would never believe I was merely dropping off a passenger and not intending to sell my cargo in the Caribbean and promptly confiscate whatever goods were in the hold."

Anna lifted a finely shaped eyebrow quizzically. "You have never been to Jamaica, Captain?"

"Yes, I have been there," Phillip admitted reluctantly. "But I'll not risk your life, nor those of my crew in a venture so foolish as this! You'll stay here at Briarcliff as you were told!"

Anna looked down at the letter in her hands, caressing the thick parchment lightly. "Charles did not forbid me to come to Jamaica. Perhaps it did not occur to him that I would be willing to make the voyage. I'll sail aboard a British vessel if that will present fewer problems, but I'll definitely go."

"You'll do no such thing!" Phillip ordered hoarsely but the bright gleam in her tawny eyes defied him still. "God help me, Anna, what am I to do with you?"

Anna tossed her curls with a saucy shrug. "Why, Captain, Charles left your money here, didn't he? Haven't you been paid in full? I'm no longer your responsibility then, am I? Can't you simply return to the *Angelina* and erase all thought of me from your mind?"

"That would be an impossibility!" Phillip replied instantly, revealing far more than he'd wished to divulge. But he relaxed somewhat when he saw she had no idea why he'd never be able to forget her. "Have you forgotten Sophia's health will preclude her from travel for some weeks? Surely you'd not leave her here alone. You must wait here for Charles, Anna, it's the only sensible thing for you to do."

Anna turned away, tired of arguing with him when he obviously cared so little for her happiness. "Will you excuse me please, I really must see if Sophia needs anything. She was resting comfortably but I should be with her when she awakens." She rose then, not waiting for his reply before she started up the path.

Phillip leapt to his feet and overtook her in two long strides. "You'll not escape me so easily, Anna. You will still have to have supper this evening and I much prefer your company to my own. Won't you please join me? Charles's cook is truly a chef and his meals are

164

very fine."

Anna gave the dark-haired man a sly glance through her thick lashes. "You've just reminded me I'm neglecting my maid's welfare shamefully when her injuries were entirely my fault. How can you now suggest I take time away from her care to dine with you?"

Phillip sighed impatiently. "I am doing my best to be a gentleman. Why will you not allow it? I know we are not friends, but tomorrow I shall return to my ship and we will most likely never meet again. Could we not be civil to each other for one night at least?"

When they reached the terrace, Anna hid the pain his casual dismissal of their relationship had caused behind a slight smile for what he said was true: Once he was gone she could do as she pleased. There was no reason to battle with him over her future since he obviously had no desire to be part of it. "Forgive me if I was rude. I shall be delighted to have supper with you if only you will see me to my room now and call for me there later. I've found this house to be as difficult to traverse as a Chinese puzzle is to solve!"

Laughing at the truth in her words, Phillip took Anna's arm and, pointing out the route as he went, guided her expertly to her room where he left her with a jaunty salute and a firm vow to return.

Lydia Shepard slipped behind a partially open door to avoid being seen as she watched the striking couple pass by. They were far too friendly in her estimation. The young woman's beauty had surprised her. The first Lady Clairbourne had been so plain of appearance she'd not thought how susceptible Charles would be to the wiles of a young woman possessing such grace and charm. She frowned petulantly, displeased to find

Lady Thorson so formidable an adversary. Briarcliff was her home, hers alone to rule and she'd tolerate no more interference from the Swedish beauty. She fingered the keys at her belt nervously. There was more than one way to obey a command and she'd see Lady Thorson's orders were followed without haste or precision. Without ever suggesting disobedience, she'd see the staff of Briarcliff made the young woman feel most unwelcome. Perhaps they'd be so effective she'd not even bother to remain to meet Lord Clairbourne but declare their engagement broken and return to her home at once. That possibility pleased Lydia greatly and with a knowing smile she hurried to the kitchen to oversee the preparations for the evening meal.

Chapter Nine

Phillip spent the remainder of the afternoon relaxing in the privacy of his room. Stretched out in a comfortable red velvet wing chair, he did not bother to rise to light a lamp when the setting sun no longer illuminated the expansive room with a subtle glow. Silent, thumbs hooked in his belt loops, he was lost in his efforts to make sense of his last conversation with the delectable Lady Thorson. Anna Ericdotter, he reminded himself with a sly smile, somehow preferring the sound of the distinctively Swedish name to her formal one. He was fooling himself, he knew, for regardless of what she called herself she was indisputably of high birth. Her finely drawn features were exquisite, her unusual coloring superb, the elegant proportions of her slender figure those of a goddess. She deserved no less than the finest prince for her husband, not a snake like Charles! Thoroughly disgusted with that sickening prospect, Phillip rose slowly, stretching to flex his sore muscles in an attempt to work out the stiffness remaining from the long ride on horseback he'd begun before dawn. It had been months since he'd ridden and not in all his life had he ever driven an animal to the limit of its endurance as he had that morning. The beast was probably lying dead in the stables and he'd have to borrow a mount from Briarcliff's stock to return to Exmouth. Not that the life of one horse was of any consequence when compared to Anna's safety, but the young woman had seemed more annoyed by his timely arrival than grateful.

"Damn!" Phillip swore bitterly. Tired of being confined, he was anxious to return to the *Angelina* but first he had to convince Anna to remain at Briarcliff. How was he to accomplish that feat when she listened to not one word he ever spoke to her? That he'd been so foolish as to kiss her again appalled him but she continually pushed him until he lost all control of his emotions. That kiss had been worth it though, he thought with a chuckle and deciding to visit the stables he left the house to see if perhaps the rented horse had survived the morning's furiously paced journey in better condition than had he.

When Anna's belongings finally appeared at her door, she thanked Mrs. Shepard graciously as if their long delay were of scant importance. As it was, however, she had little time to bathe and dress before Phillip called to escort her to supper. She could readily tell by the width of his smile he was pleased by her appearance. The deep blue of her silk gown gave her eyes the glow of sapphires which she had hoped would be becoming and his appreciative glance was proof that it was.

"Do you think Sophia might permit me a few minutes of her time? I will be leaving very early tomorrow morning and don't want to disturb her then to bid her farewell." Phillip's tone was polite as he inquired about the maid.

Anna opened the door to permit him to enter. "Of course, Captain, she will be very pleased by your concern." She led him over to the bed, then stood back while he moved to the chair she'd occupied at Sophia's bedside.

"I will be returning to the *Angelina* at first light, Sophia. I wanted you to know I hope your recovery will be both rapid and complete."

"You are leaving us, Captain Bradford?" Greatly disturbed by that news, Sophia tried to sit up but found the effort not worth the excruciating pain and lay back to catch her breath. "How will we ever manage without you, sir?"

Alarmed by the brightness of her eyes, Phillip reached out to touch the little woman's cheek lightly but found her skin cool. Deciding his concern was unfounded, he smiled and hastened to disagree. "You are in most capable hands here, Sophia. Both Mrs. Shepard and Dr. Beckwith will tend you well. Now you must simply try and sleep for it is rest you need most now."

"I know, sir, but I am so worried about my dear Anna, with Lord Clairbourne away and you gone. If any more calamities befall us to whom shall we turn?"

"Sophia," Phillip whispered softly, wanting to reassure her and not knowing quite what to say. He could not guarantee the behavior of her mistress would not present several calamities before Charles returned. "I am not abandoning you among strangers but leaving you well cared for. Briarcliff is now your home. Do not concern yourself with any matter save your own recovery for Lady Anna is confident she will be happy here, aren't you, my dear?''

Anna understood she was expected to agree and did so only to ease her servant's fears, not out of regard for the truth. ''Of course, please do not fret so, Sophia. Try and sleep and I will return shortly.'' Turning to the handsome young man, Anna asked politely, ''Would you be so kind as to summon a maid from your room, Captain? Mrs. Shepard requested I use the bellpull for service but I do not believe the one in this room is functioning.''

Puzzled, Phillip gave Sophia's hands a last affectionate squeeze then rose to give the embroidered bellpull hanging beside the bed a savage yank. ''Let's try an experiment. I'll give the one in my room a tug and we'll see whose call is answered most promptly. Wait here as Mrs. Shepard would not approve of our challenging her staff to such a race.''

Amused by the thought of playing such a trick on that austere woman, Anna stood at her door to wave as Phillip entered his own room. When she turned to face Sophia she was smiling still. ''When someone comes I'll ask him to sit with you while we are at supper. I'll not leave you here all alone.''

The petite woman yawned sleepily before arguing. ''Go along with the captain, Lady Anna. Do not keep him waiting; I will require little more than this comfortable bed in which to sleep this night.''

Rather than insist upon having her own way, Anna simply waited by the door until Phillip returned with a plump woman in a snug gray uniform, her white apron and cuffs heavily starched and spotless. "This is Lenore and she will be happy to sit with Sophia for an hour or two, won't you, Lenore?" Phillip ushered the startled woman into Anna's room and saw she was comfortably seated at Sophia's side. "We shall be dining but do not hesitate to call us should Sophia complain of even the slightest bit of discomfort. Do you understand what it is you are to do, Lenore?" Phillip wanted to make certain she did.

"Yes, sir, I am to call you if there be need." Lenore folded her hands in her ample lap and fixed Sophia with a watchful eye.

"Good. Now come, Lady Thorson. Let us enjoy your first formal meal at Briarcliff without further delay." Phillip drew Anna through the door but stopped several paces down the hall and spoke in a conspiratorial whisper. "I am glad you thought to summon a maid but Lenore came to answer my call and made no mention of yours. I will see the bells are in good working order before I leave tomorrow as I do not want you to be without the means to call for help should the need arise."

"Oh, Captain, you don't truly think Sophia is doing poorly, do you? She slept several hours this afternoon, sipped a cup of clear broth as well as several cups of herb tea. I will not leave her now if you even suspect she is in danger for she is most precious to me." Anna grasped his hands tightly as her golden eyes swept his expression searching for a deeper message than he'd spoken.

Not having meant to cause the pretty blonde such a fright, Phillip hastened to reassure her. "I am not a physician, Anna. Although I've tended many an injury aboard the *Angelina*, I'm not qualified to make any sort of prediction about Sophia's health. It is only that she seems very worried about you, and she should be spared any anxiety now. Did you mention your plans to sail to Jamaica?"

"No, of course not!" Anna was disappointed he thought so little of her judgment and did not remark upon her desire to join Charles until they were seated in the dining room. To use the long mahogany table clearly meant for entertaining dozens of guests rather than for only two people seemed pretentious to her but she'd not thought to tell Mrs. Shepard to set a table for them elsewhere. The high ceiling of the enormous room made the sound of their voices echo with an eerie ring and she found herself leaning close to the finely dressed captain to whisper. "I thought perhaps by the time you had secured a cargo and loaded it on board the *Angelina* Sophia might be feeling well enough to travel with me."

Phillip nearly choked on the rich lentil soup he'd just brought to his mouth and dropped his heavy silver spoon with a loud clatter as he grabbed up his linen napkin to cover his cough. "Lady Anna, please do not startle me so badly ever again! That subject is closed. Sophia's fragile health as well as the consideration for your own personal safety demand you remain here where no other harm can befall you!" He was clearly incensed that she would bring up her ridiculous wish to sail to Jamaica once again after he'd done all he could to make her see how foolish that hope was.

Anna patted his arm lightly with her fingertips. "Forgive me, I did not mean to ruin our last meal together as I seem to have ruined all the others. Your concern for my safety is appreciated, Captain. I understand why you cannot take me any farther and will cease to plead my cause since it is clearly pointless, a waste of my time as well as yours."

Phillip stared in sullen silence as Anna finished her soup. When he could hold his temper no longer he inquired crossly, "Were your parents not frantic they had produced so reckless a daughter? How have you managed to survive in the world without the least bit of common sense to guide your way?"

"That you disapprove of me is plain, Captain, but what would you have me do, meekly remain here until Charles finds the time or the inclination to return? I am not some witless waif who'd be content to wait for a reluctant bridegroom who may never appear. If I must spend the rest of my life as Lord Clairbourne's wife then so be it, but I'll not be ignored so blatantly as this!" Anna caught herself before she revealed any more of her despair for truly she thought Phillip impervious to her pain and that sharing her anger would bring no sympathy.

Phillip waited until their entree had been served, then lowered his voice to a more discreet level in hopes she would do the same. "I know nothing of how marriages are arranged by your class, by men and women with fine old titles and elegant estates." He gestured toward the brightly frescoed ceiling; a magnificent work of art in itself, it drew little attention in the opulently decorated room. "All I know is that I am sick to death of arriving just seconds before you meet your doom! If you can think of no reason to remain here, then arrange to visit your mother's relatives for a month or two but give up this nonsensical dream you have of going to Jamaica before . . ." When no truly horrible possibility came to his mind he paused to catch his breath and Anna supplied a concluding thought.

"Before what? Before I am killed? I do not think I can adequately describe how little that prospect frightens me."

It terrified Phillip, however. He shoved back his chair and sprang to his feet, his stance as menacing as his words. "I cannot even taste this meal let alone enjoy it! If you wish to remain then do so. If not, I will see you to your room before I go to mine. I plan to get an early start tomorrow morning and need what rest I can find!" How he could sleep that night he had no idea, but he couldn't stand to sit there another minute.

No longer concerned about the man's perpetual ill-humor, Anna glanced down at the steaming supper upon her Wedgwood plate. The roast pork was delicious, succulent and tender, the fresh vegetables scrumptious in a lightly seasoned butter sauce. She shook her head emphatically. "I'll not insult so fine a chef as the one who prepared this superb meal. I am a poor hostess I fear, but I'll not insist you stay with me if you do not wish to do so. Polite company, like affection, is a gift and I'll not be so foolish as to try and force you to like me when it is so very plain you do not."

Sinking back down into his chair, Phillip grabbed up his fork and took a bite of the roast pork and then another, attacking his supper with the vengeance he dared not turn on his beautiful companion. When Anna started to giggle her laugh contained such an infectiously pleasant sparkle he could neither ignore nor

174

resist it and after a second's pause he could not suppress his own deep laughter. "You must think me a pompous fool, Anna, but I cannot discuss your possible death with the detachment you affect. It would be a tragedy too great to even contemplate and I'll not do it, not tonight, or ever."

"I have never considered you pompous, Captain. Arrogant and demanding certainly, but not pompous." Anna smiled sweetly, flirting so easily she'd not realized she'd done it. The man was definitely well suited to command, she thought. He had a confident manner which inspired trust but it was a friend she needed so desperately now, not an overbearing master. "Forgive me for being so flippant, Captain Bradford. You can not change your way of thinking any more than I can change mine simply because what is best for you is so far different from what is best for me. If we are to part company tonight I should like your memory of me to be a pleasant one. But is there no hope we might meet again someday?"

Completely bewitched by Anna's guileless manner, Phillip searched his mind frantically for some gentlemanly response. "It is my hope that we will, Anna, for I should like to know you are safe and well."

Seizing upon his kind words as encouragement, Anna inquired excitedly, "Jamaica is far closer to your country than to this one. "If I were to visit America one day, how might I find you?"

"Would you truly wish to try?" Phillip asked softly, not daring to hope that she might. He could imagine her moving through the dense fog which frequently blankets the Eastern seaboard, her lovely smile glowing brightly from her own inner warmth as the sound of her musical voice calling his name echoed along the deserted docks. She might search forever and their paths never cross, that she would even want to try and find him brought a sorrow he found difficult to disguise and he looked away to hide the pain he was certain she'd see but never understand.

Anna's warm gaze swept Phillip's finely sculptured features slowly, completely misreading the cause for his solemn mood. "I am sorry, that was very forward of me, wasn't it?" Twisting her napkin nervously in her lap she continued, "I do not want you to spend the rest of your days dreading that I might suddenly appear to embarrass you, Captain. If you'd rather not see me ever again, please just say so."

Phillip thought it best to turn their conversation to a more practical vein as he'd obviously insulted her without meaning to do so. "I can not imagine ever being embarrassed by your presence, Anna, but I do sail to England each year so it is far more likely I will see you right here at Briarcliff than it is you'll chance to meet me on the streets of Philadelphia."

"Is Philadelphia your home port then?" Anna inquired shyly, not content to say goodbye when she still knew so little about him and he fascinated her so.

Phillip had to chuckle at her persistence. "I told you the *Angelina* is my home for I am as likely to be in the Southern ports loading cotton or tobacco as I am to be in Philadelphia or Boston. America is a vast land, Anna, the ports and cities are many. Perhaps Charles will take you there someday as he enjoys travel greatly."

"Why is it all our conversations must begin and end with that man's name? Do you regard me to be so com-

176

pletely his property that I do not even exist in my own right? Can you not look at me without seeing Charles's face in your mind?"

"No, indeed I can not!" Giving up all hope of finishing their meal in any sort of a pleasant fashion, Phillip gave his full attention to eating every morsel on his plate, then savored the dessert of sweet, juicy berries served in thick cream before he escorted Anna to her room where he bid her a terse good night. It was not at all the way he wanted to say farewell, but truly he did not wish to leave her on that night or any other and could not bring himself to tarry when the pain of their parting was so great.

Hurt by his curt rebuff, Anna slipped through her door with a gaze blurred by unshed tears. She did not immediately realize Lenore was not seated where they'd left her. When she saw her maid was unattended, she rushed to the large bed and found Sophia entangled in the bedclothes, her right arm outstretched as if she'd been trying to reach the bellpull. Her fair skin had grown pale, clammy to the touch with a slight bluish cast near her lips. When she tried to greet Anna her voice was too breathless to be understood. Badly frightened, Anna offered comforting words as she smoothed out the rumpled sheets and adjusted the feather pillows so her stricken servant might rest more comfortably before she excused herself to run to Phillip's room to plead for the assistance she prayed he'd not refuse.

Stripped to the waist, the well-built young man had no time to don his shirt as Anna rushed through his door without stopping to knock. He saw only the anguish in her tear-filled eyes and ran past her to learn first-hand what terrible thing had transpired. As he came to her bedside, Sophia tried to smile but her words were inaudible and he bent down close in order to hear.

"Do not leave my dear Anna, Captain, never leave her." The light which had shown so brightly in her blue eyes earlier that evening had faded to no more than a soft glow, her spirit visibly departing her frail body as she attempted to make him agree to her desperate plea.

Stunned by a request he could not honor, Phillip straightened up, taking the sweet little woman's small hands in his as he slid his fingertips to her wrist to feel for a pulse although he already knew the search would reveal a faint, wildly erratic beat.

Anna had followed Phillip into her room but hung back, not wishing to intrude upon so intimate a scene. "What could have possessed Lenore to leave Sophia unattended? She was trying to ring for the maid as I entered but either could not reach the bellpull or it malfunctioned again. Shall we send Frederick or one of the others for Dr. Beckwith again?"

Phillip patted the gravely ill maid's hands tenderly as he replied in a voice hoarse with emotion. "There is no need to summon him tonight, Anna. Come here and sit down beside Sophia for a moment while she falls asleep. Your attention will be all she needs."

Moving closer to the bed, Anna peered down at her dear friend's sweet face and called softly, "Sophia?" She reached out to caress the woman's wrinkled cheek lightly, then seeing her wan smile sat down in the chair beside the bed and leaned close. "I am here, Sophia. I will not leave you again. Rest quietly and tomorrow when the sun rises I will fill our room with flowers. The

178

gardens of Briarcliff are splendid, far prettier than any we ever had at home. Do you remember my mother's garden? She worked so diligently that last spring and still . . ."

Phillip stood listening quietly to Anna's calm, reassuring voice as she made Sophia's last moments on earth bright ones. Finally he reached out to touch the lovely young woman's shoulder. "She can no longer hear you, Anna. It must have been her heart, a sudden attack which struck so swiftly I'm sure she felt little pain."

Anna sat without moving for a long time, staring intently at her beloved servant's slight smile before she turned to look up at Phillip. "She did not suffer?"

"No, I am certain she did not." In truth he had no idea what a person felt when his heart ceased to beat but he would have told any lie to save Anna pain. "Now come with me, I want you to sleep in my room tonight." He lifted her gently from her chair, his arm encircling her narrow waist as he led her across the richly carpeted floor before she could argue. He hoped only to ease her grief but as he opened the door he was greeted by an irate Lydia Shepard followed closely by the neatly dressed Lenore.

The housekeeper's caustic gaze raked over Phillip's half-clothed body before she turned to the dazed beauty in his embrace. "If you think the scandalous nature of your behavior will go unreported to Lord Clairbourne, you are badly mistaken, Lady Thorson! It is obvious what your relationship must have been with Captain Bradford on board his ship but it will not continue under his lordship's roof I can assure you!"

"Mrs. Shepard, you have far overstepped your authority!" Phillip responded fiercely. "And as for you, Lenore, how dare you leave Sophia alone when you are specifically told not to do so!"

Cringing under that stern rebuke, Lenore replied in a high-pitched whimper. "I only went to call Mrs. Shepard, sir. When no one answered the bell I had no choice but to leave as the woman was struggling to catch her breath and I grew frightened she might be seriously ill!" Lenore wrung her hands anxiously, clearly distraught she'd displeased an important guest and fearing her job was in jeopardy as a result.

Exasperated by the woman's foolishness, Phillip hugged Anna closer to his side. "That is most unfortunately a gross understatement. Sophia has died in the time you left her alone to summon help. Lady Thorson will spend the night in my room without further insult, Mrs. Shepard. You will remain here with Lenore to see Sophia's body is properly prepared for burial, but not one word of any suspected scandal is ever to reach Charles's ears for it will not be Lady Thorson's reputation which will suffer but your own!" Brushing past the startled servants, Phillip led Anna down the hall to his room where he locked the door securely behind them to make certain they would not be disturbed. When he turned he found the young woman's expression troubled. She glanced over at the large bed. The sheets had been turned down in anticipation of his retiring and the lamp at the bedside cast only a small amount of light upon the pillows. The rest of the bedchamber was too dimly lit to be seen, but clearly there was only one place to sleep. "I meant what I said, Anna. You need not worry I will take advantage of your grief tonight, but you should not be left alone to brood." He tried to smile, his sympathy sincere. "I am so terribly sorry this has happened. I sensed something was amiss before we went downstairs to supper but—"

Rushing forward, Anna's golden eyes blazed with a sudden fury. "You told me there was no reason to worry! Had I known there was even the slightest chance Sophia might need me tonight I never would have left her by herself! Why did you lie to me when it cost her her life!

"I saw only her anxiety, Anna. I did not realize its cause!" Phillip was appalled she'd blame him for a death he was positive could not be laid at his feet. A point he tried to make her see. "Sophia was not a young woman. Perhaps the strain of the voyage was far greater than she let you see. It is possible the injuries she received this morning were more severe than Dr. Beckwith could discern. Undoubtedly it was a combination of factors which overwhelmed her and proved fatal, but none can be blamed on me!"

Anna stepped back quickly, struck as much by the hostility of Phillip's manner as she was by the truth of his words. "No, I am sorry, the fault is entirely mine for I wanted her to come with me so I might have some small part of home to give me comfort when I became a stranger's bride. My selfishness killed her. I am the one who killed her and all she ever showed me was love."

Phillip's anger dissolved instantly as he watched the remorseful young woman lift her hand to hide her tears. Her shoulders shook as she wept and he could not bear to watch her sorrow without trying in some way to ease it. He gathered her up into his arms, carried her over to the comfortable chair near the win-

dows and, sitting down, drew her across his lap. Her
curls shone in the moonlight and he stroked her hair
lightly as he kissed away her tears, forgetting his reserve as he whispered, "You must not blame yourself
for Sophia's death, Anna. Never do that for it will only
ruin the memories of her which I know must be most
precious to you and make your grief that much more
difficult to bear." As he spoke, his hands traced her
soft curves slowly. He wanted only to hold her close, to
cradle her in his arms. She did not struggle against
him, relaxing to accept his tender sympathy most willingly.

Gradually Anna's ravaged emotions gave way to a
peaceful calm as Phillip's inviting affection led her out
of her guilt. She raised her fingertips to his bare chest,
returning his gentle touch with a fond caress before
lifting her arm to encircle his neck to draw his mouth
down to hers. As always his kiss held an unspoken
promise of love and she hugged him more tightly, leading him again into the rapture which was within their
grasp. Enticing, playful, she traced the shape of his
lips with the tip of her tongue before invading his
slightly open mouth with a saucy abandon he welcomed eagerly for there was not the slightest bit of reti-
cence in her kiss. She was no tease but a woman so
loving she wanted to please him in every way she knew
how.

Phillip pulled Anna closer to his heart, fondly sepa-
rating her fair curls into silken strands with his fingertips as he enjoyed her deep kiss. He had never been
with so affectionate a creature, but he knew only too
well how little control he had over his emotions where
she was concerned and grew more cautious. He forced

himself to do no more than hold her but he longed to again cover her lissome body with kisses, to drive reason from her mind until she could do no more than sob his name in hoarse whispers but that was a memory he'd promised not to relive that night. At least he could savor her kiss, his mouth caressing hers gently, his enjoyment of her endless. Her intoxicating taste was more potent than any wine and when he felt her hands moving down his body with a smooth caress which grew increasingly more bold he did not move to stop her but let the pleasure swell through his loins until it became a need bordering upon pain. He recalled the real reason she'd come into his arms and reached down to lace her fingers firmly in his as he drew away. Pressing her head to his shoulder he whispered softly, "Forgive me, Anna, I meant only to hold you in my arms to ease your grief but when you kissed me I longed to recapture the joy we found before. It's wrong to seek that pleasure when the woman who was so dear to you lies dead. That you are still so eager for my affection pleases me greatly but had I not stopped you just now I would not have been able to stop myself and you would never have forgiven me, nor yourself when you awakened in the morning and remembered what we'd done on this of all nights."

His solemn words only confused Anna, filling her heart with an anguish nearly impossible to endure and she sat up proudly. "I seem to have been very selfish again if I've used the sadness of this night to take from you the affection you would not have freely given. Will you let me go, please? I've no desire to remain perched upon your knee if you find my presence such a torment. At least you were kind enough not to remind me

I am engaged to Charles and for that small kindness I am most grateful." She slid off his knee the instant he released her. "Where do you wish me to sleep? It is obvious you do not want me to share your bed."

"Anna!" Phillip whispered hoarsely as he rose, sorry now he'd not pushed his advantage for all it had been worth when he'd had the chance. Her cool rebuke provoked him sorely. "The bed is yours. Sleep in your chemise, do not return to your own room for a nightgown. This house is large and I'll find another bed somewhere, but first I want to see why no calls from your room are answered. That something should be amiss in the bedchamber prepared for you strikes me as most peculiar."

"Wait! I'm coming with you!" Anna hurried after him, not content to be left alone when there was a mystery to be solved.

Phillip unlocked his door, then held the key lightly in his palm, wondering if he could slip through the door and lock the unpredictable young woman inside where she could give him no more trouble that night. Deciding she was far too clever to let him get away with that trick he tried to explain. "I'll do no more than go down the back stairs to the kitchen to check the bells. It will hardly be a great adventure!"

"I don't care. If something was done deliberately to cause me harm, then the ploy succeeded and Sophia's death was no less than murder!"

Murder was too strong a word in Phillip's view, but he saw no point in arguing until they had some tangible proof of tampering. "Bring the lamp then and let's hurry." Phillip watched as she crossed the room, still not convinced he'd not be smart to lock her in. But he waited, then took her elbow to lead her down the hall. "The back stairs are narrow. Let me go first and then you follow."

The small oil lamp cast eerie shadows upon the walls as they moved over the thick carpet with hushed steps. Anna wondered what time it might be but did not ask, for surely any staff left to clean the kitchen after their supper had done so and gone to bed. When the wooden stairs creaked under Phillip's weight she whispered quickly, "Let me go first while you wait, then if the kitchen is deserted I'll come back up to let you know. We're making so much noise anyone still working will hear us and come to investigate."

Knowing that was the first sensible suggestion Anna had ever made to him, Phillip readily agreed. "I will wait for no more than five minutes. If you have not returned then I'm coming down no matter if there are fifty people down there!"

"I will hurry." Slipping past him, Anna's fingertips caressed his broad chest lightly, startling them both as a spark of excitement passed between them. Blushing deeply, Anna hurried on down the winding staircase, holding her hand in front of the lamp to hide the light until she reached the kitchen and found it in total darkness. She glanced around quickly and saw a door which she thought might lead to the housekeeper's apartment. She crossed the room to close it before going back up the stairs to summon Phillip. "They're all asleep." She took his hand and led him back down the stairs to the large kitchen where she could imagine the cook working with an enormous staff to prepare meals when Lord Clairbourne entertained.

"Bring the lamp. The bells are over here, I believe."

As Phillip turned, he tripped over a chair and cried out in pain.

"Hush! You'll wake the entire household!" Anna scolded.

"I should have known better than to expect sympathy from you!" Phillip straightened up, but limped badly as he crossed to the far wall.

"Are you really hurt? Anna asked skeptically. "I did not mean to sound so unconcerned if you truly are."

"I will live." Pausing to bring the chair he'd found so unexpectedly, Phillip placed it below the panel of bells which were labeled for the various rooms of the mansion. "Do you know how this contraption works?"

"Yes, by a system of pulleys and ropes. The cables run through the walls and have to be replaced frequently for if they get damp they rot and break."

Phillip nodded, surprised that her explanation was so accurate. "Yes, that's true, but no signal can be heard if the cord is cut either. Now just put the lamp aside and hold this chair for me so I do not suffer any more injuries tonight."

"I really am sorry, Phillip." Anna held the chair with great care, not wishing to see him hurt either. "Can you see anything?"

"Not yet." Phillip strained to read the faint labels. "Hand me the lamp please." Taking it carefully he studied the panel, then smiled. "Here, take the lamp. I think I've located our problem." With a sharp tug he removed one of the brass bells from its place and stepped down to show it to Anna. "Does this look as if the cord has rotted through due to mildew or even been severed by a rat's bite?"

Holding the bell near the lamp Anna examined the

end of the cord carefully. "No, this was cut with a pair of sharp scissors, I'd say. See, there is a crimp at the end of the cord and a knife would not have left such a mark."

"You are an exceedingly clever young woman, Anna. Now let us return to my room where we shall have to decide what to do next."

"I think we should keep the bell. It is evidence and we should have it."

"Yes, bring it along." Phillip replaced the chair in the center of the room and followed Anna back up the staircase without worrying about the noise they made. Once back in his room he again locked the door, then sat down and pulled off his right boot and began to roll down his blood-soaked stocking.

"You did hurt yourself, didn't you? I am so sorry. I am nothing but trouble for you it seems. I do not mean to cause you so many problems." Anna knelt by his side, ready to offer whatever assistance she could. There was a deep gash below his knee where the sharp edge of the chair seat had struck him, just above the top of his boot. It looked painful and she was certain it was.

Phillip reached out to tousle her soft curls playfully. "Go to bed, Anna. I want to stay up a while longer to think but you should already be asleep."

"You will not leave without waking me?" Anna pressed him to give his word. "Promise me that you won't."

The words stuck in his throat but he shook his head and whispered, "I will not leave without telling you goodbye."

"The bed is a wide one, Phillip. When you are tired

please share it with me. You need not fear I will presume upon your affection for me any further tonight." Their situation was a most painful one, she thought, for this would be their last opportunity to be lovers and yet the night was such an unbearably sad one making love would be impossible now.

Phillip watched as Anna extinguished the lamp. He heard the soft rustle of her clothing as she laid it aside. When she drew back the covers and climbed into his bed, he gave up all pretense of being able to refuse her invitation. He yanked off his left boot then went to the large bed and stretched out beside her, drawing her into his arms, cradling her head tenderly upon his shoulder as he whispered, "Just be still, Anna, for I want nothing more than to hold you in my arms as we sleep."

The sheets were cool, their chill a sharp reminder of the night's grim tragedy and Anna hugged him tightly, not wanting to cry again in front of him when she could not refuse his tender sympathy as emphatically as he refused hers.

Chapter Ten

No sooner had Anna fallen asleep than the hideous dreams began. Violent, twisted images filled her mind, then the highwayman's contorted face glowed in the darkness, his malevolent gaze fierce as he again drew back his fist, this time intent upon crushing her face as his other hand closed around her throat, choking her breath to sharp gasps. Terrified, Anna tried to escape his grasp, thrashing about wildly as she let out a blood-curdling shriek.

Despite being exhausted by a long and trying day, Phillip was instantly alert, his heart pounding as wildly as Anna's as he sat up and drew the trembling blonde into his arms. "Anna, what is it? What is the matter with you?"

Anna threw her arms around Phillip's neck, clinging to him as she sobbed pathetically. "It was only a nightmare, just a wretched dream but it was so very real it frightened me badly."

Phillip hugged Anna tightly until she had ceased to weep. "Dreams can be far more frightening than reality. That is why I did not want to leave you alone tonight." Seeing she had grown calm once more he stretched out across the comfortable bed and rubbed her back gently until her tension had eased. When she dozed again she was nestled against him, her head upon his shoulder. He lay wide awake trying to imagine a worse torture than the one he was suffering. The deep gash in his leg ached painfully but it was not that anguish which provided a nearly unbearable torment. He ran his fingers through her tangled curls and brought them to his lips, wondering how he could leave so dear a treasure as Anna. How could he ever find the strength to do it?

The handsomely appointed bedroom was awash in bright sunlight when Anna next awoke. She lay among the feather pillows which still held Phillip's distinctive scent, wondering if he had truly been there with her or if his comforting presence had been no more than the peace of restful slumber after her terrifying dreams. She stretched languidly, burying her face in the fragrant pillows and knew that faint tantalizing trace was all she'd ever have of him. He'd promised to say goodbye but now she hoped he had gone for she did not think she could bear to face him in the light of day when she'd have no assurance they'd ever meet again. At last she sat up and, tossing back the sheets, she gasped at the dark red stains which marred their snowy whiteness. She'd not realized Phillip had cut himself so badly, but the splotches of dried blood were irrefutable evidence that he had. "Whatever Clairbourne paid you, my dearest, it was not worth your pain." That's all she'd ever been to the man she thought sadly, just a miserable succession of the most perplexing of problems he had had no desire to solve.

Depressed by her maudlin thoughts, Anna remained seated on the edge of the bed for a long while, not wanting to return to her own room where Sophia's body was sure to be laid. She'd seen her mother's body, as well as her father's, all their loving goodness gone and she'd taken no comfort in the familiar image when it had been so devoid of life. Still, when she had loved their sparkling warmth and humor so dearly. Overwhelmed by those painful memories, she waited silently in Phillip's room hoping someone would come to bring her things. When Mrs. Shepard finally arrived, Anna was surprised by the woman's hostile tone.

The housekeeper's glance was menacing as she brought in a silver tray bearing an elegantly styled Wedgwood teapot, a cup and saucer from the same pattern, a plate of hot buttered muffins and a single red rose in a crystal bud vase. "Captain Bradford is supervising the construction of a coffin. He's sent word to the priest in Exmouth that he would like to bury your maid before noon so if you wish to attend her funeral I suggest you rise and dress immediately."

Anna clenched her fists at her sides, clearly displeased by the woman's haughty greeting, but she'd no interest in chastising her when she had so many other difficulties to face that morning. "The captain is extremely efficient. Please prepare a bath and bring my dark blue dress. It will have to do as I have no other garment suitable for mourning."

"As you wish, Lady Thorson." Despite her insolent manner, Lydia Shepard was conscientious and saw the young woman was beautifully groomed and dressed before she turned her attention to her other duties and summoned a maid to clean the lovely room thoroughly.

Following the route through the spacious home which Phillip had shown her on the way to dinner the previous evening, Anna found her way through the mansion and outside without once becoming lost. It seemed there was a pattern to the arrangement of the rooms and she was certain in a day or two she'd have mastered the floorplan completely. She skirted the lush gardens and went toward the barns from which she could hear the sounds of someone hammering with a slow, steady rhythm. To her amazement, she found Phillip and Joshua Coombes working diligently on the final touches of a well-crafted pine coffin.

"Mr. Coombes, forgive me. With all my worries yesterday I did not see you were paid as I'd promised." Dreadfully embarrassed by her oversight, Anna looked up at Phillip to apologize. "I thought Charles would be here to take care of Mr. Coombes's bill for me, but—"

"I have already paid Joshua, Lady Thorson. You need worry no longer that he will present his bill to you," Phillip remarked coolly, his manner polite but aloof.

Laying his hammer aside, Joshua offered his sympathy. "I thought I might be of some small service here, Lady Thorson, but I'd not anticipated so sad a task as this one."

Anna stepped forward to take the man's work-worn hands tenderly between her own. "Thank you for your kindness, Mr. Coombes, it is greatly appreciated." Then turning again to Phillip, Anna asked shyly, "I wonder if I might speak with you privately for a moment, Captain."

"Of course." Phillip gestured toward the pathway leading to the extensive gardens and took Anna's elbow lightly to guide her way as they strolled along. "I have arranged for Sophia's funeral. There is no cemetery here at Briarcliff but Charles supports the Anglican church at Exmouth, St. Michael's I believe it is called."

As Anna listened to him an idea came to her so suddenly she stopped abruptly, her face lit with a delighted smile. "You know the burial service, do you not? Or at least have a book with the words for a captain to recite for a burial at sea?"

Startled by the absurdity of her question, Phillip simply stared at the excited blonde for a long moment before he understood her true request. "Oh no, Anna, absolutely not! A burial at sea means just that, bodies are not tossed into the water near the shore, I'd have to be many miles distant of land to even consider such a thing." He thrust his hands into his pockets and took several steps away before he turned to regard her with keen interest. "God almighty! Where do you get your ideas, Anna? How do you continually pose such bizarre suggestions as a burial at sea for a lady's maid?"

Anna observed his expression closely for she found even his consternation intriguing, but her thoughtful expression brought a frown to his brow. "I would never have hated either you or myself this morning, Phillip. Not on this day nor any other." She felt not the slightest guilt that they'd made love on one occasion, so surely had they done so again she would feel no differently about herself or the regard she felt for him.

Blushing deeply under her steady gaze, Phillip glanced around the garden hurriedly to be certain they

193

were being neither overheard nor observed but the windows of the house were too numerous to guarantee them any true measure of privacy. "Anna, please, the fact that we have been intimate is better left forgotten for it will never be repeated, nor should it."

"I did not mean to embarrass you so badly by reminding you of it, simply to relieve your mind since you seem to frequently worry over matters I do not pretend to understand. I would like to see Sophia's body returned to Sweden for burial as England was not her home and she would not have been here had it not been for her love for me. To bury her here seems most improper. Since I have no way to pay for shipping her coffin home to Sweden though, I thought perhaps a sea burial would suffice for seafaring is our heritage and the ocean is not a stranger to us but a most loving friend."

Phillip shook his head sadly as he approached her. "I must return to Southampton immediately. In my haste to see you arrive here safely, I had to leave before taking on any cargo or giving my crew the rest they deserved. It is simply impossible for me to fulfill your wish for a burial at sea for Sophia, no matter how romantic or appropriate that desire may seem to you. Joshua will transport her coffin to Exmouth. You may ride with him of course and then he'll bring you back here to Briarcliff before he returns to Southampton."

"I see." Anna glanced down at the toe of her slipper as she scuffed it distractedly on the pebbles at the edge of the path. "All your plans are made and as usual I am not to argue but simply submit. You are in a great hurry as always and my trivial concerns must not delay you."

"You're being most unfair, Anna. I was fond of Sophia although I'd known her only briefly, but her devotion to you was commendable and I think you should show her memory far more respect than you are."

Insulted, Anna lifted her chin proudly. "I will mourn Sophia's death in my own fashion, Captain Bradford. I do not require lessons from you on the proper manner to grieve."

Frustrated by the pointlessness of their conversation, Phillip ended it abruptly. "Wait here. When Joshua and I have completed our preparations to leave, we shall go, for the morning is half spent already."

Dismayed as well as disappointed that her feelings still meant so very little to him Anna watched Phillip walk away at a swift pace, his long stride carrying him back to the barns in a few minutes time while she tried not to scream outloud over his tyrannical attitude. "If only you were taking me to Jamaica, what I ask would be a small thing," she whispered only to herself, knowing he'd neither hear nor heed any argument of hers.

Their grim task complete, Phillip saddled the horse he'd rented in Exmouth and, having already gathered his few belongings, returned to the gardens where he was delighted to find Anna exactly where he'd left her. He did no more than offer his arm as he led the way toward the house. "Joshua has taken the carriage around to the front. Is there anything you'd like to bring with you to the service, a Bible, perhaps?"

"Why, yes, thank you, I would like to bring my own. Please wait a moment while I fetch it, I'll not keep you waiting." Feeling more confident of her surroundings with each trip, Anna found her bedroom easily this time but to her amazement her possessions were nowhere to be found. She crossed the hall to the room she'd shared with Phillip only to find it also stripped bare. Puzzled, she hurried down the main staircase and out the front door where she stopped to wait as she saw Phillip and Lydia Shepard engaged in a heated argument upon which she'd no desire to intrude.

"I have packed that woman's things so they may be taken as you leave now. Do not pretend ignorance of the reason she is unwelcome at Briarcliff. A man of your experience should have known better than to bring a virgin to Lord Clairbourne's home and then bed her yourself!"

Aghast at the housekeeper's loudly voiced rebuke, Phillip lowered his voice as he saw Anna standing nearby. "Neither Lady Thorson nor I will tolerate such an insult, Mrs. Shepard. Now I insist you return her luggage to her room where it belongs for she is not leaving here with me but remaining to wed Charles!"

"He'll not have that slut for a bride!" Lydia shrieked defiantly, her bitter expression growing sinister.

Phillip drew back his hand, clearly meaning to strike the obnoxious housekeeper a punishing blow, but before he could do so Anna sprinted down the wide steps to grab his arm. "Captain, you must control your temper!" Anna had no idea what the word slut meant. It was clearly uncomplimentary, but she could not allow Phillip to give vent to his anger in so rude a fashion. "I am not yet the mistress here but I'll not allow the staff of Briarcliff to be abused."

Furious with her interference, Phillip brushed

Anna's hands aside. "Mrs. Shepard's lurid imagination will not ruin your reputation, Anna, not while I have breath to defend you!"

"Why do I require such a vigorous defense?" Anna's gaze swept the faces of both the hostile servant and the proud young man but she could see no cause for their heated confrontation. "Of what have I been accused?"

Stepping forward, Lydia Shepard again raised her voice so the household staff who'd been drawn outside to witness the commotion could hear her response clearly. "It is no mere accusation! You spent the night in the captain's bed and I've the blood-stained sheets to prove it!"

Anna heard Phillip's sharp gasp and still did not comprehend what had driven the volatile woman to such an extreme state of anger. "Mrs. Shepard, I do not understand why you are creating such a ridiculous scene over that for it was Phillip's own blood you found in his bed. He cut himself rather badly and—"

Lydia gave a high-pitched squeal of laughter, scoffing rudely at Anna's calm explanation. "So you'll not deny you were in the captain's room, or even in his bed, but only what occurred there? Shall we ask Dr. Beckwith to ascertain the truth?"

Anna's confusion was obvious as she glanced up at the tall captain's fierce expression. Clearly he was ready to tear the vicious woman limb from limb. "Do you object to the physician looking at your leg if Mrs. Shepard will not be content until she hears a doctor's report?"

Finding the Swedish beauty's innocence highly amusing, Lydia continued to add to her taunts. "Tell her, Captain Bradford. Explain if you can that it is Lady Thorson herself who must be examined, not you!" When she laughed loudly at that prospect several other members of the staff joined in, plainly enjoying their prospective mistress's keen embarrassment. They had considerable freedom with their master away for a large portion of the year and had no desire to see him remarry so attractive a young woman. That would surely mean he'd spend more of his time at Briarcliff demanding they work far more diligently than they ever did in his absence.

"Lady Thorson need not submit to such a humiliation simply to appease the suspicions of an impertinent servant!" Phillip shouted angrily, incensed more by his own stupidity than he cared to admit. Anna had not seen his bed after they'd made love; he'd remade it and tossed the stained sheets to the fishes to be certain no one else did either. He'd not realized the injury he'd suffered the previous night had left evidence which could be so easily misinterpreted. He was appalled by the unexpected turn of the morning's events for he could not possibly leave Anna in so hostile a household without even the friendship of a maid for comfort. Signaling Joshua, he grabbed the first of her small trunks and carried it around to the rear of the waiting carriage to load.

Finally realizing it was her virtue which was being discussed so openly, Anna was shocked beyond words or tears. She'd been branded a harlot and could scarcely deny the accusation although she certainly didn't consider herself as such. She had only to glance at the leering faces which surrounded her to see Mrs. Shepard had been readily believed. The men were almost drooling, barely able to hide their lust while the women nodded with satisfied smirks, eager to accept the housekeeper's conjecture as the truth. Her unexpected arrival at Briarcliff had obviously caused a sensation. She'd been attacked by highwaymen en route, then had brought death and disgrace to a respected household, and no amount of explanation on her part now would change the low opinion the servants had formed of her. She could not possibly allow Dr. Beckwith to conduct an examination to certify her virginity and her blush deepened for she had no desire to ever experience such a degrading ordeal or to explain the certain result. Forcing back her tears she ran after Phillip, hoping to change his mind. "I am sorry to have caused all this trouble, Captain. I don't know why these people are so eager to believe the worst of me but they are a surly lot and would profit from a strong hand to guide them. I am willing to stay for if I let them think I am afraid of them now how shall I ever be able to control them when I become Lady Clairbourne?"

That she had such spirit did not surprise Phillip, but while he admired her courage he could not let her make such a sacrifice. He lowered his voice to explain why. "This morning I confronted Lydia with the bell we found severed from its cord and she pretended complete ignorance of the deed, but she was lying. She runs this house; all that happens within its walls is under her direction. If Sophia's death was unavoidable it was at least hastened by that woman's neglect and I'll not leave you here when your life might be in danger too." He stepped aside as Joshua brought over the rest of her small bags. "Get in the carriage and we'll be gone!"

"But where are we going?" Anna whispered hoarsely, completely confused by his demand.

"I've no idea, now just get in and hush!" Phillip took her arm and nearly tossed her into the freshly washed and polished vehicle. He leapt upon his mount and, motioning for Joshua to follow, led the way out to the road. He set a brisk pace which he did not slacken until they'd reached the steps of St. Michael's church in Exmouth. He then sent Joshua to notify the rector of their arrival and hastened to open the door of the carriage for Anna.

Having been jostled to the point of near injury by the swiftness of their journey, Anna found it difficult to stand upright and clutched the door for support as she climbed down from the steps. She glanced up to see if Sophia's coffin had been dislodged from its place atop the carriage and, satisfied it had made the journey in far better condition than she had, adjusted the folds of her dark blue dress modestly and tried to regain her sense of balance. "I trust we have arrived in time to meet your demanding schedule, Captain."

"Close enough, but while Joshua is locating the priest we must decide what our next course of action should be." Phillip stared down at her with a disapproving frown, perplexed that a young woman of such splendid beauty and grace should be so difficult to chaperon.

When he began to brush the dust of the road from his coat, Anna remarked slyly, "First tell me just what a slut is, that is not a word my mother taught me."

"Blast it all, what do you think it means? Use your imagination!" When she made no ready retort but stood calmly regarding him with open curiosity he grew ashamed of his rudeness and apologized. "Forgive me, I brought this regrettable embarrassment upon you with my own lack of regard for propriety last night but I have been a guest at Briarcliff several times and did not realize how outraged Lydia would be at your sharing my room. It seemed only right you should not be left alone after such an unexpected tragedy but I see now my reaction was most unfortunately the wrong one."

Anna looked away, as pained as he was by the morning's bitter confrontation on the steps of what was to have been her new home. "It was merely a convenient excuse, Phillip. Had it not been that Mrs. Shepard would have seized upon something else, the peculiar way I speak English, the unusual assortment of clothing that makes up my wardrobe, or simply the fact I would never have let her intimidate me. She'd have found any excuse to force me to leave Briarcliff since clearly she regarded me as a rival to her authority." Pausing thoughtfully, Anna remarked upon another possibility. "Is she a housekeeper only, or Clairbourne's mistress as well?"

Phillip was surprised by her question but shook his head emphatically after giving it serious thought. "No, nothing so exotic as his mistress surely, at least not from any hint Charles ever gave me. I can see how you might suspect their relationship to be an intimate one however for she is attractive in a prim sort of way and he is a widower, but we must not allow our imaginations the free rein she has given hers."

Anna thought better of pointing out the woman had discerned their true relationship, whether or not her assumption about one particular night might have

201

been incorrect. "Yes, you are right. I will not mention that possibility ever again and most certainly never to Charles but what reason can I give him for leaving his home after so brief a stay? It should be clear to you I must speak with him before anyone at Briarcliff does but how am I to accomplish that unless I go to Jamaica?"

Phillip pondered her question thoughtfully, for indeed it was imperative they reach Charles before Lydia did. He had been certain the man would probably never sleep with Anna but if he had some reason to think she was not the virtuous young woman she appeared to be he might just do it. "Where are your relatives, Anna? I think it would be best if I saw you there immediately. I will run whatever risks I must to see Charles in Jamaica after my return voyage home."

"But that makes no sense, Phillip! If you'll go that far you might as well take me with you so I can seek to influence him myself! Don't you see, it's the only sensible thing you can do!"

Before Phillip could offer his first word of argument the priest arrived at his elbow, a diminutive gray-haired man in his late forties. He'd spent all his life in Exmouth and knew Lord Clairbourne well. He was eager to meet the fiancée of so prominent a man and began to provide what he hoped would be words of comfort in her time of sorrow. "Lady Thorson, I am Gerald Parker. Permit me to welcome you to our city. That you have come on so sad a mission is regrettable but I hope you will soon regard St. Michael's as fondly as you did your own church in your homeland."

"Thank you, Reverend Parker, I am most grateful for your welcome but Sophia was a Lutheran as is most

202

of the population of Sweden and—" Anna halted in mid-sentence as Phillip's hand tightened around her upper arm in a painful grasp.

"As a Lutheran clergyman is unavailable, Reverend Parker has been kind enough to agree to perform a burial service for Sophia and as I am certain he is neglecting his other duties to do this favor for us let us enter his church now so that we might begin without further delay." Phillip drew the reluctant young woman through the wide double doors and showed her to a seat near the ornately carved pulpit before returning to the carriage to assist Joshua with the coffin. The two men managed to carry the cumbersome box down the center aisle without mishap, if also without any measure of true dignity, then took their places in the front pew on either side of Anna.

Swiftly trapped in her place by their muscular bodies Anna was livid, appalled that Phillip had treated her so meanly, again disregarding her wishes as if she were a naughty child who should keep still while the adults ran her life. She'd meant only to ask the Reverend Parker to recite a Bible verse she recalled as being a particular favorite of Sophia's, not to argue with the priest over the differences in their religions! As her eyes grew accustomed to the darkness she glanced about the dimly lit stone church and shivered from its pervading chill. The Gothic structure was impressive but the high-vaulted ceiling gave the atmosphere of the imposing edifice all the charm of an ancient tomb. The windows were narrow, the sunlight which filtered through the richly colored stained glass provided no warmth and the soft scent of incense only added to the overpowering sense of gloom. In such a depressing environment Anna could not seem to concentrate on the priest's words. Phillip's voice was inviting, low and confident, the prayers for the dead were obviously no mystery to him but clearly familiar, but she felt so lost. She was a stranger in a foreign land, seated in an imposing church, a monument in stone to a faith that wasn't her own, surrounded by men she barely knew as she listened to an unfamiliar service being read for the woman who had been like a second mother to her, and yet even at that very moment she could not truly accept the fact Sophia was gone. Her death had been too sudden, one more tragedy after so many others and Anna refused to give way to tears in front of her well-meaning companions. The priest would probably expect her to weep, Joshua Coombes would show no surprise but it was Phillip whose sympathy she could no longer abide and she dug her fingernails into her palms to distract herself from the sharpness of one pain with another. She'd loved Sophia while the dear woman had been alive and that was far more important surely than shedding tears now. She walked dry eyed from the church at the conclusion of the solemn service, paying scant heed to the Reverend Parker's solicitous attentions as he described the arrangements for Sophia's burial. Then something he said sparked her interest.

"A simple marker will be fashioned of stone. Just give me the date of your maid's birth and I will see the work is completed promptly."

"How thoughtful of you, but if I write an inscription neatly do you think the stonemason could copy it accurately?" Anna turned to face the helpful priest, her voice as subdued as her emotions.

"Yes, he is a fine craftsman and can provide whatever you wish. Please come into my office where I have paper and pen you may use." The small man scurried on ahead up the path to the adjacent cottage which served as the rectory. His office was off the parlor, a small and cluttered room. He stacked the papers on the desk into neat piles so Anna would have a place to write.

Phillip leaned against the doorway of the small room, folded his arms across his chest and scowled impatiently as Anna took the chair the priest offered. She seemed deep in thought for several minutes, then drew a series of symbols he recognized easily. He had no idea what their significance might be but they were runes, the ancient writing of the Vikings and he readily understood the priest's confusion when she handed him the completed message. Suddenly he knew what she had done. Displeased, he straightened up abruptly; whether or not she had intentionally created what was surely to be another unfortunate scene he could not tell, but he could see what was coming and did not like it one bit.

"I am sorry, Lady Thorson, I do not understand what it is you want carved. What manner of writing is this?"

Anna rose gracefully, her smile sweet as she responded. "It is Swedish, of an ancient variety, an inscription to honor my maid's faithful service and constant heart."

Perplexed, the priest turned the paper this way and that, trying to recognize some pattern or letter he could comprehend. "This is an Anglican church, Lady Thorson. How do I know this is what you say it is and

205

not some message of which our bishop will heartily disapprove?"

"You will have to accept my word, Reverend Parker. It is exactly what I say it is and nothing which should give the slightest offense to anyone."

"Well, I can not take the responsibility for this by myself, for I know Sweden came late to Christianity and I—"

Phillip's menacing stance completely filled the doorway of the priest's office as he moved to interrupt. "Are you refusing to comply with Lady Thorson's wishes? If you are, say so now and we'll be gone for I have no time to waste while you and your bishop debate this issue."

Horrified by the tall man's anger, Gerald Parker stuttered nervously, "This whole matter has been most irregular, sir. That I hesitate to bury a stranger in holy ground with a headstone none can read should come as no surprise. Lord Clairbourne himself might object to this inscription and I should not like to offend him, nor any others in my congregation."

"I will not allow Sophia to be buried with no headstone as a pauper is," Anna declared proudly before turning to face Phillip. She waited a moment to compose himself and then asked, "What would you have me do, Captain, the choice is yours."

Phillip nearly strangled on his own rage, for she had managed to ask what seemed to be a straightforward question when truly it was not. "Would you permit us to use your office for a few minutes time, Reverend Parker? I would like very much to discuss this matter with Lady Thorson in private."

Glad for the excuse to escape a situation he could see

no tactful way to resolve, the priest agreed readily and fled back to the serenity of his church wiping his perspiring brow as he ran. He prayed he had not already offended the bishop by his actions that morning, but he was far more afraid of incurring Lord Clairbourne's wrath than that of his superior.

Phillip gestured toward the one chair in the crowded room and insisted Anna take it. "I should have known better than to trust you not to create some sort of disturbance here. I had hoped to see Sophia was given a proper burial, now why have you chosen to make that desire impossible?"

"Is what I asked so outrageous a request? It did not seem so to me when I made it," Anna replied quickly, not enjoying being put on the defensive once again.

Something in her manner made Phillip suspicious and he picked up the sheet of paper the priest had dropped upon his desk. "Had Sophia died at your home would you have thought of doing this? Would it have been allowed there?"

Blushing deeply, Anna looked away, her expression telling him all he needed to know. But his question demanded an answer and she responded truthfully. "The runes were of particular fascination to my father. He pursued their study tirelessly and enjoyed teaching me what he'd learned. The Vikings used their alphabet to cast charms and make spells, to insure their safety and success in battle as well as to commemorate special events as was probably the case with the stone you saw near Gothenburg. When Christianity was adopted in Sweden, the runes were suppressed for they were thought to possess magic and were regarded as witchcraft. I am sorry to say that view is still held by many today although my father was able to have my mother's tombstone inscribed with runes and I did the same for his."

Surprised by her candor, Phillip's curiosity overcame his anger. "Do you believe these letters have such power? Is that what you're doing, casting some spell to protect Sophia in the next world?"

Anna regarded the handsome man closely, wishing with all her heart he was always so understanding. "Surely the magic lies in the belief only, not in the runes themselves. I meant no disrespect to the members of St. Michael's congregation nor to any of the Anglican faith, I assure you, but perhaps I was naive not to realize the word Viking still strikes dread into the heart of an Englishman and so their writing would also be unwelcome here."

It was her eyes which Phillip could not resist. While the curve of her lips proved irresistibly inviting, it was her long-lashed golden eyes which seemed to hold the secrets of the universe and he was unable to defy the strength of the attraction which they exerted upon him now. Seeing a way to avoid an argument that could rage in ecclesiastical circles for decades, he folded the paper neatly and slipped it into his coat pocket. "We will take Sophia's coffin on board the *Angelina*. I am already so late I despair of ever reaching Philadelphia, let alone on time to make the final payment on my ship before it becomes delinquent. I will see that Sophia is buried at sea as you wished since I know we'll never succeed in having her buried here with the headstone you want, then I will take you to the home of your mother's relatives. In what part of England do they reside?"

A slow smile lifted the corner of Anna's pretty mouth as she shook her head, for that was a secret she'd never reveal. If Phillip had no idea where to send her, he'd have to take her with him to Jamaica and the joy of staying with him for even a few more weeks was worth the price she'd have to pay in his anger.

Chapter Eleven

Anna spent a miserable afternoon sitting on her bunk, her posture rigid, her hands clasped tightly in her lap. Philip had kept his promise, he'd sailed the *Angelina* out into open waters and had then provided Sophia with a second burial service before her canvas-wrapped body had been cast into the depths. It was the finality of that sad gesture which had wrenched Anna's heart in two. But if that anguish were not enough, she'd then been swiftly banished to her cabin, confined there indefinitely, Phillip had said, at least until she was ready to divulge the whereabouts of her English relatives. That meant forever as far as she was concerned, but despite her anger, the prospect of remaining a prisoner aboard the *Angelina* brought a wistful smile to her lips if not happiness to her heart.

"Set our course for Southampton, Jamie. You'll find me in my cabin if I'm needed."

"Aye, aye, Captain," Jamie replied curtly, far from pleased by the events of the last few hours. He'd been delighted to see Anna again, overjoyed in fact when he'd seen her walking up the gangplank on Phillip's arm. But his happiness had been short-lived when he'd discovered she was to be isolated, held captive aboard their swift ship.

Phillip had already turned to go but drew back, startled by the clear insolence in the mate's tone. "What is it you wish to tell me, Jamie? Just say it to my face and be done with it."

Jamie's scowl deepened; he'd no desire to provoke Phillip but he could no longer contain his fiery temper. "I do not approve of your plan, sir. Lady Thorson is just that, the finest of ladies and she should not be treated so badly on this of all days."

Equally angry, Phillip stepped close as he lowered his voice to a threatening whisper. "That lady, as you call her, is my responsibility, Jamie, mine alone and I want only what is best for her."

"I do not doubt that, sir, but to lock her up as though she were a common criminal just isn't right!" Jamie shouted, disregarding Phillip's obvious desire for discretion.

"Is there anything else you'd care to say to me, Mr. Jenkins?" Phillip's deep blue eyes darkened to a vivid purple, the depth of his rage plain in his furious glance. He was clearly daring Jamie to start a fight he had every intention of ending swiftly.

Jamie was many things, but never a fool. He'd not destroy a relationship of long standing which had always been mutually profitable over a woman, not even one so pretty as Anna Thorson. He knew Phillip to be a fierce adversary in any battle and had no wish to ever fight him. "No, sir, you have heard my complaint, I need not repeat it."

211

"See that you don't then." Phillip strode across the deck nodding as he offered encouragement to one of his crew but once he reached the privacy of his cabin his fury erupted in a long string of bitter oaths. He paced up and down slowly, his thoughts in turmoil, but he knew no way to make Anna tell him what he had to know other than the method he'd chosen. Jamie was right, of course, to treat a creature of such delicate beauty so harshly was cruel, but it was also necessary. He'd slept little the previous night. Tired beyond his considerable endurance, he stretched out on his bunk and closed his eyes. Sleep came readily but also the sweetest of dreams, tantalizing visions of his lovely prisoner flooded his mind and he moaned softly. The longing which filled his body as well as his soul brought an agony he could no longer bear to suffer in silence.

When darkness fell Anna lit a lamp and redid her hair, coiling it neatly atop her head before she sat down at the desk to wait for her supper. She'd not eaten a bite since breakfast and as the hour grew late she became frightened. She'd never dreamed Phillip could be so cruel as to try to starve her into submission. The door to her cabin was securely locked, she'd heard him turn the key after he'd thrust her inside so she had no way to leave and sneak down to the galley to prepare her own food. Crushed he'd be so spiteful, she lay her head upon her arms, sadly contemplating her fate. She was nearly asleep when she heard the sound of a key entered the brass lock. The tumblers slipped noisily into place and she leapt to her feet, then leaned back against her chair to strike a more sedate pose as Phillip

212

came through the door. He was dressed as he had been for Catherine's party, the effect of his dark formal attire even more devastating now that her feelings for him had grown so deep. It was not simply his unusual height which made him so imposing a figure, for she'd known several men in Sweden who'd been as tall as he, but rather the strength of his personality which the attractiveness of his appearance always enhanced. His clear blue eyes glowed with a confident gleam that she recognized as pure male power but she'd known exactly what his reaction would be when first she'd chosen to defy him and returned his steady gaze without flinching.

Giving a mock bow, Phillip offered an apology. "Please forgive my tardiness; the delay was unavoidable, however. John is waiting to serve supper in my cabin, I trust you are ready to dine."

It had not occurred to Anna to dress for dinner when what she'd expected had been little more than bread and water. She glanced down at her simple dress then up at her splendidly garbed companion. "I did not realize you would wish to dine with me this evening. Perhaps I should change into a more becoming dress if it is some kind of special occasion."

"If I have failed to make you feel each minute we share is special then I am indeed sorry and beg your forgiveness. As no dress does your exquisite beauty justice let us not keep John waiting any longer." Phillip walked to Anna's side and waited for her to place her fingertips upon his sleeve before he led the way to his cabin. Once there, he held her chair and when she was seated comfortably he let his hand brush her shoulder in a caress so soft she was uncertain whether or not she had felt it. But her cheeks flooded with color as she turned to look up at him. He responded with a most charming grin, confusing her all the more, but with John ladling soup carefully into their bowls she thought it best not to question her host's intentions aloud.

"Is Mr. Jenkins not joining us this evening?" Anna noted the table was set only for two and wondered where Jamie might be.

Phillip lifted a well-shaped brow quizzically. "You would prefer his company to mine? If so—" He began to rise, ready to summon the mate should she so desire.

"No, please stay. I did not mean to be rude." Anna was amazed by the sudden change in Phillip's manner; he'd never behaved in such a flirtatious fashion and she was afraid his friendliness was insincere. Too hungry to dwell on the complexities of that possibility, she lifted her spoon to her lips to sample their first course. "This chowder is delicious, John. Will you please tell Michael how much I enjoyed it?"

"Yes, Lady Thorson." The boy blushed deeply as he removed the silver covers from the platters bearing their entrees and placed them on the table. "I will be sure to tell him."

"Thank you." When he had gone, Anna glanced up at Phillip, her gaze curious. "He is so painfully shy; has he been aboard the *Angelina* long?"

"No more than a few months. He's Michael's nephew but I'd not take him before he turned eighteen as I'll not have children among my crew."

"He is eighteen?" Anna asked with surprise for she'd not realized John was her age. He had always seemed to be so much younger.

214

"Yes, but he is a long way from being a grown man, I'm afraid." Phillip filled Anna's wine goblet then his own and lifted it to touch the rim of hers lightly. "You are a remarkably perceptive young woman, Anna, so warm and caring. Why is it you have such sympathy for John and none for me?"

Startled by the intimate nature of his question, Anna took a long sip of the rich, red wine while she tried to formulate some coherent response. Finally she answered softly, "Sympathy is the last emotion you would ever evoke in me, Captain." She dared not look at him directly but found her steaming supper offered no enticement to eat. Her appetite had vanished completely under his barrage of suggestive inquiries.

"You are not hungry? Well, no matter, for I am." Phillip proceeded to eat his meal with keen enjoyment, seldom bothering to glance at his guest and after a few minutes Anna took a bite of her supper and then another. Phillip refilled her wine goblet each time he drained his own and the silence between them grew to be a comfortable one. He saw no reason for meaningless conversation if she preferred to remain silent and did not press her until they had finished their main course. He then sliced an apple into thin sections and handed half to her on a small tray. "The cheese is excellent, would you care for some?"

"Yes, please." The deep yellow cheddar was sharp, its tangy flavor a perfect complement to the crispness of the apple. When Phillip again offered her more wine, Anna drank it. She felt a blissful numbness creeping up her spine; she tried to smile, uncertain as to whether or not her lips had moved.

"Tell me something about your mother, Anna. Was

she as great a beauty as you are?" Phillip winked slyly, for he knew Anna must realize how pretty she was.

"Oh, yes, she was." Anna licked her lips slowly as she tried to find the best words to describe her parent's attractiveness. "She was not blond, but dark-haired like you, yet her skin was very fair, nearly transparent and her eyes were like mine." Realizing that was incorrect she rephrased her statement. "My eyes are like hers." Embarrassed that he'd paid a compliment to which she'd not responded in kind Anna began again, then could not remember what it was they had been discussing. "Thank you I should have said first, thank you."

Phillip took her hand in his as he leaned forward to whisper, "She sounds lovely. Did she have sisters as pretty as she was?"

"No, only one brother who died in infancy. My mother was unique, the only example of her kind." Anna took another sip of wine and tried not to giggle which she knew to be very bad manners.

"Her family was large though, cousins, aunts, uncles, people you came to visit often?" Phillip's question was casually asked, as if the information meant little to him.

"Not often, a few times," Anna corrected shyly. "We came to England together perhaps half a dozen times and I came with my father once."

"Do you recall the time I saw you in Southampton? The night could not have been more wretched and yet you and your father were out walking. Were you visiting your relatives on that occasion? Was their home nearby?" Again there was no urgency in his voice, only a calm concern.

"No." Anna shivered suddenly, chilled by the memory of that terrifying night. "That was years ago, Phillip. I've no wish to remember it now."

"Are you cold? Come here to me and I'll hold you until you are warm again." Phillip stood to assist her from her chair, then pulled her down across his lap. His touch was sweet, not confining as he picked up her goblet. "Finish your wine, Anna, it will warm your blood."

Anna sipped the soothing beverage slowly and found he was correct in his prediction. She finished the last drop, then tried to set the silver goblet on the table but missed the edge and it slipped from her grasp to topple to the floor. "Oh, I'm sorry, did it break?"

"No, of course not. These are silver rather than crystal for just that purpose; a ship is no place for fine glassware. Now tell me something more of your mother. Was she raised near Clairbourne's home, in Devon perhaps or in Cornwall?" He leaned down to retrieve the fallen goblet, then placed it on the table beside his own. "Didn't you tell me once she was from Cornwall?"

Phillip's voice was soft and low, enticing her to confide in him but Anna was too sleepy. She lay her head on his shoulder as she raised her hand to cover a wide yawn. She heard him repeat his question but could not understand why he was so interested in hearing about her mother that night. "Her name was Claire. There was a Saint Claire, did you know that?"

"Yes, I've heard of Saint Claire, there was a Saint Ann as well." Phillip placed his fingertips under Anna's chin to lift her gaze to his then regretted that gesture for her eyes' honey color drew him into a sweetness he was forbidden to savor and he grew deliberately stern. "Where was your mother born, Anna? You haven't forgotten have you? Don't you remember where your mother was born?"

Anna tried to focus her attention upon the blue of his eyes but he was too close and she saw only the inviting curve of his lips. She raised her arms to encircle his neck as she lifted her mouth to his. He drew back but for no more than an instant before he wrapped her tightly in his embrace and returned her gentle kiss with a passion he made no effort to tame.

Anna was delighted by his spontaneous show of affection and hugged him more tightly, drinking in his delicious taste with an abandon that matched his own. She wanted more of his exquisite loving and gave no thought to the consequences she'd have to face. She'd lost everything she held dear, but had found him and would never long for anything more.

Several minutes passed before Phillip came to his senses. He'd been ready to carry Anna to his bunk when his conscience had dealt him a sharp blow. He'd forced her to drink far more than she could safely imbibe and now his own mind was far from clear as to what his original purpose had been. He'd hoped only to gain information to help him find her family, not to unleash her passion by numbing whatever restraints she might have been taught to guide her behavior. Ashamed of himself for attempting so underhanded a trick he pushed her away as he rose to his feet. "It is late, Anna. I've kept you up too long; come, I'll see you safely to your cabin."

Anna leaned against his side for a moment, hoping to regain her balance before taking a step. But the cabin seemed to be revolving around her and when she took a step she stumbled.

"Anna!" Phillip caught her waist as she slipped and pressed her slender body close. "Here, I will put my arm around you as we walk. There, that's better, isn't it?" When he had escorted her to her door, he hesitated to leave and she turned to look up at him, her eyes wide with apprehension.

"Since I will be alone, would you please come in for a moment to unbutton my dress? I have no maid to help me tonight."

That she did not seem to realize he would already know that upset Phillip all the more but he thought it best if he did not comply with her request and said so. "That would be unwise. The hour is late and—"

Anna interrupted his apology with a saucy giggle. "Then undo my buttons out here please as I have no desire to sleep in this somber garment." She smiled coyly as she tried to turn, but Phillip caught her elbow and opening the door to her cabin pushed her inside.

"I'll come in then for I'll not have my crew find me undressing you! It would seem the word discreet is completely foreign to you!"

Anna continued to laugh. She was so dizzy she could scarcely stand and he seemed to be telling the most amusing of jokes. "Of course the word is foreign to me, silly. You are speaking English and I am a Swedish girl!"

"That is not in the least bit funny, Anna!" He'd gotten her quite drunk and while he had done it deliberately he could not deal with the result. She seemed to be wiggling just to confound his efforts to unfasten the tiny buttons which extended down her back. When she

219

pulled the pins from her hair he could not even find them under the cascade of glistening curls. "Anna, please! Can't you hold still? Now where is your nightgown? Why have you not bothered to unpack your things?"

"My things? There's no need to unpack if you'll not keep me with you as you should," Anna scolded crossly. "As Mrs. Shepard packed them, I've no idea where anything is. You'll have to help me look."

Phillip watched her fumbling with the lock on her trunk and drew her aside. "You sit down on your bunk, I will find the nightgown for you myself." He searched the contents of her luggage rapidly, spilling the silks and satins all about his feet but he found no lingerie until he came to the last small bag. "Here is one at least, this will have to do." He turned to hand it to her but she was curled up, snugly hugging her pillow and blissfully unaware of his presence. "Anna?" Phillip reached out to shake her shoulder but she only purred contentedly and went back to her dreams. Perplexed, he considered just leaving her there, then decided against it. Uncovered she'd grow chilled and might fall ill, to say nothing of her anger when she awoke in the morning still in her dress and remembered what he'd done to her and realized why.

"Well, Sleeping Beauty, I have undressed many a woman so you should present no special difficulties tonight." Laying the soft nightgown aside, he slipped her dress off her shoulders and immediately realized his mistake, for her creamy skin beckoned to his senses like a siren's song. He leaned down to kiss the curve of her throat lightly before he forced his mind to concentrate on the task at hand. Only by the greatest exertion of will power could he accomplish what he'd set out to do for Anna was simply too lovely to ignore. But he thought only of how sick she'd be in the morning and how he was still no closer to learning what he had to know. The anger that thought kindled was enough to distract him until he found himself faced with the chore of putting a nightgown on a nude young woman whose superb figure he'd much rather simply enjoy. His glance traveled down her graceful curves, memorizing her contours with an appreciative gaze before he drew the soft linen gown over her head. Her fingers were limp as he pulled her hands through the lace-trimmed sleeves. As he began to ease the garment down her slender body he stopped to wonder. She was sound asleep, and if he kissed her lightly or happened to give her a slight caress she would think it only a part of her dreams, but his pleasure would be none the less. He would never have another such opportunity to be alone with her and, kneeling down beside the bunk, he kissed her eyelids sweetly before his lips moved slowly down the curve of her cheek. As always her spell was the same, the mere touch of her skin filling him with a desperate longing and he trailed his gentle kisses over the swell of her breast then down across her smooth, flat stomach with no intention of stopping until he'd savored her very essence. Warm, soft, irresistibly inviting, he was lost in his own desires until her fingers moved through his dark curls with a lazy caress which drew him near and he sat up abruptly, shocked beyond words to find her golden eyes filling with mischief as she watched his face redden with a deep blush.

"If you are applying for the job of my maid, Captain, you have it."

With that teasing remark, Anna had foolishly pushed Philip past the realm of desire into the most furious anger. His blue eyes glowed with a deep purple fire as he rose to his feet. He despised her in that instant and his fierce glance hid none of his rage. "I'm in no mood for your games! As you well know, I am a man who enjoys being with a woman who holds nothing back and I've no desire to waste another minute of this night catering to your whims when you're behaving like a spoiled child who thinks arousing a man's passions is amusing!"

Anna gasped in surprise, shocked by his insult. But she knew instantly she didn't want to quarrel when what he'd suggested was so much more appealing. She made no move to adjust her nightgown but continued to focus her attention upon his face while his eyes hungrily swept her partially nude figure. "Are you speaking only of tonight, Philip. What about tomorrow or the next day?" What about the rest of our lives, she longed to ask, but she saw no hope for the future in his defiant glance.

"Tomorrow nothing will be changed. You will still become Lady Clairbourne and I am merely the first on what will undoubtedly be an extensive list of lovers." That prospect sickened him even as he spoke it but he wanted to have her again too badly to worry over what the future might bring.

Anna closed her eyes thoughtfully as she took a deep breath. She licked her lips slowly, the enticing nature of that gesture completely lost upon her. That he thought so little of her character saddened her greatly but she knew there was no way to convince him there would never be another man for her if he did not already know it. She might have to spend her life as Lady Clairbourne but she would never love any man but him. Her long lashes made her expression seductive as her gaze swept his attractive features, memorizing the even planes of his face so his striking image would live in her heart forever. Finally she whispered softly, "Since the hour is already late, let's not waste what little time we have left to share."

A rakish grin lifted the corner of Philip's mouth as he doused the lamp on the desk. "I will do my best to see we put our time to good use, Anna."

As be began to unbutton his shirt Anna rose to draw her lace-trimmed gown over her head to save him the trouble of doing it, but she got caught in the folds of the long garment and nearly tripped and fell.

"What are you doing?" Philip removed the last of his clothing then caught her arm, pulling her against his bare chest in a warm embrace.

"I wanted only to remove the gown you just put on me so sweetly, that is all." She still felt dizzy with the heady effects of the wine and her words were slurred in a sensuous purr.

"Let me help you then." Phillip gathered up the soft linen garment and pulled it over her head with an easy tug. "There, that is much better." He put his hands around her waist to draw her near, pressing every inch of her warm, flushed skin against his own. "You see, clothing only gets in the way and I want nothing between us save affection."

Anna slid her fingertips through the dark curls which covered his chest, then lifted her hands to his shoulders as she agreed. "Yes, you are always so warm, your golden skin as smooth as butter."

"Butter?" Phillip chuckled at her choice of words. "I had forgotten you grew up on a country estate but you must not compare a man's muscular build to a dollop of butter!"

Lifting her fingertips to the soft curls at his nape, Anna continued in a confident, persuasive tone yet she was so unsteady on her feet that had he not been holding her so tightly she could not have remained standing. "I was not commenting upon your physique, which is superb, but upon the texture of your skin which is even more marvelous, firm and so alive with a healthy sheen that is exactly like the gloss on freshly churned butter."

Phillip's deep laugh brought a smile to her lips and she stood on tiptoes to kiss the pulse which throbbed in his throat, its steady rhythm far calmer than the fluttering beat of her own heart. She stood in his embrace, surrounded with an excitement so vibrant she could scarcely catch her breath as she lifted her lips to his, inviting the affection she'd promised to give with no hope of receiving the same undying devotion in return. She felt so at home in his arms, as if she belonged with him, safe, where no one could ever harm her or cause her the slightest bit of pain. She loved him dearly but kept that delicious secret locked within her heart rather than reveal the depth of her emotions. She knew he would consider such a sweet admission no more than a trap she'd baited with her own body and cast out to ensnare him against his will. He would have to come to love her in his own time, to accept her love as a natural expression of her true feelings and return it without being asked so she said not another word as he gathered her up into his arms and carried her to her bunk. He lay her down very gently then stretched out beside her, letting his hands move down her luscious figure with a fond caress, his fingertips so light upon her skin she could barely suppress a throaty giggle. But fearing such a reaction would remind him again of her youth, she would her fingers in his glossy curls and captured his mouth by slipping her tongue between his lips as smoothly as if they'd been together all their lives rather than for no more than a few brief weeks.

That Anna had agreed so readily to his demands had astonished Phillip but she had pleased him more than he dared admit even to himself. Her kisses were delightful, her caress tantalizing. He forced himself to move slowly, to savor each moment to the fullest though he would rather have simply taken her with a swiftness which would have given him great pleasure but, he feared, none to her. That thought startled him, for he was not used to being considerate of a woman's feelings. Yet Anna was like no other woman, she was so precious to him he thought only of pleasing her and he waited until he was certain he had before he took his need for her affection to its natural conclusion.

Lying contentedly in Phillip's arms, Anna caressed his cheek fondly with her fingertips as she whispered, "Will you stay here with me all night?"

"I have never had a more enticing invitation, Anna, but truly I had no intention of leaving you for hours yet."

"Good." With a slow, feline grace Anna moved across him, her kisses warm as she nuzzled his throat softly. She loved the feel of his deeply bronzed skin, the smoothness of his powerful muscles when he lay so relaxed in her embrace. Her lips teased him playfully until he could no longer lie still and grabbed for her waist to press her against him.

"Dear God, Anna, how am I ever to forget you?"

"It is my fondest wish that you will remember me for as long as I remember you, Phillip." Her musical whisper drove all thought save one from his mind and Anna accepted his passion-filled kiss eagerly, responding to his desire as she always did, gratefully, joyously welcoming his loving until the fire which burned within him consumed them both in the bright flames of ecstasy.

When at last Anna fell asleep still cradled in his arms Phillip lay wide awake, holding her curved body curved snugly against his own, dreamily kissing her fingertips as he remembered each subtle nuance of her affection. She was the most splendid female creature ever born, far surpassing his dreams of her in every respect and with a sudden stab of remorse he realized her mind had been far from clear when he'd escorted her to her cabin. He had simply gotten her drunk and seduced her, there was no other way to explain what he'd done. But he was shocked to think he'd played her so underhanded a trick. When he heard the bells toll the end of the midnight watch he moved carefully from her bed and lit the lamp so he could find his clothing since he'd tossed it aside so hurriedly when he'd undressed. When once again he was fully clothed, he stook gazing down at Anna's sweet expression and knew her dreams would be far sweeter than his. But he dreaded what the next day would bring. She would hate him then, he knew that without a doubt, but still would not have missed a moment of the ecstasy she'd given him. He was a man of his word, however, and there would never be another such night for them; there couldn't be, not when he ached with desire at the mere sight of her. It would be useless to steal another minute of her passion when a lifetime of her love would not satisfy his desperate need. Perhaps it would be far better if she did hate him, for he had no life separate from the one he lived aboard the *Angelina*. That existence was both profitable and adventuresome, but no life for a woman born to be a countess to live.

Pushing his thoughts to the more practical he considered how sick she'd probably be in the morning and wishing to save her whatever anguish he could he picked up her nightgown, again slipped it over her head, pulled her hands through the sleeves, smoothed out its folds and tucked the blanket around her to keep her warm. He leaned down to kiss her goodnight, then forced himself to walk to the door where he stood for a long moment before putting out the lamp. He had not felt such overwhelming loneliness since he'd been a child, but he could scarcely force himself to leave her when she was so very dear to him and they'd had such little time to enjoy the pleasure which flowed so naturally between then. "If only I'd not let you escape me that foggy night in Southampton, Anna." But not even God could turn back the hands of time and he knew the elegant lady that beautiful child had become was lost to him forever.

Chapter Twelve

Once the *Angelina* had docked in Southampton, Phillip lost no time in securing a profitable cargo. Manufactured goods were still in short supply in America and he knew he'd find a ready market no matter what he chose to carry. Putting aside his earlier excuses, he filled the hold of his magnificent ship to overflowing. He then turned his attention to the far more difficult task of making arrangements for Anna's lodgings. He was determined to see she was left in her relatives' care, or in that of a respectable substitute. He'd toured the city on numerous occasions and thought he'd seen precisely the solution to his problems with the irresistibly lovely young woman. Once certain what he had in mind was indeed possible, he went to Anna's cabin for the first time in three days. As he had anticipated, she was not at all pleased to see him.

Anna's disdainful glance swept Phillip's lean physique slowly as he described his terms. While she was appalled by his demands, she was more confused and hurt that he'd had no time to spend with her since their intimate dinner had ended so romantically. She could recall that evening only dimly up to the point when she'd awakened to find herself lying nearly nude in his arms, but the vivid memory of what the rest of the night had been brought a bright blush to her cheeks as well as a flare to her temper. How dare the man think he could ravage her body so joyfully that night and then reject her so cruelly in the following days? She had obviously misunderstood his terms but she was not in the least bit sorry about what had happened between them and somehow she sensed that he was. That was not a question she cared to ask, however, and she responded to the issue at hand. "I am eighteen, Captain, surely an academy devoted to the education of young girls has no interest in enrolling a pupil of such an advanced age."

"You misunderstand me, Anna. You are not to be enrolled as a student, but hired as a temporary member of their faculty."

"A what?" No longer able to contain her outrage, Anna's thick fringe of dark lashes swept her brows as she leapt to her feet.

"I have a carriage waiting. Once you see the school I'm certain your enthusiasm for my proposal will increase markedly. The headmistress, Mrs. Browne, is expecting you to appear for an interview this afternoon. As your gray dress is both modest and becoming I suggest you don it immediately. I will wait for you on deck." With a sly smile, Phillip moved through her door and this time did not lock it.

Furious that he would treat her so meanly, Anna searched through her meager wardrobe for the most scandalously cut dress Catherine had given her. With a cape drawn smugly around her shoulders, Phillip would not know what she'd chosen to wear until it was too late. Pleased to have thought of so clever a way to thwart his ridiculous plan she dressed quickly and went up to meet him, her shy smile completely disarming as well as misleading.

As they traversed the distance to the school Phillip remarked upon the passing scene in a genial fashion, but when Anna showed not the slightest bit of interest he grew silent until they reached the school. He thought the ivy-covered brick buildings charming and gestured toward the gardens as he helped Anna from the carriage. "The grounds are extensive with separate dormitories for the different age groups. The more senior members of the faculty reside in the cottages you see to the left. You will be expected to live with your students for the time being."

Anna nodded absently. Since she had no intention of remaining there, the facilities were of no particular importance. The wrought iron gate was neither locked nor guarded, she noticed, making an exit as simple to achieve as their entrance. She continued to observe the buildings as they proceeded to Mrs. Browne's office but her interest centered upon escape rather than the comfortable homelike atmosphere of the school. She responded politely to the headmistress's friendly welcome, but once seated in her small office Anna let her cape slip from her shoulders to reveal a red silk dress the low neckline of which barely covered her ample bosom.

Phillip saw Mrs. Browne's horrified stare and turned to see what had caused such an improbable reaction. He could barely suppress a deep burst of laughter then as he realized what Anna had done. But he had the presence of mind to outwit her and remarked with a wide smile, "Lady Thorson has an exquisite figure as you can well see, Mrs. Browne, but it is entirely my fault she had no more suitable dress to wear this afternoon. Her luggage was most unfortunately misplaced, but I will find it before the day is out. Regardless of her present attire, I can assure you she is indeed the modest and unassuming young woman I described this morning." With a smile which held a stern warning rather than warmth, Phillip nodded slightly and waited for Anna to dispute his word. When she had the good sense to do no more than glare angrily he continued. "As I told you, Mrs. Browne, Lady Thorson has relatives here in England but prefers not to burden them with her presence while she awaits Lord Clairbourne's return. While most young women her age would rather pass the summer months in London enjoying the season's endless round of parties she has a far more serious nature and would rather earn her own living. The appointment you offered would be perfect for her as the education she received in Sweden was obviously superb."

Enchanted by the handsome young man's easy conversation, Mrs. Browne beamed warmly. "Captain Bradford spoke highly of your abilities, Lady Thorson. It is not often I have the opportunity of offering a position on our staff to a young woman of your breeding although many of our students are from fine families. Even though your stay here will be a brief one, I am certain it will be beneficial to us both. Now if you will just bid the captain goodbye, I will show you to the dormitory where you may begin your duties immediately."

"Thank you, Mrs. Browne, but would it be possible for me to speak with Captain Bradford in private for a moment? In addition to the confusion over my luggage, there is another matter we must settle as well." When Anna rose from her chair, her companions did also and the headmistress moved toward the door.

"I will wait for you at the end of the hall then, Lady Thorson, and thank you again for thinking of us, Captain."

Anna waited until the gracious woman had closed her door before she demanded an explanation. "What sort of trickery is this? I am to be left here as an orphan might have been dropped off by those uncaring relatives of yours? How dare you treat me in this fashion?"

Outraged that she'd bring up his wretched past, Phillip snarled angrily, "This is no trick of mine but your own doing! I have told you repeatedly I will take you wherever you wish to go within reason!"

"I want to go to Jamaica as you well know!" Anna responded furiously, her anger a match for his any day. But her words sounded false even in her own ears for what she really wanted was simply to stay with him.

Phillip took a deep breath and prepared for the long and bitter scene he should have known he'd not be able to avoid. "Unfortunately, Jamaica is impossible but that does not mean I won't escort you to the home of your mother's people as I have offered repeatedly to do. They are certain to take you to London for the season which I'm sure you'd find most amusing. I've attended those parties myself and can highly recommend them. Surely you'd prefer to be entertained in the coming weeks rather than staying here to tutor small children."

Anna made no response but crossed to the window behind the headmistress's desk and looked out over the high wall which surrounded the boarding school, providing the security of a prison. "Have you forgotten I am Lord Clairbourne's fiancée? Why would I wish to attend parties which are designed solely to introduce young ladies to suitable young men when I am already betrothed? Would that not be considered most improper?" Her words dripped with sarcasm, for he already knew just how little she cared for her reputation.

Disregarding the insult he was certain was directed solely at him, Phillip suggested an alternative. "It would not be improper in the least for your relatives to present you to their friends or for you to make the acquaintance of young women who would remain your friends after your marriage." He could barely speak that word without choking and brought his hand to his mouth to cover the resulting cough.

"I find it difficult to believe you are so concerned with my happiness when what I want seems to be so irrelevant here." Turning slowly, she regarded him with a cool and steady stare. "Do you want to leave me here, Phillip? Is this what you truly want?"

The sunlight caught her pretty hair with the glow of a golden halo and Phillip found it impossible to lie and so changed the subject completely. "That red dress was a nice touch. I'm afraid you shocked Mrs. Browne rather badly but I'll manage to locate your belongings I supposedly lost and see they are delivered here promptly so your attire will cause no further comment or embarrassment."

"Toss my luggage overboard if you like; the garments mean nothing to me!" Anna shouted spitefully.

"Stop it, you're behaving like a spoiled brat again when you've given me no choice but to leave you here! The *Angelina* will sail on the morning tide and when next we meet you will be Clairbourne's wife. The matter was settled before we met and can not be changed, nor should it be. Can't you see the only sensible thing for me to do is leave you here to wait for Charles?" Phillip was completely exasperated with Anna when she continually disregarded the obvious impossibility of her desires.

Anna turned back toward the window with a careless toss of her bright curls. "You were far from sensible the other night, Phillip, and I liked you ever so much better then. If you can bear to leave me here then be gone now but I'll not pretend we are friends when next we meet for clearly we are not."

Incensed by her taunting insults Phillip took a step forward then stopped. He'd not shake her for she'd never come to her senses and he'd only lose his if he touched her again. But he could not allow her to have the last word this time. "When next we meet I hope you will have finally learned to behave as a lady must, to be polite and charming no matter how miserable the situation. I made no promises to you which I've broken, nor did I ever force you to do anything it wasn't plain you truly wanted to do. I will thank you never to refer to the nights we spent together ever again; hate me for it if you must, if you find that easier than hating yourself."

"I hate neither of us, Phillip." No, indeed, that was the problem. He was dressed as he had been the first time she'd seen him; she'd thought him so handsome

234

but his arrogance had broken her heart then and her gaze was melancholy now as she approached him. "Would you please kiss me goodbye?"

Seeing no way to refuse such a politely worded and totally unexpected request, Phillip complied. He'd meant only to kiss her lightly, but Anna fit into his embrace so perfectly, her supple body languidly melting against him that he could think of nothing other than the exquisite softness of her lips as her mouth met his. He had taught her too well; her kiss was magical, smooth and enticing, drawing him ever deeper into the intimacy he'd sworn never to recapture. With a strength born of anguish he tore himself away and left the room without speaking, content to leave her in Mrs. Browne's capable hands where he prayed she'd stay until Charles arrived to claim her. He drew a heavy curtain across his mind at that point for he could not stand the thought of Anna belonging to another man when he wanted so desperately to keep her only for himself.

When John arrived at the academy late that afternoon with her luggage, Anna saw an opportunity too good to miss and quickly drew him aside, certain he'd come to her rescue if she made him understand how desperate her situation truly was. She spun a tale she was certain he'd believe but it was only partially the truth. "John, I am engaged to a man I have never met. He has gone to Jamaica to subdue slave riots which could well cost him his life. My place is clearly with him but your captain pays my arguments no heed for reasons I do not pretend to understand. If I could just reach America I am certain I could book passage to Jamaica more easily than I can from here. Won't you please help me?" She touched his arm fondly, her whole manner beseeching him to come to her aid.

John could barely lift his gaze from the creamy expanse of exposed bosom above her red silk bodice. He had never been so close to her. She was the most beautiful woman he'd ever seen, he simply adored her but was confused by her plea. "Lady Thorson, please, how can I help you? My wages are better than most, but I've no money to give you to purchase passage to America."

Seeing his bright blush, Anna stepped closer, embarrassing him all the more. "I want to go on board the *Angelina*, John. I could hide in the hold and Captain Bradford would never know I was on board. Since you help prepare food, it would be a small matter for you to provide the tiny amount I'd need to survive. Please say you'll help me, John, oh, please do for there's no one else to whom I can turn." Sparkling tears welled up in her tawny eyes at that dismal thought and she clutched his arm more tightly. "Please, John, you'll help me won't you?"

Straightening up proudly, John responded readily to her anguished plea. "While I am pleased you would turn to me, Lady Thorson, what you ask is impossible. The hold of a ship is no place for a lady so fine as you."

"If not in the hold, then where could I hide? Where are the stores kept? Is there room there for me?" Anna continued to press him. She could see he really wanted to help her and thought with enough encouragement he would agree.

"There is a storage compartment off the galley, but it is no place for a lady either!" John exclaimed.

Anna's golden gaze searched the young man's expression. She was certain she detected a wavering in his resolve and persisted. "I am not nearly so fragile as I appear, John. I managed a farm and spent many a day in the fields and caring for our animals before Captain Bradford arrived to escort me to England. I will survive for a few weeks time in cramped quarters, no matter how unsuitable they are. Now how shall I sneak back on board?"

"I did not say I'd help you, Lady Thorson!" As John looked into her golden eyes his knees grew weak. That this exquisite creature would turn to him for help and believe him capable of rendering it successfully pleased him so greatly he knew he could not fail her. "Are you truly certain this is what you must do?"

"Yes, John, it is the only thing possible. What if Lord Clairbourne were to perish and I'd never even met him? I would not have the respect due a widow but only pity as a young woman whose love was never returned. I can not bear that possibility. I will be ever so grateful. I have no money to reward you now but surely Lord Clairbourne will be pleased and see you are paid well for helping me."

After a long moment John relented. "All right, I will help you, but what shall we do with your luggage? You can not wear one dress for the entire voyage."

"Yes, that is true." Frowning, Anna looked over the things he'd brought. "If I packed my belongings very tightly, most would fit into that one trunk. Have all the provisions been loaded aboard? I know they come last; couldn't my trunk be carried aboard somehow?"

John nodded thoughtfully. "Yes, I am to pick up the last of the stores on my way back to the ship. I can hide the trunk but you must pack it now as I have already delayed too long in my return and we don't want the captain to become suspicious."

Squealing with delight, Anna hugged the startled young man. "Oh, thank you, John! I knew I could depend upon you!" She then turned to her luggage, emptying it hastily, then folding the clothes she thought most necessary into neat stacks which she laid in the trunk before locking the leather-covered chest securely. "That is ready, now all that remains is to get myself on board. What do you suggest?"

"This is our last night in port. I will stand watch since I do not want to . . ." Blushing deeply, John tried to think of some tactful way to describe the crew's usual amusements. "What I mean is, I do not want to get drunk and, and—"

"Meet women, is that what you mean?" Anna inquired softly.

"Yes, I have not ever, well, . . ." John stammered as he realized he'd admitted too much.

Understanding his embarrassment, Anna interrupted, "I know what you mean, John. How some men can consort with women who are complete strangers is a mystery to me, but apparently sailors enjoy that sport enormously. That you do not, however, is to your credit." After having been with Phillip, Anna could not imagine how any woman could make love to a man she didn't adore for it was far too splendid an act to waste on the undeserving. Reaching up to kiss his cheek lightly, she whispered. "I will sneak out of here after midnight and make my way to the docks. Watch for me for I will be there well before dawn."

"Lady Thorson, if we should be caught I shudder to think what our punishment will be. Captain Bradford is not a forgiving man."

"Nor is my nature a forgiving one and he owes me this, John, truly he does. You will not suffer for helping me, I promise you that. Now you must go before our plan is discovered."

Smiling shyly the young man lifted her small trunk to his shoulder and carried it out to the waiting wagon. He paused to look back at the school and wondered if Anna had gone to a window where she might be watching him. What she had suggested was so impossible he knew they'd be caught if the slightest mishap occurred and he prayed all the way back to the *Angelina* that everything went according to their plan.

Pleading fatigue after the long voyage, Anna managed to escape assuming her duties and sleeping in a dormitory that night and was given the spare room in Mrs. Browne's own cottage. She'd not wanted to meet the girls who were supposed to be her charges when she'd made such urgent plans to leave, for she thought it best not to disappoint them by arriving to care for them one afternoon and then vanishing that very night. It appalled her to take advantage of the sweet-tempered headmistress but she had no way to avoid it when Phillip was sailing so soon. She went to her room early but spent her time sorting out the remainder of her belongings rather than sleeping. She'd take none of her old dresses, they'd been worn out in the first place and she was glad she'd not have to meet Clairbourne in any of those. Making a small stack of those garments, she turned her attention to the warm, woolen stockings she'd not thought to include with the things John had taken. It might be very cold crossing the Atlantic and she'd be foolish not to take them. After a few moments' contemplation, she dressed in several layers of warm clothing and wrapped herself in her long, woolen cape. Too excited to rest she paced the small bedroom anxiously until she heard the clock in the hallway chime twelve. Knowing Mrs. Browne deserved some sort of explanation for her disappearance, she wrote her a brief note saying only she'd gone to join the man she loved. Surely a thought so romantic as that would sway the headmistress from anger and when she returned to England she'd send the school some sort of a donation, or at least Charles would. She'd heard no sound in the small cottage for hours and, summoning all her courage, she picked up the small bag containing the rest of her personal items and tiptoed through the little house and out the front door where she found to her horror she was surrounded by a thick, damp mist which obscured her vision completely. Frightened she'd become lost before she even reached the main gate, she moved slowly down the path hesitating at each turn for she'd not dreamed the way would be so difficult to find. It took her more than half an hour to reach the entrance where she found the gate securely chained and padlocked. Not one to quit, she tossed her bag over to the other side and, using the decorative pattern of the wrought iron for footholds, scaled the tall gate quickly. She picked up her bag and looked about; she could make out little and heard no sounds of anyone approaching. She'd thought the trip to the docks would be a tiresome walk but not the impossible feat it now appeared to be. One wrong turn would mean she'd be hopelessly lost. She had not a moment to spare or the *Angelina* would sail without her and she could not bear to think she'd come so close to leaving and had missed the chance. "Damn you, Phillip!" she whispered to herself and her anger gave her a renewed sense of purpose as she started down the cobblestone street. They'd made several turns on the way to the school, but it had seemed to her at the time to be more a matter of the cabbie's preference for roadways rather than necessary as they'd doubled back more than once. Surely if she stayed on that one street and simply followed it to its end she would be at the docks and then the *Angelina* would be easy to find.

The night was bitterly cold and her breath hung on the chill air in small, white puffs as she hurried along, nearly running when she thought she heard someone approaching from a side street. Silent, quick, she darted into a doorway and waited for her pounding heart to return to a steady rhythm before she again took to the street. After more than two hours time she had no idea how many miles she'd covered or if she were anywhere near her destination but she'd not give up and pushed on. When the sound of music first reached her ears she strained to follow the spritely tune and came to a tavern the lights of which showed dimly in the fog. That the establishment was doing so lively a business at that late hour made her certain she'd found a place which catered to mariners. Reaching up on her tiptoes to peek in the window, she saw a large room filled with men whose apparel clearly showed them to be merchant seamen. She moved back into the shadows and waited for someone to leave, for she hoped any man on his way back to his ship would take her close enough to find the *Angelina* before dawn. She waited impatiently, stamping her feet to ward off the chill and when finally a single man emerged from the crowded inn she took up his trail a few yards behind where he'd not be able to see her if he turned but where she could hear his footsteps and follow along without fear of becoming lost. The pungent smell of the sea grew stronger and, excited, she grew careless. No longer listening to the sounds of the man's boots on the walk, she gave a loud shriek when his face appeared suddenly in front of her as he reached out to grab her arms.

"Are you girls never satisfied? You've taken to chasing an honest man through the town hoping to take the last coin in his purse? Did you plan to lift your skirt for me right here? Well, did you?"

He reeked of liquor and Anna was appalled he'd mistaken her for a prostitute. She tried to pull free. "I am on my way home also and have no business to conduct with the likes of you, now let me be!"

Startled by the musical tones of her speech as well as by the clear ring of authority in her words, the sailor dropped his hands to his sides and laughed heartily. "You might be worth the last of my money, lass. Lead the way and I'll follow you this time."

"Stand aside, I'll not invite you to my home!" Furious, Anna tried to slip past the man but he grabbed for her again, shoving her rudely into the adjacent doorway.

"I like a woman with spirit. Let's see what you've got under that cape."

Terrified, Anna had no desire to be raped by the drunken sailor before she could even scream for help. When his hands began moving down her body, roughly assessing her proportions, she waited no longer. She lifted her knee in a vicious jab which sent the man

242

sprawling to the sidewalk where he writhed in agony as she leapt over him. He grabbed for her foot but his hand slipped off her ankle, only tripping her slightly and not slowing her flight as she ran at top speed toward what she prayed were the docks where she'd find John waiting to sneak her aboard the *Angelina*. She ran on and on with the scent of the sea overpowering her senses until at last she came to the water's edge, so suddenly she nearly toppled right into the ice-cold brine. Gasping for breath she looked around, hoping none had seen her dashing through the street and decided to follow. Surely the fog would lift at dawn; she'd still not have found the *Angelina* with the luck she was having. Sitting down on her fabric bag she took several deep breaths and tried to decide in which direction to go. The harbor was a large one and she'd had little opportunity to look for landmarks. How foolish she'd been not to memorize the route they'd taken that afternoon! It had been lunacy to think she could walk straight to the ship she wanted when the choices were so many. Despondent over her problem she sat dejectedly trying to decide what to do when she overheard the sound of men's voices and laughter as they passed nearby. She grabbed her bag and slipped back into the shadows but to her immense delight she recognized one of the men as a sailor from the *Angelina*, Mark was his name, she thought, but that detail was unimportant when now she had a way to find his ship. She trailed the men with far more stealth than she'd used with the sailor who'd left the tavern and in ten minutes time she spotted the tall masts of the *Angelina* in the distance and quickened her pace. She watched Mark walk slowly up the gangplank and waited until she was certain he'd had time to go below before sprinting up the ramp and into John's waiting arms.

"Lady Thorson! You gave me an awful start! Why has it taken you so long to arrive?"

"That is too desperate a story to relate now, John. Just show me where I might hide, please, as I am dreadfully tired." When he took her bag and led her through the darkness to the galley, she followed closely behind, eager to find some safe place to rest.

Lighting a lamp, John opened the door to the pantry. "Michael never comes in here himself. He sends me to fetch whatever he requires. There is nothing I can do about the aroma of onions but the few extra blankets I found might make a passable bed."

Too tired and grateful to be critical, Anna dropped to her knees then stretched out upon the old, woolen blankets and sighed contentedly. "This is softer than a cloud, John, a wonderful bed, thank you so much." Without another word she was asleep, and taking the lamp, John returned to his post hoping he'd not just made the greatest mistake of his young life.

Chapter Thirteen

Anna soon discovered the *Angelina* had a life of her own, a vitality which throbbed with the sure, steady beat of a human heart as her streamlined hull sliced through the cresting waves. Still and silent, Anna listened until she became accustomed to each creak and moan of the sturdy timbers which surrounded her snug hiding place. The pantry was small, that was true, but in addition to the tangy onions it was filled with the delectable aroma of cheeses and honey-cured hams. John had given her a knife so she might help herself if she grew hungry before he brought her supper, but she seldom touched those provisions when there were fresh oranges to savor. She napped during the day, too restless to truly sleep; at night when John was on watch she would go up on deck and sit in the shadows beside him, quietly enjoying the sight of the sparkling stars and the feel of the fresh sea breeze upon her cheeks. The four hours of his turn at watch always passed too rapidly. Once she was nearly caught when the next man came up on deck a few minutes early. It had been a scare neither she nor John wished to risk repeating and after that narrow escape Anna stayed up on deck for no more than an hour during the middle of his time on duty.

After the excitement of the first few days spent hidden in the cool, dark storeroom expecting to be caught at any moment, Anna grew increasingly bored with her confinement. She could not risk lighting a lamp to read so she spent the long hours daydreaming, Phillip appearing with maddening frequency in her fantasies. He had simply used her for a diversion, it seemed plain, but she had fallen in love with him and that made his indifference all the more painful to bear. As he never came into the galley, she did not ever hear his voice but the pain of knowing he was on board when she couldn't see him tore her already ravaged emotions to ragged shreds. She wanted to simply walk into his cabin some evening and take her place at his table or perhaps stroll around the deck at dawn for the sheer enjoyment of seeing the look of disbelief fill his eyes when first he saw her. Such a trick was impossible, of course, and hopelessly foolish to even contemplate. But still at odd moments during the night she would consider revealing her presence. It was the thought that John would be blamed that kept her in hiding for she was afraid he might be whipped, perhaps savagely beaten for helping her and she'd not allow him to suffer after the kindness he'd shown to her.

During the second week of the *Angelina*'s voyage, the sea grew increasingly turbulent as the fiercest of storms overtook them, buffeting the ship hour after hour until Anna became so sick she did not even attempt to stand let alone worry over when John might appear with her meals. She lay upon her makeshift cot and hoped the torment would soon cease for her journey was difficult enough to bear without seasickness to add to the ordeal. All hands were hard at work so Michael kept a kettle of hearty soup bubbling throughout the day and night to warm the men when they came below to rest. He spent such long hours in the galley John had few opportunities to speak with Anna and feared she had fared even worse than the rest of them. When at last the sun broke through the clouds after four straight days of rain he waited for an exhausted Michael to go up on deck before he slipped into the pantry.

"Anna?" he called softly, then taking a few steps forward he knelt down by her side and touched her shoulder lightly.

Yawning sleepily Anna sat up and tried to smile. "The weather seems to have improved at last. I've lost all track of the time in here. Is it day or night?"

"Night, the captain's broken out extra rations of rum, for the crew deserves some reward after the punishment they've taken the last few days."

"Don't you consider yourself a part of the crew, John? You have as many duties as the other men, are you not one of them?" She had grown very fond of the shy young man. His features were pleasant and if he were not yet handsome she was certain in a few more years he would be. There was an unfinished quality to both his appearance and manner she knew he would outgrow before long. He would be a fine man, she was sure of it, but clearly he had little confidence in his own abilities, a sorry situation she did her best to remedy.

John shook his head sadly as he stuttered a hesitant

denial. "No, no, but it is not what I think that matters, but what they think of me."

Anna reached out to touch his cheek lightly. "Well, they are fools then for you are a wonderful friend and it is their loss if they do not know it!"

Charmed by her easy praise, John began to laugh, then offered a surprise. "We always collect rain water for bathing, I will warm some for you if you like."

"Oh, would you please? That would be such a treat although I do believe I'll probably still reek of onions!" Once John had gone back into the galley Anna folded up her blankets and placed them atop an unopened barrel of flour. She listened for a moment at the door where she'd overheard many a conversation between Michael and John but the young man appeared to be alone and, after peeking out to be certain he was, she moved to his side. "How much longer will the journey to America take?"

"The storm blew us way off course. We'll have to make up the distance we've lost before we can begin to count the days. It is better not to count them anyway but to let them come and go unheeded. The weeks pass more swiftly that way."

"Yes, that is undoubtedly true but I can't help but be impatient." She watched him tend the fire for a while, then certain the water was warm enough she helped him fill a pail. "Here, I can carry this myself. Why don't you join the others?"

John hesitated to leave her for he enjoyed her company so greatly. "Well, I, that is—"

"Just go, John!" Anna admonished brightly. "Sit down with the men and if you act like you belong with them you soon will! Now go and try it, you'll see!"

248

Moving quickly back into the pantry, Anna stripped off her wrinkled garments. Being a stowaway certainly had its price but she felt more confident with each passing hour that the choice she'd made had been the correct one. She scrubbed herself from head to toe with the coarse soap John had provided, then searched through her trunk for fresh clothing. She had donned no more than her lace-trimmed lingerie however when she heard a sound at the door and turned to find John watching her with a rapt gaze. Not knowing how long he'd been standing there, she could not help but blush as she called softly, "Just a moment please, John, I'm not quite dressed yet."

"Let me stay, Anna, I want to be with you tonight."

The hoarse tone of his voice alarmed the pretty blonde but she responded sweetly, "That would be unwise, but give me a minute more to dress and then we can talk." They'd spent many an hour conversing but she could see by the sweetness of his smile that was the last thing he wanted from her that night. She glanced around the tightly packed storeroom, hoping the crowded conditions would quell his ardor or at least hamper his advance but he crossed the distance between then swiftly and drew her into a close embrace.

"John, please let me go," Anna whispered against his cheek. He was such a shy young man, so pleasant and dear she had no wish to hurt him as badly as she had the drunken sailor who'd accosted her on the street in Southampton, but she'd not accept his affection either. "John, let me go now. Please let me finish getting dressed." She did not struggle against his caress, but stood perfectly still hoping she could transmit her forced sense of calm to him. The knife he'd provided lay within reach but she'd no intention of using it on him no matter how unreasonable he became. She purred softly, her warm breath brushing his cheek. "You are one of the best friends I have ever had. Please don't spoil our friendship this way." She continued to speak to him, her voice reassuring and low until she heard someone enter the galley. She froze then, too frightened to draw a breath as she heard Phillip calling John's name. The pantry door was ajar and in the next instant the captain stepped through it. The look in his eyes held exactly the degree of surprise she'd expected but his expression turned quickly to one of utter disgust as he realized he'd caught John and her about to make love. In one smooth stride he crossed the small room and, grabbing John by the scruff of the neck, lifted the startled youth clear off his feet.

"I might have known I'd find you here, Anna. John has been so preoccupied of late, so distracted and unlike himself I came to fetch him so he might join in the fun, but it is obvious he's had far more with you!"

Anna gasped in dismay, shocked by his accusation. "You are mistaken, sir, for what you assume is untrue!"

Phillip shoved John aside but did not release him. "I find a half-clothed stowaway and her accomplice locked in a passionate embrace and you say I am mistaken to believe what I can see with my own two eyes? The hell I am!" With that bitter retort Phillip manhandled John once more, pushing him through the door before dragging him out of the galley. The whole scene had taken less than one minute to play but Anna was shaking uncontrollably. How could Philip taunt her so rudely? He knew John to be shy and unassuming, a trustworthy lad who'd hardly be the type to engage in an illicit love affair. Glancing down at her scant attire she could readily understand how Phillip had believed what he had but surely if he would consider the situation more fully he'd see how mistaken he was. Yet, had he not come in when he had, could she have stopped John before he'd tried for more than a warm hug? He'd certainly wanted far more for her thin lingerie had provided little barrier between them and she'd felt the strength of his desire plainly. In spite of the fact he'd never been with a woman, it had been clear he'd wanted her that night, and most desperately. Now he was in terrible trouble and it was all because of her. Dressing quickly, she combed out her damp curls then hurried to Phillip's cabin intent upon making him see she was the one who deserved to be punished, not John. Finding the room empty, she paced up and down anxiously, wringing her hands with each long stride.

When Phillip at last entered his quarters he did not even pause to take a breath before he continued his tirade. "I can not believe what an incredible fool I've been! To think the first time I saw you I thought you were an angel! You certainly look like one, but no more unangelic woman was ever born! No devil from hell will ever torment me as cruelly as you do! How could you have seduced John? How could you have used him so badly when it was plain to us all he was infatuated with you? Have you not the slightest bit of regard for others? Must you pursue this ridiculous course of yours at all costs no matter whom you must hurt to do it?"

"Stop it!" Anna screamed defiantly. "Stop it this instant! John is my friend and a good one. I'd not use his affection for me or ever abuse it!"

Phillip's blue eyes grew black with hatred as he snarled, "You don't even realize what you've done, do you? How you've manipulated a boy to do your bidding with no thought of the consequences to him!" Clearly he was outraged by such blatant selfishness as she had displayed.

"Oh, please, Phillip, you've no reason to whip him. Beat me if you must but do not hurt John! I couldn't bear it if you did."

"Isn't it rather late for such tender feelings, Lady Thorson? As I am captain of this vessel I may do as I please to discipline my crew when they flout the rules of the sea so flagrantly!"

"No!" Anna rushed forward, ready to argue all night if need be. "You must not punish John for helping me! Don't you see I am solely responsible for my being on board? This is all my own doing and none of his!" She started to reach out for his hand but dared not when he took a step backward, obviously revolted by her touch.

"Cease your pleading as I have no reason to believe you'll ever speak the truth! The *Angelina* has a brig of sorts and that's where John will remain until we reach port. And as for you . . ."

When Phillip paused Anna straightened her shoulders with grim determination, she'd take whatever punishment he wished to give without shedding a single tear. "Well, what is it you wish of me? I believe it is customary to make a stowaway work for her passage. If Michael will be without his helper I will gladly assist him in John's place."

Startled by her sensible suggestion, Phillip hesitated

252

to consider it for a long moment. "Yes, you may help Michael, but as John also served as my cabin boy I expect you to have those duties as well, to make up my bunk each morning, to do my laundry, to serve my meals and to tend whatever task I assign."

Greatly relieved he'd not chosen to flog either of them, Anna found it difficult to suppress a wide smile. "I am used to hard work, Phillip. I will do whatever you require without complaint."

"From now on you will address me as Captain Bradford, Lady Thorson and when your day's work is finished you will sleep here in my cabin where I can be certain you will be into no further mischief!"

The pretty blush excitement had brought to her cheeks faded instantly as Anna glanced over at his bunk. There was no other bed in the cabin and she could not agree to what he had just suggested after the callous way he had treated her. Did he truly believe she had seduced John? Did he consider her no better than a whore now and plan to simply enjoy her favors again and again? Sickened by that thought she hastened to argue. "I invited you to share my bed but if you are now demanding that I share yours then I must refuse, for that is no longer a pastime in which I wish to indulge with you."

Furious that she had misunderstood him so completely, Phillip scoffed at her worries. "I said you'd sleep in my cabin, not in my bunk, no matter how greatly you enjoy it!" Anna's hand struck his cheek so swiftly he had no time to block her blow and he restrained himself from returning it by the barest of margins. "Striking the captain of a ship is considered an act of mutiny, Anna. Do you realize what the penalty is

253

for that?"

"It can be no worse than the punishment I've already suffered from you!" Anna responded heatedly.

"I assure you, if you prefer death to sleeping with me again I will most willingly arrange for your execution!"

Preferring to ignore his threats, Anna showed not the slightest sign of fear as she returned his fierce gaze. "What, pray tell, would you say to Lord Clairbourne when next you meet? You're already been paid to take me to him, I want only for you to uphold your part of the bargain!"

"Oh, believe me I will! That blasted storm blew us so far south I'll gladly set our course for Jamaica simply to be finished with you once and for all!" Phillip shouted at the top of his lungs, livid with the strikingly beautiful young woman he'd never been able to control.

Astonished he'd finally agreed to a request she considered so reasonable, Anna was tempted to hug him but dared not be so bold. "Thank you, that is very generous of you and I will praise your name endlessly to Charles but I'll still not be your mistress for this voyage."

Stepping closer Phillip whispered hoarsely, "You are the last woman on earth I'd ever hire as my mistress, the very last! Now fetch your belongings. Bring whatever you've been using for a bed and place it as far away from my bunk as possible so I'll not trip over you as I rise in the morning! Now go, do as I say!"

"Yes, sir!" Anna replied with a careless toss of her bright curls. She'd show him a thing or two before they reached Jamaica! If she disgusted him so be it, she'd be with Charles at last and no matter what sort of life he gave her it would be better than the last few weeks in Phillip Bradford's company had been. He'd given her none of love's joy but only its sorrow and she had had more than enough of his arrogant moods and cold manner.

Phillip seldom drank with his crew, but that night he joined the group sprawled about the deck and gave them a brief report of the evening's events. They all simply stared, mouths agape as he told them Lady Thorson had been discovered on board and John had been confined to the brig for arranging that bit of trickery. When not even Michael had the presence of mind to ask any questions he turned smartly and walked away as if returning to his cabin were what he really wanted to do. Jamie was asleep so he'd have to face him in the morning but he already knew what the mate would say. He would take the side of a beautiful woman in any argument. Frowning deeply Phillip paused at his own door, then thinking such chivalry misplaced he went on through without knocking, determined to show the impossible Lady Thorson no mercy whatsoever.

Equally cool, Anna pretended to be asleep. She'd tossed her dress and lingerie over one of the chairs at the round table and had put on a nightgown for the first time since she'd snuck aboard. The layered blankets were no more comfortable a bed in his cabin than they had been in the pantry but at least her surroundings held only the fresh clean scent of the sea rather than the earthy aroma of onions!

Phillip ignored Anna's presence as he prepared to retire. He removed his shirt, then remembered such an unusual circumstance as the discovery of a stowaway deserved a notation in his log. Pulling up a chair he sat down at his desk and tried to compose some reasonable statement, but found that nearly impossible. How did one calmly report a beauty like Lady Anna Thorson had been found aboard and would be spending the remainder of the voyage working as his cabin steward and the cook's helper? It would take more energy than he possessed that night to chart their new course and he decided to leave that chore for the morning. He turned to look over his shoulder at Anna and saw she hadn't moved since he'd come in; the few blankets she had were thin and he knew from bitter experience the floor was hard and cold but damn it that was all the consideration she deserved. He'd done his best to take care of her, to leave her well provided for in Southampton and she'd made a mockery of his efforts. Worn out by the troubles she presented, he snuffed out the lamp then stripped off the rest of his clothing. But as he lifted the covers to slip into his bunk the softness of the woolen blankets seemed somehow obscene and he carried the top one over to Anna and carefully tucked it around her shoulders before he returned to his bed. He stretched out on his back, and propped his head upon his hands, suddenly wide awake. As he stared up into the darkness he saw Anna's face as clearly as if they'd been standing on deck at noon. Her golden eyes shown with a taunting fire and he cursed softly under his breath as he tried unsuccessfully to force her distracting image from his mind.

"Captain Bradford?" Anna whispered softly. "Thank you for your kindness, I will not disappoint you again."

"Save your breath and go to sleep, Anna, for I've no hope that you won't disappoint me endlessly," Phillip replied crossly. He did not trust her out of his sight, but he'd never admit even to himself how desperately he had missed her. It was not simply the one incredible night they'd spent making love either; there was a charm about her that surpassed even the most erotic of his desires, but he could not think of the proper word to describe that delicious appeal. She was simply all any woman could ever be to a man and he reminded himself for the hundredth time that that man was a titled Engish gentleman and not him. Finding not the slightest bit of comfort in that dismal thought he turned his thoughts to the voyage ahead. It would be a lengthy one and who could say what might happen between them when the days grew warm and the nights were softly scented with the fragrant Jamaican wind? A slow, satisfied smile curved across his handsome mouth and he fell asleep almost instantly, his mind filled with the most tantalizing dreams of what the next few weeks might bring.

Chapter Fourteen

Anna made good on her promise; she was up and dressed, in the galley ready to help Michael prepare the crew's breakfast before Phillip awakened the next morning. After having spent so many days hiding in his pantry, she felt as though she already knew the cook, but the portly man was clearly embarrassed to have her assistance.

"Lady Thorson, I am certain you know how to prepare a most delicious porridge, but I can not bear to see you do it!" He wiped his perspiring palms on his grease-stained apron then continued to gesture helplessly.

Anna put her hands on her hips, tapping her foot impatiently as she attempted to make the man understand her plight. "The captain has agreed to allow me to take John's place here, a most generous gesture on his part, one for which I am most grateful. If you can not bear to have my help, though, I have no choice but to tell him so now and suffer whatever other punishment he selects." Turning away abruptly, Anna wiped a nonexistent tear from the corner of her eye.

"My dear lady, please, please stay!" Michael overturned an empty flour barrel and motioned for her to be seated. "This is all so unexpected. The work is too hard, you can not even lift the supplies I need, let alone carry them! This galley is too warm for a lady's delicate constitution and what man could eat knowing you had prepared his meal for punishment?"

Anna nodded absently as the agitated man gave excuse after excuse for excluding her from his galley. When she could stand to listen to no more she held up her hand. "Be that as it may, I am here and ready to work at whatever task you wish to assign. Surely the captain's needs should be seen to promptly. Does he eat his breakfast first or should I take him some hot water so he can shave? He is always well-groomed and I do not want to disrupt whatever routine he might have."

"John takes him his breakfast first but—"

Standing up, Anna reached for the silver tray John had always carried. "Then give me whatever you have prepared and I'll take it to him." Her command was too reasonable to be ignored and she smiled as Michael gathered fruit, cheese, biscuits and a pot of tea. "Thank you, Michael, I know I can do all that will be required of me if you will just give me the chance." Without waiting for him to argue that point, Anna picked up the tray and swept out of the galley.

Phillip sat up as Anna came through the door. He'd expected her to be the one who slept late and he was not quite certain what he wanted to do now that she'd caught him still in his bunk. Scowling, he watched her cross the room, the graceful swing of her slender hips as inviting as always.

Anna placed the tray on the table and turned to face the young man. "Is there anything else you require Captain?" A smile lifted the corner of her pretty mouth as she noted his embarrassment and rightly guessed its cause. It was obvious from his bare chest he usually slept in the nude and the previous night had apparently been no exception. While they had shared the most delicious intimacies, it had all been under the sensual veil of darkness and now his cabin was flooded with sunlight. "If I am to occupy your cabin we are undoubtedly going to find ourselves in this same situation fairly often. Would you like me to turn around or shall I simply leave while you dress?"

Her question struck Phillip as wildly amusing and he chuckled as he reached for the edge of his blanket, ready to throw it back. "The choice is yours, Lady Thorson, for I am not nearly as shy as John." A fact he thought she should damn well know.

Anna moved closer, staring coldly as she replied in a low voice filled with anger, "I'll not allow you to make fun of him! What you assumed about us was completely untrue but I won't let you ridicule him!"

Phillip lifted a dark brow quizzically. "I don't wish to discuss last night again so skip your excuses for that tender scene I interrupted. I'll not believe a word you say." Returning to their present problem he asked pointedly, "Now do you wish to leave or stay?"

"I have not the slightest desire to remain here, Captain. I will leave you alone to eat and return in a moment with the hot water you need to shave. Would you like me to do it, my father taught me how."

"I'd sooner grow a beard than let you near me with a

razor in your hand!" Phillip replied sarcastically.

Moving toward the door with a jaunty step, Anna purred softly, "It is your choice, of course, but you are so very handsome I doubt a beard would harm your looks in the slightest."

She was gone before Phillip could reply but he laughed as he leapt out of his bunk and dressed quickly to avoid another such ridiculous scene. The young woman had no end of nerve it seemed but there was no point in his parading in the nude in front of her when he'd sworn not to make love to her again. The absurdity of that vow made him laugh all over again and he ate his breakfast in a surprisingly optimistic mood.

By suppertime Anna was exhausted; she'd worked all day long at one task or another and could barely stop yawning long enough to carry the evening meal to Phillip's cabin. When Jamie met her at the door and took the heavy tray she thanked him warmly for his help.

"The pleasure is mine, Lady Thorson, for we are unlikely to ever have so attractive a cabin steward ever again." Jamie winked slyly, hoping her newly reduced status might work to his advantage.

"I am hungry even if you two are not. Just serve our meal, Anna, and leave us to enjoy it." Phillip drew his chair up to the table and nodded impatiently at his two companions.

Aghast at his friend's rudeness, Jamie inquired hurriedly, "Isn't Anna, I mean Lady Thorson, going to dine here with us?"

"No, of course not. You did not expect John to take his meals with us so why should she?" Phillip pointed out logically.

Jamie looked back and forth between the captain and the lovely blonde, his confusion clear in his troubled gaze. "But she is—"

Stepping forward, Anna guided Jamie toward the table. "There is no need to argue, gentlemen. I have already eaten and can recommend this fare highly." She continued to praise Michael's cuisine as she served their plates, then after filling their silver goblets with wine left them to return to the galley where she climbed upon the overturned keg and yawned sleepily. "You have such long days, Michael. How are you able to do it?"

Laughing, the cook put away the last of the cutlery he'd used to prepare supper. "I like my work, that's a fact, but I've been at it since I was a lad and do not find the hours overlong. Captain Bradford does not scrimp when it comes to feeding his crew as many a captain does and that makes for a happier crew and a far more popular cook!" The good-natured man's laughter was brief as he noticed Anna again attempting to cover a yawn. "I told you this galley was no place for a lady to be, miss. Will you not allow me to speak with the captain about your duties now?"

"No!" Anna responded indignantly. "What he asks of me is only fair. I am a stowaway and must work to pay for my passage, I've no other choice."

Michael pursed his lips thoughtfully weighing his options thoroughly before he spoke. "Me and the other men were thinking that if each of us were to put in a little something, your way would be paid and you'd not have to work. Mr. Jenkins would give you his cabin again too. It isn't right for you to have to share the Captain's quarters."

Blushing at the transparency of his thoughts, Anna had to smile. "Why, Michael, how dear of you to suggest such a sweet solution to my problems but I don't believe Captain Bradford would accept your money and I can't accept your charity either. I'll pay my own way by working, I know I can do it. How is John? If only I could take him his meals I could—"

This time Michael interrupted sternly. "No, miss, that is forbidden. Bradford is a reasonable man, but I'll not disobey him and risk losing my job aboard the *Angelina* for it's the best I've ever had."

"No, I would not suggest that either, Michael, but please tell John I am thinking of him, that I won't desert him. Would you please tell him that for me?"

After a moment's hesitation the cook agreed. "Aye, I can do that much."

Anna gave him a hug as she left the galley and, taking her shawl to wrap snugly around her shoulders, she went up on deck to stroll about for a while, not knowing when she should return to Phillip's cabin. But she was more tired than she'd thought possible and yawned repeatedly as she waited. When she could stay awake no longer she rapped lightly upon the captain's door.

"Anna? You needn't knock at my door, simply come and go as you please." Phillip stood aside so she might enter. Jamie was gone, the plates had been cleared from the table and he'd been reading but didn't seem disturbed by the interruption.

When he sat down with his book, Anna wondered if he'd purposely chosen a chair facing the corner where she'd made her bed. He was a bright man, surely it was no accident he'd not selected a chair where his back

263

would have afforded her some degree of privacy. It seemed the tables had been turned and she did not like the feeling one bit, but she was too tired to wait for him to douse the lamp to undress. If he'd thought to embarrass her she'd not give him the satisfaction and with a slow, graceful turn she began to disrobe, dropping her blouse casually upon the trunk which contained her clothes before slipping off her skirt. When she glanced up, Phillip was watching her with rapt attention. "Is something the matter, Captain?"

"Don't you have the midnight watch tonight? Why bother to undress?"

Anna could not bring herself to believe he was serious. "You expect me to stand watch?"

"Of course, you're taking John's place, aren't you?" Phillip let his eyes wander down her slender figure with an insolent laziness and tried to ignore the rapidly mounting beat of his heart which filled his ears with a near-deafening roar. He gripped his book tightly and forced himself to continue. "I should find you some more suitable clothing, the nights are very cold and—"

Seething with anger, Anna interrupted swiftly. "I know the temperatures are low, I've been up on deck whenever John has had the midnight watch. If I must take his turn I will and you needn't worry I am too frail to stand the night air without falling ill." As if that had ever been his concern she thought bitterly.

"I won't. You're obviously a prime example of Swedish womanhood and undoubtedly hardy despite your fair coloring." Pretending again to concentrate on his book, Phillip attempted unsuccessfully to force Anna's tantalizing presence from his mind.

Confused, Anna sank down upon her trunk and

stared coldly at the handsome man. "Why do you pretend to despise me when just the opposite is true?"

"What?" Phillip's expression filled with alarm. His book slipped from his grasp and fell into his lap, a sharp corner jabbing him painfully.

"You heard me. You delight in insulting me at every opportunity. I would simply like to know the reason why."

Tossing the book down upon the table, Phillip rose slowly to his feet and came forward, his mood clearly bitter. "I told you before that I do not enjoy playing nursemaid to an impossibly self-centered child so it should come as no surprise that I have not changed my mind, Lady Thorson." After pausing a moment to allow time for her to fully absorb that insult he continued, "Nothing in my wardrobe will fit you, but I think one or two of my crew might have clothing close enough to your size to be wearable. It is ridiculous for you to work in the galley in silks and satins. Go to sleep and I'll see you have suitable attire by midnight."

"How thoughtful of you!" Anna replied crossly, too tired to care what she wore. When Phillip stalked out of the cabin she lay down upon her bed, covered herself with the extra blanket he'd provided and was sound asleep by the time he returned.

Since the men rotated shifts, by careful scheduling Phillip managed to see he and Anna seldom crossed paths, but he could not avoid her at mealtimes when she continued to serve him with a gaiety that made eating nearly impossible. Her superb figure proved to be even more distracting in the masculine garb he'd provided, the curves of her elegant form in all the wrong places, and he regretted he'd ever told her to put away her own gowns. The crew had taken to her presence with an enthusiasm he should have expected, yet hadn't and their ceaseless efforts to spare her any extra work or discomfort annoyed him tremendously. Then one afternoon he found her climbing the rigging with Jamie and could no longer control his temper.

"Anna, come down here this instant!" Phillip shouted into the wind, furious that the mate had allowed such a thing. But that was a matter he'd wait to take up with Jamie when they could discuss it in the privacy of his cabin.

Anna frowned with deep concentration as she came down the rope ladder. Going up had been far easier and she had to be very careful where she placed her feet so as not to slip and fall. The men could all climb with the ease of monkeys and she'd envied them so, but she could see by Phillip's stern glance she'd displeased him as greatly as always. "Yes, Captain Bradford, is there something you need of me?" Dropping to the deck, Anna faced him squarely, her pose confident, as if she'd been doing nothing which could bring the slightest censure.

"I do not want to see you behaving so foolishly ever again. Women simply do not, I mean they must not . . ." Phillip hesitated, uncertain how to put his command in a sensible fashion. When Anna continually did such outrageous things he could not seem to stay ahead of her. "I thought you were busy doing my laundry this morning. Isn't that enough of a job for you?"

"I have finished, Captain." Anna smiled sweetly. "I merely asked Jamie a question or two and he thought it would be better simply to show me than to try and explain only with words."

266

Jamie laughed at her candor. "That is the truth, Captain. I was attempting to explain why the distance we can see is increased when we move from the deck up to the top of the mast."

"Dear God, you were not going to put Anna in the crow's nest!" Phillip moaned in disbelief. He found Anna in Jamie's company all too often but this was too much to bear.

"No, not yet, I thought she should understand how we raise and lower the sails first," Jamie boasted proudly.

"Oh, I see, Lady Thorson plans to make a career of being a merchant seaman and you were just instructing her in the basics?" Phillip was so angry he could barely catch his breath to hiss that question.

"Why, Captain Bradford, you know I am to become Lady Clairbourne. Surely Charles would not allow his wife to pursue such a vocation."

"Neither will I! This entire voyage has been ridiculous from beginning to end and this farce must stop immediately. You are being punished and yet you act as though you were enjoying the most wonderfully amusing cruise! Enough! I expect to find you in the galley or in my cabin doing some useful work but I'll not allow you to cavort through the rigging like some, like some! . . ." When no truly appropriate insult came to his mind Phillip turned away and strode off, leaving both Jamie and Anna holding their sides to stifle the sounds of their laughter.

"I am sorry, Mr. Jenkins, we are both going to suffer, I'm afraid. I should have known Phillip would be unhappy to see me climbing up so high."

"Unhappy is not the word for his mood, Lady Thorson. He is furious with us but your extended stay on board is proving more difficult for him than for the rest of us it seems." Jamie flashed his most charming grin; he did not mind being in trouble if Anna were in it with him.

Ignoring his admiring glance Anna continued to watch Phillip traverse the length of the deck. He was willing to give her nothing it seemed, not even a kind word. "Why is that, Mr. Jenkins? Why does he find my presence so very objectionable?"

"He is a proud man, Anna, one who can be trusted to keep his word, to behave with honor whatever the situation. He is not a man who would court another man's fiancée."

Her golden eyes blazing with anger, Anna disagreed sharply. "Would he ever bother to court any woman? Or would he not rather take his pleasures wherever he can find them with no thought of the sweetness of love or the true meaning of honor?"

Startled by her question, Jamie could only stare as Anna moved away, returning to the galley as she'd been told to do. Her odd assortment of castoff clothing did nothing to hide her luscious figure and he knew Phillip's anguish all too well. They were still many days from Jamaica but he promised himself the minute they made port he was going to find a woman and pay her well to make him forget the beautiful Anna Thorson completely.

Her work in the galley finished for the time being Anna took Phillip's freshly washed and dried shirts into his cabin to fold and put away. They smelled of sunshine, and the softness of the fine linen was a delight to her fingertips. She checked the buttons carefully and, finding one missing from a cuff, laid the shirt aside to repair. When Phillip entered a moment later she asked him where he kept his needle and thread and he produced a small tin box with an assortment of needles, thread of finely spun flax and a half dozen perfectly formed mother of pearl buttons.

"Just what I need, do you mind if I work in here?" Anna hesitated to remain. He had just told her she should be either in the galley or his cabin but still she had never felt welcome in his quarters. "I can go up on deck to sew if I'll be in your way here."

"No, I would prefer you worked here." Phillip gestured toward the table. "Sit down, I did not plan to stay." He went then to his desk to consult one of his charts and paid her no further heed.

Anna took a chair at his table and quickly attached the new button with a few deft stitches, then knotted the thread tightly and snipped it with her teeth. "There you are. Is there anything else of yours which needs mending?"

"No," Phillip replied curtly, not really certain whether there were or not.

"You're most welcome, Captain Bradford." Anna tried to suppress a teasing smile but her eyes lit with a merry sparkle. She replaced the needle and thread in the small box then folded the soft white shirt carefully but left it upon her lap.

"Thank you," Phillip offered grudgingly. "I could have done that myself."

"It was no trouble. You have a handsome wardrobe. These shirts are beautifully made, the stitches so minute they are nearly invisible upon the fabric."

Having completed his calculations Phillip returned

the chart to its place before turning to face her. "A woman in Philadelphia makes them for me. I bring her the linen and she makes the shirts a half dozen at a time."

"Is she your mistress?" Anna inquired softly, too curious not to ask about so important a matter, yet she dreaded hearing his reply.

Phillip shook his head emphatically as he laughed. "No, were she my mistress she'd have no time to sew!" He'd not describe the seamstress for she was a dear little, old woman he doubted had ever been any man's mistress, at least not in his lifetime. "Whatever makes you ask such an impertinent question?"

Anna licked her lips coyly, forcing herself to portray a detachment she did not feel. "It seems likely that you would have a mistress somewhere, Philadelphia would be as good a place as any. A woman who does handwork so fine as this would be a great treasure."

"Oh, indeed she is, Anna, but is that how you think a man chooses his mistress? If so, you have been misinformed." A slow smile spread across Phillip's well-shaped mouth as he leaned back against his desk and folded his arms across his chest, apparently content to discuss the topic fully. "Very badly misinformed I'd say."

"You can not possibly think me still so naive as that, Captain. I understand a man selects a woman for her charms and beauty but you did not answer my question. If the woman who makes your clothing is not your mistress, is there another who is?"

Phillip found Anna's direct gaze most unsettling, but answered truthfully. "No, I see no point in providing for a woman's lodging and comfort when I could visit her so seldom. The advantage would all be hers, not mine."

"Why, Captain, you make such an arrangement sound more like a business partnership than an affair of the heart."

"That's all it is, Anna, a man provides for his mistress's comfort and she provides for his, the romantic involvement is slight." Phillip shrugged nonchalantly, the matter a clear-cut one in his view.

Anna nodded thoughtfully. "Yes, I think I see what you mean for if a man truly loved a woman he'd make her his wife wouldn't he?"

"Surely you know love is not the main consideration when a marriage is arranged." Her own situation was an example he didn't care to cite.

"So in your view, there is no place for love in either a marriage or an affair? Don't you believe in love at all, Captain?" She could not look at him without remembering his intoxicating kisses and magical touch which had promised far more than his words ever had.

Not wishing to tread upon such dangerous ground, Phillip regarded her critically with a disapproving frown. "There you sit in clothes which belong to lord knows whom, calmly discussing the merits of employing a mistress as if it were a fit subject for a lady to talk about at afternoon tea, which by the way, you have neglected to serve!"

Knowing instantly their discussion was over, Anna rose and placed his neatly folded shirt in the drawer with the others. "How thoughtless of me, I will see to it immediately. But before I go, I would like to ask you if I might not see John to—"

"No!" Phillip crossed the distance between them in

one fluid stride and grabbed her shoulders in a firm hold. "If I ever catch you with him again, you'll both be exceedingly sorry!"

"You did not 'catch' me with him as you keep insisting you did!" Anna argued vehemently. "You still don't understand what you saw and I doubt you ever will since you seem to know nothing of true affection, of—"

Phillip lowered his head, capturing her mouth in a brutal kiss which ended her argument instantly. But when she did not fight him, he found her pliant form impossible to resist and pressed her gently to his heart, relaxing his hold upon her at the same time he deepened his kiss. He wound his fingers in her golden curls and was lost again in her delicious taste, consumed with the burning need he'd tried so long to deny.

Anna had no more success in controlling her passions than Phillip had with his and they were soon sprawled across his bunk, entangled in an embrace from which neither could have withdrawn. When he could not seem to remove her ill-fitting clothing fast enough, she helped him rather than have the few garments she wore hamper his advance. She wanted him to make love to her again, to feel the power of his strength through every nerve of her body, to be enveloped in the same marvelous sensations which had been such a delicious surprise when he'd first taught her the secrets of making love. Riding the crest of his mounting excitement she lured him higher and higher until at last he shuddered with a final surrender and buried his face in her tangled curls as he let the ecstasy she'd given him roll through his body, leaving him too filled with the warmth of deep contentment to move away.

She held him gently in her arms, her pleasure as deep as his as her fingertips continued to caress the satin smooth skin of his shoulders slowly moving over the powerful muscles coaxing the taut fibers to relax under her cool touch. But when he finally drew away her satisfied smile brought a frown to his brow she'd not expected. "Is something wrong, Captain?"

"Yes, I'd say every blasted thing is wrong!" He'd planned to have her again, but never like this, not with a passion so hot he'd been consumed in its flames, no more able to control his mind than his body. He yanked on his clothes with furious haste then slammed the door of his cabin as he left her, still so stunned by the grip she held over his emotions he could think of no explanation for her power save witchcraft and wondered if the Vikings had been able to cast such potent spells with their runes.

Hurt by his hostile rejection when she'd enjoyed his affection so greatly, Anna made no move to leave Phillip's comfortable bed. She lay languidly, absorbing what remained of his fiery warmth and whispered softly to herself, "Dear God, Phillip, how can I ever marry Charles after having known you?" She forced away the hot tears which burned her eyes as a weakness to which she'd not submit, but she knew each day brought her closer to marriage with Lord Clairbourne, and not one bit closer to the man she loved.

Chapter Fifteen

Anna leaned against the rail, drinking in the beauty of the sparkling heavens. Dawn was still several hours away but she considered the time past midnight as the best of all. Her eyes swept the scene before her slowly. There was no separation between the sky and sea for the stars' light was reflected in the water with a brightness which was nearly blinding on a night so clear as that one. It was a marvelous sight. Phillip had cautioned her to be alert when she stood watch but she found herself so entranced with the excitement of the dazzling sky, she thought little of the danger to a ship moving at top speed through the darkness until something out of the ordinary caught her eye. She strained to see more clearly but could not, yet she was certain it was not simply her imagination. It had to be another ship, moving parallel to the *Angelina*, and as she tried to make out its shape she grew frightened. The weather had been warming gradually with each new day, the shade of the ocean was growing more blue and

Phillip's tales of pirates came quickly to her agile mind. Seized with a sudden terror, she ran for his cabin, slamming the door loudly before she knelt by his bunk and gave his shoulder a brisk shake.

"Phillip, come quickly, there is a ship stalking us, come and see!"

Despite having had no more than a few hours sleep, Phillip was swift to respond. Anna's voice teased his senses and he reached out to take her hand as he came fully awake. "You needn't shout. What is wrong that can't wait until morning to be reported?"

Anna left her hand in his as she continued excitedly, "There is a ship moving along with us. It lies to the south, following our course exactly. Could it be pirates, Phillip, could it?"

Phillip chuckled for the innocence of her question was so unlike her. "Give me a moment, Anna, I will dress and come look for myself for the odds are great whatever ship it is means trouble for us."

"A British man-of-war perhaps? Oh, Phillip, what will you do?"

"If you do not move aside so I might leave my bunk I can do little!" Phillip scolded impatiently, thinking little of her fears when he had no proof anything was amiss.

Anna rose to her feet and hastily went to the door. "I will wait just outside. Please hurry for if it is an enemy there is no time to lose in preparing our defense."

"Since when have you imagined yourself to possess the cunning of an admiral?" Phillip sneered sarcastically. "I can defend the *Angelina* quite well without your help." The very idea of her offering suggestions for a battle plan appalled him.

"Just hurry!" Anna pleaded as she left his cabin. She fidgeted nervously with her oversized sweater, rolling and unrolling the sleeves while she paced back and forth. When Phillip at last appeared, she ran along by his side, racing to the port rail where she'd first sighted the mysterious vessel. The sky had grown lighter with the promise of the coming dawn but nowhere was there any sign of the ship she'd seen so clearly. "It was there, Phillip, I swear it was!"

Phillip stood silent for several minutes, scanning the vastness of the sea with intense interest. "Did you see it well enough to count the masts at least?"

"No, I saw only the whiteness of the sails. I saw them plainly against the skyline, I know I did!" Anna protested heatedly. "How could the ship have just vanished?"

Raising his voice, Phillip persisted in his interrogation. "Was it a square rigger or fore-and-aft rigged as the *Angelina* is?"

"Square, of that much I'm certain. That means she must carry more men than we do, doesn't it?" Anna's voice trembled with emotion. They'd be outnumbered, she was sure of it.

"If a ship actually existed, it might," Phillip replied sternly. "Just keep your wits about you this time. If you see something else, be certain you can at least describe it accurately before you come for me."

As the tall man turned away Anna reached out to catch his arm, grabbing his elbow in a frantic grasp. "You will not stay with me a while longer?"

"Why? To waste the night when I could be sleeping? Goodnight, Anna, do not disturb me again until you bring my breakfast."

"Aye, aye, Captain!" Anna cried out, her tone as sarcastic as his. He'd not believed her, not one bit. He thought her foolish for having awakened him. But she could not stop shaking for she knew she had seen a ship which could very likely threaten all their lives and she'd not been able to make Phillip believe her. She gripped the rail tightly, sick with fear, for she knew had she not been on board the *Angelina* would already be safe in port in Philadelphia. If any harm came to her captain or her crew Anna knew she'd never forgive herself for causing it.

Despite Phillip's curt rebuff of Anna's report, he rose early and with characteristic calm stayed on deck all morning so he'd know first-hand if trouble were brewing. He knew the young woman to be both bright and perceptive, but she was unfamiliar with the sea and could not be expected to give the most accurate of reports. Yet he was certain if she'd seen something then most likely someone else would see it too and soon. All ships followed approximately the same routes as they traversed the globe so it was no surprise when another vessel came into view, but he was uneasy all the same for the chances of sighting a friend in those waters were slight.

Anna did not have a turn at watch the following night but went up on deck anyway for she was far too restless to sleep. Phillip was at the helm and she sat down nearby, hugging her knees as she waited for him to comment upon her presence. He was leaning into his task, his stance proud, his gaze intent upon the stars but his expression was easy to read. He was clearly troubled.

"What is it Captain? The wind is good; why is your

mood so dark?" As dark as my own, she thought sadly.

"Leave me be, Anna, I'm in no mood for your questions tonight," Phillip ordered wearily.

"I have thought of a plan though. I think the ship I saw was British and if the *Angelina* is boarded we should simply say I am Lady Clairbourne rather than merely Charles's fiancée. If I demand a safe escort to Jamaica, they will have to let you proceed without further question."

Phillip stared straight ahead for a long moment, then began to explain slowly as if he were speaking to a small child. "The ship was not seen today although many watched for it. The British have no reason to play a game of hide and seek with us, so if there really were a ship nearby, which I still doubt, it was not from the Royal Fleet." After pausing to gauge his course he continued, "Do you honestly think the British Navy is so full of fools they would look at you and believe you are Lady Clairbourne? Most likely they will mistake you for my cabin boy!"

Anna glanced down at her thick sweater and baggy pants; a knit cap covered her glossy curls. She supposed Phillip's prediction was true. "Since you provided my present wardrobe yourself, it is rude of you to make fun of it. I still have my own clothes and the prettiest ones too. They will believe me to be Lady Clairbourne readily enough, you needn't worry they won't," Anna boasted proudly. She was not in the least bit ashamed of her disheveled appearance, it was simply irrelevant in her present situation.

"All right, let's say they accept your story as the truth, then it is logical to assume they will invite you aboard so they might take you to Jamaica themselves rather than giving the *Angelina* an escort."

"If they suggest that I will gladly agree, for then you and your men would no longer be in danger because of me," Anna explained softly.

"Do you really expect me to believe our welfare concerns you?" Phillip scoffed loudly. "It is far too late to convince me of that, Anna."

Anna rose gracefully, drawn to him despite his taunting words. She laid her hand gently upon his shoulder as she reached up to kiss his cheek sweetly. "There is only one thing I wish you to believe of me and if you still do not understand the depth of my regard for you then I fear you will never be convinced."

Phillip was too astonished by Anna's sudden affection to make any sort of a reply as she moved away into the shadows. She was gone in an instant but he stood motionless, unable to leave his post to give pursuit. His throat tightened into a painful knot as he whispered only to himself, "Dear God, Anna, if only you knew how dearly I love you." Far too dearly, he knew, to ever ruin her life by speaking those words out loud.

As the night progressed the temperature dropped steadily and a heavy mist enveloped the *Angelina* in a damp shroud. From under the cover of the dense fog a ship suddenly emerged, a three-masted frigate in full sail. It bore down upon the sleek schooner with a deadly grace, coming along side with more than a dozen guns firing in thunderous bursts of flame. The first volley shredded the sails on the *Angelina*'s forward mast, sending the heavy canvas crashing down upon the deck spreading burning embers in hellish profusion.

Anna leapt from her bed, terrified by the sudden explosions which rocked the ship. She grabbed for her clothes, donning them quickly, ready to take up arms herself.

Phillip cursed loudly as he rolled from his bunk. He'd slept in his clothes to be ready to respond instantly should the need arise but no call of alarm had been given. "Stay here, Anna. No matter what happens, do not open that door!"

"No, I'm coming with you. I can fight too, I'm not afraid!" The ship was listing crazily to port and she had no intention of being trapped below deck if the *Angelina* went to the bottom.

"Never!" Phillip vowed hoarsely. "I'll not rely upon a woman to defend me!" Then yanking on his boots he grabbed for the saber he'd left by the door.

Anna ran to his side, her mind focused on the most immediate danger. "If you'll not let me fight, what about John? You'll need everyone. You must set him free; he's trapped and he'll surely die if you don't release him!"

Phillip shoved her aside as he'd no time to argue with a headstrong young woman, but he quickly made his way through the smoke filled passageway to the storage compartment which served as the brig. Jamie was already there, his shirt torn and charred; he'd not yet felt the pain of his burns in his haste to see to the young man's safety. "They came from nowhere, the bloodthirsty cowards!" He had to shout to be heard above the din on deck.

"I should have heeded Anna's warning. God help us now, Jamie, for it is our own fault we are so unprepared." Turning to John he issued a terse command. "Run to my cabin and stay with Anna. She's dressed as a boy and if she is captured don't let anyone discover that she's not!" The fire in his eyes was enough to send the youth flying away, but Phillip wasted no more of his energy worrying about Anna when their situation was so desperate, their chances for survival so very slim.

Anna refused to sit meekly in Phillip's cabin while the crew of the *Angelina* fought to their deaths. She knew exactly what her fate would be should she fall into the pirates' hands and began a frantic search through Phillip's belongings for some weapon to use in her own defense. She turned as John came through the door then enlisted his aid. "We need weapons. Help me find a knife at least so I might slit a throat or two!"

John bolted the door and leaned back against it, aghast at the Swedish beauty's threatening words. The room was strewn with the captain's clothing as Anna had left no drawer unopened. "He has pistols in his desk, the bottom drawer. I'll get them." He'd no idea how to load them but to his amazement Anna did.

"Of course, I've seen him use these." The pistols were very finely crafted, their mahogany stocks inlaid with sterling silver and she lifted them carefully from their velvet-lined box. They were the ones he'd carried when he'd saved her from the highwaymen on the way to Briarcliff so she knew their aim to be true. "You take this one, aim for the heart and—"

"Lady Anna!" John's hands shook as he realized she expected him to kill a man, but he did not flinch as she showed him how to load the weapon. That she was wearing a sailor's clothes had surprised him but he did not bother to ask where she had gotten the outfit on such short notice. He looked down at his own tattered breeches which were none too clean then recalled the severity of their situation and gave no more thought to his attire. "Captain Bradford told me to wait here to protect you. Perhaps our crew will defeat these marauders and—"

Anna shot him a withering glance. The ship was still listing badly, taking on water and in danger of sinking and he expected a victory as if this were no more than a brawl being fought in some waterfront tavern rather than all-out war? "We'll be lucky to escape with our lives, John. Now look, you must shoot to kill, we have only one shot apiece and if we show the slightest hesitation these villains will kill us."

John straightened up to his full height, but he was no more than two inches taller than she. "The captain believes me capable of defending you and I do, too. I'll not fail you or him."

Impressed by his determination, Anna smiled as she gave him a warm hug. "I have missed you, my friend. Now come, we must waste no more time."

John moved to the side to block her way. "No, we must stay in here!" His words were drowned out by yet another deafening roar and Anna was swept from his arms, thrown against the door as the *Angelina* gave a fearful shudder. "Lady Anna!"

Dazed, Anna raised her hand to give herself a moment to clear her head. "Do you see now, we must go up on deck, we have no other choice if we are to survive."

Badly frightened, John lay his pistol aside as he lifted the shaken young woman to her feet. "That was too close, Anna; we'll be boarded now for certain."

"Then our only hope will be to take to the lifeboats

and there are none in here!" Anna wrenched herself free of his grasp and slipped through the door into the midst of the fight. She heard John gasping for breath as he followed closely; they were nearly suffocated by smoke by the time they reached the deck. The flames of the burning wreckage from the fallen sails licked at their ankles and leapt at their clothes engulfing them again in billows of dense smoke which stung ther eyes and choked their throats. The pirates were already swarming over the deck of the *Angelina* but paid little attention to the two, mistaking them for harmless cabin boys in their rush to quell the resistance from the more fomidable members of the ship's crew.

When John saw they had attracted no notice he led the way half-dragging half-carrying Anna to the starboard rail. The lifeboat had already been lowered to the water but he hesitated to leap over the side with the young woman in his arms for fear she might slip from his grasp and drown. They stood poised looking down at the empty boat, each trying to gauge the distance to the water when they heard Phillip call Anna's name in a desperate cry which carried in the smoke-filled wind like the scream of a banshee. He approached them slowly, blood streaming from a deep wound in his left shoulder which had turned his once-white shirt to crimson but he was still on his feet, the prospect of admitting defeat unthinkable for him still. Anna watched in horrified fascination as he came toward her. Dazed by pain he did not hear the bearded man approaching him from behind. Clad in a fine red velvet coat, black breeches and highly polished boots, the villain lacked the manners to match his elegant attire. In his right hand he held a wooden club which he swung in a slow arc, dealing Phillip a savage blow to the back of his head, knocking him to the deck where he lay sprawled in his own blood, more dead than alive. Laughing gleefully, the pirate drew back his boot to kick the fallen captain in the face, meaning to finish him off for good before claiming the *Angelina* as his own.

Coolly, Anna leveled her pistol and, using both hands to steady her aim, pulled the trigger. A look of astonishment filled the bearded man's eyes in the second before he fell dead, his bewilderment clear as he realized he'd been mortally wounded just as he'd thought triumph was within his grasp. Suddenly a second man appeared from the clouds of smoke brandishing a bloody sword only to meet the same gruesome fate as John fired a round which pierced his skull, dropping him instantly onto the bloody heap of his shipmate's body.

Rushing forward, Anna struggled to pull Phillip away from the two dead men. John came quickly to her side but stopped only to take the sword from his captain's hand. He stood ready to fiercely defend the fallen man and Anna for sounds of hand to hand combat filled the air as thickly as the ashes from the burning sails and he dared not leave them alone to seek help. He heard men calling names, the vilest of insults hurled back and forth, but could see nothing with the flames blocking his view. When another pirate came running toward them he raised his sword ready to kill again but the man slid to a halt, stricken by the sight of his dead comrades. He turned abruptly, fleeing in the direction from which he'd come. Startled by the man's unexpected retreat John turned to look back over his shoulder at Anna. "Is the captain dead?"

"No, only unconscious, but he's cut to ribbons, John, and I can do little for him here." Anna held Phillip cradled in her arms, holding him close to her heart as she tried to stem the flow of blood which oozed from the gash in the back of his head. "He didn't want us to leave, John. He was looking at me when he should have been thinking of his own safety. Dear God, please don't let him die," she prayed softly. "Please don't let him die."

"We'll not leave him behind if we must abandon ship, Lady Anna, no one would leave him behind." John wheeled as he heard footsteps approaching but the encounter ended as swiftly as the previous one with no attack coming from the pirate who gawked at the two dead bodies at the boy's feet and then fled in terror. "What can be the matter with these fools, Lady Anna?" John knew they could not be terrified of him so what had frightened them into running away? Though no more of the enemy approached them, the deck was filled with the sound of men dashing about the flames, shouting back and forth. Then as swiftly as the assault had begun it was over, the villains returning to their own vessel where they cut loose the ropes which had held the *Angelina* captive then drew away.

Jamie Jenkins finally found them, his face now bloody from numerous blows but he'd suffered no great injury. "John, my God, man, you have killed their captain and saved us all!" He stepped over the fallen man in the bright velvet coat, ready to spit in the fiend's face when he realized Anna would not admire him for so disrespectful a gesture.

"He was their captain?" John asked incredulously.

"Yes, a butcher of the worst sort from what I saw,

whatever his name," Jamie responded with a contempt-filled sneer.

"Lady Anna killed him. It was the other man I killed." John knelt beside Anna, laying the sword aside as he took Phillip's left wrist in his hand to search for a pulse. "Lady Anna deserves all the credit if the victory is ours."

Anna looked up at Jamie, a fierce gleam of vengeance lighting her golden eyes. "Are our port cannon still able to fire, Mr. Jenkins?"

"Well, yes, of course, but—"

"Then why are you standing here? Give the order to fire while the bastards are too disorganized to fight or they may return on the morrow to kill us all!"

The truth of her words was too obvious to be ignored and Jamie sprinted down the deck, dodged the flames of the still-smoldering sails and shouted orders to assemble whatever manpower he could to fire every last round they had available. Arguing amongst themselves as to whom would assume command, the surly lot aboard the frigate did not notice the *Angelina*'s change in course until her guns began to fire, ripping gaping holes in the ship's starboard side. Jamie wasted no time aiming for the masts, instead bombarding the ship's wooden hull until flames and smoke from the enemy craft obscured his view. He waited no longer to catch the wind with every last inch of sail he could raise, leaving the sinking pirate ship awash in the *Angelina*'s wake.

Chapter Sixteen

Jamie and John lifted Phillip carefully and carried him to his cabin as soon as the mate was certain the fires which had burned so furiously upon the deck were completely out. The pirates had wanted the *Angelina*'s cargo and their cannon volleys had been well aimed only to disable, not to sink the heavily laden ship. The damage to her hull was minimal and with diligent pumping she was able to hold an even trim while all the holes along her port side were filled and sealed with tar. The work went on all day, yet none of the weary crew uttered a word of complaint as they knew their own survival depended upon the soundness of their ship.

At nightfall Jamie went again to Phillip's cabin, hoping to find the captain's condition improved but there had been no change. He drew a chair up close to Phillip's bunk and gave his friend's hand a reassuring grasp. "He has not awakened even once, Lady Anna?"

"No, I have treated his wounds as best I can but the head injury is obviously the most severe. He may sleep—" biting her lower lip savagely to force away her tears, she continued bravely— "He may sleep forever."

Jamie frowned, as troubled as she by the grave nature of Phillip's injuries. "We have never had a physician on board. Phillip has always been the one with the knack for healing but he uses words of encouragement more than medicines and we have naught in our medical supplies to help him now."

Anna nodded, recalling the way Phillip had put Sophia at ease. "Yes, I understand what you mean. His manner always inspires confidence. He treated my maid most tenderly when she was ill." Anna was seated on the edge of Phillip's bunk, dressed in a soft blue gown with her glowing curls falling loosely about her shoulders. It was her effort at giving the appearance of calm even though she had grown increasingly anxious as the hours passed without her patient having regained consciousness. "John seems to be very good though. Today I watched him bandage many a wound I could not have touched myself. There does not seem to be one of the men who was unhurt except for him, but thank God none were killed."

"I did not take you for the squeamish sort, Lady Anna. You and John worked so swiftly to tend all the injured I did not realize the sight of blood bothered you in the slightest. Would you rather I stay here with Phillip tonight? You have worked as hard as the rest of us and deserve some rest. You may use the spare bunk in my cabin if you like," Jamie offered with a charming grin. He ached all over but considered his burns and bruises slight injuries compared to the captain's.

Anna combed the thick curls away from Phillip's

288

forehead and laid her palm against his bronze skin. "He is not feverish or delirious, just so deeply asleep I have not tried to awaken him. Thank you for your offer of help but I will stay with him myself since I brought this misfortune to the *Angelina* and can never make up for his pain."

The concern which filled the blond beauty's delicate features brought a quick argument from Jamie. "No voyage is without its own dangers. You gave us a clear warning when you were on watch two nights ago. Phillip was skeptical of your report but I was the fool who completely disregarded it. I thought we were prepared to face any emergency which might confront us but an attack at dawn found us woefully unready to defend ourselves. Had you not killed their captain—"

"Mr. Jenkins, please. Were I not on board you would be enjoying yourself in some tavern in Philadelphia this very night, not sitting here trying to take the blame for this tragedy."

"I'll not let you assume that blame either, dear lady," Jamie insisted firmly as he rose wearily to his feet. "Phillip has not been unconscious long, less than a day. Tomorrow he may awaken to complain of no more than a severe headache."

Anna was not nearly so optimistic. "Let us pray that is true." She bid the mate goodnight but did not move from her place at Phillip's side. Not one of his crew who was able to walk had failed to come to his cabin to ask about their captain's condition. Each had spoken only the highest praise for the young man they served and it had soon become clear to Anna Phillip's courage in the face of even impossible odds had been the key to the pirates' defeat. A band of ruffians of the rudest sort, they had been eager for what they thought would be easy spoils. They had had only their own insatiable greed to inspire them while the crew of the *Angelina* was one bound by mutual trust and respect. They would have fought to the last man while the cowardly seagoing bandits had fled the moment they realized their leader had been slain.

Anna caressed Phillip's cheek fondly. He'd had no time to shave that morning but the slight growth of his beard scarcely marred his attractive appearance and she leaned down to kiss his lips lightly. He'd apparently fought off several knife-wielding attackers at close range for in addition to the deep gash in his shoulder his arms were slashed in half a dozen places. She'd bound his wounds after carefully cleansing them and hoped they would heal rapidly and leave only slight scars. That he had such obvious courage and then had been clubbed from behind as he'd called to her pained her greatly for no matter what Jamie had tried to make her believe she knew she was responsible for the *Angelina* being in such southern waters and therefore was to blame for the attack.

Concerned that Phillip rest as comfortably as possible she lifted the sheet which covered him and folded it back to check the linen bandage on his shoulder. It was unstained, spotless still although she knew he'd lost a considerable amount of blood before she'd begun to tend him. When John had helped her to undress the handsome young man she'd not felt the slightest bit of embarrassment as they'd stripped away his clothing. His breeches had been drenched with blood and John had simply placed a towel over his loins since they'd not wished to put him into his bed wearing such gory

290

attire. She smiled now as she thought of it. Both she and John had been so worried about Phillip neither had thought their task improper but she knew the young man had no idea she'd seen Phillip completely undressed before. That passion-filled afternoon seemed far distant but she could not bear to think he would not recover fully when he was so fine a man and had deserved none of the terrible abuse he'd suffered that day. He had a powerful build, his torso well-muscled and firm from years of strenuous labor and she let her fingertips comb the dark curls which covered his broad chest with a lazy caress. His skin was warm, alive despite his deep sleep and instantly she remembered the night she'd awakened to find him covering her body with light kisses. She would have made any promise to have convinced him to stay with her then, yet she had not dreamed the bargain they'd made would be so difficult to keep. Her commitment to Charles would stand between them for all time it seemed, yet her father's promise held scant meaning with Phillip so near death.

Phillip might have no more than a few hours left to live but Anna wanted to share those precious moments as closely as she could. Crossing the cabin quickly, she bolted the door then doused the lamp before slipping off her dress and slips and tossing them upon her trunk. Clad only in a creamy silk chemise she lay down beside Phillip and drew him into her arms, covering them both with his thick woolen blankets as she pressed her slender body along the length of his. She wanted only to hold him close, to pretend for a few brief hours that he loved her as deeply as she'd come to love him. In the morning she prayed that by some miracle he would awaken; he could be as mean to her as he wished and she'd not fault him for it. With a small contented sigh she snuggled closer still and in a moment was sound asleep, exhausted by the gruesome ordeal she'd survived that day, but even in her dreams her arms remained tightly clasped around the man she loved.

As the bells tolled the beginning of the midnight watch, Phillip felt little other than the agonizing pain which filled his whole being with anguish. For one dreadful moment he was certain he'd died and had been cast into the fires of hell but as he grew more fully awake that impression faded as the pain in his head lessened to a dull throb. He tried to shift his position slightly but found his way blocked by the warmth of a supple form he recognized instantly as Anna's. He tried to remember what had happened to him and how he'd come to be in such misery. He'd fought off one burly pirate only to find three more waiting to take their turns at killing him but somehow he'd managed to survive their best efforts to hack him to tiny bits with their blades. Then in his mind's eye he saw Anna at the rail, John coaxing her to jump and he could hear himself shout. He'd wanted to stop her for surely she'd drown or be lost in the vastness of the sea if he didn't make her stay with him where she belonged. When she'd turned to look at him the fright in her eyes had been for him, not herself and he'd wanted only to take her in his arms and protect her from the filthy villains who swarmed over the *Angelina* like a plague of locusts. But he'd not been able to reach her, someone had stopped him before he'd reached her side and he was overcome with sadness as he realized how greatly he must have failed her. He nuzzled her soft curls, breathing in the delicate perfume of her warm young body with a hunger he saw no reason to deny. He'd come too close to death that day to restrain the desire which blazed within him with a heat greater than the flames he'd braved on the *Angelina*'s deck. He moved slowly so as not to cause himself any more pain as he pinned the fair beauty beneath him and buried his face in her luxuriant curls. He had never wanted any woman more than he continually wanted her, and he meant to have her again before she could slip from his grasp.

Anna lifted her arms to encircle Phillip's neck as his kisses aroused her from her slumber. She was delighted to find him in so affectionate a mood and returned his teasing kisses with unabashed abandon. She wanted only to ask where he'd found such strength when she'd been afraid he might never awaken, but he gave her no opportunity to speak at all as he wound his fingers in her curls and deepened his kiss. She'd climbed into his bunk with no thought of the consequences should he awaken to find her draped around him as snugly as his blankets, but his loving was all she'd truly wanted that night. He shifted slightly then, still cradling her in his arms as he began to slowly trail the lightest of kisses down the elegant curve of her throat, savoring the silken softness of her creamy skin before he peeled away her chemise and lowered his mouth to the smooth swell of her breast. With one quick tug he managed to remove the only garment she wore and he tossed it carelessly over his shoulder so no barrier remained between them.

Anna tried to hold him gently. Though she longed to

slip her fingers through his dark curls to press him close to her heart, she dared not for fear she'd cause him pain. His kiss was so enticing, teasing and sweet, she relaxed against him as he ran his hand along her side tracing her shapely curves before drawing her hips against his own. "Phillip," Anna whispered seductively. While she enjoyed his delectable kisses, she wanted the promises he never gave. Yet she dared not speak of love herself when she knew he'd only laugh at her unwanted devotion. She had called his name, softly, hoping only to inspire him to say something sweet in return.

Having no wish to converse on any subject, Phillip took her hands firmly by the wrists to press her back against the pillow. "You're mine, Anna. You've always been mine and you know it as well as I do. Now hush!"

"Hush?" Anna asked softly. "Is that all you wish to say to me?" She held her breath praying he'd speak the words of love she longed to hear but he simply lowered his mouth to hers, smothering her complaint in a lingering kiss that filled her slender body with desire and drove all thought of protest from her mind as he drew her passionate spirit to a peak which quickly matched his own. She clung to him then, wanting all he could give of the pleasure which flooded her veins with a pounding ecstasy that left her graceful body his to claim, pliant and warm. She welcomed his increasingly intimate touch with a tantalizing caress of her own, driving him past all restraint. He moved swiftly to end her play with the ultimate act of love.

The cabin was as dark as the depths of the sea, while the *Angelina*'s gentle motion followed the undulating currents which guided her upon her way, that easy rhythm a sharp contrast to Phillip's powerful grace. He had again conquered Anna's defiant spirit but he sought to capture her very soul, to bind her life to his for all time. He was lost in pleasure, plunged to its depths, captivated by the same joy she always gave and he did not release her even when his passion was fully spent and his thoughts again turned rational. He held her locked in his arms kissing her flushed cheeks softly as he whispered, "My dearest Anna, paradise can not be more enjoyable than your love."

Although his manner was loving, Anna felt only betrayed. It had not been rape. She could never accuse him of that when her weakness for him was so very great, but he had again taken every advantage of the love she felt for him without offering anything in return. "I am happy if I have pleased you at last, but I'll thank you not to refer to me as 'yours' as though I were no more than an article of clothing or some piece of furniture. Besides, we both know if any man has the right to call me his it is Lord Clairbourne and not you."

"What?" Phillip grasped Anna's shoulders firmly and gave her a sound shake. "How can you believe I'd still let you marry him? How can you believe that of me?" That their destinies were inseparably interwoven suddenly seemed so clear to him he was furious with her lack of insight although he'd always gone to great lengths to conceal his true feelings from her. "How many times must I make love to you before you'll understand I mean to keep you for my own? Tell me and I will start counting, a hundred times, a thousand? What is it you need before you'll see what is so obvious to me? What must I do to convince you you'll always belong to me, only to me!" Since that truth escaped her while she lay in his bed he did not know what it would take to convince her to whom she now belonged.

Startled by his unexpected anger Anna nonetheless persisted, "Since you have always made it plain you do not believe in love, should I consider that an offer to provide for me as a man usually cares for his mistress rather than a proposal of marriage?" She was so confused she had no idea how he might reply.

Phillip had always known only one choice was possible with a lady so fine as Anna. He would have to offer marriage for anything else would be an insult she'd surely refuse. "I want you for my wife, my beloved. If this proposal is poorly timed and most awkwardly delivered please forgive me for with you in my arms I can think only of making love."

With a squeal of delighted surprise, Anna wrapped her arms around his neck and returned his deep kiss with a slow, luscious slip of her tongue which explored his warm mouth with a taunting laziness before she released him. "I know exactly when I fell in love with you, it was when I went to your cabin to apologize for my behavior when we were on our way to England. You were soaking wet from the storm but you were so sweet to me that I simply couldn't resist you. You'll never know how dreadful it's been for me to think I'd have to marry Charles when I love you so dearly."

"Believe me, Anna, I know exactly what torture you've suffered, now hush," Phillip whispered softly for he'd never reveal how long ago he had fallen in love with her. He kissed her again and again, this time intent upon giving her the greatest of pleasures. His touch was knowing, sure, cupping her full breast

296

lightly before his hand slid over the flatness of her stomach then moved slowly through the triangle of blond curls between her thighs. He thought only of pleasing her again as he'd never bothered to please another woman. With a sharp stab of guilt he realized he could not even count let alone name the many women with whom he'd slept, but he'd loved none of them, had forgotten each as the darkness is forgotten with the break of dawn. Why had the words been so impossible to speak when he wanted to yell them at the top of his lungs? "I love you, Anna, I love you so." The blood coursing through his veins drowned out the sound of his own voice in his ears but he knew she'd heard him. God how he loved her and with a strength close to violence he took her again, swiftly sealing his proposal of marriage with a desperate grace for he could not bear to think how close his pride had taken him to losing her forever.

The darkness enveloped Anna in a liquid warmth but she wished only that it were noon and the cabin flooded with the brightest sunlight so she might see Phillip's joy as well as feel it. She held him tightly, her fingertips moving down the rippling muscles of his back before sliding over his narrow hips with a slow, tender touch. She could not seem to get close enough to him even though there was not an inch of space or shred of cloth to separate them. The confusion which had plagued her mind in the past weeks was gone, replaced by a happiness so precious she dared not give it a name. But she was certain no woman had ever loved a man more than she loved Phillip. She loved his strength as well as his tenderness. His loving was exquisite, eager acceptance, delicious warmth, an excitement so spontaneous and delightful she wanted it to last forever. His love was the most magnificent of gifts, one she planned to savor with undying devotion but his lips were too hungry for hers to allow her to make such a sweet promise in words. She answered instead with her lissome body, welcoming his with an undisguised pleasure which lured him deeper and deeper into the very essence of love.

When Phillip at last lay sleeping in her embrace, Anna could not bear to rest with the precious memory of his words of love so new in her heart. Her slender fingers combed through the tangled curls at his temple with a fondness she no longer had to hide, for if she were to be his wife then he would be her husband, the dearest of husbands she knew instinctively now that each had revealed the truth of their emotions to the other. His love had brought a rapture beyond her dreams and she could not stop smiling as she hugged him once again. That a night filled with the splendor of love had followed a day of such horror astonished her but she could not wait for the dawn, for to see Phillip smile as he spoke of loving her and what their life together would be would bring a glimpse of paradise and almost indescribable joy.

Phillip awakened slowly, the layers of contentment peeling away so gradually he could not tell where his dreams left off and consciousness began anew. He heard Anna singing softly to herself as she moved about his cabin and readily understood her happiness for he felt elated still, but as he tried to sit up a sharp burst of pain sliced through his brain with the precision of a steel blade and he had to lie back, stunned by the sudden agony which had been so unexpected. He had difficulty catching his breath and called hoarsely, "Would you bring me some water please?"

Anna rushed to his side, for he'd slept long past the time she'd expected him to wake; it was nearly noon. When he did not sit up she slipped her arm under his head to lift his lips to the cup. "There you are. I know you were feeling very well last night, How do you feel now?"

Phillip sipped the water slowly then took several deep breaths before lying back down. "Is it morning yet, Anna?"

"Why, of course it is morning, past that really but you know well enough how your cabin looks when the sun fills it with light." She sat down beside him and reached for his hand, lacing her fingers tightly in his. "What difference does the hour make? You must rest for several days at least before you try to return to your usual schedule. Jamie is supervising the repairs with the men who are able to work. He was here this morning to see you but we didn't want to wake you when you were sleeping so soundly."

Phillip tried to listen attentively as Anna described the previous day's casualties. He was grateful no men had been lost but was pained to hear several would need a long rest before they returned to their duties. He lay very still, waiting for his vision to clear but he could not seem to make his eyes focus on her face. He could see her golden hair, the creamy peach tones of her fair skin, but could not discern her pretty features. Although he did not want to frighten her, he could not hide his own anxiety from her perceptive gaze.

"What's wrong?" Anna brought his hand to her lips and kissed his bruised knuckles tenderly. "Would you like me to call Jamie so you might speak with him yourself?"

"I can't see, Anna. As close as you are to me I can't see your face clearly." There was no way he could lie about what had happened to him and he saw no reason to try.

Anna leaned down, peering into the blue of his eyes as if she could see what the matter might be and remedy it. "Do you see nothing at all, Phillip, just darkness? Or am I simply blurry, hazy as if your cabin were filled with a heavy mist?"

Shocked by the accuracy of her description, Phillip nodded before he thought to consider his headache and the pain returned to torment him anew. When he could again draw a breath he replied slowly, "Misty, that's the way you look, as if we were on deck in a dense fog."

"I understand, I should have expected this considering how severely you were beaten yesterday. I saw the man hit you. He swung a club with the full force of his strength. That the blow should have affected your vision somewhat isn't surprising."

"Anna," Phillip scolded crossly. "I am no better than blind, can't you understand that!"

Anna placed her palms on his shoulders to make him lay back and listen. "I am sure it is not permanent, Phillip. We had a groom once who struck his head upon a rock when he fell from a horse and he experienced the same difficulty with his sight for several days but eventually he could see as well as he ever had. Please don't worry so over this, I know it won't last," Anna reassured him calmly. She had wanted to speak of their future, of love, but that Phillip should be blind for even a short while appalled her and she was far

300

more frightened than she would let him suspect.

Never a coward, Phillip took a deep breath and let it out slowly. "Don't tell anyone about this yet, Anna. Not even Jamie must know what has happened to me."

"But Jamie is your best friend, he'd not disappoint you in any way. Surely you know he can be trusted with any secret."

"No! Tell him nothing about this or anything else!" Phillip commanded sharply.

"Oh, I see. What you asked me last night is to be forgotten, is that it?" Anna asked pointedly, not about to let him forget the love they'd promised to share forever. Forever, she thought bitterly, forever to him apparently did not mean more than one night.

"I'll not force you to marry me if I'm blind, Anna. I'd never do that. Now just go away, leave me alone for a while." Phillip turned his face away and closed his eyes, sick that fate had played him so cruel a trick as to have allowed him to propose to the only woman he'd ever loved and then to have stolen his sight when she'd accepted. Dear God, he thought to himself, how could he possibly provide for Anna if he could not see the stars to navigate or read his charts to find his way?

"Phillip, don't you dare even think that! What if I had been the one who'd been hurt? What if I were blind today, would you love me any less? Would you throw away whatever chance we have for finding happiness together if I were the one who could not see?"

Phillip's mouth was set in an angry line as he made no reply; her question was ridiculous in the extreme. Were she both blind and deaf he would never stop loving her. If she could not walk he would spend his life carrying her wherever she wished to go, but he could not bear to think of her devoting her life to caring for him if he were truly blind. She'd stay with him out of pity of course. He knew she would never ask to be set free and he could not stand the thought of her languishing at the side of an invalid for the rest of her life. "Leave me alone, Anna."

Anna started to argue, then thought better of it. "I will be happy to since your mood is so foul, but first I must change the bandage on your shoulder. Do you think you could sit up?"

"Oh God," Phillip moaned softly, but he gave it a try and struggled to a sitting position. The excruciating pain again tore through his head and sliced down his neck but he paid it scant heed. "Just give me a moment and I'll move over to a chair."

He had paled noticeably as he sat up and Anna was certain he'd probably faint if he tried to walk alone. "Please let me help. While you're up I think I'll change the linens on your bed so you'll be able to rest more comfortably. Here, wrap this blanket around yourself so you won't get chilled." Anna then slipped her arms around him and led him over to the chair he usually used and saw he was comfortably seated.

"It was not getting chilled which concerned me, Anna," Phillip teased with little humor. He laid his arms upon the table and rested his head upon them, his whole pose as dejected as he felt.

"You are the handsomest man ever born, Phillip, and you needn't be embarrassed with me, for it is far too late for such modesty between us now," she offered sensibly. Although she longed to stay with him she knew he'd reject any display of affection as unwanted sympathy and so left his side to take clean linens from their drawer beneath his bunk. She quickly ripped the rumpled sheets from his bed and tossed them in a heap by the door. "I'll tell Jamie you're awake but feeling poorly which you obviously are; he'll be so happy to speak with you again he'll not notice anything's amiss if you don't tell him."

"Just see that you don't either, Anna," Phillip cautioned sternly. "How many days did I miss, only one?"

"Yes, we did not even try to wake you yesterday for fear of increasing your pain." Anna tucked in the corners of the sheets then spread the blankets over the bunk to finish her task neatly before turning back to him. "The wound in your shoulder is deep. I really must be certain it's begun to heal properly." She had not bothered to bandage his head for she knew that while scalp wounds might bleed profusely they healed rapidly.

Phillip raked his hand through his dark curls as he sat back in his chair. "Go ahead, do whatever you must but be quick about it because I don't think I can sit here much longer."

"If you're not well please come back to your bed and I can do it here," Anna offered helpfully.

"You better call Jamie, Anna. I can't even stand up, let alone walk on my own." The tiredness in his voice gave his words the clear ring of truth; he wasn't asking for sympathy, just stating a fact in plain language.

Anna wasted no time calling for the mate but went to his side herself. "It is no wonder you're ill, my darling, but I can help you back to bed if you'll let me."

"No!" Phillip shouted as he shoved her away rudely. "I don't need you!" He had never felt more wretched, sick to his stomach, his head splitting with

303

pain and his heart ripped to shreds with the same agony he knew he was causing her. "It is better to end it now, Anna, than to continue to pretend we can ever be man and wife if I'm blind."

Shaken by his bitterness, Anna nonetheless straightened her shoulders with a determined gesture as she replied. "It is pointless to debate that issue today, we can discuss our wedding plans in a week or two when you've regained your strength, but not today." She peeled away the layers of linen she'd so carefully wrapped around his shoulder and found only the topmost clean. The gash was still oozing bright red blood but she forced herself to lie for his sake. "It's bleeding slightly. I'll just have to bind it more tightly this time."

Phillip could feel the warm liquid trickle down his chest and disagreed. "You should have cauterized it while I couldn't feel anything. It will hurt like the devil to do it now."

Anna's stomach lurched sharply and she gripped the back of his chair to force away the nausea his suggestion brought. "I'll not burn you, Phillip, I won't do it." She'd seen that done, a blade heated in the fire until it was red hot would sear a wound and stop the bleeding, but the stench of burning flesh was enough to make not only the patient pass out but the physician as well from what she'd witnessed. "I'd never do that to you."

"Perhaps you're right. Bleeding to death here in my cabin will at least be swift, not the endless torture blindness will be."

"Stop it! You're not the type of man to enjoy such self-pity and I certainly don't want to hear it!" Anna had the fresh bandages close at hand and went to work on his torn shoulder immediately. "It is no wonder

304

you're bleeding with the way you behaved last night but as you said you had only one thought on your mind and I'll certainly not fault you since I was the cause of it. I know I am wrapping this tightly and it will be uncomfortable but you're the only husband I'll ever have and I've no intention of allowing you to bleed to death before we can be married!''

Phillip tried to laugh for her words were so hilariously funny, but he found the effort exhausting and could do no more than smile. The cabin seemed to tilt suddenly, making him so dizzy he nearly slid from his chair but Anna caught him, bracing his body against her own as she finished binding the gruesome wound, then used her fingertips to apply additional pressure. The mist before his eyes went from gray to red as he fainted but she held him in her arms until Jamie arrived and could carry him back to his freshly made up bunk and the peaceful oblivion of sleep once more.

Chapter Seventeen

Anna sat beside Phillip, slowly spoon feeding him a nourishing broth while Jamie paced up and down the cabin gesturing for emphasis as he recounted the pirates' attack. He and the crew had been discussing little else for two days and the tale had grown increasingly more dramatic with each retelling.

"I have never seen such chaos! The smoke was so thick you could not tell if the man by your side were friend or foe but—"

"We did not lose the cargo in the forward hold though?" Phillip asked impatiently, clearly tired of hearing about the battle when the problems they now faced were no less acute. He'd slept for almost five hours after passing out in Anna's arms but he was still so tired he could scarcely swallow the soup she seemed determined to feed him. That Jamie was in so talkative a mood only presented another aggravation he'd sooner miss.

"No, the cargo was unharmed. We sustained some damage to the deck and lost many yards of canvas but stop interrupting me, I was just getting to the most exciting part!" Turning rapidly Jamie continued his pacing as he gave his report the embellishment of a tall tale. "Their captain was a wild-eyed fellow, bearded and fierce in both his appearance and manner but he made the mistake of disregarding the threat Anna posed to his safety. Why he never even glanced her way and—"

Embarrassed by Jamie's vivid description of an event he had not even witnessed, Anna interrupted him with a lilting giggle. "Mr. Jenkins, please, you were not with us, how do you know he didn't regard me with the greatest of trepidations?"

"What is he talking about, Anna. Did the brute harm you in some way?" Phillip looked up at her, his expression pained although his clear blue eyes saw little.

"Did she not tell you herself?" Jamie exclaimed in disbelief. "Anna killed the fiend before he could finish you off, my friend, shot him dead and when his first mate came running to see what had happened John put a quick end to his villainy too. There they were, those two looking so innocent and dead bodies littered all around them!" He'd not mention that Phillip's injuries had added to the horror of that ghastly scene too.

"Is that true, Anna?" Phillip tried to remember. She and John had been standing at the rail as he approached, he'd not noticed they were armed, but how could they have been? "Where did you and John get weapons?"

"From your desk. The pistols are beauties; I cleaned them and put them away where you'd kept them while you slept yesterday morning." She had welcomed the

307

distraction when he'd lain so still she'd had to listen closely to be certain he'd still been breathing.

Phillip shut his eyes tightly to force away the gory scene his imagination painted with brilliant colors in his mind. He'd wanted to save Anna from harm, that had been his only thought, to reach Anna and protect her. Not only had he failed miserably in that effort but she'd managed to kill the man who'd nearly killed him and had turned the tide of the battle in their favor. It was clear she didn't need his help to survive when she was so formidable an adversary in her own right.

"Phillip?" Anna touched his cheek lightly with her fingertips. "The battle is better left forgotten, you must eat to grow strong again. The wound in your shoulder is no longer bleeding but you really must finish this soup to regain your strength. I'll send Jamie away if speaking with him is too great a strain on you.'

"Have you assumed command of the *Angelina*, Anna?" Phillip snarled sarcastically. He'd never had less appetite and didn't care at all about getting well but dutifully opened his mouth when she brought the spoon to his lips knowing it would take less energy to eat than to argue.

"She'd make a fine captain, sir. It was her idea to fire on the pirates before they were out of our range. Blew them right out of the water, we did, too. That ship will no longer keep honest men from making a fair profit in these waters. Sunk she was, along with her whole filthy crew."

Phillip groaned in frustration. "Didn't you have sense enough to fire on the vessel yourself without waiting for Lady Thorson to give that order? Damn! I might as well have her for my mate if she has so much

308

more sense than you!"

Jamie laughed at his captain's anger. "She is much prettier to look at too!"

Anna knew better than to tease Phillip even if Jamie did not and hastened to end the play. "I think you better go now, Mr. Jenkins. Tomorrow there will be plenty of time for you two to plan strategy and discuss the repairs which still must be made."

Jamie looked down at his friend. Phillip was perhaps a bit pale but that was understandable. He had never approved of Anna's sharing his quarters though and thought perhaps this might be a good time to change that arrangement. "I have not sent John back to the brig, sir. With so many injured he is needed too badly. Since he fought so well I think you might pardon his crime and let us all get on with the voyage. There's no need to make Lady Anna work in the galley now either." Gathering all his courage, Jamie completed his speech. "I think she should take my cabin again as it is most improper for her to share yours."

Phillip waited for Anna to disagree and when she did not speak he had no way of knowing what she might be thinking since he could not see her face well enough to read her expression. He had no choice really; he needed her help if he were to continue to fool the others. "No, Anna must stay here for the time being. She is a fine nurse and I, well, I need her still."

Knowing how much that admission had cost him, Anna smiled widely as she turned toward Jamie. "Please do not continue to concern yourself with my welfare, Mr. Jenkins, for I am most comfortable here. Now I think you really should leave and let Phillip get some more rest."

Scowling unhappily Jamie turned toward the door. "Well, I've said what I wanted to and if neither of you sees the danger in your living arrangements I have no choice but to drop the subject and go!"

Anna waited until the mate had closed the cabin door before she spoke. "You see, he did not even suspect anything is wrong although I really don't think you should try and continue to fool him."

Phillip was tempted to sit up and simply throttle the feisty blonde but knew the agonizing pain which would return to his head wouldn't be worth it. "I am tired, Anna. Go up on deck if you like, I'll be all right here by myself."

Laying the now-empty bowl and spoon aside, Anna reached for his hands and took them firmly in her own. "Please don't be so discouraged, Phillip, your blindness won't last. But even if it did it would make no difference to me, I would love you still."

"It is not a question of love, Anna, but of what is best for you." Phillip drew her hands to his lips and kissed them tenderly. "I want only the very best for you and a blind man could never provide it."

Even though his tone was reasonable, Anna knew his thinking was not. "Why do you continually tell me that you know what is best for me? I love you and you don't seem to have the vaguest understanding of what that truly means. What is best for me is simply to be with you! All I will ever need to be happy is your loving and you can still provide that very well."

Phillip shook his head slowly. "Don't tempt me for I don't feel nearly as well as I did last night." He hoped she'd respond to teasing since the tremendous obstacle his lack of vision presented escaped her so completely.

Maybe that was the secret. He'd simply take each day as it came, refusing to make any plans for the future which included her and eventually she'd accept his decision as the best for both of them and be grateful for it.

Anna leaned down to brush his lips lightly with hers. "I did not mean to tire you. I chased Jamie away so you could rest. Go to sleep and I'll see you in the morning."

"I wish I could say that with such confidence." Phillip pulled the blankets up to his chin and turned away. He was exhausted and hoped she'd think him already asleep and leave him alone.

Perplexed by his melancholy goodnight, Anna touched his dark curls with a gentle pat then returned his bowl and spoon to the galley. The night was so crisp and clear she strolled around the deck then leaned against the starboard rail to enjoy the sight of the stars, forgetting her problems for a while in the beauty of the night. When John came to her side she smiled fondly. "Jamie has you hard at work again it seems."

"Yes, Mr. Jenkins told me Captain Bradford did not object but I will not believe it until he tells me so himself." The young man leaned back against the rail, his pose a relaxed and confident one. The fact he'd suddenly become one of the strongest members of the crew had done wonders for his self-esteem.

"It is true for I heard their conversation and the captain was not displeased that you have returned to your former duties." At least he'd made no such comment and she couldn't believe he'd send John back to the brig after Jamie had let him have his freedom again. "It will be a while before Phillip is strong enough to work so you had best believe what Mr. Jenkins tells you while he is in command."

"The captain is all right though, isn't he?" John asked anxiously.

"Yes, he will recover fully from his injuries, I'm sure of it. All he needs is time to rest and regain his strength."

John stood by her side, silent for a long while as they did no more than watch the moonlight's sparkle upon the water. Then gathering all his courage he began to apologize. "The night the captain found us together, well, what I am trying to say is, I never should have tried to force myself upon you, to . . ."

Anna lifted her hand to his shoulder to reassure him, "We are friends still, John, you need never mention that night again for nothing happened for which you must be sorry. I know how much you like me and we are friends still, aren't we?"

"Is such a thing possible, Lady Anna? I am no more than a cook's helper and you will soon be a nobleman's bride."

Startled by that prediction, Anna drew away. "No, we are simply a young man and young woman who are friends, no more than that, John. Now please excuse me, I must see if the captain is resting comfortably." She left him where he stood and hurried to Phillip's cabin hoping he'd still be awake. But he was breathing deeply, sound asleep, and she'd not wake him to make him listen to her foolish fears. She considered her engagement to Lord Clairbourne a thing of the past and wanted his reassurance that he did as well.

In the following days Phillip was polite whenever he spoke to Anna, painfully proper; he made not the slightest demand upon her time and never failed to thank her when she performed some small service for him. When he felt well enough to leave his bunk he walked around his cabin for long stretches during the morning and afternoon but did not go up on deck for fear he'd trip over a coiled line of rope or someone's else's feet. It was the clumsiness he couldn't stand; it had been a week since the pirates' attack and he could still not see his own hand in front of his face. "It's not going to happen as you keep insisting it will, Anna. My vision is never going to be any better than it is this very minute. It is useless to hope that it will improve!" He took hold of the back of one of the chairs at his table and flexed the muscles in his arms until his shoulder began to ache painfully and he had to stop.

Anna was tired of offering encouragement when Phillip reacted to every kindness as though it were an insult. He was a difficult man on the best of days, when he was so depressed she had no hope of raising his spirits. She'd not wanted to return to his bed when he was so miserable. She'd waited instead for him to invite her to share his nights as he'd asked her to share his life but he was behaving as if he had never proposed and she had not wanted to question him when he was so preoccupied with his own problems. Her life seemed continually in turmoil regardless of her best efforts to make her existence a happy one. Nothing was going right and she was exhausted with her attempts to please Phillip, to keep him amused and his mind filled with optimism. "What is the very worst that could happen, Phillip? You own the *Angelina*, or you will at the end of this voyage. You will still have the income her cargos bring even if you have to rely upon another to be her captain."

"What sort of life would that be for me? I am not some fat old merchant who enjoys counting his gold! I would go mad in a week if I were forced to stay in port while the *Angelina* sailed under another man's command!"

She'd just changed the bandage on his shoulder and he'd not bothered to put on his shirt. He stood there clad only in his tight-fitting pants and boots, his skin as deeply tanned as any pirate's and the look in his blue eyes twice as wild. He still wouldn't trust her with his razor, so had been forced to let his beard grow but she thought it enhanced his well-defined features rather than detracting from them. She could not look at him without thinking how strong and handsome he looked, and how dearly she loved him. Her voice teased his ears softly as she asked, "Where had you planned for me to live, Phillip? Did you not plan to make a home with me somewhere?"

Phillip turned his back on her, unable to admit he'd made no plans at all since he'd lost his sight. "Will you please call Jamie for me, I want to speak to him about a matter I've just remembered."

"Of course, I'll be happy to call him, but you'll not answer my question before I go?" Anna held her breath, praying he'd give her some small hope that their future could still be a happy one they'd spend together.

"I'll not lie to you, Anna, and nothing I'd like to promise you now will ever come true. Just go get Jamie for me. That's all I want from you right now."

"Yes, Captain," Anna replied coolly as she slipped out his door. She'd not give up her dreams regardless of what he said but why couldn't he see his blindness was

314

her problem too, their burden to share, not a hardship that he had to suffer alone as if she did not love him and want so badly to make him happy.

Jamie had learned all Phillip had attempted to teach him in their numerous voyages together and was enjoying his time in command enormously. He stood at attention, delivering his report with what he hoped was both efficiency and wit. "With the damage we sustained I can not rig the ship fully so our time is far less swift than we were making but we should reach Jamaica within a week. We'll approach the island from the north, then we can drop anchor near the mouth of the Rio Bueno without arousing the notice of the British authorities in Port Royal, escort Lady Thorson to Lord Clairbourne's plantation, then weigh anchor and be gone all in a day's time."

Anna looked from one man to the other. It was her life they were so calmly discussing as if she were not even present and it was all she could do not to scream at them to stop. She'd not marry Clairbourne, knew in her heart she never would have married him even if he had been at Briarcliff waiting for her to arrive as she'd expected him to be. She wanted to see him though, to meet him and refuse his proposal in person, not in a letter or spoken message for that would be too cruel. "Gentlemen, I wonder if I might not interrupt for a moment?"

Phillip raised his hand in a forceful gesture. "Let us finish please, Anna." He was seated on the edge of his bunk, using the excuse of another severe headache to avoid looking at the charts Jamie had laid upon the table. "Your plan is a fine one, Jamie, but I'll not risk taking Lady Thorson to Charles when the ship is still not fully repaired. There are many islands on my charts, lands with fresh water and no inhabitants. Choose any you like and set the *Angelina*'s course for it now as I want my ship in top form before we enter Jamaican waters. The British are far worse than pirates when it comes to confiscating cargo and taking prisoners whom they'll insist are their own citizens who've deserted the Royal Navy.''

"That's why I planned to make our visit to Jamaica so brief, but stopping en route at an island would give us all time to rest as well as to make repairs." Jamie studied the charts with great care, the Caribbean was filled with islands but to choose one which also served as home port to a gang of pirates would be a calamity he wished to avoid at all costs. "Let us just continue on our course and investigate the first land we sight, for I too would like to know we can outrun any who might wish to stop us."

Anna strolled over to Phillip's desk while the men continued to discuss their plans. Jamie had written in the ship's log each day that Phillip had been ill and she supposed he'd want to do so again since he was there now. She opened the leather-bound journal and thumbed through it to pass the time, looking back for the pages Phillip had written himself. His notations were brief, comments on wind and sea conditions, course headings; it was not the content of the book which enthralled her but the neatly penned words. She recognized the handwriting immediately and felt faint, sick with the knowledge of how Phillip had tricked her. She went quickly to her trunk, slipping her hand along the side to the pocket where she'd placed Charles's letter.

Phillip frowned as he looked up. He could hear Anna rummaging through her trunk if not see her and could not imagine why she wished to change her clothing at that precise moment. "What are you doing, Anna? Couldn't you go up on deck if you find our conversation so uninteresting?"

"You two never bore me, Phillip, not in the slightest!" Anna insisted as she carried the single page over to the ship's log. She had not been mistaken, the writing was Phillip's all right, unmistakably his and she sank down into one of the chairs at his table, too angry to cry. But the second Jamie left them alone she rose to her feet and went to Phillip's side. "Why did you do this to me, why? I thought Charles had truly been concerned about me and it was no more than a joke of yours! How dare you lie to me! Is that all it's ever been between us, nothing but lies?"

Mystified by her hysterical outburst Phillip got to his feet and faced her squarely. He could make out her golden hair, it was a bright spot in the mist which swam before his eyes but he didn't need to see her face clearly to understand her mood. "I have no idea what it is you're complaining about, Anna. Can't you be more specific so I would at least know why you're yelling at me so loudly?"

"Oh!" Anna waved the letter furiously. "You wrote this letter you gave me yourself! Charles left no letter at Briarcliff for me so you wrote one yourself! Don't bother to deny it either because your handwriting is too distinctive for his to match yours so exactly by coincidence." Anna was livid, trembling with rage. The man had tricked her most cruelly and she hated him for it.

Phillip shrugged. He'd loved her even then, not

317

wanted her to be disappointed and so had seen to it that she wasn't. "I won't deny that I wrote it. It was a mere oversight on Charles's part that he didn't leave some sort of message for you. I'm sorry you discovered the truth since it pleased you then."

"Yes, it did please me. It made me feel as though I were engaged to a real man instead of a stranger who was no more than a name! But it wasn't true!" Anna ripped the letter to shreds and tossed it in his face. "There, I don't want your lies!"

Phillip did not move. He stood quietly waiting for Anna to run o of insults before he remarked slyly, "Why were you saving that letter if you're so in love with me?"

Anna stepped back, tempted to slap the smirk from his face but something stayed her hand at the last possible moment and instead she laid her fingertips upon his bare chest. "I had forgotten I had it until I noticed the writing in your log. Charles means nothing to me, truly he doesn't, but I do still want to go on to Jamaica to refuse his proposal of marriage in person. How could you let Jamie continue to believe I'll marry that man now? Don't you see how impossible that would be?"

Phillip placed his hand over hers and gently pushed her away. "It will be a couple of weeks at least before anything must be settled one way or the other, Anna. What Jamie believes doesn't matter."

Anna's golden eyes held only the glow of anguish as she looked up at him. "Apparently what I think doesn't matter either but I will never become Lord Clairbourne's bride no matter what you might think is best for me, I want you to understand that now, Phillip. I won't marry that man or any other, I simply won't."

Phillip refused to argue, he simply turned away and again stretched out on his bunk to rest. His head still hurt, and if the pain were no longer excruciating it was still present, a dull, throbbing ache which never ceased and he closed his eyes to escape again into the world of dreams where Anna was truly his and not the slightest difficulty barred their way to a lifetime of happiness.

Anna stared intently as Phillip dozed. The tension in his features relaxed and he was so handsome she could not tear her eyes away. She knew he was too proud to accept her love when he thought he had little to offer in return but he was so terribly wrong. "You are all I'll ever want, Phillip, just you." She ran from his cabin then, ran up on deck to the gaiety of the sunshine and clear blue water, a beauty she longed to share with the man she loved.

The nights were the worst for both of them. Phillip was never able to sleep the night through but lay on his bunk pretending to be so that Anna would not attempt to draw him into a conversation. He loved the sound of her voice, the musical tones were enchanting and he would never tire of the sweetness of her thoughts, but it was unfair of him to use her dreams to fill his heart with hope when their future had disappeared with his vision. All her words were encouraging whether she was only discussing his clothing for the day or the fairness of the weather. He longed to share her enthusiasm. He wanted to believe her, desperately he wanted to believe that he would soon recover his sight, but the plain truth was he could see no better now than he could the first afternoon after the pirates' attack. He had learned to use what sight he had, that was all, to recognize vague outlines for the objects they were. He had found it easy to recognize people by the sound of their voices. Jamie's was breathless, always filled with excitement as if he'd run all the way to his cabin with the most wonderful of news. John's voice was higher, more hesitant, never ringing with the brash confidence the mate's never lacked. Each member of the crew had a distinctive characteristic to his voice that made him easy to identify and he'd made no mistakes. Nor had he told Anna she need not provide him with the clues she always gave. Whenever anyone came to his cabin she would say his name, pay a compliment or issue a warm greeting so he would know who had come to call. She had done that from the beginning without being asked and he'd never even thanked her for her thoughtfulness. She was a woman like no other, a great prize but he could give her no future worth living and that sad fact filled him with a despair too deep to hide.

He was past anger now, past all emotion except pain as he reflected upon the life he'd led. His childhood was a painful blur, best left forgotten. He'd grown to manhood rapidly, tall and strong; he'd earned a man's wages from the day he turned fifteen. His mates had quickly taught him how to spend those wages too he recalled with a chuckle, first with drink and then with women. The first woman he'd had had been no more of a woman than he'd been a man. An innkeeper's daughter with a curiosity that had matched his own, they had spent a most enlightening week together but the next time he'd visited that port the girl had been married and pretended not to know him when they met on the street. After that he had confined his romantic adventures to women who accepted his money and gave him full value for it. It was far better that way for a sailor could not promise to be true to any woman when his travels were constant and his home no more than a small sea chest he could carry upon his shoulder from one ship to the next. They were all the same after a while, the women and the ships, until he'd caught a glimpse of the *Angelina* and decided one day he'd own her. His life had had a purpose after that. He'd saved his money diligently, advanced rapidly and soon had made first mate. With that experience to recommend him, the rest had been easy for the merchant marine had great need of ambitious young men, and he'd made good use of every opportunity he'd received. Yet as he lay in his bunk his achievements offered no comfort. It was Anna's pretty face he remembered most clearly, and he ached with loneliness, wanting to call to the lovely young woman who lay sleeping close by. All he would have to do was call her name softly and she would come to him, he knew that she would, but he dared not speak her name and choked with bitterness at the cruelty of his fate. He remained silent, awake and alone, as heartbroken as she that they could not be together.

Anna tossed and turned as she tried to find a comfortable position. More blankets had been found so she now had no complaint as to the hardness of the floor, but still she could not sleep. During the day the cabin was so often filled with others she had little difficulty keeping up her pretense Phillip was slowly getting well. But at night when she was alone with her own thoughts her doubts betrayed her, frightening her badly with the dreariness of her future. She had told

321

Phillip the truth, she'd take him for a husband or have none. Lord Clairbourne would have little problem attracting another bride for Briarcliff was a magnificent estate and many a young woman would delight in having so splendid a home regardless of how little she cared for her husband. Turning again Anna lay upon her stomach and propped her chin upon her hands. She truly believed Phillip would soon be well but she could not seem to convince him of that fact and the waiting was nearly impossible to bear when he had withdrawn from her so completely. He was polite, but distant, as if they'd never even kissed let alone made love so many times. As her sorrow overwhelmed her, tears welled up in her eyes and trickled down her cheeks. He had been so dear when they'd thought they would have a lifetime of love to share instead of no more than a few brief occasions of stolen love. She'd not change a minute of it though, for it had been worth it to her and she continued to savor each precious memory to the fullest. Phillip was the best of men and he'd loved her with all his strength and if his beautiful promises had lasted only one night then she'd not fault him for it as surely he'd known so little of love he did not understand the depth of her devotion or the strength of the tie which bound them now.

By the end of his second week of rest Phillip felt well, except for his poor vision he had no other complaint. His headaches were gone and his shoulder no longer pained him. He now found his self-imposed confinement in his cabin unbearable and paced with the ceaseless motion of a caged tiger until Anna insisted he stop.

"Let's go up on deck. I will stay by your side and no

one will discover your secret." She had been reading aloud but it was clear he was far too distracted to pay any attention to the novel she considered most entertaining.

Frowning deeply, Phillip considered her suggestion an impossibility. "Jamie is sure to ask my opinion on the work the men have accomplished. What can I possibly tell him that will make any sense?"

"I'm sure I don't know but please let's just give it a try." Anna took his arm and with persistent coaxing finally drew him through the door. "You're at home upon the deck at night, this will be no different."

"Night?" Phillip asked skeptically. "Night is nothing like this confusion, Anna, believe me it isn't."

"I will not argue the point. Simply give me your arm and we will do the best we can." That he was reluctant was no surprise but once they reached the deck Anna found it a simple matter to guide his way with slight pressure from her fingertips. When Jamie called to them she moved to the rail where Phillip could hold on securely while they talked.

Phillip breathed deeply, the salt-scented breeze filling his lungs with a zest for life he'd nearly forgotten. "Has it only been two weeks, Mr. Jenkins? I'd say your progress has been remarkable considering the way the *Angelina* looked when last I saw her."

Jamie looked around with an astonished glance for the deck was still charred from the fires and every man he could spare sat with needle and thread trying to patch what canvas they had into usable sails. The *Angelina* had never looked so woebegone as she limped along in the light breeze and since Phillip had always been a perfectionist to hear him paying compliments now was staggering. "Thank you, sir, we are all doing our best to return the ship to top form."

"That is plain for all to see, Mr, Jenkins, but do not let us distract you from your duties." Phillip dismissed the mate with a wide smile.

Jamie bid Anna a good afternoon and went down the deck trying to take some pride in what he was certain was still an awful mess. At least he'd kept the ship afloat and that fact pleased him greatly.

"You see, I knew you could do it!" Anna hugged Phillip warmly, forgetting all thought of propriety in her delight for he was smiling at last. She hoped he would continue to be in such good spirits for the remainder of the day.

Phillip's expression grew stern as he pushed Anna angrily away. "You know the truth even if Jamie doesn't, but you mustn't make things impossible for us both with such foolish displays of affection."

Anna turned to grip the rail, her knuckles white as she poured all her strength into simply holding on when she wanted to run away as fast as she could. But there was no place to hide and no one to whom she could turn now that Phillip continually refused her love. She embarrassed him now, that was plain in his every gesture and word. What a fool she had been to ever believe he had loved her when he could not even bear to feel her touch.

For Anna to be so silent was unusual and Phillip knew he'd been too abrupt and tried to apologize as he whispered, "I do not want any gossip about us, here on board the *Angelina* or anywhere else, Anna, try to remember that. It is to your advantage as well as mine that you are thought of as no more than my nurse."

"You must forgive me, Captain, for I can not hide my emotions so easily as you do. When I said I loved you I meant it with all my heart, but you are ashamed of that affection now, aren't you? The men of your crew are our friends, whom would they tell if they saw me in your arms? Since I disgust you so completely I will ask Mr. Jenkins if I might not move into his cabin again as he suggested so you will not be forced to endure my company unless you truly want it."

Phillip grabbed Anna's wrist so suddenly she had no time to flee. "Do as you please but first you will help me walk back to my cabin without incident, do you understand?"

"Yes, sir," Anna replied bitterly, sick to death of his desire for secrecy upon a matter which concerned the welfare of them all. He was blind all right, but it was not only his eyes which did not see, but his heart as well.

Chapter Eighteen

Returning to Jamie's cabin felt somehow like coming home and Anna's spirits rose considerably now that she felt she had some measure of control over her life once again. If Phillip did not already appreciate how much she had done to make his life easier he would soon, of that she was certain. But when he awakened her by pounding furiously at her door the first morning she'd not been with him, she was more annoyed than pleased.

"What's wrong, Phillip, are we under attack again?" Anna yawned sleepily as she peeked around the edge of her door. He seemed genuinely disturbed about something but she couldn't resist teasing him.

"They've sighted land and Jamie expects me to come up and give him some sort of opinion on whether or not this island will make a good place for us to stay a few days."

"I see, well, come in while I dress so no more time is wasted." Anna opened the door, then drew him inside and pushed him toward the extra bunk. "Sit down and tell me what is required and then I'll keep watch for you."

"Are you just going to dress right here in front of me?" Phillip asked incredulously.

"We shared the same cabin for several weeks, Phillip, and if that is not enough to make such intimacy not in the least bit shocking need I remind that you have undressed me yourself on more than one occasion? What is the difference between that and being here while I put on my clothes?"

"None, I suppose, it is only that—"

"Yes, I know, it is most improper for young ladies to entertain gentlemen callers in their bedchambers but we have no choice in the matter, do we? Now what is required of this island, a sheltered harbor, fresh water, what else?"

"Those are the main concerns. We'll send a small party ashore to check the water supply before we let everyone leave the ship; that way the entire day won't be lost if we must go on."

As she listened Anna tossed her nightgown aside, slipped on her lingerie, splashed cold water from the pitcher kept on the desk on her face, hurriedly brushed her teeth, then pulled her dress over her head before she began to brush her long hair with furious strokes. "Just a moment longer, I am almost ready." She had never dressed with such haste and hoped he understood she was moving as quickly as she possible could.

Phillip rubbed his hand over his eyes. For a few seconds he'd almost thought he could see her but it must have been his imagination, for the mist which filled his gaze had returned as thick as ever. "What color is your

327

dress, Anna?"

"It is a pale green like new grass. Why?" Anna sat down on her bunk to draw on her stockings and slippers, hurrying still so Jamie would not come searching for Phillip before she was ready to accompany him on deck.

Deciding not to mention that for an instant he'd seen her clearly enough to have been certain her dress was green, he changed the subject. "Are you ready to go?" Impatient to go up on deck, he stood and walked to the door.

Grabbing her shawl, Anna came forward to take his arm. "Yes, let us hope this island proves to be exactly what you'd hoped to find."

Phillip scowled as they went through the door. "Even if it isn't, I'll never know it!"

"Oh, hush, just listen and then you can decide what is best." Anna strolled by Phillip's side to where Jamie and several of the men were using a spy glass to study the terrain of the island in the distance. "Can you estimate the size of that bit of land fairly accurately, Mr. Jenkins?"

"I'd say it is perhaps three miles long, half that wide. What do you make of it, Captain?"

When Jamie extended the spy glass, Anna reached for it quickly. "Oh, please let me see first, may I, Captain?" She lifted the long black cylinder to her eye and exclaimed happily. "There seems to be quite a bit of foliage. Does that mean there's fresh water?" She remained looking out at the island, sweeping the whole length with a watchful eye for something Jamie had missed, but other than sand and lush greenery she found nothing upon which to remark. When she finished she held the spy glass for a long while before handing it back to Jamie. He did not realize Phillip had not used it.

"This looks like a good spot for a few days' rest, Mr. Jenkins. Let's put a small party ashore to survey the land more fully, locate water if there is any and then we can drop anchor if their report is promising." Phillip lifted his hand to shield his eyes from the sun's glare as he pretended to regard the island with rapt attention.

"Right away, Captain." Jamie already had a shore party in mind and called their names rapidly, assembling the group as a lifeboat was lowered to the water. The surf was light and the men reached the beach swiftly, scrambled out of the boat then dragged it up on dry sand before turning to wave to those left behind on the *Angelina*.

Anna waved then whispered, "They've reached the shore, do you want to wait here or should we go below for breakfast while we're waiting?"

Extending his right arm, Phillip smiled warmly as he issued an invitation. "I would prefer to eat. Would you be so kind as to join me, Lady Thorson?"

"Why, thank you, sir." Anna took his arm and guided him around a tangle of rope which blocked their way, deftly leading him back to his cabin without mishap. "So far so good, they should be back in an hour or so, shouldn't they?"

"Yes, that was clever of you to ask Jamie about the island's size. It gave me a better idea of what I was supposed to be seeing."

Anna stepped out of the way as John came through the door carrying the tray with their tea, fruit and biscuits for breakfast. "Good morning, John, did you

329

have a chance to look at the island? How does it seem to you?"

"You must ask the captain that question, Lady Thorson, for I know little about islands other than that they are small bits of land surrounded by water." John blushed slightly, embarrassed by his own attempt at humor.

Phillip laughed as he moved toward the table, sliding into his place after he'd heard a soft rustle of fabric and knew Anna had taken hers. "There is little else to know, John, but if we are lucky there will be fresh water to replenish our supply and perhaps some edible fruits as well. As long as there are no signs of other men I will be pleased with the place and insist we drop anchor for a few days."

"We could all do with the rest, sir." John could not understand why the well-built young man had not returned to the command of the *Angelina* when he appeared so fit, but not daring to ask what the captain would surely regard as an insolent question he saw their table was laid properly for breakfast and left them alone to enjoy the meal.

Anna poured their tea and munched a small biscuit thoughtfully. "Could we go ashore if the others do? It would be so nice to lie in the sun and relax without the constant roll of this ship to remind me where our journey is leading."

"You may go ashore if you like, Anna. Once we're certain there's no danger about, you may go exploring for I doubt you could get lost on so small a piece of land."

"You'll not come with me?" Anna asked softly, hoping he'd not refuse.

"I must stay here. It would be too difficult for me to fool Jamie there. I'd not know where to step and would probably fall on my face within ten minutes."

"Of course you wouldn't!" Anna protested swiftly. "If we took off our shoes and walked along the damp sand, the path would be flat. We could walk all the way around the island if we wanted to, that would be fun, couldn't we try and do it?"

Phillip had to marvel at her persistence. He would enjoy the walk, it wasn't the thought of the exercise which bothered him but the prospect of her enticing company which made him hesitate to agree. "Let's wait and see what the shore party says before we make any plans for the day."

Anna sighed impatiently, but realizing he'd not said no she agreed. "All right. Do you like to swim?"

"Swim?" Phillip set down his teacup with a loud clank. "Can you swim, Anna?"

"Certainly I can! Sweden is located on a peninsula as I'm sure you're well aware. We're nearly surrounded by the sea and my father thought it was ridiculous so few people knew how to swim when their lives could well depend on their possessing that skill. The water is not warm enough to stay in for long, but we did swim in the summertime, we really did."

"What else did that marvelous father of yours teach you, Anna? He seems to have had no end of talents." Except for managing money, Phillip remembered, but for once he was polite enough not to share such a sarcastic comment.

Anna waited a long moment before she replied, her voice a tantalizing whisper. "You have taught me such wonderful things yourself, Phillip, you taught me how to—"

"Anna!" Phillip shouted hoarsely. "Spare me the beauty of your memories. That is over and finished between us, it has to be!"

Stunned by his hostility, Anna folded her napkin neatly, laid it beside her plate and left his cabin without further comment to return to the deck. She watched the men traversing the small island and when they seemed satisfied they had examined it thoroughly they returned with an enthusiastic report. Fresh water was plentiful, the harbor deep enough for the *Angelina* to come in close, and the lagoon filled with large fish. It was the finest of islands in their view and all hands made ready to go ashore as soon as Phillip gave the order.

Anna went ashore with the second boatload of supplies. Michael had built a fire on the beach to roast freshly caught fish for lunch and the atmosphere was that of a lively summer picnic. The men seemed embarrassed by her company but she did no more than smile as she walked past them for she had no intention of spoiling their fun with her presence. They would have to be too careful then, too proper in their speech and actions when she knew they needed to relax without any constraints for a change. She moved behind a thick clump of bushes to remove her slippers and stockings and left them on dry sand so she might lift her skirt and walk at the surf's edge. The white sand reflected the sun's light with a bright sparkle. She had never seen the sea so magnificent a blue, as azure as the cloudless sky it was transparent, warm as a kiss as it lapped at her ankles with playful nibbles. With a happy laugh she began to run, splashing water as her

332

footsteps fell lightly upon the damp sand. On and on she ran until the group from the *Angelina* was far behind; she was elated by her freedom after so many days spent aboard the ship where her travels had been so restricted. When at last she grew tired of such strenuous exercise she sat down upon a small rise, hugged her knees and calmly enjoyed the beauty of the Caribbean sea. She could no longer see the sails of the *Angelina* but her solitude did not frighten her. She'd often ridden through the forest alone after her mother's death or strolled along beside the fields and let the hours slip by unheeded she's been so content with her own company. Sweden was a marvelous country, a verdant green in summer, covered by a sparkling blanket of white snow in the winter. She considered her homeland the best of all places to be but this small island had a charm so different from what she'd known all her life she found it quite fascinating despite its diminutive size. The air held the sea breeze's heady perfume; the white sand was so fine it blew in the slight breeze as she strained it through her fingers. Would Jamaica be so captivating a place? It was much larger, she knew, but wouldn't the sea which surrounded it still be as blue as sapphires and the sand as pale as new-fallen snow? Phillip would know, but he'd never described any of the Caribbean islands to her and she'd not thought to ask him. Oh, why hadn't he come with her when the day was such a perfect one? The thought of him sitting alone in his cabin brooding dejectedly filled her with sadness. What amusement would he have to pass the long hours the rest of them would spend in the warmth of the sun? Then with a sudden jolt of alarm she remembered the pistols. She'd replaced them in the bottom drawer of his desk so he'd have no trouble finding them. He'd been so depressed, so angry that he couldn't see well, was he despondent enough to use a bullet from one of the pistols on himself?

Terrified to realize she had abandoned him when he needed her most, Anna raced back up the beach, sprinting with long, graceful strides until she reached the lagoon where the *Angelina* floated at anchor. The lifeboat the men had been using to ferry supplies from the ship to the beach was again being loaded and she dared not wait for it to return to the shore to take her back to the ship when at that very moment Phillip could be lifting a pistol to his head. Ripping off her dress and slips, she dove into the water, leaving the men nearby standing with mouths agape as she swam with clean, even strokes out to the *Angelina* and, without pausing to catch her breath, grabbed the rope ladder hanging over the side and climbed up to the deck.

Jamie stared in astonishment as Anna came toward him. Her long, golden curls clung to her shoulders in damp ringlets while her silk camisole and pantaloons were transparent, giving her the sensuous grace of a Grecian statue. But to his utter amazement Phillip sat by his side regarding the young woman's approach with a calm detachment he could not effect. He quickly unbuttoned his own shirt and draped it over Anna's bare shoulders. "Lady Thorson! You might have drowned! Why didn't you wave to us? I would have sent the boat for you immediately. Where are the rest of your clothes?"

Rising to his feet Phillip tried to grasp the gravity of the situation which Jamie's excited questions clearly described. "Anna is an accomplished swimmer. She'd not drown in so short a distance with so many nearby to save her."

"But still!" Jamie gestured helplessly. No mermaid had ever been more lovely. He could not understand his captain's composure; he considered the risk she'd taken a most dangerous one.

Offering his arm, Phillip bowed slightly. "Lady Thorson, please allow me to escort you to your cabin where you will undoubtedly wish to put on dry clothing."

Not only was Phillip in no danger, he'd obviously been enjoying himself talking with Jamie. Anna felt utterly ridiculous standing there in a growing puddle when her haste had been so totally unnecessary. How Phillip had gotten from his cabin up on deck she couldn't guess but Jamie was nearly drooling as his dark gaze swept over her slowly and she had no wish to remain on view in her dripping attire which she was certain was no better than being completely nude. She accepted Phillip's offer gratefully but when they reached her cabin he surprised her by following her right inside.

"What did you want to prove, Anna? What was so damn important that you had to cast off your clothes and swim back to the *Angelina*? I thought you wanted to spend the whole day on the island. What made you change your mind so quickly? Were you already bored?"

Anna turned away, not about to reveal the truth when her haste had been so pointless. "I was merely being foolish it seems, as you insist I always am."

Puzzled that she'd make such an admission, Phillip reached out to touch her shoulder and found the soft

335

muslin of Jamie's shirt sopping wet. He could readily imagine how she looked: The thin fabric would be clinging to her luscious curves, and he could easily understand the cause of the mate's excitement for Anna was always lovely and even wringing wet he knew she would be irresistibly appealing. He leaned down to pull the blanket from the spare bunk then draped it gently around her shoulders. "I am sorry to be so clumsy but I do not want you to become chilled." When Anna relaxed against him, he wrapped his arms around her in a warm hug, content to hold her if for only a moment, but he could not resist nuzzling her damp curls with a light kiss.

"You are not in the least bit clumsy, Phillip, you needn't apologize." Anna wanted that sweet moment of tenderness to last forever but all too quickly he drew away.

Realizing he'd been dangerously close to forgetting the reserve he'd forced himself to display, Phillip changed the subject abruptly. "How did you find the island? Was exploring it the adventure you hoped it would be?"

"No, not without you it wasn't," Anna admitted hesitantly for she was certain of his reaction. She held her breath waiting for him to make some bitter retort but he surprised her.

"I am as tired of sitting in my cabin as you must be. If I could manage to get up on deck by myself this morning then I'm willing to risk a fall or two in the sand. Put on some dry clothing and we'll go back to the island together in the boat. I won't make you swim both ways."

"Really?" Anna turned around quickly, her golden

eyes sparkling with delighted surprise. "You will come with me, truly you will?"

"Yes, I'll wait up on deck, but hurry, the best part of the morning is already gone."

Anna reached up to kiss his cheek lightly. "I'll not be a minute but you may wait here again if you like."

Moving toward the door so he'd not be tempted to change his mind, Phillip disagreed. "Absolutely not, Anna. I may not be able to see you clearly but I can still think and I'd rather not dwell upon the beauty I'm missing, if you don't mind." He opened the door and stepped through it before she could offer any further enticement to remain, but once up on deck he regretted his decision for he grew increasingly impatient when she did not rapidly appear and he found it nearly impossible to concentrate upon Jamie's rambling conversation.

Having left her slippers on the sand, Anna had no choice but to go barefoot. The gown she'd chosen was a modest one of pale rose muslin which exactly matched the pretty blush in her cheeks. As she approached them with light running steps she looked no more than sixteen, so sweet and vulnerable Jamie had to turn away for his thoughts of her had recently been so far from innocent he was ashamed of himself for indulging in such indecent fantasies about so fine and chaste a young woman. Phillip saw only the warm pink glow of her dress and glad she was ready at last gave Anna a hand so she might climb over the side and down the ropes safely to the boat. He walked slowly along the deck, his hand trailing along the rail until he found the spot where the rope ladder was secured. He could still climb with remarkable agility but Anna took his hand to draw him down upon the seat beside her. Her gesture was so natural the two men at the oars thought nothing of it but Phillip understood she had helped him once again to find his way. There seemed to be no end to the quiet, sure assistance she was able to render and he sat silently by her side trying to think what he had left to offer in return.

Anna whispered softly as they left the lifeboat, "The men are simply sitting on the beach, a few are fishing but most look too tired to do more than rest. I hope you won't scold them for their idleness."

A slow smile crossed Phillip's lips as he shook his head. "I am no tyrant, Anna. I do not keep my crew in chains or threaten them with the whip. Our main purpose was to stop and rest so they are following my orders exactly as it is." He waited a moment and when a friendly voice called his name, he turned and waved. "There, they can see I don't mind them enjoying their leisure, now where shall we go? You shall have to lead the way so it should be your choice."

Anna looked down the beach in the direction she'd taken, then chose the opposite. "That way is pretty, but let's try this instead." She took his hand without thinking then dropped it quickly, certain he'd be displeased by the familiarity of that gesture.

Phillip jammed his hands into his pockets and took a step before he asked gruffly, "Well, are you coming with me or not?"

"Yes, I'm coming." Anna lifted her skirt and ran after him, her bare feet making soft impressions in the wet sand alongside the deep indentations from the heels of his boots. They walked along the shore for several minutes, neither caring to speak until Anna recalled her curiosity about Jamaica and inquired about the island. "Is Jamaica so pretty as this, Phillip? Does it have sparkling white sand and clear blue water? Is the weather so fair and warm?"

Phillip chuckled at her enthusiasm, understanding it well. "I first saw Jamaica at the end of the war, for many who'd been loyal to King George left America to go there where they'd still have the Crown to protect them. I was about ten then, had never been out of the Colonies, but after surviving so many naval battles I thought I knew all there was to know about the world. The beauty of the Caribbean was a complete surprise to me however, the warmth of the sun and wind most welcome after the long New England winters. I seriously considered staying in Port Royal when my ship made ready to depart."

"What made you change your mind?" The breeze blew a curl across Anna's eyes and she smiled happily as she brushed it away. She had hoped Phillip would relax if they got away together but she'd hardly dared hope he would reveal something of his past.

"The captain's name was Hoffman. He was a burly man, perhaps six feet in height and solidly built. He'd given me my freedom to explore the port and I think he suspected what I was thinking for the night before we were to sail he simply picked me up by the scruff of the neck, tossed me into his cabin and locked the door. I had no choice but to leave then and it was several years before I returned. By then I'd set my mind on owning my own ship and had no desire to earn my livelihood in a Caribbean port." Frowning slightly Phillip continued, "It seems impossible now that I could have been so young that the brutality of the island escaped me so completely."

"Brutality? Whatever do you mean, Phillip?"

"The island's economy is based on the export of sugar, a crop raised at an enormous price in labor, but it's the slaves who pay it, not the owners of the plantations. They prefer to reside in England and grow fat on their profits while their slaves are kept alive on Jamaica at near-starvation rations."

Anna grabbed Phillip's hand to make him stand still for a moment. "Is that the way Charles behaves too? Does he mistreat his slaves so shamefully as that? The prospect of owning other human beings is most distasteful to me, but to then neglect the poor creatures so cruelly should be a crime!"

Phillip sighed sadly. "Charles is the worst of the lot, Anna. It is no wonder he has riots on his hands. He comes to Jamaica more frequently than most of the plantation owners, but only in the interest of seeing production is high, not out of any concern for the welfare of the poor souls who work his land."

"But that is horrible, Phillip. What can we do to put a stop to such a travesty?" Anna's tone was serious, she could not tolerate cruelty of any sort, certainly not in the man she was supposed to marry, even though that would no longer be the case.

Gesturing widely, Phillip's hand swept toward the water. "You could as easily change the color of the sea as you could change a man like Charles. It is a hopeless task and one you must not even contemplate attempting."

Anna's pretty lips were set in a grim, determined line. "No, I will do whatever I can to see the man learns the error of his ways. But let's not argue about him again. Let's just keep walking for a while since the day is so pretty."

Glad to avoid so pointless a debate, Phillip strolled on agreeably until the toe of his right boot struck a rock half-buried in the sand. He would have tripped and fallen had Anna not grabbed his arm to help him remain upright. He stood still, trying to force back his anger rather than let her see his frustration. But he had little self-control and did not fool her in the slightest.

"I am so sorry, I should have been watching the path instead of the birds overhead. It's my fault you tripped, not yours and I'll be more careful now," Anna offered apologetically for she did not want him to turn back.

Phillip looked out toward the water. He could see the reflected gleam of the sunshine, the blue of the clear sky, even the lush green foliage which began at the sand's edge. He could see the bright colors, the patterns of light and shadow but none of it was clear enough to be of any use and his throat closed in a painful knot as he disagreed. "I will not be treated like some pathetic puppy who must be led on a leash so he does not fall into mud puddles!"

"Good lord, Phillip, no one would ever call a man like you pathetic, don't be ridiculous!" Anna threw up her hands in frustration, pushed to the end of her patience by his self-pity. "We've come a considerable distance, no one can see us, let's go for a swim!" Not waiting for him to offer an objection, Anna skipped on ahead, shedding her dress then loosening the ribbon ties on her lace-trimmed lingerie. "You and your men go without shirts when it's warm, it must be heavenly to feel the heat of the sun on your bare skin."

"Anna!" Phillip exclaimed with clear exasperation. He was frantic she'd been so foolish as to discard her clothing for the second time in one day. "Ladies simply do not frolic on the shore without proper attire!"

"Is that a fact?" Anna draped her soft dress over a piece of driftwood and continued to tease him. "We are quite alone here, Phillip. You won't tell anyone that I've committed such a breach of propriety, will you?" She was nude in a matter of seconds and, brushing past him, ran into the surf splashing playfully as she began to swim. "Please come and join me, we could have a race if you swim as well as I do!"

Phillip cursed under his breath then tore off his shirt before sitting down to pull off his boots. "I'll come in all right, but only to pull you out!"

Anna wasn't in the least bit afraid of his anger and called invitingly, "Take off all your clothes too, it's ever so much nicer here in the water without them." The sea was as warm as a bath and she had never had such a wonderful time swimming.

As he got to his feet, Phillip tried to see where she was but the sun was too bright on the water for him to find her. "Do you mean you're not wearing anything at all?" He knew if he could keep her talking he could follow her voice and he strained to pinpoint her location.

"Phillip, really, you mustn't be so stuffy! You sound rather like my Uncle Gustav and you're not like him at all!" Anna swam out a bit farther then rolled upon her back and floated parallel to the shore. "Please come swimming with me, don't spoil what could be the most perfect day we'll ever live."

A wicked gleam filled Phillip's blue eyes as he de-

342

cided to play her game, after all. Here was the loveliest of young women inviting him to pursue her through the waves, but perhaps she did not realize how he'd end her sport. In a moment he'd stripped off the rest of his clothing and was in the water, his long, powerful stroke carrying him rapidly to her side. The ocean floor sloped away from the shore at a gentle angle; they could go some distance from the edge of the surf and still be able to touch bottom. Where they were he could stand easily but he was certain she'd have to stretch to reach the sand with her toes and he locked his hands around her waist in a vicious jerk, bringing her slippery body abruptly against his own, shocking her with the force of his embrace.

"Are you trying to drown me?" Anna raised her hands to his shoulders just in case that had been his purpose. She thought his expression a trifle too stern and wanted him to be as happy as she was that day. "Phillip, let me go. I'm sorry I teased you if I made you angry with me again but—" His mouth covered hers so quickly she had no opportunity to escape his grasp before his purpose became shockingly clear. She'd not known what he seemed determined to do was even possible in the sea but the suddenness of that realization brought an end to her panic and she wrapped her arms around his neck as she returned his savage kiss with a mischievous hug. His strength was no longer frightening when she knew it would end in pleasure, but her joyous acceptance of his affection amazed Phillip and he was the one to draw away.

"Is it a race you want or this?" Phillip did not loosen his hold upon her as he took a step backwards. He wanted the water to support her weight so she'd have

343

no choice but to cling to him tightly. "Mermaids lured sailors to their deaths; is that the fate you have planned for me?"

Anna leaned back to dip her long curls in the sea so when she shook her head the water clinging to the golden tresses flew about them in a sparkling shower of bright droplets. "I want you alive, my dearest. I'd never let you drown, as long as I have the strength to save you you'll always be safe with me."

Phillip chuckled at her promise since she'd already saved his life once. "Did I ever thank you for dispatching the pirate who very nearly killed me? I should have said it, if I did not—"

"Hush, Phillip," Anna whispered seductively as she began to kiss his face with light, playful kisses. His beard was soft, growing low upon his cheeks it accented his even features handsomely while his dark curls dripped salty water, flavoring their kisses with the taste of the sea. She wanted to be truly his once again, to be held and loved with the same tender passion he'd always given. The sea which swirled around them drew them ever closer with a sensuous caress of its own.

Phillip's kisses turned wild then, filled with the hunger he'd endeavored so unsuccessfully to suppress. It had been agony for him to refuse the love she offered so willingly and he forced all thought of the impossibility of their marriage from his mind as her supple form melted into his, drawing him ever deeper into the warm, soft sweetness she'd given only to him. His fingertips caressed her throat, feeling the throbbing beat of her pulse grow wilder until he could no longer concentrate on any sensation other than the deep pleasure which swelled within him, until he thought his heart would burst with the passion he could no longer control. How he could have existed for so many years without knowing what love between a man and woman was truly meant to be he couldn't imagine but Anna was the most loving and vibrant creature ever born and he adored her, saw her beauty so clearly in his mind he did not miss his sight when she flooded his other senses with a rapture too exquisite to name.

Anna's slender limbs were coiled around Phillip so snugly she could feel the rhythm of his heart beating in time with her own, the frantic tempo thundering in her ears more loudly than the incessant roar of the sea which held them gently suspended in its liquid grasp. He enfolded her in the lightest of embraces, enveloped her with loving so delicious she would never have her fill of his affection until at last they both lay in the sand at the surf's edge, exhausted by pleasure and too content to care if the water which lapped over them presented any real threat of their drowning. When Anna could bear to move from Phillip's side she leaned down over him, the tender tips of her breasts brushing his broad chest lightly as her lips coaxed him from his dreams. His smile was slow and sweet as he drew her down into his arms to return her generous affection with a lazy kiss which promised they'd spend many more such delightful hours together.

"I love you, Phillip, so deeply and dearly, with all my heart I love you." As Anna whispered she glanced up, wanting only to remember the beauty of their surroundings but she saw a flash of white disappear behind a palm tree and knew it had not been a sea gull's feathers but a man's shirt. Mortified that someone had been watching them make love, she sat up and shaded her eyes as she looked up and down the beach to make certain no one else was nearby.

Phillip was now so attuned to Anna's moods he sensed her alarm and sat up too. "What is it? Not a sea serpent, I hope, as I brought no weapons to defend you."

"It was nothing, the noise of the birds startled me, that's all," Anna lied convincingly, far too embarrassed to admit the truth. But it hadn't been her imagination, someone had seen them but was it someone they could trust to keep such a tantalizing secret to himself? "Let's get dressed, we've been away from the others for a long while and I know you don't want them to become suspicious about us."

"No, I most certainly do not. But I intended to do no more than keep you company when we set out for a walk but you distracted me so completely I lost all track of time." Realizing he had no idea where his clothes might lie, Phillip frowned sullenly for that simple problem reminded him of the hopelessness of his situation so graphically he turned away rather than allow Anna to see the tears in his eyes. He'd never display such weakness in front of her.

Confused by Phillip's sudden change of mood when he'd been in such delightfully high spirits, Anna was nevertheless in too great a hurry to dress to worry over it. She went first to pick up his clothing, then returned to drape it over his shoulder. "Here, you needn't wear your boots, I'll carry them for you." She left him to dress. She shook the sand from her chemise and pantaloons before pulling them on quickly; her dress got no more than a brush of her fingertips before she slipped it

346

over her head and fastened the tiny buttons. There was nothing she could do about her damp curls but she hoped the sun would dry her hair before they rejoined the others. When she turned, Phillip was also dressed; he stood staring out at the sea she knew he couldn't really see and, wanting to distract him from any sad thoughts, she ran to take his arm, chatting brightly about the beauty of the sun-drenched island as they continued their walk.

Chapter Nineteen

As they enjoyed Michael's delicious roasted fish that evening Anna let her eyes wander slowly over the crew hoping for some telltale sign which would reveal the identity of the man who'd seen her with Phillip. At the very least he'd observed them lazily relaxing in the shallow surf, reclining nude in each other's arms. At the worst, he'd been watching them for a long while and she blushed at that possibility since what they'd shared had been meant to be the most private of amusements. Yet that someone had seen them did not diminish the glow of love which burned so brightly in her heart, she still felt its splendid warmth.

Phillip was as nervous as Anna but for an entirely different reason. At night he was completely helpless for he had not even the play of light and shadow to help him find his way. He and the lovely blonde were seated with the men who were relaxing around a blazing fire as they ate, joking amongst themselves as he'd provided plenty of ale to sate their thirst and lift their mood. A sailor's life was a lonely one but tonight he knew they would feel a closeness he envied, for while they respected him he was their captain and no longer one of them as he'd been in his youth. Those carefree days were long behind him and he leaned over to whisper to Anna. "Let's go back to the ship, this is no place for you to spend the night."

"Oh, couldn't I please stay? I'll go off by myself if you think I should but I'm not afraid. We've seen the whole island and there's nothing about which could harm me."

Sighing wearily Phillip rose to his feet and extended his right hand as he rephrased his request in the form of a command. "You will return to the *Angelina* with me now, Lady Thorson, as you will be ever so much more comfortable in Jamie's cabin than here on the beach." And so will I, he thought slyly.

Everyone was looking her way now, their eyes curious. Only John was too busy cleaning up the remains of their meal to pay her any attention and she had no desire to embarrass Phillip by arguing with him in front of his men. "I'm sure you're right, Captain, how thoughtful of you to consider my comfort." As she took his arm and walked by his side to the boat, two men scrambled to their feet and rushed to take up the oars so Phillip would not have to row the boat himself.

The short boat ride took only a few minutes and then Anna found herself alone again with Phillip as they crossed the deck. The men were still taking turns at watch for he'd not leave the *Angelina* unattended after dark, but the presence of another man on board didn't bother her. Phillip had said little during the afternoon; he'd spent his time talking with his crew, paying particular attention to those who still bore the signs of the

349

pirates' attack, but he'd made so few comments to her she did not know what to expect of him that night. Did he want her to stay in his cabin again, or would he come to hers? Would it be too bold of her to inquire as to which was his preference or should she simply wait and see what he did? He was such a perplexing man, she never knew from one moment to the next what his mood would be. Finally when she could bear the uncertainty no longer, she blurted out the question which preyed so heavily upon her mind. "Phillip, you are not sorry about what happened between us today, are you?"

"That is a strange question, Anna. Whatever makes you ask it of me?" Phillip knew he'd told her repeatedly that such romantic encounters were finished between them only to take her again with a delight he'd made no effort to hide. He wasn't in the least bit sorry he'd made love to her, only that he'd not been strong enough not to succumb to her charms when he still had no way to give her a home. That thought depressed him thoroughly but the damage was already done and he'd no way to undo it now. But he'd never say he was sorry they'd made love when he'd enjoyed it so very much.

"I do not want to be a burden to you, Phillip. I could not bear it if you thought of me only as a responsibility you could not shirk."

"Let's go to my cabin where we can talk all night if you wish, there we'll be in no danger of being overheard." Phillip took her arm but as usual she led him where he wished to go. "I've rum at least, if no wine. Would you like some of that?"

"I tasted it once, it's rather good isn't it?" Anna

350

knew where the small cask was kept and, taking two silver cups from atop his desk, filled one for him and a tiny amount for herself. The fiery liquid burned her throat and she set down the cup as she began to choke.

"Try taking small sips, Anna, don't just toss it down your throat like a shot of whiskey." The young woman was clearly unused to drink, he thought with a smile, but he'd not make the mistake of getting her drunk ever again. "Come sit beside me and help me decide what is best for you, for clearly we can not continue to live as we have."

Anna's heart fell. It was true then, he didn't want her to be his wife, all he wanted was for her to be willing whenever he was in the mood to make love. "There's no reason for us to have such a conversation when it is obvious you have already decided what should be done. Goodnight." With that breathless goodbye she ran from his cabin to Jamie's where she sat stiffly upon her bunk, hot tears rolling down her cheeks. She'd not beg him to marry her when it was so plain he didn't want to do so. It was all so unfair; if only she'd been able to get a clear shot at the pirate before he'd hit Phillip, then he'd not be blind and he wouldn't have to think of her as only another torment when he had so many. Love was supposed to be wonderful, not this wretched sorrow which became more difficult to bear with each passing day. But she'd not be so weak as to cling to the possibility Phillip still loved her when clearly he didn't. "If only I had never left Sweden," she whispered softly, if only she had run away when first her uncle had told her she was to go to England to marry. If she had only known then what she knew now she would have saddled a horse and ridden as far away as the animal could have carried her rather than to have attempted to honor her father's promise when each step she took seemed to be in the wrong direction. Phillip had not simply broken her heart, he had crushed it into a thousand jagged pieces and she did not know how she could face the rest of her life if he would not be at her side to share it.

The door of the small cabin flew open with a loud crash as Phillip came through it and as if that noise were not enough to have attracted her attention he then slammed it shut as he began to speak in a threatening whisper. "The next time you run out on me I swear I will turn you over my knee and give you the thrashing you deserve!"

Anna leapt to her feet as she responded defiantly, "You ever lift your hand to strike me and I'll hit you right back! Your threats don't frighten me in the slightest!"

Confused by the fury of her temper, Phillip leaned back against her door and folded his arms across his chest. "You don't frighten me either, Anna, but I've had enough of your childish tantrums. I'm not leaving here until we understand each other completely so you might as well sit down while you listen."

"How are we ever to understand each other if you do all the talking while all I'm permitted to do is listen?" Anna paced up and down in front of her bunk too upset to sit calmly with her hands folded primly in her lap while the man she adored explained for the hundredth time why they couldn't marry.

The lamp on the desk lit the small chamber with a soft glow, Phillip could see Anna's silhouette as she moved back and forth. He didn't need to see the proud line of her back clearly to know how she felt. "I am a reasonable man. I will let you speak first. Go ahead and say whatever you wish and I will listen without interrupting."

Anna placed her hands on her slender hips as she walked up to face him. For once his lack of vision was an advantage to her for she was certain he could not tell she had been crying. "I think the life we could have together would be paradise and for you to throw it away simply because you can't see well for a few weeks is lunacy! I think your blindness is only an excuse; you wanted me because I'm pretty but you don't have the simplest grasp of the true meaning of love. I won't allow myself to be used!"

Phillip was able to contain his anger by the greatest force of effort he'd ever expended on such a cause. He'd promised to be silent and he remained so, but how Anna could misunderstand his motives so completely he didn't know. When at least she turned away and was still he asked pointedly, "Is it now my turn?"

"Yes!" Anna replied obstinately. She wanted only to put her hands over her ears so she wouldn't have to listen but he'd listened to her as he'd promised to do and she would have to afford him the same courtesy.

Phillip took a deep breath and when that wasn't sufficiently calming he took another. "Perhaps you have a point, but you must remember I asked you to marry me and made love to you before I knew what had happened to my sight."

"You've got it backwards, Phillip, you made love to me first!" Anna shouted, forgetting her promise to listen quietly.

Phillip would have liked nothing better than to put

his hands over Anna's mouth to make her be still but he restrained himself from being so foolish. "What is the difference? I made love to you because I love you. The fact that you are surely one of the most beautiful women ever born has nothing to do with my feelings by the way. I did not want you to feel 'used' today, only loved. I have done all I can to fight the attraction which exists between us and I've lost. I can't stay away from you and I don't even want to try anymore. But how in God's name can I provide any sort of life for you if I'm blind? I'll not beg on street corners hoping to receive enough pennies to keep you in clean rags! To want you so badly and to not be able to have you is the worst torture any man has ever suffered but I'll not have you believe I don't love you or that the time we spent making love today was not most precious to me." As he turned to open the door Anna rushed past him to push it closed then threw herself into his arms.

"If you still love me then nothing else matters, truly it doesn't!" She kissed him with a hunger more desperate than his own and he knew she had won again. She was going to get everything she wanted and he had no way to stop her when he loved her more dearly than life itself. Her nimble fingers were all over him, removing his clothing with a speed he'd not thought possible but he did his best to help her before he found himself tearing at her dress with the same frantic haste she'd displayed. "Dear God, Anna, how can you doubt my love?" His mouth sought hers eagerly. Her rum-flavored kiss was delicious and he could not seem to release her long enough to carry her the short distance to her bunk. He wanted only to make her understand the depth of his devotion, to feel the power of his love throughout her being so she'd finally believe the truth of his words. If he could not reach her with logic he would use passion but he had to try, again and again he had to try and convince her how dearly he loved her. He knew there were many more ways to make love than he'd shown her and he wanted to teach her all there was to know of the love they shared. When she pulled him down across the bunk he tore his mouth from hers and let his lips slide down her slender throat, across her delicate collarbone to her high, firm breasts but this time he did not linger at their soft, flushed peaks. He wanted more than he'd ever taken from any woman, complete intimacy, total surrender. His mouth moved over the dimples at her navel to the golden triangle of curls which drew him lower still. She made not the slightest move to resist his erotic kiss and he grew more bold, seeking the ultimate satisfaction, savoring the warm, honey-smooth sweetness of her graceful body with enormous delight. He could feel her excitement, the tiny tremors of ecstasy which swept down her spine, and he tightened his hands around her waist, holding her fast so she'd not escape the slow, easy rhythm of his tongue as he drew her senses to the heights of rapture, to a realm of pleasure beyond imagination. Her fingers were woven in his dark curls, drawing him ever closer until no secret remained hidden and in that final shattering instant she belonged more to him than to herself. The joy which throbbed from within her trembling body gave him the greatest thrill he'd ever known for surely this was the purest form of love, totally unselfish, with no thought of return other than the contentment of knowing he'd pleased her as greatly as any man ever could.

Reason returned slowly to Anna's agile mind but as Phillip began to kiss her cheeks tenderly she whispered an enchanting question. "Would your joy be as deep as mine if I did that to you?"

Too stunned to respond for a moment, Phillip remembered how quick a pupil he'd attempted to instruct and answered truthfully, "Yes, for surely our senses must be the same, the pleasure as rich, the joy as deep for one of us as for the other." But he'd thought only of the giving, not what she might do in return and he held his breath, uncertain whether or not he truly wanted such a remarkable response from the woman he loved but then it was far too late for she had already slid from his arms. Her playful kisses moved down his ribs with a purpose he could not resist and he rolled over on his back eager to accept whatever expression of love she cared to give. Her silken curls brushed his stomach with a sensuous caress as her lips burned his flesh with the heat of her passion, her tongue driving him past all thought of resistance, luring him to the brink of madness, drawing a deep moan from his throat before she sent him rushing into an ecstasy so magnificent he thought his sanity a small price to pay for such a splendid gift of pleasure.

Anna smiled with deep satisfaction as Phillip's blue gaze met her own. "I will never leave you, never. No matter what tragedy befalls us, I will never stop loving you as dearly as I do tonight."

Phillip pulled her down into his arms, hugging her so tightly she could scarcely draw a breath. They had become lovers so skillful in bestowing pleasure he knew they could never return to the stilted awkwardness he'd imposed upon them in the last two weeks.

They belonged together and he no longer had the will to deny what was clearly meant to be his destiny. Anna was his life, the breath which filled his lungs, the blood which poured through his veins. She was his very soul he loved her so and he began to make love to her again, this time letting the power of his lean body bring the rapture to its peak as his lips never left hers. But his unspoken promise was understood, he belonged more to her than to himself and at last she knew it as well as he did.

It was past ten when Anna awoke the next morning; Phillip had left her side just before dawn but she felt his presence still. The contentment which made her long to burst into song was too delightful to contain and she leapt from her bed and made it up quickly she was so anxious to find him. She would have to be discreet in her greeting for she understood his desire for propriety but it would be difficult not to simply throw herself into his arms when she loved him so greatly. She sat in front of her mirror and tried to affect a nonchalant expression totally without success. Her complexion was radiant, her happiness bursting forth and she knew she'd have to rely upon Phillip to speak first so she would have to do no more than make a demure reply. When a knock came at the door she rushed to open it but rather than the man she loved she found John holding a breakfast tray.

"Good morning, Lady Thorson."

John stepped past her and placed the tray upon the desk. "The captain has already eaten and gone ashore but he begs you to wait for the boat this morning rather than swimming to the island." He was clearly embarrassed by that message and turned without once look-

357

ing her way.

Anna thought John's manner most peculiar, then recalled he'd been occupied the previous evening either with the supper preparations or clean-up and she'd not seen him glance her way once. Had he merely been busy or was there another reason for his aloofness? She stepped in front of him to block his way as she asked, "Won't you please stay and talk with me for a moment, John?"

John focused his attention upon her bare toes. He'd seen her slippers someplace but couldn't recall just where. "Michael will be calling for me, Lady Thorson. I must go."

Anna reached out to touch his sleeve lightly. "John, while the captain and I were walking around the island yesterday we stopped for a while and I thought I saw someone watching us although I caught no more than the glimpse of a shirt sleeve. Was it you?"

John's cheeks flooded with color as he tried to elude her grasp. "I don't know what you're talking about, Lady Thorson, please excuse me."

"Please call me Anna. You did before, what has changed between us that you must be so formal?" Anna was sure now, positive it had been John who'd seen them making love and she could imagine how he'd felt. But she wanted him to understand what he'd seen had been the truest expression of love, not simply some lust-filled encounter. "I am not angry, John. If you were out walking, just enjoying the day then you could not have predicted what you might see, but if on the other hand you followed us, hoping to discover a secret we wish kept then I am very disappointed in you."

John looked up then, his eyes filling with tears as he confirmed her suspicions. "The captain is so strict with you, not even polite, why would you have given yourself to him?"

Anna smiled wistfully as she tried to explain, "We are very much in love, John. He has tried to hide his feelings and so have I. Please don't tell any of the others what you saw as it would hurt us both very badly and I know you would never want to do that."

"I'll never tell anyone and I wasn't following you either. I just came over the rise and there you were. I turned away immediately so it was no wonder you didn't see my face." He was so ashamed, but truly he had been walking, looking for fruit to supplement their supper when he'd come upon them and he'd run away rather than watch the woman he adored make love with another man. He had always known she'd never love him but to see her with Phillip had broken his heart and he couldn't bear to answer her questions.

"This must be our secret, John. Phillip doesn't even suspect you saw us together. Please don't let this be the end of our friendship for you are very important to me."

John nodded dumbly. He wanted only to leave the small cabin where no matter where he stood he could not escape her soft touch. "I must go."

Anna opened the door for him but Phillip was on the other side, his rakish grin disappearing as he realized she wasn't alone. "John just brought me my breakfast. Do you have any other work for him, Captain?"

"Yes, I wish to take Lady Thorson fishing. Find me something to use for bait, John."

"Yes, sir." John nearly ran he left them so suddenly

and Phillip leaned against the doorjamb as he turned to watch him go.

"What's gotten into him?"

"He's a very sensitive boy, Phillip. He's only eighteen and understands very little of life it seems."

"While you at eighteen are of course an expert?" he pointed out skeptically.

"Stop teasing me, or I'll not come fishing with you after all," Anna threatened playfully. "Just let me eat my breakfast and I'll be up on deck."

"I will give you five minutes and not a second more or the boat will leave without you." Phillip winked slyly and turned to go but he had to use his hand to guide his way and hoped Anna wouldn't notice what slow progress he made.

Anna closed the door softly then leaned back against it. She was glad Phillip had not been jealous of John, that was a good sign at least. But she was still upset the young man had discovered they were lovers. It was a difficult secret to keep and she was afraid it was only a matter of time before every man on the *Angelina* knew exactly how close she and their captain had become. That would hurt Phillip far more than it would hurt her, so with a determined frown she drank her tea and, grabbing up two biscuits, went to find Phillip before he made good on his promise and left her behind.

This day was as glorious as the last and Anna sat holding her fishing pole while Phillip slept in the sand beside her. The scars on his arms showed as thin, pink lines against his deep tan and she turned away rather than recall the horror of the day when she'd held his bleeding body in her arms and begged God not to let him die. It was a memory she had tried to suppress but it took only a glimpse of those scars, or the sight of his unseeing glance to bring the tragedy back into sharp focus. Forcing herself to concentrate on her task, she had landed three plump fish by the time Phillip awakened.

"Somehow I was certain you already knew how to fish, Anna, and I can guess who taught you." He leaned back on his elbows and chuckled as she displayed her catch.

"My father, of course. Since he had no son, there was no one else to receive the benefit of his knowledge and I like to think I've put it all to good use."

"Oh, yes, you most certainly have," Phillip remarked agreeably.

Curious as always Anna inquired softly, "If you went to sea when you were eight how were you able to attend school, Phillip? Did you simply have tutors?"

"I have never set foot inside a schoolhouse, but I guess you could say I had tutors, not the usual sort for a young boy but I learned my lessons all the same."

Astonished, Anna continued to question him. "You write beautifully, and your cabin has many fine books which appear to have been read frequently. You have the manners of the finest gentleman and—"

Laughing at her compliments Phillip explained, "I am thirty-two years old, Anna. I've had plenty of time to pick up anything I missed as a youth. Does my shocking lack of formal education bother you? Were you hoping I could read Latin and Greek as the scholars do?"

If he'd forgotten he could not see well enough to read she'd not remind him and she hastened to change the subject. "I am sure there is a place in the world for all of us, Phillip, dashing sea captains as well as somber scholars and I do not wish to change anything about you for I am greatly pleased with you just as you are." When he pulled her down into his arms, she kissed him sweetly but then slipped from his grasp and got to her feet. "I don't want these fine fish to spoil when it may be all we will have for supper. Don't you think we better start back?"

"What are a few fish compared to my happiness, now come back here!" Phillip commanded sharply but she stood where she was.

"That you spend so much time with me must be causing comment. I am only trying to be discreet as you continually criticize my behavior as being too forward and lacking in judgment."

Phillip moaned with frustration. "Now you have decided to behave like a mature woman, now of all times!" He brushed off his breeches as he got to his feet. "What am I to do with such an exasperating female?" He turned quickly in the next second as he heard Jamie calling his name loudly.

"You may thank me later, sir," Anna whispered calmly but she was as startled as he. They had escaped being caught in the most compromising of situations by the barest of margins and she could not believe they had been so lucky. She walked along beside Phillip as they returned to the place the *Angelina*'s crew had taken upon the beach. It seemed Jamie needed no more than advice but he was anxious to complete the repairs to the ship and wanted the captain's opinion on the work. Anna tossed her catch to John and while he did not smile warmly at least he did not ignore her. She accompanied the men to the ship and pretended a rapt interest in all they discussed for she did not know how Phillip could make suggestions on things he could not see.

"We have sanded away the charred portions of the deck but now the surface is uneven, water will collect in the depressions and—"

Phillip nodded patiently as he listened but his choices were few. "A slight problem, Jamie, just varnish the bare spots and we'll replace whatever planks need to be replaced when we reach home. The *Angelina* is a beauty and she will be still with a few minor imperfections. I am more concerned about the sails as we really must buy more canvas and they'll charge us a fortune in Montego Bay."

"Aye, that is true." Jamie smiled warmly at Anna, thinking she'd be interested in the port. "That is the most likely place for us to buy provisions after we take you to Lord Clairbourne's. It is the largest port on the northwest of Jamaica and he ships the produce from his plantation from there."

Anna turned pale at the mention of the man's name for she'd given him such little thought in recent days she'd nearly forgotten why they'd come to the Caribbean in the first place. "Montego Bay? Is that named for one of the Spanish explorers?" She hoped the question did not sound too foolish but she dared not discuss Charles with the mate.

When Jamie did not respond immediately, Phillip supplied the correct answer. "The Spanish are responsible for the names of many places, but while they cultivated sugar cane they also exported large amounts of cacao, hides and lard. *Manteca* is the Spanish word for lard and somehow the bay got that name which eventually was mispronounced Montego and that's what the port is still called today."

Fascinated by so detailed a response, Anna marveled at the intelligence of a man who'd never attended school in his youth and yet had managed to simply absorb knowledge wherever he traveled until his education could be considered most complete. "Thank you, you've quite satisfied my curiosity and if you gentlemen will excuse me I think I'll go to my cabin and rest. All the exploring we've done today has left me very tired."

"Of course, you'll join us again for supper won't you?" Phillip inquired hopefully.

"Yes, I'll see you then." But Anna hesitated to leave him alone with Jamie. They seemed to have finished their discussion and she knew he could find his way around the *Angelina* unaided but still she did not want to go.

"What is it, Anna, is there something you need?"

Only you, she thought to herself, but she left him with no more than a slight caress upon the arm and went to her room where she slept soundly until sundown and then had to hurry to dress properly for supper before Phillip came for her. She at least had her slippers once again and smiled slightly as she picked up her shawl. She might appear to be the most proper of young ladies but she could not wait for nightfall when she'd feel safe to make love with Phillip no matter where he chose to do it.

The few days they'd planned to stay on the island stretched into more than a week and Anna counted each glorious hour she spent with Phillip as the best of her life. He was never stern with her now, never demanding but always gentle and sweet, seeing that she was amused, pampered, loved with such tenderness and affection she knew the depth of their relationship must no longer be a secret to anyone, yet none of the men dared make the slightest teasing remark to their captain for they knew without risking it what his reaction would be. It was clear from his example that Lady Thorson was to be treated with the utmost respect and they did so but the glances they passed between themselves were knowing and sly.

Only Jamie Jenkins seemed intent upon making speedy progress. After the third time Phillip told him to take his time he began to follow his captain's example and spent the early morning fishing and relaxing in the sun and turned his mind to the *Angelina*'s needs for only a few short hours in the afternoon. A lazy calm pervaded the warm atmosphere and all seemed content to let the days roll by uncounted for the soft breeze and bright sun lulled them into a peaceful complacency they enjoyed too thoroughly to leave.

When his vision had first begun to clear Phillip had been afraid to hope Anna's prediction was coming true. He said nothing to her but slowly the mist which had obscured his vision began to lift. When he could again see the beauty of her smile, the sparkle of her golden eyes, the flutter of her long, dark lashes as she kissed him he knew it was time to leave the island but dreaded the moment they'd have to set sail for Jamaica as if it were the date for his own execution. The perfect solution to his dilemma presented itself one afternoon as he sat on the beach watching Anna sleep. Her body was curled softly next to his and he reached out to touch her glossy curls lightly. He would never tire of the sight of her, she was so lovely, her tan now a deep golden glow making her striking light eyes all the more astonishing. Her hair was streaked with highlights, her cheeks kissed with tiny freckles and she looked so young and dear he could no longer wait to wake her and, stretching out beside her, drew her into his arms, kissing her pretty mouth with a teasing playfulness until she at last opened her eyes and returned his smile. "Is it time to go back to the others already?"

"Yes, but there is something I must ask you first and I want you to consider your answer most thoroughly before you reply."

Anna reached up to touch his dark curls. His hair had grown too long; it dipped over his ears and down his neck. But she'd not offered to trim it for him when she thought it so attractive. "Why are you so serious, my love, do I not regard all your requests as thoughtfully as I should?"

Phillip hugged her tightly as he laughed. "No, indeed, you do not, but you must this time." He got to his feet quickly and leaned down to help her up but kept his arms around her waist. He could not suppress a rakish grin as he began to explain. "I want to leave here tonight. We can reach Jamaica in a day or two. With the patchwork quilts we've got for sails. I want to buy what canvas we need in Montego Bay and while we're there I want you to marry me."

"But Phillip!" Anna began to argue, thrilled and yet frightened all at the same time.

"Just listen, I will take you to Charles as I promised for I know you feel he deserves to hear the news you must give him from your own lips, but I want you to already be my wife when you meet him."

"No, please, don't ask that of me. I can't refuse to marry him because I am already married to you. That just isn't right and I can't do it." Anna frowned unhappily. "Please, I want to marry you so badly but please let me refuse Charles's proposal first. I must insist upon it."

Phillip lifted a dark brow quizzically. "You insist upon it? Are you simply giving me that excuse or have you decided you'd rather not spend your life with a blind man after all?"

Anna shook her head emphatically. "What must I do to convince you I will love you forever regardless of how well you are able to see?" She wrapped her arms around his neck and hugged him with a desperate passion. "I adore you, Phillip, but can't you understand I owe the man this courtesy? It is a matter of honor that I refuse his proposal before I accept yours. It can be no other way."

Phillip stepped back and regarded her closely, the tears which welled up in her pretty eyes touched him with a sorrow as deep as her own and he reached out to wipe them from her lashes. With that easy gesture, she realized instantly that he could see.

"Phillip, you can see again, can't you?" Anna was astonished but it was suddenly plain from the bright sparkle in his eyes as well as his grin that he could see clearly and as she thought back over the last few days, she knew he had been fooling her for some time. "You scoundrel, you absolute scoundrel! Why did you trick me this time?'

Phillip laughed at her indignation since it was so justified but he hastened to explain. "I wanted to be certain that it wasn't just my imagination. I wanted to see again so badly and when I thought my vision was returning I was afraid to mention it for fear I was mistaken, but I can see and I will never tire of looking at you."

"Then it is time that we leave." Anna looked down the beach with a longing glance. "We have been so happy here that I do not want to go."

"Nor do I for exactly the same reason but we will still be together, Anna, and what difference will the place make? I know Charles will be furious that I've married his fiancée but I'll risk his wrath and I care not one bit what bad manners I might have shown."

Anna took a step away and then came back to him and took his hand. "No, I will not let the man blame you for anything. I want you to escort me to his plantation and I will tell him that I've no wish to marry him or anyone else. I will be so dreadfully obnoxious and spiteful he will be delighted to see me go and then we can be married when we reach Philadelphia where the news of our wedding will never reach his ears. That way I will have honored my father's promise by going to him but I will break the engagement immediately and leave the island with you."

Phillip was not a bit pleased, but he could tell by the determined light in her eyes that Anna would insist upon getting her way. He could think of only one last possibility which would make her change her mind and used it. "It will be a long while before we reach Philadelphia, Anna. Is there not a good reason why we should be married as soon as possible?"

Anna's cheeks flooded with color as she stammered, "I am not certain, Phillip, not really. There might be a reason but it is too soon for me to be positive." She was horribly embarrassed by his question. Perhaps it was a most natural one for a man to ask his wife but they were not yet married and she had planned to keep the possibility of a child to herself until they were.

Phillip thought her blush charming. They had made love so often he did not understand how she could have escaped becoming pregnant but he had not thought his question would upset her so. "All right, but I would appreciate knowing whether or not I'll become a father as soon as you can make such an announcement for certain." When she did no more than nod shyly, he gave up all hope of arguing with her about anything. "We will still stop in Montego Bay as I'd planned. I know we are going to have to leave Jamaica with a haste the angels will envy and I'll not risk being overtaken. You are mine, Anna, truly mine now and I'll not risk your life if Charles guesses the truth and comes after us with every vessel the Royal Navy has afloat in Caribbean waters."

"Thank you, Phillip." Anna smiled with relief, delighted he'd seen her way was the best. "You know I am clever. He will not even suspect we are on speaking terms. You'll see. I will spend no more than one day with the man and he will be overjoyed to see me go." She hugged his arm tightly as they walked up the beach. "I'll be just awful, Phillip. He'll think me so spoiled and demanding he will probably give you a bonus for taking me away!"

"My dearest Anna, treat him no differently than you used to treat me and I know he will be glad to see you gone!" He dodged her playful jab to his ribs and, taking her hand, ran up the beach laughing as he pulled her along. What difference would a few days make, or a few weeks for that matter as she was already his wife in every way that mattered. Saying goodbye to Charles was no more than a formality he'd have to let her perform. Charles didn't frighten him one bit when he knew Anna had already made her choice, she was his and he promised himself she'd never regret she'd become Mrs. Phillip Bradford rather than a countess.

Chapter Twenty

Anna stood on deck the *Angelina* as the crew dashed around her. She was as impatient to leave Montego Bay as Phillip but she could understand the men's confusion for after their extended vacation on the island he had worked them unmercifully. She was supposed to be paying close attention; he expected her to learn the names of all the sails and she'd been astonished to find each had a separate name depending upon the mast to which it was attached and its relative position to the others. She thought the word sails descriptive enough but he insisted she memorize the correct terms. The *Angelina* was fore and aft rigged, that she understood, it had jack-yard topsails, triangular sails set above the main gaffsail. The first mast was the foremast, the center the mainmast and the last the mizzenmast. She whispered the words with such concentration Phillip walked over to her side delighted to see her studying so diligently.

"Show me a jib and I'll dismiss class for the day," he offered with a wicked grin, as if he were certain she'd fail that test.

"I'll do better than that, sir." Anna lifted her hand to point as she explained. "The bowsprit is the spar which extends beyond the bow, to which the fore staysail and the jibs are set. There is a flying jib, an outer jib and an inner jib."

"If half my crew were so bright as you I believe I could make the *Angelina* fly, Anna." Phillip then flashed the charming smile he reserved especially for her. She was the most remarkable woman in every respect and he had no doubt she would master any assignment he gave in record time. "I want to weigh anchor and sail on the evening tide. It is no more than thirty miles up the coast to the Rio Bueno. We'll leave the ship in the bay and go up the river to Charles's plantation at first light. That way you'll have the entire day to be obnoxious and we can sail at dusk."

"Good." Anna frowned slightly, the final stages of her plan still evolving in her mind. "Will you excuse me please, I want to go to my cabin for a while."

Understanding the complexity of their situation Phillip nodded agreeably. "Until supper then, Lady Thorson."

Anna turned to smile as she started below, his teasing expression was a promise of another marvelous evening and she could scarcely wait for the sun to set.

Jamie watched the pretty blonde skip across the deck, happiness lighting her sweet features. Something was afoot and he could no longer contain his curiosity. He approached Phillip cautiously and seeing the taller man's ready smile felt confident enough to ask, "Do you really plan to hand that bewitching creature over to that ghoul Clairbourne?"

Phillip's expression changed instantly to one of the utmost hostility. "That is a matter for Lady Thorson and Clairbourne to decide between themselves, Mr. Jenkins, no business of ours."

Although he was offended by that curt rebuff Jamie persisted. "I'd propose to her myself if I thought she'd have me, but if she looked at me the way she looks at you I know I'd have her safe in Philadelphia before Charles ever heard we'd been here."

Reminding himself he needed only one more day to preserve their secret Phillip restrained himself from simply striking the mate for being so insolent. "Your concern is appreciated, Mr. Jenkins, but the matter is not in your hands to settle which, if I may remind you, the *Angelina*'s progress is. I suggest you see to the duties for which you're being paid."

Jamie walked off with a brisk step. The whole crew was counting the hours for none wished to see the lovely Anna Thorson leave them. There was not a man on board who had not fallen in love with her but why couldn't Phillip see she had eyes only for him?

Anna responded demurely to Jamie's polite conversation at supper but she was ecstatic when the mate excused himself and left her alone with Phillip. She left her chair then to sit on his lap and wrapped her arms around his neck as she kissed him. "I'll never be able to sleep tonight. May I stay here with you?"

Phillip shook his head slowly. "In five minutes time I want you to walk sedately to your cabin and pretend to be asleep for at least an hour. That will give me time enough to appear on deck and allay the suspicions that seem to be running rampant among the crew. It is only for one more day, Anna, and then they will all know the truth about us."

Since he did not seem in the least concerned about revealing such a scandalous secret, she lifted her fingertips to his lips. "Not the whole truth I hope for I would still like to arrive in Philadelphia with some reputation left."

Phillip set her down gently before he rose to his feet. "A man need only to look at you to see you are a lady, Anna. Do not fret there will be gossip." Gossip seemed too small a word to describe what he knew would be a scandal so sensational it would fascinate two continents, to say nothing of the numerous islands of the Caribbean.

"Must I wait an entire hour?" Anna purred coquettishly.

"Tease me like that and I'll make it two, now run along!" Phillip gave her a playful swat to move her toward the door but he loved her charmingly flirtatious ways and was not at all certain he could wait a full hour to see her again. As it turned out, in only forty-five minutes he was in her bed.

"Let me rub your back. You are far more nervous than I am tonight." Anna moved astride Phillip's hips, her fingertips massaging the tension from his shoulders as she bent down to kiss the back of his neck softly. "It will all be over by this time tomorrow night but tell me, what is Charles most likely to dislike, a prim, serious type, or a childlike vixen? I want to present the worst possible alternative so I'll be certain to make him despise me."

"I had no idea you considered yourself so fine an actress, but I think you should simply be yourself." When she cuffed his ear playfully he turned to look up at her. "I'm not teasing you, just be yourself and be brief." He spoke then in an imitation of her voice. "No, Charles, I have no wish to marry you, thank you for your gracious proposal but I must refuse. Goodbye." Seeing her smile at his efforts he continued. "Just tell him something like that and we'll go. There will be no point in prolonging the scene when the outcome is already determined."

Anna moved her hands down his spine, carefully pressing each vertebra with a silken caress. "Yes, of course, I should be honest in my manner but that will be difficult to achieve when I have no intention of revealing the truth."

Phillip laid his cheek upon his hands and relaxed as he listened to her voice. He had always loved her pretty speech which was so unusual, as unique as the rest of her charming personality and every bit as inviting. "Just be brief, Anna, that's all I ask. Don't give him the opportunity to fall in love with you as the rest of us have."

"Us?" Anna asked softly. "Do not flatter me so, sir, or I shall become most conceited and difficult to please."

With a devilish laugh, Phillip grabbed for her waist, pulling her down beside him where he could gaze into her marvelous eyes as he watched her passion grow. "I know how to please you, lady, you know that I do." Her lips were soft, opening eagerly to accept his kiss and he was lost in his desire, captivated by her warmth. He did not release her until the first light of dawn filled the sky and he had to race back to his cabin before John came to awake him for the day and found him missing from his bed.

Twisting her hands nervously in her lap, Anna turned again to glance up at Phillip for reassurance. He'd arrived at her door that morning clean-shaven with his hair newly trimmed, so proper a gentleman in his appearance none could have faulted him. As always she thought him almost painfully handsome but now she was trying to concentrate on his words. The Rio Bueno had been named by Columbus he told her, the water was fresh, welcome refreshment for the explorer's weary crew and she marveled at the courage of the man who'd set out to prove the world was round rather than flat. How people could have been so foolish as to doubt the truth of his assumption she did not know, but any thought was a welcome distraction as the minutes sped by and Clairbourne's plantation came into view. She was doing her best to appear calm for Phillip's sake as well as her own but her heart raced with excitement and she felt faint from the oppressive heat. The sea breeze did not extend so far inland and she wondered how the slaves could work under such humid conditions. Just sitting in an open boat she was miserable. How could Charles possibly expect men to work all day in such heat?

Phillip helped Anna from the boat and gave her hand a warm squeeze, the only gesture of affection he dared give when he had no idea who might be observing them. But he knew she understood. "Come, it is a short walk to the house and you will be able to rest there."

Anna placed her fingertips upon his sleeve and whispered, "I am not tired but terrified! Let's just get this over with, I do not even want to stay for lunch!"

"You must try and display some manners, Lady

Thorson," Phillip cautioned sternly but the light in his blue eyes was a mischievous twinkle.

Anna tried to return his smile but her lips trembled slightly. She was ashamed to display such a lack of courage. She forced herself to concentrate upon the spacious home built upon a rise overlooking the river. The house was Georgian in style, wooden shingled with multiple roofs. The ground floor was constructed of stone; shady verandas surrounded the second. The many windows were covered by louvers which could be adjusted to catch even a slight breeze. And though the comfortable home was surrounded by lush hibiscus in full bloom, the bright red flowers did nothing to raise her spirits and a chill of dread shot down her spine making her shiver almost uncontrollably despite the warmth of the day. Phillip had sent one of his men on ahead to announce their arrival and as they approached the flower-lined path Charles came down the steps to greet them. He was followed by a pretty young woman with flashing black eyes and a skin of a creamy light brown. In sharp contrast to Lydia Shepard's caustic personality and cold demeanor, the Jamaican housekeeper was dressed in bright colors and smiling warmly in welcome.

Anna looked up at Phillip, her eyes filling with confusion as she realized the tall, fair-haired man walking toward them was her fiancé. While not so tall as Phillip, he was above average in height, trim and fit, his clothes elegantly tailored to show off his athletic build. His fair skin held a healthy tan, complementing his features which were even if not strong. His eyes were a soft, sparkling brown, holding only the hint of the golden flecks which filled her own. He was a handsome man and she knew he could not possibly be more than five or six years older than Phillip. She'd expected a far more mature gentleman and could think of no way to greet him as his gaze swept over her with a delight she found far more frightening than anger. Dear God, she thought, how could Phillip have imagined the man preferred counting money to being with women when he was regarding her figure with an admiring glance that barely concealed what she could only describe as lust? When he spoke, his voice held an arrogant sharpness which dismayed her all the more.

"When I hired you to escort Lady Thorson to my door, Bradford, I had no idea you would take the assignment so seriously." Laughing at his own joke, Charles gave the captain no further notice as he continued to appraise Anna's beauty with an appreciative stare. "You are perfection, my dear, as splendid a beauty as you father swore you'd be."

Anna finally remembered to extend her hand and he bowed slightly as he lifted her fingertips to his lips. He wore an unusual ruby ring on the little finger of his right hand. Although she caught only a glimpse of it, she was certain it depicted a golden serpent coiled around an apple and thought a scene from the Garden of Eden a most astonishing motif for the man to wear. His eyes held a mocking light as his glance lingered a moment too long at her bosom and she said the first thing which entered her mind. "My uncle said we were cousins, is that true?"

"Why, yes, our great grandmothers were sisters. We met only once, however, when you were no more than a child so I will forgive you for not remembering me." With a satisfied grin he drew her to his side, effectively blocking Phillip's way as he turned toward the house. "Let me show you inside, Anna, but you needn't stay, Bradford. Come back this evening to dine with us and I'll give you a most generous bonus for bringing me so ravishing a bride."

Anna turned back to give Phillip a reassuring smile. "Yes, please join us then, Captain." She nodded slightly, hoping he would understand her desire to speak with Charles privately and she saw by his confident expression that he did. He left without argument and she allowed Charles to escort her indoors though she was grateful when he asked his housekeeper to prepare rum-laced refreshments to be served on the veranda. She took a sip and then another, welcoming the numbness the intoxicating beverage would bring. The fact Charles had proved to be nothing like the man she'd imagined had upset her greatly.

The Englishman finished his drink quickly, then leaned back against the carved railing which surrounded the wide porch and explained proudly, "This is one of the most successful sugar plantations in the Caribbean. I built aqueducts to bring water from the river to power the mill and our production has increased significantly every year. It was regrettable I had to leave England before you arrived but I could not allow conditions here to deteriorate any further than they already had. I am proud to say I have restored order. The slaves are no longer openly rebellious so I think we should return home as soon as passage can be arranged. I have no desire to remain here for the summer as the weather is most disagreeable and we will be far more comfortable at Briarcliff."

Business seemed an unusual topic for him to discuss

at their first meeting but Anna was curious. "I understood you had come because of some difficulties with your workers. Have their grievances been addressed?"

"Grievances?" Charles scoffed in disbelief. "I own these black creatures, Anna. They are like animals, pets, they have no right to present grievances and I would not listen to them if they did. They are my property, exactly like that chair upon which you're resting belongs to me. They have no rights whatsoever. Where did you ever get such a ridiculous notion?"

Startled as much by his insistent manner as she was by the stupidity of his thoughts, Anna hastened to disagree. "The young woman who served these refreshments seemed like a person to me, are you saying she isn't?"

"Cassie is half white, and therefore free under our laws. How some Englishmen can keep black mistresses is a mystery to me but their children are free and permitted to marry."

"Your slaves do not marry?" Anna could see no logic to the man's words but persisted in her efforts to understand how the plantation functioned.

"Does a tomcat take a bride? These creatures have no need for our sacraments. They breed, of course, which I encourage, but they do not seem to be particular about with whom they mate." He sneered as he spoke, his dislike for the unfortunate creatures who called him master plain in his expression. "If you are finished I will show you something of the plantation before lunch."

His statement was not a politely worded invitation but a command and Anna put her hand in his rather than begin an argument when she thought it highly possible they would have an even more violent disagreement before the day was out.

Charles summoned a horse-drawn buggy which he drove himself as he gave Anna an extensive tour of his holdings. He was extremely proud of his success and boasted continually, but Anna saw only the terrified gaze in the eyes of his slaves rather than the lush fields of sugar cane. The dark-skinned men wore only light-weight cotton breeches and she did not see one whose back was unmarked by numerous scars from what appeared to have been savage beatings. "These men have all been whipped. Why?"

Charles shot Anna a disapproving glance. "The man I had employed as overseer was found drowned in the river. His death was no accident, however. I would rather have hanged a few of the Africans as an example to the others but they cost nearly one hundred pounds each and are worth far more to me alive than dead."

"You would hang men whether or not they are guilty of this suspected murder?" Anna asked incredulously, amazed that the expense rather than the immorality of his plan had influenced his decision.

Exasperated, Charles snarled impatiently, "The man did not fall into the river, he was deliberately drowned, which is merely one example of the stupidity of these creatures. Jamaica is an island; there is no way for them to escape and they are only wasting their time causing mischief. Each man I own was whipped severely, those suspected of being the leaders of the rebellion saw their wives sold to one of my neighbors and their children to another. With their families scattered to the four winds they will be docile enough in the future and the others will not risk the same punishment."

Sickened by his calm description of what she regarded as unspeakable cruelty Anna could only whisper. "I thought you said they had no wives. Are you telling me now that they do?"

Pulling the horse to an abrupt halt, Charles glared menacingly. "I do not like your questions, Anna. They are impertinent in the extreme and I suggest you consider them more fully and keep them to yourself in the future for I'll not spare you from punishment just because you are my wife should you displease me by being as disobedient as my slaves dared to be!"

Appalled by his insipid threats, Anna was glad to keep her thoughts to herself. The sun was high in the sky, the hour approaching noon and she had no desire to see any more of the plantation. They continued, however, until they had stopped at each point in the production of sugar. The field hands had the most menial jobs, digging the fields to plant the cane, tending its growth, then cutting and transporting it to the factory at harvest time. Jobs in the factory were no less strenuous as the cane had to be ground at the mill then boiled with lime in the steam-filled boiling houses. When the juice was reduced to a thick syrup it was stored in the curing house in hogshead barrels weighing nearly fifteen hundred pounds, ready to be exported to markets throughout the world. Charles explained the process in a matter-of-fact monotone, ending finally in front of the curing house. "I do not expect you to display any further interest in the workings of the plantation, now let us return to the house for lunch. My new overseer, Daniel MacDonald, will be there as we use that time to discuss our problems and I want you to meet him."

"Will your sons also be joining us?"

"Yes, they are fine lads. Thomas is the younger, he is five; William is seven. They resemble me rather than their mother which is fortunate but you may judge for yourself and tell me if you don't find them handsome."

Clearly the man had no respect for his late wife but Anna was still shocked he'd not shown her memory more regard when she'd given him two sons. "I have been looking forward to meeting your children," she replied hesitantly, beginning to worry that they'd be as ill-mannered as their father.

As for the overseer, she hadn't known what to expect from him but he met them in front of the house. He was immense in size, tall and broad, with bushy red hair which gave him a somewhat comic appearance, but his cold blue eyes held the same fierce glint as a bulldog's and Anna withdrew her hand from his sweaty grip after no more than a second's pause. He looked like the sort who relished delivering the whippings Charles ordered and she wiped her palm on her skirt hoping he would not see how repugnant she had found his touch.

They found the two little boys already in the dining room, seated on the edges of their chairs fidgeting impatiently as they waited for Mr. MacDonald and their father. They had Charles's dark eyes and fair hair but their bodies were chunky, thick at the waist rather than sleek like their father's. William, the bolder of the two, slipped from his chair to give Anna a closer look.

"Is this woman to be our new mother?" He looked her up and down slowly, his inspection very thorough but his lips puckered up in a sour scowl.

Anna smiled at the seriousness of his question but evaded it. "You must be William. How do you do?"

William made a funny face, clearly disgusted. "Why is your speech so strange?"

"Lady Thorson is from Sweden, but she will learn to speak properly quite soon, William, so we will simply ignore her peculiar accent for the time being." Charles spoke softly to the child, as if the pretty blonde at his side had not just been insulted most rudely while his overseer laughed out loud at the child's remark.

Trying to make the best of an awkward situation, Anna extended her hand and William took it gingerly then dropped it and stood aside to let Thomas take his turn at meeting her. The younger boy frowned unhappily and when Anna smiled sweetly and offered her hand to him he drew it quickly to his mouth and bit her index finger so deeply it bled.

Tears rushed to Anna's eyes as she tore her hand away. "Why, you naughty little brat!"

Charles grabbed her arm tightly as he issued a stern rebuke. "You will not criticize my sons in any way as they are not yours. They are spoiled, that is true, but I enjoy indulging them and have no intention of doing otherwise. Now let me show you to your place and we will have lunch together." Patting Thomas lightly upon the head as if he were a delight rather than a demon, Charles sent the boys back to their places.

Anna looked down at the blood which was dripping through her fingers. "I would like some soap and water please. You may begin without me as I have no appetite now."

"I will show her to her room, sir." Cassie had seen the unfortunate incident and stepped forward quickly to render assistance.

"As you wish." Charles and Daniel MacDonald

took their places and after saying grace quietly began to eat their meal with enthusiasm. That his son had caused his fiancée a deliberate injury obviously did not concern him in the least.

Cassie led Anna upstairs to a pretty, sun-drenched room where she directed her to be seated at the dressing table while she brought a pan of warm water and a bar of perfumed soap. "Those boys are a handful, and the master is to blame."

Anna let her hand soak in the soapy water and in a few moments the painful bite was clean and she could bear the dull ache without any more tears. "Thank you, Cassie. I have always enjoyed the company of small children but I have met none so ill-mannered as those two."

Cassie touched Anna's soft curls lightly. "You are very pretty. The master will like you, he needs a woman, I think."

Blushing deeply at that thought, Anna glanced over at the large bed. "Is this to be my room?"

"Yes, do you want to rest? I will bring some laudanum if you like."

"Laudanum?" Anna knew the drug to be a solution of opium in alcohol and while it was used to aid sound sleep she thought it unnecessary for a nap. "No, I shall not need it. This bite will not pain me long."

Cassie shrugged. "I will fetch it anyway." She returned quickly and put the small bottle down on the dressing table where the blue glass shone in the sun casting a sparkling reflection upon the walls. "Now where are your clothes?"

Anna understood the housekeeper's curiosity. After all, her arrival had been completely unexpected and her absence of luggage was decidedly odd. "My clothes? Well, I was not even certain Charles would be here so I left them on the ship for the time being." She'd worn the soft gold dress Sophia had helped her select for her first meeting with Charles and brushed the folds of the skirt lightly as she thought of the dear little woman and how much she missed her. "This dress will be all I'll need today. Thank you, Cassie, I'll be fine now and I'd like to rest."

Once the helpful servant had left, Anna wrapped a towel around her hand and lay down upon the bed but was too anxious to rest. She missed Phillip dreadfully and wanted only to return to the *Angelina* as soon as possible. It would be hours before he came back for her but she could hardly stand to wait. That Charles was so young and his appearance pleasing had been a surprise, but he was not someone she'd even care to know, let alone marry. He was arrogant and cruel, insensitive to the pain of others. She went over the speech she'd prepared several times and when she was certain he'd be finished with his lunch she tiptoed down the stairs hoping to find him alone. When she saw him seated in his study reading to himself, she rapped lightly at the door. "May I please speak with you for a moment?"

"Why, of course, come in, it is time we had a talk." Charles marked his place carefully then laid his book aside as he rose to greet her. "Please come and take this chair for it is the most comfortable."

Surprised by his courtesy, Anna sat down and leaned forward, hoping to finish all she had to say before he interrupted or she lost her courage. "Lord Clairbourne, I—"

"You needn't address me in so formal a manner, my

386

dear. My name is Charles and that is sufficient between a man and his wife."

Anna didn't know how to respond to that remark so simply continued, "When my uncle informed me of your proposal I was very flattered but understandably quite surprised as we had never met. At least I did not recall that we had and I thought it advisable that we meet to make plans for our future before we married rather than after. When you were not at Briarcliff I had no choice but to come here and I convinced Captain Bradford to bring me." That was not really the truth of the situation but she thought the lie a small one.

Charles nodded impatiently. "I can see you are here, Anna, and Bradford is never averse to doing something for a price. I'm sure he knew I'd pay whatever your journey cost. He is a resourceful man, but America seems to be filled with his kind. His resemblance to a man in the House of Lords is too close to be coincidental but I doubt he knows his father's name himself."

Anna was appalled by the man's crude innuendo. "I know he was orphaned. What makes you think his father was not a man named Bradford?"

Charles waved away her objection as unimportant. "He is a bastard all right. Many a young nobleman toured the Colonies then returned home to England without once giving another thought to the comely wenches they'd seduced. Like many born out of wedlock, Bradford is handsome and clever but certainly no fit company for a young lady of your fine background and I am sorry you had to spend so long on board his ship where I'm certain you were bored to distraction.

Now we seem to be getting off your subject if you had one. Please continue."

The details of Phillip's heritage did not matter to Anna but she was nonetheless shocked Charles would compliment him in one breath and then insult him the next. "My point was, is, that while my father wanted only what he thought was best for me, I have absolutely no desire to ever marry. My objection would be the same regardless of whom he had chosen for my husband, so I beg you to consider our engagement broken. I doubt many outside our immediate families ever knew of the arrangement you made with my father so there need be no embarrassment to either of us when we do not marry."

Charles frowned as he rocked back on his heels, his expression growing bitter. "There seems to be some sort of misunderstanding, Anna, while your father and I agreed completely. I met him several times, usually over a gaming table."

"Yes, I know his passion for gambling but that has nothing to do with us. I can not marry you, Charles, and I would like for you to accept my decision graciously as a gentleman should." That he was no gentleman in spite of his wealth and title was obvious to her but she hoped to appeal to his vanity since he appeared to have an abundant quantity of that fault.

Charles cocked his head slyly as he continued in a low mocking tone, "That you consider me capable of such generosity is appreciated. Now I expect you to listen to me without further interruption as if you were the lady you claim to be."

Anna's displeasure was clear in her glance but she'd known he'd be angry and wanted only to get the wretched scene over with swiftly and leave. She nodded politely and folded her hands tightly in her lap, prepared to sit for however long it took to make him see she'd never change her mind.

"The last time I saw your father he lost a considerable sum and when it came time to settle his losses he made those of us at the table a proposition. He said he owned only one possession of more value than what he owed to us and he offered it then, simply auctioned it off to cover his debts and left. I never saw him again, then heard he had died soon after he'd returned to Sweden."

Confused, Anna forgot her promise and asked breathlessly, "Are you speaking of our home? My uncle told me there were many debts to pay but I did not realize he'd had to recover a mortgage on our home."

Charles walked over to his desk and taking a key from his pocket unlocked the top drawer. He withdrew a carefully folded document from a parchment envelope she recognized and returned to face her. "I brought this with me as a precaution, for I did not want it to fall into the wrong hands while I was out of the country." With a slight smile he finished his tale. "What your father sold that night, Anna, was you."

Anna took the single sheet he offered and read it slowly. Her father's hand was easily recognizable on the marriage contract, the promise despicable but undoubtedly his. So this was the extent of her father's love, a bitter realization which pierced her heart with the force of the sharpest arrow. Several minutes passed before she trusted herself to speak without screaming. "This is an enormous sum of money he mentions here.

You thought I would be worth that much?"

"When a healthy black male capable of years of hard labor is worth one hundred pounds, I suppose ten thousand might seem like an exorbitant sum to pay for a white woman who will provide no more than pleasure, but you must not underestimate your value to me, my dear. You must also realize this was a simple business exchange. I took something he said was worth the sum he owed me rather than insist upon the amount in cash which would have been an extreme embarrassment to him. He had a debt which needed to be paid and I needed another wife. We were both quite pleased with our arrangement."

"Well, I am not!" Anna leapt to her feet, her father's neatly penned note still clutched tightly in her hand. "You have been in the slave trade too long but you can not buy me!"

"I must correct you my dear, I have already 'bought' you and you will become my bride unless you are prepared to repay the money your father owed me. That is the only way I will release you from our engagement."

"You expect me to give you ten thousand pounds for my freedom?" Anna's long, thick lashes swept her finely arched brows as she looked up at him. He could just as easily ask her for a million since she had not even one pound to her name.

"It is unfortunate I had to reveal this disgrace to you, that I will admit, but it did not occur to me you would wish to break our engagement when it is such an advantageous one for you."

"Did my uncle know about this? Did he know the truth about your so-called proposal?"

"But, of course, he is your guardian, Anna, and the

390

marriage contract is a legal one." Charles smiled with the same glee a cat turns upon an injured bird. There was no way she could escape him and he knew it.

Anna turned away, sick with shame. She had walked into a trap baited with her own body and she felt wretched through and through. She had always thought her father loved her as dearly as she loved him but it was obvious he had loved gambling far more or he never would have sold her future to cover his debts as if she'd been no more than an attractive piece of property. Her uncle would never cover this debt for there was nothing of value left to sell, nothing except her! Oh, Phillip, she thought sadly, her heart wrenched in two, I can't expect you to pay such an extravagant ransom either. He'd told her with such pride that he'd own the *Angelina* free and clear after this voyage but he was long overdue with his final payment to the bank in Philadelphia already and she couldn't ask him to go further in debt for her sake.

Charles saw the tears filling Anna's golden eyes and saw no reason to prolong their discussion when he'd clearly crushed her hopes to resist him. "I have already sent for the priest as well as what friends I can gather to help us celebrate our marriage. I must have your answer now. Either you will raise the sum you owe me before the priest arrives or you will marry me when he does. Which is it to be?"

Anna's glance filled with hatred as she turned back to face him. "You would marry me when you know I will become your wife only because I must? You want a bride you must take by force rather than love?"

An evil smile crossed Charles's lips as he took the note from her hands. "With pleasure, my dear, for I

391

intend to get my money's worth from you, every single penny."

"You may not live that long!" Anna responded fiercely, her rage against the horror of her fate unhidden.

Charles leapt forward, grabbing her shoulders in a painful grip, his fingers digging into her flesh like an eagle's talons rip into its prey. "Don't you ever dare to threaten me again, Anna. Don't even consider raising your voice to me or I'll see you suffer in ways you can't begin to imagine. No one crosses me, no one, most especially not my wife!"

I'll never be your wife, Anna thought instantly, you'll own no more than an empty shell. But she kept that spiteful comment to herself. She'd marry him to pay her father's debt, but he'd never have a wife.

Chapter Twenty-one

For his second trip up the Rio Bueno that day Phillip brought along several more men. He'd armed them well and gave them strict orders to wait downstream from Charles's dock. They could tell by the seriousness of his expression he wanted no questions asked and they waited quietly in the darkness, their apprehension mounting as he strode up the path to the house.

Not knowing what to expect from Charles, Phillip had prepared for the worst. When he left the plantation that night Anna would be with him but he hoped whatever fantasy she'd spun for the arrogant earl had been sufficient to release her from their engagement. That the house was so well-lit confused him, for why should Charles wish to entertain on this of all nights?

Cassie rushed to open the front door, delighted to see the handsome American again. "Good evening, Captain, may I bring you some champagne?"

Knowing Charles was never so extravagant, Phillip could not imagine why he'd decided to share the expensive French wine so generously but he recognized several of the men standing nearby and thought perhaps he and Anna had chanced to arrive on the eve of some special occasion. "Will I be expected to offer a toast?" He had no gift for poetic declarations and did not want to become involved in any such contest for every toast he knew was a favorite of mariners and unfit for a social gathering where ladies were present.

Laughing excitedly, Cassie showed off her sparkling smile. "A toast to the bride and groom of course!" She was gone in a flurry of ruffled skirts as she went to bring the promised wine and Phillip stared after her, too shocked to follow and question her any further. Damn it all, he swore to himself, had Anna not broken the engagement after all but let Charles invite his friends to celebrate their forthcoming marriage? He searched hastily through the small groups of people talking together in the spacious room, anxiously looking for the pretty young woman and finally caught a glimpse of her blond curls on the opposite side of the room. She was surrounded by ladies but he wanted to speak with her immediately and started in her direction, dodging the numerous servants who were scurrying about carrying heavy trays of succulent island delicacies. When he saw Charles heading toward him, he slowed his pace to a more sedate one and tried to hide his concern behind a friendly greeting.

Charles responded with a solid slap to the taller man's back as he shouted to be heard over the noise of the party. "Come into my study and I'll give you that bonus I promised, Bradford, for it is not every day that a man marries and I am in a most generous mood as a result."

"What?" Phillip exclaimed loudly, certain he could

not possibly have understood the fair-haired man's remark. When those standing nearby all turned to stare, he repeated his question with more courtesy. "I beg your pardon, what did you say?"

Charles grinned even more widely as he repeated what he'd said. "You of all people should not find the news so surprising. After all you brought Anna to me for just that purpose." He turned toward his study gesturing for Phillip to follow but the astonished captain grabbed his arm to draw him to an abrupt halt.

"Anna has married you. She married you today?" Phillip could not believe his ears. Surely the man was telling an outright lie.

"Yes!" Charles announced proudly. "More than an hour ago in fact. Why is that such a shock to you? I distinctly recall telling you I wanted to marry the young woman before she'd been at Briarcliff an hour. Why should the fact we're on Jamaica have changed my plans?" Lowering his voice, Charles continued in a conspiratorial whisper, "She is so delectable a beauty I saw no reason to spend another night alone when she is so willing to share my bed."

A fiery red haze descended over Phillip's eyes; only Charles's smug grin floated before him, a taunting, hideous smirk he wanted to rip from the leering man's face. But as he doubled up his fist and drew back his arm, Daniel MacDonald stepped between them, blocking his punch before he could throw it.

Charles seemed to find the incident very amusing and chuckled as he introduced his new overseer. "I do not believe you have met Mr. MacDonald, Captain Bradford, but he is a man of many and diverse talents. A most capable overseer as well as a bodyguard. I must remember to ask my wife why the news of our marriage should have affected you so profoundly as I am certain it will be an entertaining story. Now as the matter of your bonus, perhaps I should wait until tomorrow morning when I can give you a full accounting of how much I think Anna is truly worth."

Phillip's volatile temper exploded within him and had he been able to reach the English lord he would have torn the man limb from limb with his bare hands. But the presence of the brute MacDonald made such a deed impossible to attempt. A thousand insults came readily to his lips, each increasingly more obscene, but the words would never harm Charles so he did not waste his breath in speaking them. If Anna truly wanted such an unprincipled ass for a husband then he did not even know her, nor did he wish to. "Keep your blasted money. I wouldn't touch a penny of it!" With that bitter retort, Phillip turned and shoved aside the bystanders who'd gathered in hopes of watching a fight. He left the house and swore he'd never return, by God, he'd not ever set foot on Jamaica again after that night! He could not face his men with the news of Anna's treachery and walked off in the opposite direction from the river, trying to get his temper under control before returning to his ship. The night was warm, the sensuous Jamaican wind scented with the heady fragrance of night-blooming jasmine but the beauty of the island only increased his torment. How in God's name could Anna have stooped so low. How could she have betrayed his love in so despicable a fashion? Had her sweet promises of love all been lies, fabrications she'd told simply to pass the time when she'd become bored on their journey? The longer he walked, the more furious he became until an idea entered his mind that was so devious he could not resist using it. He returned to the impressive home then, circling it stealthily to find what he needed. A trellis on the side extended from the ground to the veranda, supporting the weight of a profusion of native orchids and in a matter of seconds he had scaled the flower-decked ladder and swung himself up on the wide porch.

He'd been inside the house several times, knew the arrangement of rooms and went first to Charles's suite where he helped himself to the bottle of champagne and two crystal flutes which sat upon a silver tray waiting for the bridal couple. "Sorry, my friend, but you'll not need these tonight and I will." Checking the hall first, he slipped into the room which adjoined the master's, certain it had been given to Anna. Her dress hung in the wardrobe and he was sorry he'd not had a better look at her to see what she was wearing. But he could not imagine that Charles would have had a wedding dress on hand and dismissing her attire as unimportant, he glanced around the room to be certain he'd missed nothing. She would surely enter alone, slowly unbuttoning her gown before going to the dressing table to brush out her hair. He walked over to the mirror and was surprised by the sight of his own reflection. He rather missed his beard and decided to grow another for Anna had always said she liked it. As he turned away swearing softly to himself for being so foolish the sight of the small blue bottle caught his glance and he set down the champagne and glasses so he could examine its contents. He recognized the scent of laudanum readily enough but could think of no reason for Anna to need it. But he could put it to a good use. He set it aside as he uncorked the sparkling French wine and pouring himself a full measure sat down to wait for Anna.

Downstairs the party grew increasingly more boisterous as the guests quenched their thirst with Charles's seemingly endless supply of champagne. Anna lifted her hand to her temple in a vain attempt to massage away the sharp pain which had plagued her all day. She had not eaten a bite but had had more glasses of the cool, sparkling wine than she could count. If she were drunk that night so much the better, but soon she began to feel ill and, excusing herself from the small circle of ladies whose names she could not seem to recall, she left the festive gathering and went upstairs to her room. She'd met everyone, neighbors who had come from miles around when Charles had summoned them and she saw no reason to prolong what had to be done. But as she closed her door quietly Phillip called to her.

"It is about time you appeared, Countess." He rose from his chair and crossed the large room to fill a crystal flute with champagne for her. It would not suit his purpose to frighten her and he smiled slightly as he turned back to hand her the wine. "Shall we drink to your happiness?"

Anna swallowed to force back the wave of nausea which filled her throat. "I've had too much already." She could not believe he was taking the news of her marriage so calmly. She'd expected him to come crashing through the front door of the house at any moment, yelling at her, calling her vile names. She had been certain his reaction would be a violent one but she'd never imagined he would simply propose a toast as if they were no more than casual acquaintances rather than the dearest of lovers.

Phillip approached her slowly, his smile still warm. "But I insist, I want you to drink this to the last drop, Anna."

Anna's hand shook so badly, the delicate, long-stemmed goblet nearly slipped from her grasp but Phillip moved swiftly to help her. His warm hand closed gently over hers.

"You have every reason to be nervous tonight, Anna, but this will help you, believe me it will." His gaze scanned her flushed features intently, hoping for some clue as to why she'd changed her purpose so completely once she'd entered Clairbourne's home. If she'd been beaten there were no marks on her face, but her glance held such confusion, her golden eyes were filled with a pain so intense he felt as if he could reach out and touch it. With his coaxing she finished the champagne and he took the empty glass and set it aside with his own. "Tell me the truth now, Anna, I will accept any explanation for this travesty as long as you tell me the truth."

Anna listened carefully to the rich mellow tones of his voice. He had such a soothing manner, but she had difficulty following his words. That he wanted the truth was plain but the enormity of her father's betrayal was a secret she'd take to her grave. She wanted to provide some explanation for her marriage since he deserved one, but it was a senseless act she'd been forced to perform and it was impossible to justify it now in any rational terms. The words stuck in her throat when she tried to speak and then she could not even catch her breath. She saw his lips move as he pressed her to explain and thought only of how dearly she loved him and how desperately she wanted to kiss him for one last time before it was too late to enjoy any sensation.

"Anna?" Phillip had been standing close for just such a purpose but when she fainted so suddenly he had to grab for her waist to keep her from slipping to the floor. Wasting no time then, he yanked off the ruby ring Charles had placed on her finger and tossing it upon the dressing table he lifted her to his shoulder, crossed to the French doors which opened out onto the veranda and quickly climbed over the rail. He descended the trellis, keeping to the shadows as he carried Anna back to the boat he'd left waiting. They were well on their way down the river before Charles had even noticed Anna was no longer chatting politely with the wives of his friends.

As the *Angelina* came into view, the men at the oars strained to increase their speed, exhaling in hoarse rasps as they saw their hurried flight nearing its end. Phillip held Anna in a gentle embrace, fondly cradling her slender body upon his lap as he kept his fingers upon her delicate wrist. Her pulse was steady but he was worried. He'd been so angry with her he'd poured the whole damn bottle of laudanum into her champagne. He knew her tolerance for alcohol was slight and doubted she'd be any more resistant to the effects of the drug. She was sleeping so deeply he knew she'd be asleep for a long time but he'd not meant for her to never waken. He wasn't proud of himself for drugging a woman who was already clearly inebriated but that was a small crime compared to hers.

As the boat came alongside the *Angelina*, Jamie

leaned over the rail to help Phillip lift Anna safely onto the ship. Completely limp her slight weight presented an awkward burden and he hoped they'd not caused her any pain. "What has happened to Anna? Has she fallen ill?" Phillip had been silent all day, pacing the deck waiting for sunset but Jamie had no idea what had occupied the captain's mind if it were not the enchanting blonde and he'd not dared to mention her name again. When Phillip gave no reply to his question, Jamie followed him but when he carried Anna into his own cabin Jamie stopped at the door. "Her belongings are still in my cabin, sir. She may use it again, I do not mind bunking with the men."

Placing Anna gently upon his bunk Phillip turned back to face the mate squarely. "Come in and shut the door, Mr. Jenkins. Your cabin isn't needed for there's no point in prolonging the masquerade Anna's engagement to Charles forced us to live." Straightening his shoulders proudly, Phillip continued, "Anna is my mistress and has been for some time. She will occupy my cabin now because this is where she belongs."

Gesturing helplessly toward the sleeping young woman, Jamie was too astounded to do more than stutter. "But, but, but what has happened now? Is she not still engaged to Clairbourne?"

"No, now she is his wife and I've just kidnapped her so I suggest you give the order to weigh anchor before his lordship arrives and makes all our lives more difficult. Set a westerly course. We'll bypass Cuba and make for New Orleans."

Jamie tore out the door, screaming orders as he ran. He'd not refuse to obey the captain's command but the peaceful night had suddenly taken on a terrifying aspect he wished most desperately to escape. He could scarcely believe what Phillip had told him was true for Anna had such a radiant glow of innocence about her he'd never dreamed she wasn't the demure noblewoman he'd admired from what he knew had not been all that respectful a distance. He'd known she cared for Phillip, as it was obvious to all, but that the captain had taken advantage of her youth and inexperience appalled him. Clairbourne would come after them, he knew that without question. But the man would expect them to flee to the northeast since their home port was Philadelphia and would most likely try to overtake them as they slipped between the eastern end of Cuba and the western tip of Haiti when in fact they'd be many miles away. Surprised as always by the captain's cleverness, Jamie left the mouth of the Rio Bueno and, posting a lookout to be certain they weren't being followed, gave all his attention to pushing the *Angelina* to her top speed. Her new sails were stiff, catching the wind easily and he smiled, confident they could outsail any pursuers that night.

Having sent Jamie to see to their departure, Phillip stood with his hands on his hips, glaring fiercely as he tried to decide what to do with Anna. Lady Clairbourne, he thought with a sneer. She was indeed a countess now and his anger nearly choked him in a furious burst of obscenities he saw no reason to squelch. How in God's name had Charles managed to produce such a beautiful gown? Not only was it new, but it was exquisite, low-cut in the bodice, yet high-waisted. Tiny tucks decorated the neckline and seed pearls adorned the embroidered lace which trimmed the sleeves and hem. The creamy peach shade of the satin showed off

Anna's golden tan to perfection and he had to force himself not to reach out and caress her cheek. He was certain no woman had ever been more lovely, then he recalled her pretty tan covered her whole body with an even glow from head to toe. They'd gone swimming each day, never bothering to clothe themselves for the sport. As his sight had been so poor it had not been an erotic pastime until he'd touched her. He smiled with that memory, for he'd never been able to avoid doing so for long. She'd led him through the waves in endless games but he'd always caught her and then . . . He forced his mind past the next image which filled his senses with longing for it was too dear to recall when she'd chosen to marry Charles with such ridiculous haste.

"Why, Anna, why?" Why would she have turned her back on the love they'd shared when he'd thought they'd have their whole lives to spend together? That riddle tormented him unmercifully for he had loved her so completely he would never have given her up for any cause. But at her first opportunity she'd left him without even the courtesy of a goodbye. They'd been parted for no more than a few hours and she had betrayed him with a speed he found truly astonishing. He'd not known so faithless a female even existed upon the face of the earth, let alone imagined Anna to be so selfish and conniving as she'd proved to be.

"Love!" he swore softly, pronouncing the word as if it were filthy. He'd been so damn smart, scorning love as unnecessary for a man and the first time he'd allowed himself to feel the beauty of that tantalizing emotion he'd been cruelly betrayed. An act of treason paled by comparison to what she'd done to him for surely loyalty to another human being was more important than loyalty to one's native land. The penalty for treason was death, but that was far too mild a sentence to pass upon Anna for what she'd done to him. She'd made him dare to believe in love, to dream for a future filled with contentment and then had dashed his hopes by marrying a man he'd not even considered a rival.

His head began to ache with the familiar pain he'd thought would no longer trouble him but he knew there would be no way to gain relief from that misery until he found a way to silence the anguish which screamed in his heart. Physical pain was a trivial annoyance compared to the agony she'd inflicted upon him that day. He continued to pace, his long stride carrying him up and down beside the bunk where she lay, until he could no longer stay awake but the prospect of sharing his bed with her was strangely repugnant. "It seems I have a poisonous viper for a mistress!" he exclaimed softly, knowing from now on he'd always be wondering what mischievous thoughts filled her pretty head, what new treachery lurked in her unfaithful heart. He'd been warned now and he'd never trust her out of sight again. Making love to her would never bring the same joy, for the sweetness of her surrender had been no more than a sham. She was the very worst of women, a beauty with a heart so cold the devil himself would envy her and he hated himself for ever having been so weak as to have loved her.

Since he'd need every bit of his energy to elude Charles's pursuit, Phillip knew to avoid sleep was senseless, but he'd have to undress Anna, for her gown left too little room in the narrow bunk for him to rest omfortably. He had to sit down on the edge of the bed and lift her up, propping her limp body across his knee as he unfastened the hooks which ran down her spine. They were tiny, the fastening stiffs, but as he eased the lovely garment off her shoulders he saw the deep purple bruises Charles fingers had made upon her creamy skin and was filled with remorse for the bitterness of his accusations. "Dear God, Anna, what happened to you in that cursed house?" He pulled her arms from the long sleeves, looking now for further signs of abuse and found the bite marks Thomas Clairbourne had left. Then he eased the gown from her body before placing her head again upon the pillow and smoothing her tangled curls away from her delicate brows. She'd had no time to explain anything before she'd fainted which had been more his fault than her own. He cast his own clothing aside and joined her in the bed, pulling her close to his heart as he brought her fingertips to his lips. He'd make Charles pay and pay dearly for hurting her. Forgetting his own pain, he let the rapture the closeness of her slender body always gave to his carry him to the world of dreams where betrayal was a word never spoken and heartbreak a sorrow unknown.

Chapter Twenty-two

Phillip made no attempt to awaken Anna before he left his cabin the next morning. He left her sleeping contentedly in a tangle of bedclothes after he'd made certain the large amount of the drug he'd given her had done her no real harm. He went about his usual chores but he kept a sharp lookout for any sign of other ships for he did not put any revenge past Charles. The more distance they could put between themselves and Jamaica before their course could be discovered the better he would like it. But he left nothing to chance that morning and under his command the *Angelina* did come very near taking flight, her graceful bow slicing through the waves as the wind caught her sails pushing her ever more swiftly toward the safety of an American port.

When he could no longer bear his curiosity, Phillip returned to his cabin and pulled a chair up beside his bunk. With but gentle coaxing Anna opened her tawny eyes but for a long moment there was no gleam of recognition in their amber depths. She sat up then clutching the rumpled sheets to her breast as she realized she was completely nude. She pushed her curls away from her eyes and peering intently at Philip asked calmly, "What am I doing on board the *Angelina?*"

Phillip shrugged noncommittally. "Where else did you expect to be this morning?"

"Nowhere," Anna admitted softly. Her head ached so badly she could barely focus her eyes on his taunting smile but the last thing she remembered was swallowing champagne she didn't really want to drink while he helped to steady her hands. "My God, Phillip, what have you done?" She was frantic then, for surely he'd killed Clairbourne and would suffer the most dire of fates as a consequence. "What have you done?"

Leaning back in his chair with an air of exaggerated boredom, Phillip was slow to reply. "What I have done is merely put things back the way they were meant to be, but I would like to have you explain why such an action was necessary. I gave you too little opportunity last night to explain behavior I can only describe as bizarre but I have plenty of time today so you may take as long as you like to make me understand why you would have been so foolish as to marry Charles when I had the distinct impression that was the last thing you planned to do yesterday." He sat up then, his mood no longer playful as his anger returned to fill his flashing blue eyes with a fury she could not mistake.

Anna looked down at her left hand, surprised to see Charles's ruby ring was gone from her finger. "His ring was too big but he had no other. I hope I haven't lost it." She looked around then, twisting the blankets nervously as she searched through their soft folds for the missing ring.

"What happened to your hand?" Phillip nodded slightly, curious, for if he were not mistaken the bruises on her right index finger had been made by teeth. "Well, speak up, what happened?"

"I should not have lost that ring. Charles will be very angry with me." Anna could not seem to grasp what had happened to her; that she was again with Phillip was so unexpected she could not push her mind to any other thought.

"Anna?" Phillip reached out to take her hand in his but his grasp was light, his touch as tender as always. He could see she was still on the edge of sleep and thought perhaps if he pressed her she might reveal all he wished to know without realizing any questions had been asked. "I can't believe Charles would bite you, but clearly someone did. Was it one of the boys, William or Thomas?"

Anna licked her lips slowly, trying to recall the little child's name. "They did not like me, Phillip. Maybe they were expecting to see their own mother once again but they were not pleased to meet me, not at all."

"Obviously not." Phillip slid his fingertips to her wrist, counting the beat of her pulse silently in his head. "I think you had too much to drink last night. You should be more careful, Anna, ladies of your breeding should not drink until they pass out as sailors do."

Anna pulled her hand from his and rubbed it across her eyes. "I should not have lost that ring, for I've no way to replace it."

Exasperated that she could not seem to get beyond that ridiculous ring Phillip spoke harshly. "You did not lose it, you left it behind for Charles to find. Now go back to sleep and I'll speak to you later when you've managed to clear your mind."

Yawning sleepily, Anna lay back down, closed her eyes and was sound asleep again before he could reach his door. Something was wrong, she could remember that much, but at least she hadn't lost the ruby ring. Charles had said it was worth a fortune and she knew she would never have been able to buy him another.

John stepped aside as Phillip came up on deck but gathering all his courage he followed the taller man and asked, "I would like to take Lady Thorson some breakfast if you will allow it."

"She's still asleep, so you needn't bother, John." Phillip saw the unspoken accusation in the boy's eyes and attempted to reassure him. "I know how this must look to you, but—"

"You need not explain, sir, for I know the truth." John left without waiting to be dismissed, his cheeks burning with a bright blush but he'd not let the captain take him for a fool.

Knowing no purpose could be served in speaking to the young man when his feelings were so transparent, Phillip let the matter slide. The whole crew had been watching him rather strangely that day but he supposed that was to be expected. They knew him to be serious and determined, so hard-working a man they'd not expected him to dash off to rescue Anna with such heroic methods as he'd chosen but he cared little for their confusion when he had her safely hidden in his cabin where Charles could never again even catch sight of her, let alone have the audacity to call her his wife.

By evening Anna's mind was far too clear and she

was badly frightened. She'd not even tried the door but knew she didn't want to still be in his bunk when Phillip returned. None of her possessions were in his cabin, not even the dress she'd worn for the wedding. Everything was gone, her lingerie, stockings, slippers and the lovely dress were nowhere to be found, but she had no intention of sitting in his bed without a stitch to wear while they talked. His clothing was too large for her that was true, but it was at least clothing and, donning one of his well-tailored shirts, she rolled up the sleeves and left her legs bare. The weather was still warm, the cabin stuffy and she made up the bunk and sat down at the table with a book to wait for Phillip to appear but she had no idea how she could face him after what she'd done. All she knew was that she would never ask him to choose between her and the *Angelina* for no matter which he chose he would be heartbroken. "Oh, Phillip, I had no choice, none at all my darling."

Anna's lack of wardrobe had been no accident but Phillip was surprised she'd helped herself to his. The oversized shirt only made her femininity all that more appealing and he wondered what he'd been trying to prove by taking away her clothes. He'd intended only to make her stay put for the afternoon but he found the look in her eyes strangely disconcerting as if he were the one who'd wronged her rather than the other way around. "Since you're obviously feeling better, let's not waste any more time getting to the truth." He pulled out his chair and sank down into it, more tired than he'd realized until that moment, but he shook off his fatigue as he leaned forward. "Just tell me how you happened to marry Charles yesterday, that's all I really want to know."

Anna closed her book slowly, unable to meet his steady gaze. "All that matters is that I did marry him and while I can't remember how you took me from his house to bring me on board the *Angelina*, I know you shouldn't have done such a foolhardy thing for now you and all your men are in danger again and I can't allow you to take such risks because of me."

"You can't allow it!" Phillip shouted angrily. He had done his best to hold his temper, to be reasonable even when there was not the slightest shred of hope such a generous attitude was justified. "Have you no idea what you've done?"

Anna looked up slowly, her golden gaze clouded by thoughts he couldn't read. "Yes, I've married Lord Clairbourne and it was wrong of you to take me away from him."

Phillip leapt to his feet, unable to remain seated when she'd provoked him so greatly. "Well, Countess, perhaps you forgot one small detail. You had already promised to marry me!"

"If you think the sequence of events is so important then you must remember that my marriage to Charles was arranged before I had even met you. You used to be fond of reminding me of that fact, as I recall."

"You'll offer no excuse at all for letting me think you loved me? For making me believe what we had was worth more to you than all of Charles's millions? Can't you bring yourself to ask for my forgiveness for such a despicable deception!" Phillip was ready to wring her neck. He was past anger and the bitterness of his outrage was clear.

With a sad, sweet smile Anna replied, "But I do love you, Phillip, don't ask me to deny the truth of my emotions for I will never do that."

"Oh, I see, you love me so dearly you just happened to marry someone else to pass a boring afternoon? Do you honestly expect me to believe such an outrageous lie?"

"Believe whatever you like but I will always love you."

Phillip crossed the cabin to lock the door then came back to face her as he stripped off his shirt. "Then prove it!"

Confused, Anna frowned. "What sort of proof is it you require if my word is not enough?"

"You damn well know what it is I want. Now get into my bed and be quick about it!"

"That would prove nothing you don't already know," Anna argued logically.

"What I know is no man has ever had a more perverse mistress than you but I have learned to depend upon your considerable talents for giving pleasure and have no intention of giving them up."

"You love for me is no more than a habit then?" Anna rose gracefully to her feet, unable to sit quietly while he insulted her so cruelly.

"You'll never hear me speak the word love again, Anna, not until the day I die. I won't ever believe in that ludicrous myth ever again!"

Anna glanced over at the neatly made up bunk, she could understand his anger but surely going to bed with her was no way to express it. "You have every right to be angry with me but truly I thought the choice of whom I married was mine to make when it was not. Marrying Charles was something I had to do, a matter of honor which had nothing to do with my love for you."

"Of course not, why would it? I am merely the man you promised to love forever, no matter what calamity befell us you swore I'd never lose you and now you twist the vow until it is no longer recognizable by stating you married Charles as a matter of honor! My God, woman, have you not the faintest idea what honor truly is?"

He was furious, but she had known he would be and yet truly she'd had no choice, none at all. She stood calmly before him, her stance proud, her gaze level. She'd make no excuses, nor would she plead for him to understand a problem so difficult she could not even begin to explain it. He'd had no family to love and protect him, he'd always been on his own so how could be possibly understand she had had to honor a promise her father had made no matter how disastrous and painful the results? "I do not expect you to forgive me for this. It would be far better if you despised me, sent me back to Jamaica and never let any thought of me ever cross your mind again. Forget me, or pretend I am dead if that would be the easier solution."

That she could reply with such calm detachment astonished Phillip. She apparently had a heart of granite despite her enchanting ways and he was thoroughly sickened to think how desperately he had loved her. "Give you back to Charles? You're not serious! You are mine now, Anna, and a woman of the most extraordinary talents, talents I'll never let that fool Clairbourne savor!" He grabbed for her waist then, drawing her close in a tight embrace that held no tenderness as he slipped his oversized shirt from her slender body. She was his woman, faithless but so lovely he

413

could not let her go no matter what her crime. He lifted her into his arms and carried her to his bunk, intent now upon making her the slave to his loving he had become to hers. As he lay down beside her his caress was bold, demanding, sure in its purpose as he drew her into a close embrace from which she could not escape. He knew her lissome body as well as his own and delighted in her silken skin which was so smooth against his bare chest. He knew how to arouse her passion with tantalizing kisses but now he wanted to teach her a lesson she'd never forget. Their bodies had been made for each other; they melted together so perfectly, ecstasy always came without conscious effort. But this time he wanted to capture her will not her heart. Pleasure was a trivial goal compared to the bond he wished to forge, for he wanted to fuse her very soul to his so she would not even contemplate, let alone ask to be set free. He wanted her to be his down to the last drop of blood in her veins, to the smallest thought in her lively mind, to the softest breath in her lungs he wanted all of her delectable spirit to be only his and he knew he had the stamina to accomplish such a feat with his body alone and moved with a sure, swift power to convince her his will would be supreme.

Rather than struggling against his strength, Anna relaxed in Phillip's fierce embrace, his kiss was brutal, bruising her lips but she lifted her arms to his shoulders, pulling him closer still. Her fingertips moved slowly up his neck to comb through his newly shorn curls, so soft and thick they were as shiny as her own. She held him with so gentle a touch that gradually his fury lessened, the anger fusing with desire and she let her hands wander slowly down his sides, softly drawing him near as she enjoyed the warmth of his deeply tanned skin. He was so alive, his body sleek, the powerful muscles which crisscrossed his back taut as they flexed in response to her feather-light touch. She had thought the rapture of his loving was a joy lost forever and she wanted only to return the pleasure his slightest touch gave to her. She moved beneath him, guiding him, luring him with a languid, feline grace which ended in a honey-smooth sigh of surrender.

Stunned by a seduction so compelling he had lost all thought of his original purpose, Phillip drew away, poised on the brink of an act he knew would surely hasten his own demise rather than hers. He had wanted to make her dependent upon him, to create within her heart a need equal to his own but he had failed so completely in his quest he'd remembered nothing but how dearly he loved her.

A soft, sultry glow filled Anna's eyes, turning their amber shade to a vibrant brown. "I love you," she whispered so quietly he heard not a sound but he saw the words clearly upon her lips and gave up all resistance to her magical allure. He knew she had to be lying but it no longer mattered. He lowered his mouth to her throat where his lips caressed the soft throb of her pulse lightly before returning to her mouth with a kiss of heart rending sweetness. His mind no longer tormented him with thoughts of her treachery when her body was so willingly his. He felt only the excitement which flooded his veins with a delicious warmth, setting his blood aflame with his need for her. She gave all he could ever hope to take and then so much more. Again and again she enveloped him with loving so exquisite he could not bear to release her and he buried his face in her golden curls, nuzzling her throat with playful kisses, so grateful for her gift of pleasure he did not trust himself to speak more than her name and that he whispered with the reverence of a prayer.

Anna hugged Phillip tightly, afraid to let him go for she wanted that blissful moment of perfect peace to last forever. "It is paradise with you, Phillip, and now all I will ever know of heaven."

As Phillip looked down at her troubled gaze, a single tear escaped her thick lashes and rolled slowly down her cheek where he caught it in a gentle kiss. "You are no fallen angel but the dearest of creatures. Why do you think heaven's gate would be closed to you tonight or ever?"

"Adultry is a sin as great as murder, is it not, and the punishment as severe?" Anna had no wish to remind him she was now Clairbourne's wife but it weighed heavily upon her own mind.

Phillip broke into a wide grin, his deep laugh taunting her cruelly until he saw she did not understand what he found so amusing. "Charles told me he'd give me a bonus based on his appraisal of your worth after he'd spent the night with you. I saw he never got that chance and since your marriage was not consummated you are not his wife and can not possibly be accused of committing adultery."

Anna's cheeks flooded with color for what Phillip said was true but it really didn't matter. "I must go back to him, Phillip. I made a promise to God as well as to him and I must go back."

Phillip shoved himself off the bed, pulling on his hastily discarded clothes as he snarled through clenched teeth. "He won't want you now, you silly

416

little fool! It's me he'll come after and for only one reason. But why I ever thought the risk of death would be a small price to pay for your love I'll never know! It is long past the hour for supper and I am famished. Get up and I'll summon John to bring whatever Michael has saved for us."

"I would prefer to bathe and dress first. Perhaps you have made no secret of our relationship now but I will not behave in so wanton a fashion as to flaunt it in front of John or any of the rest of the crew." Anna sat up and attempted to comb her tangled curls with her fingers but gave up the effort as too painful. "I need my things. I do not mind bringing the water for my own bath but I must have some garment to wear to do it."

Phillip stared coldly at the disheveled young woman. She had never been more lovely, the warm glow passion gave her lightly tanned skin made him long to gather her into his arms once again but he turned away and walked to the door. "You are right, of course, there is still a value in discretion and I will bring all you need myself for I fear John is too shocked by what's happened to be of any service to us."

"You should not underestimate him so badly, Phillip. He has known for weeks exactly what our relationship is and you did not suspect it." Anna spoke softly, her voice a warm purr. "Surely you are not still jealous of him when you never had any reason to be."

Phillip was appalled by her revelation. "How in God's name did John know. Did you tell him?"

How he came by his knowledge was a secret she'd not reveal. "I am certain our love was apparent to all who saw us together, Phillip. He is a sensitive young man and saw the truth in our glance. I'll say no more about it other than to ask you to respect his feelings."

Phillip walked back to his bunk, seething with anger once again. "That you would ask me to consider another man's feelings when you have absolutely no regard for mine is a bit contradictory, don't you think? You think only of yourself, Anna, it is that simple and I am going to learn from your example, believe me I am!"

Anna sat silently watching him as he made several trips to bring her belongings before he brought in the small copper tub she used for bathing. He provided hot water, soap and towels all without uttering a word, performing each task as if it were most painful. He left her then so she might bathe and dress in private but it was not a gesture of courtesy but one of rejection and she felt only sorrow rather than being pleased by his kindness.

Anna ate her dinner slowly, deliberately chewing each tiny bite so many times her jaws began to ache. She could bear Phillip's anger because it was justified, but his silent indifference was like a knife piercing her heart with a thousand wounds and she found that pain unendurable. Finally she lay her knife and fork across the side of her plate and asked, "What do you plan to do with me, Phillip? Where are we going and what will happen when we arrive?"

"I will tell you my plans since there is no one you can inform to prevent them." Phillip's glance was cynical as he accused her of deceiving him if it were it possible. "We are bound for New Orleans. It is a fascinating port, part of the territory gained from France two years ago, in 1803, for a mere fifteen million dollars.

418

Napoleon needed the money to finance his endless campaigns through Europe and President Jefferson was only too glad to have the additional lands as many Americans had settled along the Mississippi River when Spain held title to the region. When ownership reverted to France, these people wanted to insure they'd still have access to the port of New Orleans to ship their goods. Rather than merely invading the port, Jefferson sent James Monroe to France to negotiate for its sale, but Napoleon offered to sell not only the port but an enormous block of land as well and all at a bargain price."

Anna nodded thoughtfully. "Yes, land is precious to every country and especially so to yours which is so newly independent. Is that your plan then, to make your home in New Orleans rather than Philadelphia?"

"Only for the time being. I have debts I must pay so I will have to return to the East Coast eventually, but I have mentioned my obligations to you before and you did not think them important."

Anna swallowed the angry retort which came to her lips and remained silent. She had been most unsympathetic to his problems when all she'd wanted to do was meet Charles and end the uncertainty of her future. What a stupid fool she had been to involve Phillip in her life when the results had been so disastrous for them both. He did not realize she would never ask him to choose between his precious *Angelina* and her love but that was a secret she'd not reveal even though it made her seem selfish when in fact her marriage to Charles had been a completely selfless act. "You did not say what you plan to do with me but regardless of what you believe I do not think we can legally marry."

Phillip tossed down the last of his wine and set his silver goblet upon the table with a loud thump. "How can you possibly think I'd still be interested in marrying you? That would be even more preposterous than your marriage to Charles!"

Stunned by the viciousness of that insult, Anna rose to her feet, ready to flee to the deck rather than take such uncalled for abuse. "Please excuse me, I have been confined here too long and would like to enjoy the night air, alone." She turned to leave but Phillip overtook her before she could reach the door.

"I can not allow you to roam the ship alone, Countess. There is too great a danger you might suffer some injury and I would never forgive myself if that occurred." Phillip's voice dripped with sarcasm as he escorted her through the door. Once up on deck he led her to the starboard rail where he kept a confining hand upon her waist. The night had an extraordinary beauty, warm and clear with a wind which caressed his cheek as seductively as Anna's kisses and he quickly regretted he'd not let her go for a walk alone.

Anna saw only the stern line of the proud man's jaw and knew a discussion on any topic would lead to further argument. She stood at his side, breathing deeply of the warm tropical air and wished with all her heart she could explain her reason for marrying Charles. But her loyalty to her father's memory was too strong and her eyes filled with tears as she considered how little her parent must have loved her. It was plain Phillip no longer loved her either and she felt doubly abandoned as she stood close by his side, an unbridgeable distance from his heart. Surrounded by loneliness, all her options gone, she gazed down at the sparkling water

420

which beckoned with a deadly invitation she found hypnotically attractive. The cresting waves seemed to call to her softly, coaxing her to leap to their depths and she turned away, shocked by the level of her own need for the oblivion that act would offer, for the peace of the grave seemed the only joy left open to her now.

When she turned away Phillip reached out to take her hand in his, gently pulling her back to his side. "Are you ready to go back to my cabin so soon?" His voice was a teasing invitation of what he obviously expected to occur, his words slurred by the wind but easily understood.

Anna looked up at her handsome companion and nodded shyly for it was now evident what the pattern of their days would be. Clearly he hated her for leaving him but his pride as well as his passion would not let him send her away. She had been exiled from his heart if not his bed but the real closeness they'd shared was gone leaving only the taunting reminder of the beauty that had been lost. She had become his mistress, it seemed, a woman kept for pleasure, for continual amusement. But the joy she'd always felt in his strong embrace would be the same for her feelings for him had not altered and she walked back to his cabin without the slightest bit of apprehension. As soon as he'd closed the door she whispered softly, "Lock it, please, Phillip, for surely we do not wish to be disturbed tonight."

The liquid purr of her voice surprised him but Phillip had given up all hope of understanding the young woman and slid the bolt into place as she'd requested. "Jamie will not disturb us and it seems John has already been here to clear away the remains of our meal. We will be quite alone." He stood by the door as Anna began to disrobe. Her gestured were as graceful as a ritual dance and he wondered if she realized the effect her casual strip tease was having upon him and if it were intentional. She sat down on the edge of his bunk to roll down her silk stockings, revealing a perfect pair of shapely legs and he turned away to pour himself some rum rather than allow her to see the depth of his desire in his expression. That he had such little restraint where she was concerned annoyed him tremendously. He wanted to be able to take her whenever he wished but she could control his moods far too easily. She aroused him with no more than a glance and he debated with himself whether or not to relieve the man on watch simply to make her wait but knew he'd be punishing only himself and he was not that foolish.

"How does a mistress behave, Phillip? You must teach me," Anna asked in an inviting whisper. "You are the best of teachers so surely you can tell me what is required." She was now clad only in her chemise, curled upon his bed in a sensuous pose, her mood obviously far more relaxed than his.

"No woman was ever a better mistress than you, Anna. When we get to New Orleans I will tell Yvette Molyneaux to ask you for lessons."

"Yvette? Who might she be that she needs instruction from me?" Anna wondered aloud.

"You will meet her soon enough, wait and see." Phillip evaded her question deftly as he approached the narrow bed. It was far too small for a couple so athletic as they, he thought suddenly, and he wished for the sunlit days they'd spent on the island where a lack of space had never been a problem when they'd wanted to make love. He tried to replace that expression in his mind with one far more crude but when he looked at Anna's pretty smile he could not even bring himself to think in such base terms, let alone speak them. With her it would always be making love but he'd sworn never to speak that word again and meant to keep that bitter vow even in his thoughts.

When he sat down beside her, Anna moved quickly to help him, her touch light as she unbuttoned his shirt. But when she reached for his belt, Phillip put his hand over hers. "You must not be so impatient. I have been undressing myself for a good many years and can accomplish the task tonight as well."

"As you wish." Anna moved off the bunk, her glance an admiring one for his tan was as extensive as hers now, his once-white hips a golden brown. He was so muscular and fit she found the sight of him most enjoyable but when he reached for her chemise she drew away.

"A mistress is never modest, by the way. Put out the lamp and come here." Phillip stretched out upon the comfortable bunk to wait for her but she surprised him once again when she sat down by his feet so she might trail the most enticing of kisses up the inside of his thigh. Her lips were soft, her sweet breath light upon his skin and he knew all was lost for once again he was more her prisoner than she would ever be his. He could not control the vibrant flame her affection kindled within his heart any more than he could suppress the fire which spread through his loins at her touch. She inspired a passion too delicious to deny and he let her move over him, winding his fingers in her long curls to hold her near as a cresting ecstasy swept through him with a brilliance he was compelled to share. He lifted her into his arms, hugging her tightly as he rolled over to pin her beneath him so he might finish with a joyous abandon what she had begun, knowing her enjoyment would be as deep as his own. She fell asleep again cradled in his arms but he could not bear to leave her even in his dreams and lay awake for hours trying to unravel the mysterious spell of her love.

Chapter Twenty-three

As they neared the Louisiana coast the mild weather began to deteriorate and the seas grew increasingly turbulent sending waves crashing over the bow, drenching all who ventured on deck. The chill winds howled through the sails with an eerie wail and Phillip recognized the signs of the approaching hurricane and knew only with more luck than he'd encountered of late would the *Angelina* be able to escape its fury. They were running ahead of the storm by a margin of hours. He paced the deck nervously watching the dark clouds gather on the horizon.

"We'll make it, Captain. I'd lay a wager on it." Jamie gripped the rail to keep his balance, but his mood was good despite the impending storm.

Phillip frowned anxiously as he shook his head. "This is the most ill-fated voyage ever begun, Mr. Jenkins, and I'll not risk a penny on a prediction of its outcome." He'd passed the days since they'd left Jamaica in a constant turmoil of conflicting emotions but he'd thought they had escaped whatever danger might be pursuing them until the storm had suddenly appeared to hamper their progress. He and Anna now lived lives so intensely separate and yet so entangled he scarcely knew what each new day would bring but he'd not risk the young woman's life if there were any way to avoid it. "We should reach New Orleans before noon. I'll take Anna to Yvette's while you locate a warehouse for the cargo. With any luck we can get a good price for the goods and ride out this storm up the coast where we won't sustain the damage we would if we lay at anchor in a crowded harbor. I only pray time is on our side."

"Why do you pretend it is the safety of the cargo or the *Angelina* which concerns you when we all know it is Anna?" Perhaps due to the worsening weather Jamie felt in a reckless mood and spoke more freely than he usually dared.

Phillip simply stared, his bright blue eyes narrowing to menacing slits before he nodded slightly. "Think whatever you like, I am responsible for the welfare of all three." He was still able to hold his emotions tightly in check with his crew. It was only with Anna that he found himself unable to behave in a responsible manner. He'd become a sullen tyrant by day but he had to admit the effects of her intoxicating affection turned him into the most tender lover each night. She'd still explained nothing about the time she'd spent with Charles but he knew that's where the answer to her betrayal had to lie. Something had happened that day which had changed Anna from a willful girl to a woman who would forsake his love in the name of honor and that ridiculous decision tore at his conscious mind in each waking hour until he welcomed sleep the way a man dying of thirst welcomes a drop of water. How she could have changed so completely in the space of a few hours time was a riddle which gave him no peace and he was looking forward to putting her ashore where he hoped a few days in her own company would make her realize how foolish she had become. He'd had her trust once, as well as her love and he desperately wanted to regain that confidence again, for he planned to keep her with him forever and knew neither of them could survive the strain under which they were currently trying to live. Anna had grown more distant each day and he missed the sparkling light which had filled her eyes when she had looked up at him. Now he saw only the reflection of the unspeakable sorrow which he was certain filled his own gaze.

Anna packed her belongings neatly into her trunk and was ready to leave the *Angelina* the minute they reached New Orleans. Phillip had told her to be prepared to go ashore and she did not question his demand or test his patience. He did not bother to summon a carriage but carried her trunk upon his shoulder while she carried her fabric bag for the short walk to the Hotel LaMer where he'd told her she'd be staying. He'd neglected to tell her how long she'd have to remain there and she felt certain that oversight was no accident. As they walked down the narrow sidewalk she glanced up at the brightly painted buildings. They were decorated with ornate wrought-iron balconies but the louvered windows reminded her instantly of Charles's home on Jamaica and she shuddered with a sudden chill of foreboding which she could not dispel. She noticed there were slaves here, too, men working along the docks and scurrying up and down the streets and she wanted to ask Phillip if their lot were better in his country than on the Caribbean islands. But his expression did not invite comment so she kept still.

The small hotel was located close to the docks and once inside Anna gave the place a wary glance for it did not appear to be the sort of establishment which was accustomed to serving ladies. The entrance way was small, the walls adorned with a garish damask of brilliant crimson. The woman who greeted them at the front desk wore makeup in such theatrical amounts Anna wondered if perhaps she were performing in a musical production at a nearby theatre and only worked at the hotel part-time.

Eyeing the handsome captain with a saucy toss of her flaming red curls, Yvette cooed enthusiastically, "Captain Bradford, I am delighted to see you as always, but what have you here, your own—"

Phillip interrupted before Yvette spoke a word he was certain would send Anna into screaming fits of temper. "I am in a great hurry, Madame Molyneaux. Have you a room where Miss Thorson might stay for a few days while I am occupied at the port? She would like something quiet, where she could rest without being disturbed as our voyage has been a most strenuous one."

Yvette smiled as she looked Anna up and down slowly with an appreciative glance. She thought her unique coloring exquisite as was her figure, but she saw a reserve in the young woman's bearing which made her think she would be most difficult to please. "Of course, Captain, she shall have our finest accommodations if that is what you desire. I can guarantee privacy as well as elegance, as you know."

"That is precisely why I am entrusting Miss Thorson to your care." Phillip took Anna's arm to guide her up the stairs to the second floor where Yvette unlocked the door to a surprisingly luxurious suite. The rooms were spacious and well-appointed and he was certain Anna would be comfortable there until he returned. "Miss Thorson will take her meals here. If there is anything she requires please send someone to purchase it for her and I will cover the expense."

Anna walked to the windows and looked down at the busy street, uncertain what to make of the overly glamorous Madame Molyneaux or her hotel. "I can go out without getting lost if I am provided with the directions, Captain Bradford. I do not need to be waited on hand and foot."

"I am thinking only of your safety. The storm may be a severe one and I do not want you to risk injury or illness by venturing out. I will return when the weather clears and we can make our plans then."

Anna turned slowly, regarding him with a suspicious glance. She had no idea what sort of plans he wished to make but with the French woman standing by his side she had no desire to explore the subject. She guessed Madame Molyneaux to be in her forties; her bright green gown was as extreme in style as her makeup. While her manner appeared to be friendly, Anna did not feel comfortable in her presence and, preferring to be alone, she bid Phillip a terse farewell. "Until after the storm then, Captain, goodbye."

When she turned back to the window, Phillip was overcome with a sorrow so great it crushed his chest with a pain so terrible he could not catch his breath. He could not even speak the word goodbye and instead walked to her side to pull her into his arms. His kiss was demanding, his mouth seeking the reassurance which was so lacking in her glance. She stiffened in his embrace rather than return his affection and, angered by her cool rebuff, he released her abruptly and walked to the door. "Come with me, Yvette, I want to settle the bill for Miss Thorson's lodgings now."

Left alone Anna could do no more than pace nervously but at least she had sufficient space in which to walk for a change. She licked her bruised lips and thought again how little she appreciated Phillip's expressing his anger with passion. It was completely misplaced emotion but a point which escaped him entirely. At least he had never struck her although she'd seen that idea cross his mind so clearly it was unmistakable. What a terrible mess she'd made of everything and here she was again, left behind with strangers while he went off to take care of business matters which always commanded top priority as far as she could see. Crossing to the windows again, she looked up at the sky. Sea gulls circled lazily overhead, their raucous squawking heralding the coming storm and she shivered despite the warmth of the room. When she heard the door open she turned hoping to see Phillip returning to apologize but it was a petite dark-skinned maid in an attractive blue uniform.

"I have tea, mademoiselle, or is it madame?" She curtsied politely as she placed the small silver tray on the table.

Uncertain as to how she should be addressed, Anna replied softly, "My name is Anna, please call me that." She'd no intention of calling herself Lady Clairbourne but somehow anything else seemed dishonest.

430

"I am Lucille," the young woman offered sweetly. "Is there anything else you need? If not I will see to your wardrobe."

"You may unpack my trunk. There's nothing else I require." Anna sat down to sip the refreshing mint-flavored tea and watched as the maid placed her gowns in the wardrobe. Catherine's cast-offs had certainly seen a lot of use but they were lovely still, sweetly scented with sachet and not in the least bit worn. The dress she'd worn for her wedding had never appeared and rather than ask Phillip what he'd done with it she had kept silent for there was no reason for her to treasure it.

"Your dresses are very pretty, nicer than any the others have. You will be very popular here."

"Popular, Lucille? With whom? I know not a soul here in New Orleans." Other than the men of the *Angelina* and she already knew she was well liked by them regardless of their captain's neglect.

Lucille giggled as she closed the wardrobe and came forward. "This is the best room, so you are an expensive woman. The others will all be jealous."

Anna placed her empty teacup on its saucer and asked curiously, "There is no reason for anyone to be jealous of me, Lucille. Whatever are you talking about?"

Lucille shrugged as if the answer were obvious. "It is always the same, each time Madame Molyneaux hires a new girl, the others become jealous and cause trouble but in a few weeks time they will accept you and things will be as before."

Since Lucille clearly thought she knew what they were discussing when she most certainly did not, Anna tried to draw her out. "I know why I am here, but who are these women who work for Yvette and just what is it that they do?"

"Oh, mademoiselle, they will do anything for which a man will pay, you must know that!"

Smiling calmly, Anna nodded. "Of course, I am sorry to have kept you from your other duties. You may go now, Lucille, thank you." How she could have been so incredibly stupid as to have walked in the front door of a bordello Anna did not know, but she had no intention of remaining in such an unsavory establishment. How could Phillip have played her so underhanded a trick? She knew then he was never coming back for her, that's why he'd kissed her so roughly. He'd wanted only to hurt her and he most certainly had! She might have been given the best room, and doubtless with Phillip's praise she'd command the top price but she'd be damned if she'd stay! He'd told her once she could give lessons to Yvette but she'd not understood just what kind of instruction he had meant. Furious she went to the wardrobe and grabbing her fabric bag jammed it as full of clothing as she could since she'd have to carry it herself. She dared not send for a carriage to carry her trunk when she had nowhere to go and as usual not a penny to pay for her expenses when she got there. How could Phillip have done this to her? Tears filled her eyes as she answered her own question. She was the one who had failed him and no promise of love could make up for the fact she'd married Charles. He despised her for that and had left her to fend for herself but she'd starve to death before she'd become a whore! No matter how little he thought of her she'd never sell to other men what she had given so gladly to him.

Knowing there had to be someplace she could seek shelter, she stopped a moment to think. A church was a possibility or since the city had so recently belonged to Spain and France there had to be a Catholic convent or two where the sisters would listen to her story and offer sanctuary. It was already beginning to rain, a light shower which would soon grow heavier and since she had to walk there was not a moment more to lose. She tied her cape snugly under her chin and, bringing the hood up to cover her bright curls, picked up the heavy tapestry bag and opened her door. At least she had not been locked in, she thought gratefully, as she walked quickly to the end of the hall, choosing the back stairs rather than those Yvette had used to escort her to her room. She tiptoed down the steps, pausing at the bottom to listen for someone nearby. But hearing only the lively clatter of pots and pans from the kitchen she slipped out the back door and sprinted down the alley. Surely no convent would be located near the docks so she chose the opposite direction, dashing through the increasingly heavy rain, leaping over the growing puddles as she scanned the roof line for the sight of a church spire. On and on she ran, not daring to stop to ask directions until she rounded a corner and narrowly missed being crushed beneath the wheels of a ramshackle old wagon being pulled by a horse who appeared to be as terrified by the unexpected encounter as she.

The man driving the wagon leapt from his seat to be certain Anna was uninjured for she was obviously a fine lady and he was horrified he'd come so close to harming her. When she did not respond to his effusive apology in French he switched to English. "Forgive me, I did not see you." He exclaimed loudly to be heard over the driving rain. "Are you all right?"

"No, not at all!" Anna was thoroughly drenched, her mood as miserable as the afternoon, but she drew her cloak more tightly around herself and, shifting her bag to ease its weight, started on down the street.

"Wait!" The man ran after her, slipping and sliding through the puddles. "Where are you going?"

Surprised by his interest, Anna looked at the man more closely. She guessed him to be about Phillip's age but there his resemblance to the dashing captain ended. His face was unshaven, his dark hair overlong, his worn coat patched at the elbows. He was obviously of humble means but his bright brown eyes held the light of genuine concern and she replied truthfully. "I have nowhere to go, that's why I must hurry."

"But you can not run through the streets in this rain!" He reached out to take her arm. "You must come with me."

Anna glanced back at his wagon. He reminded her of the farmers she'd known all her life; they were honest men, sincere in their promises and she quickly made her decision. "I would like to come with you if I will be no trouble."

"None at all, but let us hurry." He helped her up into the seat of his old vehicle and, climbing up beside her, clucked to his horse. The rain made it impossible to converse but the journey out of the city and along the narrow trail into the bayou where he lived took more than an hour and they were both freezing cold, their teeth chattering loudly by the time they reached his small log cabin. They unloaded the wagon quickly before he unhitched his horse and led him around back to a small shed.

"What will your wife say about me?" Anna asked hurriedly as he rejoined her on the porch for she could well imagine the woman would not be pleased to see her.

"I have no wife!" The man laughed heartily for he knew no woman would want to share his life. "I am a trapper, often gone up the river. I have no need of a wife."

Anna followed him through the door, stamping her feet to keep warm as he lit the fire in the large stone fireplace before returning to the porch to bring in his provisions. The single room held an unmade brass bed, a table and chairs which were strewn with clothing. A heap of furs filled one corner. The alcove by the fireplace which was used for preparing food was stacked with dirty pots and pans. All in all the place was a fright. It was obvious he needed the services of a maid if not a wife, but she would not be so rude as to make that comment. She had never ever been in so small and poor a home but on that afternoon the house was warm and dry, quite ample in spite of its lack of order.

"I had furs to sell, food to buy so I chanced the trip into town," the friendly man explained as he brought in the last bag of flour. "I should not have gone out in this weather but if I had not, where would you be now?"

When he gestured for her to come close to the fire Anna did, grateful for the warmth it afforded. She didn't realize he'd asked her a question until he repeated it.

"You must tell me: From where did you come and

where are you bound?"

"I am from Sweden," Anna offered hesitantly. "That is all I can state with any certainty now. I had no destination when we chanced to collide."

"It is lucky that we met then," he replied happily for now he could see Anna more clearly. He was astonished by her beauty. Her creamy complexion was flawless, her long-lashed eyes of a haunting golden shade and her blond hair a silken cloud which caressed her shoulders seductively. He began to worry about her damp clothing. "Take off your cape and it will dry here by the fire." He gathered up his own belongings from the chairs so she might have a place to lay her cloak. When he saw her dress was also soaked he picked up her small bag. "Do you have other clothes? You must not stay in that wet dress or you will become ill."

Having no desire to disrobe in front of the helpful stranger Anna shook her head. "No, my things will dry quickly."

The man peeled off his coat and hung it upon a peg near the fire. "You are my guest and I will not harm you. Now you must change your clothes."

Looking around for someplace which might provide a degree of privacy, Anna found the openness of the small dwelling disconcerting. There was nowhere she could stand that she would not be in full view.

Seeing her glance sweep his humble home the man quickly reached for his coat. "While you dress, I will check the firewood stacked on the porch." With a sly wink he went to his door certain she would understand why he was leaving.

"I will hurry, for I do not want you to risk pneumonia simply because of my modesty." As he left, the man's infectious grin warmed her heart as surely as his blazing fire warmed her blood. As soon as she had donned another set of garments, she wrapped her shawl tightly around her shoulders and called him back inside. The man then poured hot water from a kettle he'd placed over the fire and served tea. "Thank you for your hospitality. I don't know what I would have done had I not met you."

"Permit me to introduce myself, I am Jean Paul La-Casse. As you can see I am but a simple trapper but I bid you welcome to my home." He beamed with real pride, his wide smile most charming.

After a slight hesitation, Anna decided it would be best not to reveal her true identity and she responded with the first name which came to her mind. "Please call me Angelina, and I am most happy to meet you, Monsieur LaCasse." The irony in her choice of names amused her but she dared not speak the truth.

"Well, my dear Angelina, this storm may last many days but you will be safe here with me. There is plenty to eat. We can pass the time by talking as it is not often I have a guest so pretty as you." Pausing to grow more thoughtful, Jean Paul asked perceptively, "From whom were you running, a man?" He'd almost said husband but he'd noticed she wore no ring.

Anna gave her full attention to her teacup and did not reply for several minutes. "It matters not, Jean Paul. When the storm subsides I will leave, I will not be a burden to you here."

That such a pretty creature could think of herself as a burden to any man was preposterous and Jean Paul hastened to disagree. "But I insist you stay until you have some more suitable place to go. I will not send

437

you out to wander the streets again!"

Anna sneezed loudly, then reached into her pocke[t] for her handkerchief to hide her tears. "You are ver[y] kind, and I am so grateful for your help." When sh[e] sneezed again, he rose to add more wood to his fire. H[e] had a large stack ready and stood for a moment warm[-] ing his hands.

"I am sorry to say I do not cook well, perhaps . . ." He left his question hanging in the air, hoping sh[e] would volunteer to help him prepare their supper.

"May I help you then? My cooking is passable, or s[o] I've been told." Truly she had done very little in th[e] way of cooking but had watched Michael closely an[d] had learned a lot from him. "What would you like t[o] serve tonight?"

"Soup, I think. It is such a cold night. If you wil[l] make the soup, I will make the biscuits."

"That is only fair." Anna gathered together a few o[f] the vegetables he kept stored in a bin, simmered them with a bit of ham and thought the resulting soup deli[-] cious. His biscuits were feather light and they spread them with honey for dessert. "Thank you, Jean Paul, this was the most delectable meal I have eaten in a long while." Her compliment was sincere for while Mi[-] chael's cuisine was excellent, she and Phillip had sel[-] dom spoken as they ate and she'd been too worried over his angry silence to taste anything. Just thinking of how he'd abandoned her at Yvette's brought an ach[-] ing sense of loss she couldn't hide from the kindly trap[-] per, but she stood quickly and began to clear their table to distract herself from her sorrow. She washed all the dishes, cleaned pans which looked as though they'd been dirty for months then sat down again in front of the fire and watched the flames dance as the wind continued to gather intensity outside.

Jean Paul frowned as he looked out the window. "This storm is a fierce one, early for a hurricane but clearly it does not know that." He stood for a long while then turned slowly to offer a suggestion he hoped she'd accept. "We will be warmer if we share my bed."

"No, thank you," Anna replied softly. "I have slept on the floor before, tonight I will be happy to give you the bed."

"How can that be so? Who has made you sleep on his floor, I will challenge the brute to a duel tomorrow!" Jean Paul threatened dramatically.

"Is dueling not forbidden here?" Anna teased sweetly, pleased he'd want to defend her so heroically. "My comfort is a small matter, certainly not worth the risk of a life."

Frowning, Jean Paul spoke sternly, "You must sleep in the bed, I insist." But looking toward it he was embarrassed for it was an untidy mess. "This is the day I meant to change the bedclothes, I will do it now."

Anna watched with a mischievous grin as he hurriedly made up the bed. He did at least have an extra set of clean sheets and she promised herself she'd see he had a freshly laundered set of bedding when she left.

"There!" Jean Paul thumped the bed proudly. "My father brought this bed all the way from Canada just to please my mother. I hope it will please you."

"It is obviously a marvelous bed but where will you sleep?" Since she'd turned him out of his own bed she hated to seem unconcerned about his comfort.

Gesturing toward the pile of furs in the far corner, the young man chuckled. "Those make a fine bed. I will move a few closer to the fire and be fine. Are you tired?"

"Very. Do you mind if I go to sleep now? I will be happy to talk with you in the morning." Anna stood up and stretched lazily as she covered a wide yawn.

"I will see to my horse before I go to bed." Jean Paul went out into the stormy night to give her time to get ready to retire as well as well to be certain his horse was not suffering too badly. The shelter he'd built for the animal had but three sides, but fortunately the beast was shielded from the wind as well as most of the rain and was contentedly munching the grain he'd left for him. When he returned to the cabin fifteen minutes had elapsed and the pretty blonde was already in his bed, nestled down among the covers sound asleep. He tiptoed to her side, tempted to reach out and touch her soft curls, but he dared not disturb her slumber. She might awaken and be frightened of him and that was something he'd not risk. What an extraordinary young woman she was, so sweet and unassuming when she had the beauty of a princess. Perhaps she really was a princess, he thought sadly, a beautiful princess running away from someone or something which terrified her. He had little hope of keeping her with him for long. Forcing himself away from her bedside he arranged the soft pelts in a comfortable mat and lay down to rest, but sleep did not come easily and many hours passed before he closed his eyes and began to dream of Angelina and how easy she would be to love.

Anna awoke with a terrible headache. Coughing and sneezing, she climbed right back into bed as Jean Paul refused to allow her to get up when she was so ill. He brought her tea and some biscuits with honey and, building up the fire, sat down to wait until she might ask for something more. That she'd fallen ill was a tragedy but the gale force winds continued to blow the freezing rain against his small, sturdy home and he dared not leave her to summon a physician for he knew none would be likely to venture out in such dreadful weather. He'd have to wait for the skies to clear but he prayed if he kept the lovely Angelina warm and dry she would not be so ill that he could not restore her to good health quickly. He had learned a few remedies from the Indians he'd encountered in his travels. Taking out his small pouches of dried herbs, he attempted to concoct a tea which would cure her sickness.

When she awoke later Anna drank all the bitter brew he had ready, though it made her gag, and lay back upon the pillows. "I think I would rather be sick than take any more of your medicine, Jean Paul, but thank you." The brass bed was warm and soft, almost luxurious and she smiled easily. "Now tell me something of Canada where you were born." She listened contentedly as he spoke, for his soft accent was pleasant to hear. But before he had completed his tale she was sound asleep again.

Anna did not feel well enough to leave the bed the following day or the next. She was dizzy and weak, too ill to do more than lie still while the young man worked to restore order and cleanliness to his home. Once that task was accomplished he turned his attention to himself, heating water to bathe before he trimmed his hair and sharpened his razor to shave. He then put on a new shirt he'd been saving for just such an unexpected occasion and was well-pleased with his efforts. Anna's smile was all the reward he required.

Anna was surprised to find Jean Paul's transformation so complete. She would not have recognized him had she not known it was he. "How handsome you look. I am so sorry I am unable to get up and dress. I did not mean to cause you all this trouble." She tried to sip the cup of evil-tasting tea he had again prepared since he swore it would make her well, but she doubted it had any curative powers when it tasted so awful.

"The storm has almost passed, but while the wind is gone it is raining still. I could not set traps in such foul weather so if you were not here I would be very bored."

Anna smiled as she returned the almost empty cup to his hands. "I will try to get up tomorrow, perhaps by then—"

"You will do no such thing!" Jean Paul exclaimed. "I forbid it! You will rest for a week at least for it is plain you are too weak to walk about without fainting and you might injure yourself badly."

"But I must try and take care of myself. You have been so kind but I know I am imposing upon your hospitality and should leave as soon as I am able."

Pulling up a chair, Jean Paul argued. "Why should you leave if as you say, there is no place for you to go?"

Frowning slightly, Anna tried to explain. "I have been giving my future a great deal of thought. As I told you I am Swedish and I think if I could find some work in New Orleans I might be able to save enough money to pay for my passage home."

"But surely a young woman so pretty as you need not work!" the Frenchman cried out in astonishment.

"My appearance has nothing to do with this, Jean Paul. My English is good enough for me to work as a governess, or perhaps there is a dressmaker who can use another woman who is handy with a needle. I am usually strong, willing to work hard for my pay. There must be something I could do to earn my own way honestly."

"I will not hear of it. If you wish to return to Sweden then I will trap enough furs to send you. You need not do menial work when furs are worth as much as gold," Jean Paul declared proudly.

That he would wish to help her pleased her enormously but Anna could not accept his charity. "You have done too much for me already, Jean Paul, and I am only a stranger you chanced to meet in a storm."

Lifting her hand to his lips, the young man disagreed. "Can you not see how much you mean to me? I do not want you to ever go, but if you must, I will see you have money enough to travel as a lady should. Now do not argue with me for the matter is settled and you must rest, my angel." Leaning down to kiss her forehead lightly he whispered, "Sweet dreams."

As he left her bedside, Anna forced back her tears. She had been so lost and alone when he'd offered to take her into his home but she could accept neither his affection nor his money. "You are the angel, Jean Paul, truly you are," she called after him and although he laughed at her compliment she had meant it with all her heart. She had come to care for him, too, but if she told him the truth about herself would he be so eager to offer assistance? Deciding he deserved more honesty than she'd given, Anna vowed to tell him all he needed to know when she next she had the energy to converse.

Chapter Twenty-four

Phillip was in an exuberant mood. He'd gotten a higher price than he'd expected for his cargo, by moving up the coast he'd managed to keep the *Angelina* from suffering any severe damage during the storm and now he wanted to see Anna so badly he could not wait another minute. The docks were littered with debris but he leapt over the wet heaps as he made his way up the sidewalk. The damage caused by the wind and rain was evident everywhere but he ignored it as he hurried along. He had to keep reminding himself to slow down for he did not want to arrive at Anna's room out of breath and let her see how anxious he'd been to see her again. He paused for a few minutes at one corner, then walked with a carefully measured stride as he approached Yvette's hotel. He was totally unprepared for the scene he found there. At first he thought he'd taken a wrong turn and went back to the corner to read the street sign but there had been no mistake. The Hotel LaMer was simply gone as was the row of small shops which had been on the same side of the street.

Men with shovels and picks were sifting through the ruins, piling the usable lumber to one side. The once-elegant structure had been reduced to no more than a small mountain of rubble, splinters littered here and there with still-recognizable bits of furniture.

Phillip ran to the nearest man and grabbed his arm in a frantic grip. "What happened here? What in God's name happened?"

The man saw Phillip's fine clothing and straightened up, hoping he might be rewarded for his information. "It was a hurricane, no less, sir. The rain water collected on the roof when the drains became clogged with leaves and the hotel collapsed under that weight, pushing down the adjoining buildings as it fell. Happened at night so none saw it in time to save those inside."

Terrified by what he was certain was true Phillip looked about anxiously. "Where is Yvette Molyneaux and the guests who were in her hotel?"

The workman gestured helplessly. "Madame Molyneaux is in the Hospital of Our Lady as are several of her, her . . ." He stuttered nervously, trying to think of some polite term to describe her employees.

"Blast it, man. I know what they are. Now where is this hospital?" Phillip inquired crossly.

"It is no more than three blocks to the north, a large brick building on the corner. You can not miss it."

Not waiting for further directions, Phillip dashed away, this time running with no thought of propriety as he raced up the storm-ravaged street. Anna would not have been in the Hotel LaMer had he not taken her there so she'd be safe! Safe! The word rang in his ears. a bitter accusation.

When he came to the Catholic hospital he found it crowded with victims of the recent tempest. Patients filled the hallways, poor wretched creatures who had owned little and had lost even that. He stepped over them, offering apologies until he found a tiny black-robed nun seated at a cluttered reception desk.

After introducing himself briefly, Phillip explained, "I am looking for a young woman. She might have been brought here from the Hotel LaMer. She is very blond, pretty, she may be calling herself Anna Ericdotter or Thorson or perhaps Clairbourne, I do not know which last name she might have given."

The elderly nun eyed Phillip suspiciously since she knew exactly what sort of establishment the LaMer was reputed to be. After scanning her admissions lists closely she shook her head. "I am sorry, but there is no one here by any of those names, Captain."

"But she must be here, she must!" Frantic, Phillip remembered Yvette. "Where is Madame Molyneaux? She is here, I know that for a fact."

Having no time to argue with distraught visitors, the nun gestured. "She is in the women's ward, to your left but—"

Not caring to hear her objections to his visiting Yvette, Phillip entered the crowded ward and began searching for his friend. But he did not even recognize her until she lifted a pale hand and called to him.

"Captain Bradford, how good of you to come."

"Yvette, is that you?" Her face was bruised and swollen, for once devoid of makeup. Her elaborate hair style had been brushed out, leaving her red hair limp against her pillow. Smiling to cover his shock at her battered appearance, Phillip pressed her for informa-

446

tion. "Where is the young woman I left with you?" He glanced at the occupants in the adjacent beds but recognized none of the women who were regarding him with rapt interest.

"Both my legs are broken, Captain, and my beautiful hotel is gone. If I have lost track of a guest or two it is not my fault."

"No, of course it isn't." Phillip reassured her warmly. "Your misfortune pains me greatly but where can I find my Anna? Have you no idea where she might be found?" He smoothed back her bright red tresses gently, his concern sincere.

"I had my own duties. I told Lucille to see to your lady's comfort."

"Well, then, where is Lucille and I'll question her."

Sighing sadly, the injured woman closed her eyes to shut out the terror of her memories. "It was so sudden, Captain, the noise of the wind deafening. One minute we were all warm and dry and in the next the roof caved in on us before we had a chance to flee. I fear Lucille is dead with most of the others."

"No," Phillip's expression hardened into a determined frown. "Anna can not possibly be dead, she can not be dead." He squeezed Yvette's hands tightly as he said goodbye. "Try and rest, I will come to see you again tomorrow."

Yvette smiled faintly. "There are few men so good as you, sir, I hope you find your Anna soon." But as she watched him walk away she had little hope he'd find the aristocratic blonde alive.

Phillip left the busy hospital at a near run, upsetting the same unfortunate souls he'd disturbed on his way in. He went back to the ruins of the Hotel LaMer and aft r questioning several of the men working there found their foreman. "I am looking for a young woman." He began slowly.

"Aye, mate, and who isn't?" The foreman responded with a deep chuckle.

"Damn you!" Phillip grabbed the front of the startled man's shirt and lifted him clear off his feet. "Now, listen, have you found any bodies in this wreckage, anyone at all, man or woman?"

Knowing better than to anger so strong an individual further, the foreman nodded rapidly. "There were three bodies found yesterday, all women. They were taken to the morgue."

Phillip's deep tan paled to a ghostly pallor as he set the man down and stepped back. "Who found them? I'm looking for an exceptionally pretty blonde. Is there someone who can describe the women who were found?"

All the men had stopped their work to listen and two came forward to offer what they knew. "There was a blonde, at least I think she was a blonde. They'd been crushed, covered in mud; why, I was standing on one dear lass for ten minutes before I saw she was a person, or had been, that is."

Displaying more courage than he felt, Phillip thanked the men then asked for directions. "Where is the morgue, I'll have to go and look myself." He nodded as they explained then repeated the directions to be certain he'd understood the building's location. His voice was the calm, dull monotone of a man who has lost everything he holds dear yet must go on with no time to grieve. It sounded hollow in his own ears but he cared little how it sounded to those nearby. He made his way slowly this time, pushing himself to keep going, his dread mounting with each beat of his heart. He climbed the marble steps of the imposing building and pushed open the door. It was a cold place, both in appearance and temperature, reeking of strong soap, the stark facility obviously overtaxed by the recent disaster. Finding a clerk, he asked for a roster of victims.

"If their names were known, sir, they'd not be here."

"May I look for myself, then?" The horror of that prospect sickened him thoroughly but Phillip could think of no alternative.

Wiping his hands on his tattered apron, the clerk pointed down the hall. "We've more than usual, forty-three so far but there will be more by nightfall as buildings collapsed all over the city and the wreckage is still being searched. Just go on through that door and tell them Peter said you'd come to identify a woman."

"Thank you." Phillip forced himself to enter the next room where bodies were laid end to end in neat rows upon the cold stone floor. Wrapped in white shrouds, they were identical and it was impossible to discern whether they were young or old, male or female. They had all shared the same ghastly fate and awaited silently to be claimed.

An elderly man who'd been writing at a desk in the corner turned to greet him. "You've come on a sad errand, sir. Which is it you want to see, man or woman?"

"A young woman, she's very pretty, blonde . . ." The acrid stench of death pervaded the room despite its chill and when his voice faltered he could not go on.

"I am sorry to say none of my guests is pretty now, but the women are nearest the door."

"I heard three were brought in from the Hotel

LaMer. Where are they?"

Squinting to get a closer look at the tall man, the clerk shrugged. "I put tags on their toes, but where I laid them I don't recall, you better let me look first as it is not a pleasant sight."

"I can stand it." Phillip knew he was going to be sick the minute he left that room but that was a slight torment compared to what he feared had happened to Anna. He had never wanted to do anything less, but he knew knowing for certain that Anna's body lay beneath one of the morgue's sheets could be no worse than the suspense which gripped him now as he surveyed the gruesome scene. "I was not in the city. I didn't realize the storm was so severe or that so many lives were lost."

Philosophical after his many years at the morgue, the clerk shrugged. "I no longer ponder why such tragedies occur. I only do my job for the casualties. Perhaps you know we do not bury our dead in the ground here. We are so near the sea we can not dig a hole without striking water." Noticing his visitor's anxious glance, the man cut short his lecture and returned to their original purpose. "Now it was a blonde you wanted to find, wasn't it?" Without waiting for the reply the man began walking along the first row, stopping to read the tags which bore little more than the location where the body had been found. "Ah, is this the woman? She was pulled from the wreckage of the Hotel LaMer."

After forcing himself to look, Phillip shook his head, the woman was blond all right, but not a natural one. She was several years older than Anna with hair as straight as a string rather than softly curled. She was

450

nude under the sheet, very pale, very dead and he shuddered with relief. "No, that isn't her. You needn't help me, I can check the others myself." He did it too, looking at every face. Many were young, perhaps sweethearts, wives or someone's mother. They'd been filled with life only a few days before and now they lay like so many limp dolls, alone and unclaimed on the cold floor of the morgue. When Anna was not among them, Phillip said a prayer for the souls of the others and, thanking the helpful attendant, rushed outside into the sunlight where he took several deep, gasping breaths of fresh air. If Anna weren't at the hospital, or at the morgue, was she safe or still buried beneath the rubble which was all that was left of the once-elegant Hotel LaMer? It would take the few men working there days to sift through all the debris but he could not bear to wait another minute. Returning to the *Angelina* he assembled a party of men to help him search. Jamie came along as well as John, but all who volunteered were as eager as he to discover what had happened to Anna. Although they worked diligently for two long days they found no trace of the attractive blonde. Exhausted by their efforts, they returned to the *Angelina* where Phillip gave them each a generous bonus for their labors and several days liberty but there was no way he could reward himself when his quest to find the woman he loved had proved so fruitless. She never did as she was told, never followed even his smallest direction. Had her willfulness saved her this time, or had she merely lost her life in another part of the city? Phillip had thought he had suffered every possible anguish at that defiant beauty's hands but now he knew the torment was just beginning, for if he

451

could not find Anna either alive or dead he knew her memory would haunt him until his last minute on earth and with his final breath he would whisper her name.

Chapter Twenty-five

Jamie raced up the gangplank, knocking several members of the crew out of his way as he dashed to the bow where Phillip stood leaning against the rail, gazing out at the gulf waters. He hadn't moved in hours and Jamie had to shake his shoulder to bring him out of his trance-like depression. "Captain, you must come with me. I've met the most remarkable man. You must hear his tale, come quickly!"

Phillip straightened up, or attempted to. He had not slept in so long he'd forgotten the location of his bunk. "I care little for making new friends, Jamie, and I'm sure I would not be amused by any man's tales today."

Jamie disagreed emphatically. "No! This story will intrigue you greatly for the man met a beautiful, young blond woman the first night of the storm and is seeking passage to Sweden for her now!" Jamie's brown eyes lit with triumph, certain he'd have Phillip's interest now.

"Where is he?" Phillip looked toward the rubble-strewn docks. The waterfront still lay in disorder and men with shovels and brooms were hard at work attempting to clear the entrances to their shops.

"He is at a tavern just up the street. I overheard him asking about passage to Europe and told him I knew a captain who might consider taking a passenger so far as Sweden. He is waiting for us, but we must hurry!"

Phillip rubbed his hand over the dark stubble which covered his chin. "No, bring the man here but do not appear too eager. Give me time to make myself more presentable. If it is Anna he has found then God knows what she told him. I do not want to arouse his suspicions."

"Aye, that is a point I'd not considered. I will buy him an ale or two then suggest he come here to speak with you." Jamie turned and sprinted back the way he'd come, dodging past the same men with whom he'd collided on his way to Phillip's side.

Phillip strode nonchalantly into his cabin, closed the door and leaned back against it. It had to be Anna, dear God who else could it be? He managed to shave without cutting his throat by the barest of margins, then bathed quickly and put on a clean white shirt and dark pants. John had polished his boots until they shone with a bright gleam. When Jamie returned he was neatly groomed and dressed, apparently the most prosperous of captains hard at work at his desk.

"This is Jean Paul LaCasse, Captain Bradford. I thought perhaps you might be able to help him once you heard the pathetic nature of his request," Jamie explained dramatically, obviously moved by the trapper's plight.

Phillip rose to offer his hand. "How do you do, Mr. LaCasse. Now what is your problem?" Taking his chair at the table, he gestured for Jean Paul and Jamie to join him. Jamie had not described the man but Phillip was startled to find him so young and pleasant in appearance. He forced away the jealousy which brought a dull ache to his stomach and attempted to appear only mildly interested in his guest's troubles.

"I have no more than a minute to explain, Captain, for Angelina will soon awaken from her nap and be distressed to find me gone." Jean Paul perched on the edge of his chair, his intention to remain only briefly very clear.

"Angelina?" Phillip inquired politely. "Who is this Angelina, Mr. LaCasse?" he could scarcely speak for the pounding of his heart. It thundered in his ears, making coherent thought nearly impossible for the fact Anna had taken the name of his ship astonished him. "Perhaps if you were to start at the beginning of this story I would understand your plight more readily."

"Yes, of course. Well perhaps you know how dreadful this last storm was, I have never heard such terrible winds howling through the trees and—"

Phillip raised his hand. "We were just outside New Orleans ourselves and experienced the fury of the hurricane first-hand, you needn't describe it. Now please tell me how you met this Angelina."

Frowning slightly as he gathered his thoughts, Jean Paul began again. "She simply walked out of the wall of rain and into the path of my wagon, lost and shaking with a chill. I convinced her to come home with me where we shared a hot meal before I gave her my bed." He paused a moment then to look at his companions, his manner conspiratorial as he continued. "That she is a beauty is true but I would not dream of taking advantage of so young a woman when she was in such great distress."

"We understand, go on." Phillip was ready to pull the man from his chair and shake the tale out of him if he would not hurry up with it, but restrained himself with great effort and smiled in an encouraging fashion.

"She lay ill for more than three days, burning with fever. I could not leave her side to summon a physician for fear I would find her dead when I returned. I treated her as best I could with the herbs I had handy. I have been on the river for many years and have some skill with the Indian remedies I've learned."

Alarmed, Phillip leaned forward. "The woman is recovering?"

"Yes, but she is very frail, her illness more of the spirit than the body. I thought if only she had the hope of returning to her homeland she might have more of a will to live after what she's suffered."

"What sort of hardships has the woman endured, Mr. LaCasse?" Phillip held his breath, then relaxed as he realized Anna must not have revealed his name or the man would gone shrieking from the ship the moment they were introduced.

Jean Paul was undecided as to how much he wished to confide in the captain and his mate but since their manner seemed so sincere he continued. "It seems Angelina was forced to marry a man she would not have freely chosen to wed. She is from a fine family and it is not uncommon for marriages to be arranged for reasons other than love but in her case it was a great tragedy."

"She was forced to marry the man?" Phillip asked skeptically. "How, was she led in chains to the altar?"

"No, of course not." Jean Paul waved aside his question with an emphatic gesture. "Were you to meet Angelina you would not doubt her word, Captain. She had no choice but to leave a man she loved to marry one she did not."

Phillip cast a skeptical glance toward Jamie that the Frenchman could not help but see. "I know the tale is a fantastic one, but there is more. No sooner had Angelina married than she was abducted by her lover, but unfortunately he turned out to be no more honorable a man than her new husband. That scoundrel brought her here to New Orleans and left her with Yvette Molyneaux. The sign above the woman's door may read Hotel LaMer but all know it is a brothel. Perhaps you have seen the place?"

"I have heard of it," Phillip admitted hoarsely.

"Well, Angelina would not accept such a disgraceful life and fled as soon as the rascal left her alone. Having little experience with hurricanes she did not realize the storm would be such a violent one. She hoped to find a church to seek sanctuary but swiftly became lost. It was fortunate we chanced to meet when she needed a friend so desperately to help her. I have done what I can but all she truly wants is to return to her homeland where she might earn her own way honestly. I would like to see her realize her dream."

Phillip rose from his chair and began pacing beside the round table. "That is indeed a fantastic tale, Mr. LaCasse, from beginning to end." Anna had still given no reason for her marriage to Clairbourne so the man's story made things no more clear, but how could she possibly have misunderstood his intentions so completely as to have imagined he'd left her with Yvette to earn her livelihood as a whore? He was thoroughly disgusted. If that was all she thought of him, then perhaps she should return to Sweden and for all he cared she could swim!

Jamie watched Phillip's anger grow to a dangerous level and spoke to distract the trapper. "Passage to Europe is expensive. Does this young woman have the fare?"

"No, she has nothing, but I will gladly pay her way for she has become very dear to me in the few days she's been in my home. I have never married, have no children I know of and she is the sweetheart I have never had." Jean Paul blinked back his tears, ashamed to have displayed such emotion in front of strangers, but he saw to his relief that they appeared to be too preoccupied with their own thoughts to notice his lack of control.

"You should speak with the woman, don't you think, Captain? Be certain she wants to make the voyage and is well enough to survive it?"

Phillip nodded, for indeed he did want to meet this Angelina and soon. "Yes, of course, I have time now. I will come with you since you were returning home, Mr. LaCasse."

"I have only my wagon, Captain, you'll need a horse."

"If any survived the storm, I will rent one. It is a small expense." Phillip nodded to Jamie, sending him off on the errand from which he returned swiftly with not one mount but two.

"I would like to come along, Captain, the exercise would be good for me after so long at sea." He whispered softly then so only Phillip could hear, "I will see

458

Jean Paul does not disturb you while you talk with 'Angelina.' "

Phillip nodded agreeably, for he understood Anna could hardly be expected to welcome a visit from him if she truly believed she'd been abandoned in a brothel! He mounted the rented horse and followed close behind LaCasse's wagon, not letting him get more than a few feet ahead for fear he'd lose the man and be unable to see Anna after all. The trapper led them on a narrow trail which left the city to angle northeast into the surrounding bayous. More than once Phillip looked back, hoping to memorize the route, but the terrain presented a hopeless maze. When at last they reached Jean Paul's small dwelling, Jamie pulled a pistol from beneath his coat and pointed it at the Frenchman.

"Now listen carefully, my friend. We know your Angelina and mean her no harm. As long as you sit quietly on the steps of your home you'll come to no harm either."

Jean Paul's eyes grew wide with sudden insight as he realized who the two men must be. "You snakes! Why—"

"Sit down!" Phillip commanded sharply. "I mean only to speak to the young woman you know as Angelina. If she wishes to remain here I will not take her by force." He waited to be certain the man would obey his order then pulled the latchstring and entered the wooden home. A small fire glowed on the hearth giving the single room a pleasant warmth as well as light. He approached the bed slowly, expecting a fiery burst of insults from its occupant but Anna was sleeping soundly, a tattered quilt pulled up to her chin. He stood watching her for a long moment before he reached out to touch her cheek with a fond caress. Her skin was cool, whatever fever she'd suffered now gone and he drew up a chair and sat down beside her. "I feared you were dead, you little fool, and here you are sleeping peacefully without a care to trouble your dreams!"

Anna's eyes flew open at the sound of his voice and she sat up clutching the covers to her breast as she came fully awake in an instant. "How dare you come here? How dare you?" She looked around the small cabin quickly, hoping to see Jean Paul but finding they were alone.

"That is precisely the question I wished to ask you, Countess."

Anna gasped sharply, insulted as though he'd struck her, her eyes flashing with angry sparks. "I am not Clairbourne's wife, you know I am not!"

Phillip got to his feet and began to unbutton his coat, his motions slow and deliberate. "Through no fault of your own!" He cast his coat aside and then pulled his shirt off over his head.

"What are you doing?" Anna's tawny eyes swept over his powerful frame as he continued to disrobe, her glance turning from indignation to curiosity.

"Isn't it obvious? I plan to share that bed with you. I thought you were dead, Anna, that I have found you safe and well is certainly cause for celebration." Realizing she did not know what had happened at the Hotel LaMer he continued. "Yvette's hotel was destroyed in the storm and I thought I'd lost you. I inquired at the hospital where she was taken, looked at bodies in the morgue, spent two days shoveling mud hoping with all my heart I would not find your beautiful body buried beneath all the rubble. I think you owe me this after all I've been through."

Appalled, Anna argued. "You sound as though you are disappointed to find me alive! I owe you nothing and I'll never pay any man for what he's done for me as you wish to be repaid!" She was outraged by his contemptible assumption and clearly had no intention of inviting him into her bed.

"Jean Paul adores you in case you have been too ill to notice. He keeps a neat house for a bachelor but there is only that one bed. Are you saying he hasn't been sharing it with you?"

"That is no business of yours!" Anna responded hotly, making him suffer again without realizing it. "Now, where is Jean Paul? What have you done to him?"

"Not a thing. He is right outside with Jamie, passing the time of day in a good-natured fashion. Now enough of your questions." Phillip slipped into the bed and tried to draw Anna into his arms but she pushed him away. "Anna." Phillip's anger melted away as his fingertips touched the silken skin of her cheek. "Listen to me carefully. I have no family anywhere anymore so I must rely upon my friends to help me no matter how unsuitable they might be as companions for you. I took you to Yvette Molyneaux's because I thought you'd be safe there. I simply wanted for you to have a warm and dry room in which to wait out the hurricane. LaMer truly was a hotel but in addition Yvette provided amusements for those who requested them. It did not even occur to me you would ever imagine you'd been left to earn your living in a brothel until Jean Paul told me so an hour ago." Phillip leaned down to kiss her

461

throat, softly caressing her cool skin with his lips. "I can not believe you truly thought I'd given you to Yvette to sell to other men. I refuse to believe you'd think so little of me."

Anna turned slowly to face him, her expression filled with a curious mixture of sorrow and amazement. "I know how much you've come to hate me, Phillip. You needn't pretend to have feelings for me I know you no longer want to have."

Phillip wound his fingers in her golden curls, pulling her lips down to his but his kiss was light, gentle and loving rather than possessive. "Does that feel like hatred to you, my impossible beauty?"

Anna turned away again, unwilling to give any reply when all their encounters ended in disaster. "Please don't kiss me, Phillip. You'll only make everything worse."

"I have never forced you to make love to me and I won't now. I want only to hold you in my arms until you understand how foolish you were to run away from me." He wrapped her in a warm embrace, cradling her head upon his broad chest while he tried to distract himself from the desire which flooded his senses with maddening intensity.

Anna lay tense and unyielding at his side. "You kissed me so roughly, truly I thought you had gone away, had left me forever."

Phillip chuckled as he gave her an affectionate hug. "I could not leave you even if I tried, Anna. But I will forgive you for trying to leave me since this time it saved your life. Calling yourself Angelina was a nice touch, by the way. Had I had any doubt it was you Jean Paul had found that would have settled it."

Anna glanced up, looking at him more closely. He seemed more tired than she'd ever seen him and she was sorry she'd caused him this new pain after all the others. "How did the *Angelina* fair in the storm? Was she badly damaged?"

"No, we will be ready to sail in a day or two now that I've found you. We had to replace several spars, untangle miles of rigging but there was no damage to the masts or the hull," Phillip explained confidently then began to laugh as he sat up to push her down upon the pillows. "We have never had such a ridiculous conversation in bed, Anna, nor do I wish to continue it. My patience with your willfulness has reached its end."

"But, Phillip, we are still in such terrible danger. Everything is against us, even the weather which nearly took my life and could have destroyed your beautiful ship."

"Enough, woman, enough." Phillip lowered his mouth to hers, stilling her fears with a deep kiss he did not end until she had relaxed in his arms. Soft and enticing, her arms encircled his neck, inviting his passion with irresistible affection and he felt the same sweet surrender she always gave and knew she was truly his once again. Warm and enchanting, her kiss was delicious but reluctantly he had to pull away. "You must promise never to leave me again, Anna. You must promise me that."

Anna gazed up at the man she adored and shook her head sadly. "I'll make no such promise when it could cost you your life."

"I am responsible for my own life as well as yours!" He tightened his hold upon her, pressing her slender body along the length of his as he demanded she accept his command, but her expression did not change. Calm, serene, she seemed to see a future so bleak she'd give no promise to share it but he could no longer resist the temptation to possess her body even if he could still not conquer her defiant will. "Anna," he whispered softly, his hold possessive as he moved to take her for his own, to give her the rapture she always lavished upon him. When she moved beneath him slightly, to welcome his advance not to avoid it he could no longer remember what it was he wanted her to say. His mouth sought hers so eagerly she began to laugh, a low, throaty giggle which stole his heart anew. He loved her so desperately nothing mattered to him, not their humble surroundings or continual problems. He felt only the exquisite pleasure of the moment and the perfection of the love which flowed between them with such perfect harmony. The reality of her affection was so much better than the dreams which had filled his lonely nights after they'd first chanced to meet. She was so alive, filled with a playful warmth and his alone.

Anna clung to Phillip, feeling his joy as deeply as her own but it did not ease the terror which filled her heart. Their love could destroy him yet he'd not agree to let her go. She'd been a fool. Again and again at every turn she'd done the wrong thing but oh how dearly she loved him and how desperately she longed to be his wife. She held him clasped in her embrace, unwilling to ever let him go yet praying she'd find the strength to make him understand why he had to give her up.

Chapter Twenty-six

Phillip's loving glance never left Anna's sweet features as he dressed. She was sleeping so soundly he hated to awaken her again for Jean Paul's use of the word frail to describe her appearance was all too accurate. If making love overtaxed her strength he knew they'd have to delay their departure from New Orleans for he'd not take her on an extended voyage if she were so likely to become exhausted. Sailing the *Angelina* required his full attention yet with her on board he knew he'd be able to concentrate on little else. "Well, my beauty, fit or not I want you to come with me. Now wake up and we will go." He shook her shoulder lightly to arouse her and she smiled warmly this time as she opened her eyes.

"Give me a minute or two please. I'll get dressed and then I want to talk to Jean Paul for he has done so much for me and I do not want to leave without thanking him properly." Anna stretched lazily as she sat up but she made no move to leave the comfortable bed while Phillip stood so near.

"You needn't tell him goodbye. We'll see him again for I'm certain he'd like to attend our wedding." Phillip smiled slyly, pleased with himself for finally realizing he'd been foolish to tell her he'd no wish to marry her when that had been all he'd ever really wanted to do.

"Our wedding?" Anna asked incredulously. She licked her lips nervously and then forced herself to ask a question which had been worrying her greatly. "Phillip, you know I am not truly Charles's wife, but what if he swore that I were? Couldn't I be arrested for bigamy if we married?"

"What?" Phillip ran his fingers through his dark curls as he tried to imagine where she'd gotten such a dreadful idea. "Why would he want to do that, Anna?"

"To make trouble for us which it most certainly would. You don't think he'll want me now but I have no such hope that he won't. At the very least he'll want to repay you for what you've done to him and I've no hope that he'll want to spare me from the fury of his anger. If we marry it will only make everything so much worse than it already is, can't you see that?"

"No!" Phillip shouted loudly. "What I see is that you are a woman so gorgeous and loving I can not resist you and I want you for my wife!" He was sick of problems, thoroughly disgusted with the way everything continually went wrong for them. "Do you want to marry me or not?"

"Of course I want to marry you, but not if either or both of us will go to prison for it!" Anna pointed out quickly. "Please, Phillip, let's wait awhile, until we are certain what Charles will do."

Placing his hands on his narrow hips, Phillip scowled impatiently. "I have no intention of fathering a tribe of bastards, Anna, and I want you to marry me now."

What little color there had been in Anna's cheeks vanished at that taunt but she'd not give in on so important a matter. Whether or not what Charles had said about him was true, she could see he was serious in his demand. "We have months yet before that will happen, Phillip. Please don't be so angry with me because I can't agree to marry you yet."

Startled, Phillip pressed her for the truth. "You are certain then that we'll have a child, positive?"

"Quite frankly, I have had so many more difficult problems to contemplate in the last few weeks I have lost all track of the time. Perhaps, perhaps not, we'll simply have to wait and see."

"You are lying to me, Anna." Again he felt like adding, but didn't. "Just get up and dress please, do you need my help to gather your belongings?"

"No, for I have precious little left. Why don't you wait outside and I'll do my best to hurry." Anna bit her lip anxiously, not about to admit she was not telling him the truth.

Knowing only too well that he'd get nowhere by arguing with her, Phillip leaned down to kiss her cheek sweetly before he turned to go. "I will be outside. I owe Jean Paul an explanation for I let him bring me out here under completely false pretenses." He left the cabin as neatly groomed and dressed as he'd been when he'd entered but his relaxed expression made what he'd been doing all too plain.

When Anna came through the door half an hour

467

later the three men were talking quietly together. They turned too quickly to greet her and she could readily see they'd been talking about her by their sheepish expression. "Well, gentlemen, I am ready to go if you'll allow me a moment to speak privately with Jean Paul."

"Of course." Phillip grabbed Jamie's arm and led him over to the horses where they pretended to check the cinches on their saddles while Jean Paul came forward. His expression was curious, and she reached out to take his hand between hers. "I know Phillip must have spoken to you about us. I misunderstood him, it seems, but I am so very happy to have met you." She smiled as she gave him a sweet kiss upon the cheek. "I hope to see you again before we sail."

"I will remember you always, Angelina, may I still call you that? You may come to me for assistance at any time." Jean Paul brought her hands to his lips as he winked slyly and whispered, "Your captain is a fine man, I will entrust you to his care but I am very jealous."

"Bless you, my friend." Anna hurried to Phillip's side while the Frenchman brought her tapestry bag. Phillip lifted her up into his saddle then swung himself up behind her while Jamie took her satchel to carry. They were gone in a moment, following their own tracks back through the bayou while there was still plenty of light.

Anna leaned back against Phillip's chest and yawned sleepily. "I am so sorry but I can't seem to stay awake."

"I will forgive you. Close your eyes and rest." He held her tightly around the waist and gave her a warm squeeze, so happy to have her in his arms again he did

468

not care if she slept the whole way. But as they entered the street which led to the docks he pulled his horse to so abrupt a halt she awakened immediately.

The British man-of-war lay at anchor beside the *Angelina* and her red-coated troops were swarming over the schooner's decks while their officers stood aside talking earnestly with a fair-haired man Anna recognized instantly as her husband. "Oh no, Phillip, he's found us. What shall we do?" She turned to look up at him and was frightened by the intense light in his blue eyes. Clearly he already had a plan in mind and she didn't like the looks of it one bit. "Phillip!"

"Jamie, I want you to take Anna back to Jean Paul's. It's of sufficient distance from the city to avoid discovery and search." As if to accent his command, he drew the hood of Anna's cape over her bright curls before he gave her one last lingering kiss, his mouth very soft and gentle upon her lips, his passion now most tender rather than violent.

Anna clung to him, furious that he'd send her away rather than allow her to face Charles with him. "Must I go so far? Isn't there somewhere nearby that I could stay?"

"Nowhere I'd trust now that the LaMer is in ruins. Now go, there is no time to lose!" With a sure grasp Phillip lifted Anna from his horse and handed her over to Jamie, who wrapped his arms around her securely before turning his mount around to retrace the route they'd just completed. Anna looked back to watch as Phillip approached the *Angelina*. He leapt from his horse's back and with a confident stride went up the gangplank to confront the British officers whose troops filled the deck.

"Have the British any legal right to search the *Ange lina?*" Anna asked Jamie breathlessly.

"No! But that didn't stop them, did it?" Jamie made as swift progress as he dared for he knew Phillip would need all the help he could get to avoid the most desperate of situations. He tarried no more than a minute to enlist Jean Paul's aid and then was gone, heading back into the city for the second time that afternoon.

The trapper was overjoyed to have his delightful visitor back so soon but the prospect of having to defend her against an English earl and more than one hundred British troops appalled him. "You will always be welcome in my home, you know that, Anna, but perhaps we should flee up the river before your whereabouts are discovered."

Anna waited until Jamie had vanished from sight before she turned to face the Frenchman. "No, I have no intention of hiding like a frightened rabbit! I want to go back into New Orleans right now. Will you take me?"

"What are you saying?" Jean Paul gestured helplessly. "Your captain sent you here to me where you'd be safe!"

"Yes, he always does what he thinks is best for me which is always just to leave me behind!" Anna paced rapidly up and down in front of the small cabin as she tried to make Jean Paul understand her concern. "I want to be there if there is trouble since I am the cause of it. It isn't right for Phillip to take all the blame for this alone."

Jean Paul had not realized Anna was so high-spirited a young woman but he did not hesitate to deny her request. "No, it will be dark soon. We will start supper and remain here for the night. In the morning perhaps Mr. Jenkins will return with word, or the captain may come for you himself. If we hear nothing by noon then I will go alone since I can ask questions without arousing any suspicions where you could not."

Anna sighed unhappily, frustrated that his suggestion was so logical. "I won't let Phillip suffer for this, Jean Paul, I simply won't. I love him far too dearly to let him be hurt."

Placing his arm protectively around her shoulders, he gave her an affectionate hug. "Come, let us go inside. Perhaps you are well enough to prepare another pot of soup if I will make the biscuits." His eyes twinkled merrily for he cared little what problems Phillip Bradford faced when he had his Angelina back again.

Although she tried, Anna could not fall asleep that night. She tossed and turned, so distraught over Charles's arrival she could not even close her eyes, let alone rest comfortably. Finally Jean Paul got up and lit a lamp.

"Let us talk of anything but I can not rest with you jumping up and down in that bed!" He pulled a fur around his shoulders and placed another log upon the fire. "Now tell me of your home, for I have never heard about Sweden and wish to learn all there is to know."

Giving up all pretense of sleeping Anna sat up and hugged her knees. "Our history is a long and exciting one, Jean Paul. I do not believe I can do it justice in one telling."

"Then tell me only the beginning and I will be satisfied for tonight." Sitting down so he could face her, he kept her talking until she yawned so frequently she

471

could not continue. She bid him a fond goodnight then and lay down this time to sleep soundly until long past dawn.

Jamie Jenkins was a clever young man. He left the *Angelina* in midmorning and wandered through several ship chandlers' shops picking up items to complete the schooner's supplies. He appeared to have no real purpose in mind, then when he was certain he'd not been followed he ran straight for the livery stable to rent another horse and rode the long way out to Jean Paul's cabin.

Anna was outdoors, having just laundered the bedclothes as she'd meant to do before leaving the trapper's home. When she heard Jamie approaching, she ran to meet him, grabbing hold of his horse's bridle while he jumped down from the animal's back. "What's happened? I can not wait another minute to hear it!"

Jamie put his hands gently upon her shoulders while he caught his breath but he had much to explain. "Phillip's been arrested. It's far too complicated a tale to repeat but Charles has the whole city in an uproar. He claims his beautiful bride was abducted and brought here to New Orleans against her will."

"And he had Phillip arrested?" Anna put her hands over Jamie's, hanging on to him tightly as her eyes studied his troubled expression.

Jamie attempted to speak calmly, to describe an absurd situation in a rational manner. "Charles was able to convince the authorities that you had been abducted and slain. Justice seems to be swift here and a Judge

Sanchez will try Phillip for murder in three days time."

"Murder!" Anna shrieked. "But that's ridiculous, when I am very much alive!" She looked toward Jean Paul for help. "I am a stranger here. Will you come with me so I can tell this judge I'm alive? He will have to free Phillip then."

Jean Paul frowned as he joined them. They all huddled close together beside the horse, each so intent upon Phillip's fate none thought of seeking a more comfortable location to talk. "Is that not what your Englishman wants? To bring you out of hiding?"

"Of course," Jamie agreed as he offered his hand to Jean Paul. "Charles doesn't really believe Anna is dead, he's just trying to make things impossible for her as well as for Phillip."

"This is terrible!" Anna exclaimed as she looked first at one man and then at the other. "How can you discuss this so calmly? Phillip is in jail and I'm supposed to be dead! Whatever are we going to do?"

"Nothing," Jamie cautioned. "Phillip can take care of himself no matter what his circumstances. Charles has no proof a murder's been committed, he might have forced a trial but he'll never get a conviction."

"Oh, I see. I'm just to wait and let Phillip stand trial for my murder? Is that what you're suggesting, Mr. Jenkins?"

"It is not my suggestion, but Phillip's order, Anna. You are to remain here and stay out of mischief for once."

Anna turned away, livid with Phillip's edict as well as with Jamie for bringing it, but after a moment's hesitation she turned back. "He's wrong. From what I saw Charles doesn't do anything simply for the sport of

473

it. He'll see Phillip hangs, that's what he truly wants and I have no intention of sitting out here while it happens!" Seeing she had their full attention she continued, "Do you know an attorney, Jean Paul? At the very least we must have the best man in New Orleans to defend Phillip when this ridiculous case is heard."

Jean Paul shrugged helplessly. "I know no such person. I am what you see, a trapper, not a wealthy man with influential contacts. I do not know any attorneys, competent or otherwise."

"Then who would?" Anna persisted. She watched the men think for several minutes but when they could come up with no names she offered one. "What about Yvette? Wouldn't she be likely to know someone who might help us?"

Jamie swore under his breath. "Undoubtedly, but she is in the hospital, so badly injured she can not render any assistance in this matter."

"And why not? I could go to see her, ask her for the name of an honest man we can trust, for Charles is sure to bribe anyone else. Do you know in which hospital Yvette is recuperating?"

"Yes, but Phillip said this is not to concern you, Anna. He'll not let your good name be ruined by this scandal."

"What is so special about my name? I care little what gossip there is about me when Phillip is in danger of hanging! Now let us go into the city immediately so I can speak with Yvette!" Without waiting for Jamie to agree Anna leapt upon his horse's back and would have left without him had he not had the good sense to jump up behind her.

"You must not leave me behind!" Jean Paul insisted

and pausing to put no more than a bridle on his horse he rode bareback into New Orleans.

Yvette stared up at her three visitors. She knew Jamie as an amusing fellow always eager for a good time but she'd never seen him in so serious a mood. While she remembered Anna vividly there was none of the reserve in the young woman's manner she recalled from their first meeting. As for the young man with them, he had greeted her so politely in French she was quite charmed by him, but the reason for their sudden appearance at her bedside completely mystified her.

"What we need, Madame Molyneaux, is some expert legal advice and we hoped since you are well-versed in the intrigues of this city that perhaps you would be able to recommend someone," Jamie explained hurriedly. The women's ward offered little privacy and he was angry with himself for not insisting Anna wear her cape for she was too striking a young woman not to attract notice no matter how much they needed discretion. He wanted to take her back to Jean Paul's as quickly as possible before some new complication appeared.

Yvette nodded slightly as she considered their request. "Phillip has been to see me several times this last week, Miss Thorson. I am happy to know he has found you safe but I am most distressed to think his troubles have been compounded. There is a man who has been helpful to me in the past. I can think of no more qualified attorney but whether or not he will take Phillip's case I can not say."

"Just give the man's name and I will consult him this very hour, Madame Molyneaux. If you'd rather I did not mention your name I will not," Jamie offered considerately.

"We are such old friends it will not matter." Yvette smiled sweetly, her memories obviously very warm. "His name is Alexander Bennett and if any man can untangle this mess surely it is he."

"Oh, thank you, Madame Molyneaux." Anna squeezed her hand tightly. "I hope you will be well soon."

"I have no hope of that, Miss Thorson. But what of you, have you suitable attire to wear to the trial?"

Remembering the woman's outlandish garb, Anna hesitated to reply, but could think of no polite way to avoid her question. "I have a dress or two left, they will have to do."

"Nonsense, you must look as though you are being cared for extremely well, pampered lavishly, my dear. My dressmaker will be able to supply the very thing, elegance and good taste. Now I know what you are thinking, but my wardrobe suited my profession and you may trust her to create something which will suit your needs as well. Her shop is located only two blocks from where my hotel stood. You must hurry as there is no time to lose. Listen carefully and I will tell you exactly what to say."

Anna paid close attention when she realized the older woman's advice was sound. "Thank you, I will come back to see you soon." Bidding Yvette goodbye, Anna and Jean Paul promised to return to his home after visiting the dressmaker's while Jamie headed straight for the attorney's office where he called upon every bit of charm he possessed to persuade the man to take up Phillip's cause.

476

Alexander Bennett was a man in his early fifties, balding and stout. He gave no appearance of being the shrewd man Yvette had insisted he was. His office had sustained only minor damage due to the storm but he had been too busy seeing to his friends' needs to look after his own. "What I need is a broom, sir, not a client in such desperate need as you describe." He gestured toward the documents he had stacked upon several chairs to dry. His office had never been in such sorry condition and he was most distressed by the lack of order.

Jamie tried more flattery since his first appeal for help had not yielded the result for which he'd hoped. "You were recommended as the finest attorney in the city and Captain Bradford deserves no less. This is a matter of love, of the right of a man and woman to follow their own hearts. Lord Clairbourne is the villain here. He is the one who deserves to be occupying that cold, damp cell, not Phillip Bradford!"

Alexander pushed his chair over to his roll-top desk and sat down wearily. "Your regard for your captain is obviously sincere, Mr. Jenkins, but the question is simply whether or not Lady Clairbourne was kidnapped. Now answer that one if you can."

Jamie had explained the situation in the best terms possible and he hesitated now before admitting the truth. "Yes, she was, but she does not object. She has not charged Captain Bradford with any crime, only Lord Clairbourne has."

Alexander Bennett squinted, his small, gray eyes piercing for he was confused by Jamie's conflicting remarks. "I do not like the sound of this, my young friend. An English lord is not without power, even

477

here."

"But he will not have you on his side!" Jamie exclaimed confidently.

Bennett laughed at that compliment but shook his head. "Neither will Bradford unless I am certain we can win."

"But he is innocent. He is in jail charged with the murder of a woman who is alive!"

"A minor point," Bennett explained. "There is this other charge also. All the judge need ask is if the lady left Jamaica with Bradford willingly or not. Now did she walk out of that house full of guests celebrating her marriage in view of someone who can serve as a witness or did he carry her out screaming and only later win her consent for his actions?" Bennett nodded slyly, as if he were sure Jamie would know how a man might gain such approval from a beautiful young woman.

"You misunderstand the situation, sir. No one saw them leave because Clairbourne would have stopped them had he known what was happening. But Anna wasn't screaming, she made no objection at all!" Jamie could swear to that but he'd not mention she couldn't have spoken even if she'd tried.

"Look, the facts are on Lord Clairbourne's side, and I'd say your captain is in grave danger of hanging."

Not amused by that dreadful pun, Jamie gave up his efforts to win Bennett's sympathy. "Then you're not half the attorney I was told you were!" He started for the door clearly disgusted by the man's lack of interest in seeing justice done. He'd find another attorney, and another if he had to but he'd not allow Phillip to hang for any crime. The courthouse was near the harbor, a few well placed cannon volleys might have to do the

478

trick if the legal system couldn't. He tugged on the door handle but the office door was stuck fast, warped by the storm and he couldn't loosen it.

"Wait a minute, Mr. Jenkins. I will at least come with you to speak to Captain Bradford myself before I make my final decision. If nothing else I should like to meet a man who has the audacity to kidnap an earl's bride on her wedding night." He winked as he got to his feet for truly little else was being discussed in New Orleans that day and he was as curious as everyone else.

Scowling angrily, Jamie was tempted to leave alone but Yvette had said to settle for no one else and he had no idea where to go next if Alexander Bennett would not help them. "I will introduce you, sir, but I strongly suggest you never make such an uncalled-for remark to Phillip."

Alexander gave the door handle a quick downward jerk which dislodged the jammed door as he chuckled. "You may rely on me to know better than to insult a prospective client, my boy. Now let us hurry for should I decide to take this case I will have little time to prepare."

The two men walked to the jail with brisk strides and after a brief conversation Alexander Bennett knew he'd no wish to miss in participating in so unusual a trial where the defendant was accused of murdering a woman who was alive. But the abduction charge worried him, for he saw no way for Phillip to escape punishment for that crime when he refused to deny he'd taken Anna from Clairbourne's plantation in Jamaica.

The morning of the trial was overcast and cold, depressing all who still worked to salvage what remained of their storm-ravaged homes and businesses. The prospect of spending a few entertaining hours at a murder trial involving an enormously wealthy English lord and his new bride in the most shocking of scandals was greatly appealing and the courtroom was filled to capacity long before the elegantly clad earl and his escort of British officers arrived.

Phillip had not been surprised by the large number of spectators but their keen interest in his case struck him as being ghoulish, as if they wanted to be certain they caught sight of him before he went to the gallows, a destination at which he had no intention of arriving. It was clear by the hostile stares which met his glance that Charles's slanderous lies had already branded him guilty in the townspeople's eyes but he was counting on the judge proving to be a more open-minded individual than the members of the crowd obviously were.

Judge Etienne Sanchez represented the local blend of cultures well. The product of a marriage between a high-spirited French beauty and a somber Spaniard, he had the advantage of being trilingual and held his position upon the bench due not only to his considerable judicial talents but also to his ability to try cases involving the vast majority of the residents of the Louisiana territory. Tall and dark, reed-thin and sharp-featured, he had a perpetually dour expression which gave clear warning he'd tolerate no levity whatsoever in his court. That the present case had attracted such notoriety disgusted him thoroughly and he wanted only to get it over with swiftly. All rose as he took his place at the front of the room and he began the proceedings promptly. Lord Clairbourne testified with the icy calm of a practiced widower, followed by the British officer who had led the search of the *Angelina* which had yielded no trace of the missing Lady Clairbourne.

Phillip had given Alexander Bennett little in the way of tangible help in his defense. He refused to testify nor would he allow Anna to be called. But Bennett had dealt with many a proud man in his long career and had used his own judgment in the matter. When the prosecutor had finished with his portion of the trial, having firmly established in his estimation that the newly wed Lady Clairbourne had been abducted and murdered somewhere between Jamaica and New Orleans, Alexander Bennett called only one witness: the supposedly deceased Lady Anna Clairbourne.

The confused burst of conversation that announcement brought dropped instantly to a startled silence as Jamie escorted Anna into the room from the corridor outside where they'd been waiting. The mate knew Phillip would flay him alive later for disregarding his orders so blatantly, but he'd decided his captain's life was worth saving with whatever means necessary and he'd gladly face what punishment he had to.

Phillip sat up suddenly, his face filling with rage as he realized what his attorney had done. Every eye was firmly fixed upon the hauntingly beautiful blonde; where she'd gotten such a stunning new outfit on such short notice he couldn't imagine, but then she continually supplemented her meager wardrobe in the most unexpected ways. She looked every inch the countess the crowd had been so eager to believe murdered and he could not tear his gaze from her face. Her fair hair was coiled atop her head in a attractive sweep of curls only slightly covered by a veiled hat adorned with the brilliant green and golden plumage of the pheasant. The honey beige of her expertly tailored suit complemented her unusual coloring as well as her superb figure to every advantage. She was composed and serene in her manner, as if she were arriving to attend a benefit concert rather than a trial for a capital offense.

Phillip leaned over to whisper in Alexander Bennett's ear. "I told you not to involve Anna in this, I forbid it!"

Chuckling, the attorney explained, "I've not lost a client to the gallows in thirty years, Bradford, and I'd no wish to see you spoil my perfect record."

"Damn you!" Phillip hissed loudly.

"Silence!" Judge Sanchez slammed his heavy wooden gavel soundly upon his podium. "You'll be quiet, Captain Bradford, or I'll have you gagged and bound to your chair!"

Phillip sat back as he nodded slightly, clearly having no desire for such extreme restraints. But he was outraged to think Anna would have to testify for him when every word she spoke would damage her already tainted reputation beyond repair. The whole trial was a farce in his opinion, a travesty of justice since the question should have been settled between him and Charles without any outside interference. He considered the man's insistence he be charged with Anna's abduction and murder no more than a demonstration of his fiendish lust for revenge which was no less than obscene since Anna was the once who would suffer the most.

The prosecutor for the city of New Orleans stepped

forward as soon as order had been restored to the courtroom. "Since Lady Clairbourne has come forward, we wish to drop the charge of murder, your honor, and proceed with the evidence to prove she was abducted from her home on Jamaica by Phillip Bradford and brought to this country by force."

Astonished by so unexpected a turn of events, the judge turned to Alexander Bennett to inquire dryly, "I assume you will offer no argument if the murder charge against your client is dropped, Mr. Bennett?"

"None whatsoever, your honor. In fact, I move all charges be dropped due to the total lack of evidence in the prosecutor's possession."

Displeased to think his court was being used to pursue a private matter, Judge Sanchez disagreed. "Motion denied. Swear in the witness."

Anna was uncertain what to do as the name Lady Clairbourne was again called. She hesitated to admit she was Charles's wife when she wanted so desperately to deny it, but knowing she had to testify to clear Phillip's name she moved forward gracefully and placed her right hand atop the Bible held by the bailiff. She had given the matter of swearing to tell the truth considerable thought. There was more than one way to be truthful and she planned to give the most liberal interpretation possible.

The prosecutor looked around the crowded courtroom as he moved back to his place, relishing what he sensed would be a great triumph on his part. Bennett could present whatever evidence he wished, but there was no way to dispute the fact the young woman had been taken from Jamaica because there she sat for all to see. Clairbourne had promised him a large reward for his efforts should he win the case and he had already decided how he wished to see that money spent.

Alexander Bennett bowed slightly, his manner respectful as he approached the witness stand. "I know testifying here today will be a great ordeal for you, Lady Clairbourne, but I would like for you to simply tell us the story of how you happened to leave Jamaica, in your own words."

Anna looked up at the dark-eyed judge. He seemed to be such an irritable individual she hated to make an issue of her name but she simply had to do it. "May I be addressed as Lady Thorson, your honor, for while Charles and I did go through a wedding ceremony, we have never lived together as man and wife and are therefore not married so I have no claim to his name."

The entire room erupted in a burst of laughter at that question, for men and women alike were astonished that a woman of such fine breeding would openly discuss such an intimate matter. Judge Sanchez pounded furiously with his gavel in a vain attempt to restore order but he had to threaten to clear the courtroom entirely of spectators before the raucous group finally grew still. "You are the Lady Clairbourne in question here, are you not?"

When Anna looked up at him again he saw only the shimmer of unshed tears which lit her amber eyes with a bright sheen. While New Orleans was a city noted for its beautiful women, he knew he'd never met another to compare with her. She was as perfect an example of the elegance of nobility as he had ever seen. The sudden thought that French judges as well meaning as he had sent women of her class to the guillotine gave him a feeling of such sorrow he completely forgot what his question had been and prompted her gruffly, "Well, go on, I am waiting."

Anna spoke in so low a tone all but the judge had to strain to hear. Her voice was breathless as she replied. "Yes, I am she."

"Good, that is one less confusion at least. Now please tell us what transpired on your wedding night." When that question brought further peals of boisterous laughter from the assembled crowd, Sanchez realized his mistake and rephrased his inquiry more discreetly. "Just tell us how you happened to leave Jamaica."

"I will be brief, but I must begin long before that night, to the day in early spring when my uncle first brought me the news of Lord Clairbourne's proposal." She was concise, the recounting of the numerous adventures of her journey heart-rending and in every word she made Charles's neglect more apparent while Phillip's continual assistance was spoken of in the fondest terms. It was a spellbinding tale, from the violence suffered at the hands of highwaymen to bloodthirsty pirates defeated by a brave captain and his heroic crew. Her manner was sincere, her words so convincing not one of the curious crowd was unmoved or doubted Phillip's innocence by the time she paused to draw a deep breath.

"By the time I finally reached Jamaica I knew I could not possibly marry Lord Clairbourne and went to his plantation intent upon breaking our engagement and leaving the island immediately."

"I am sorry, but I do not understand. You did say you had married Lord Clairbourne, did you not?" Sanchez asked hoarsely, his confusion justifiable.

Anna forced herself to answer, to keep telling her

story although she could barely find the breath to speak and feared she might faint before she told all that had to be revealed. "Yes, Charles explained our engagement was not one which could be broken."

At Charles's urging the prosecutor leapt to his feet. "I object, your honor. The witness may enjoy relating her entire life history but it has no bearing here. The simple fact is Lord Clairbourne's bride was spirited away from his home by Phillip Bradford. He has obviously seduced the young woman, her own testimony is clear evidence of that fact and he deserves no less than death for so despicable a crime!"

Judge Sanchez gave the prosecutor a withering glance. "Are you objecting to the question I just asked the witness myself, sir?"

Realizing he'd made a grave error, the embarrassed man disagreed. "No, not at all, only that her response will be unnecessarily detailed and biased in the defendant's favor, your honor."

Appraising the handsome, well-built defendant more closely, the jurist decided the question of seduction was not one he cared to pursue. Perhaps it was his French blood but the fact that pretty young women fell in love with handsome men seemed far too natural a phenomenon to be considered a criminal offense. "Objection overruled." Judge Sanchez then rapped his gavel to silence those who'd used the few minutes of his exchange with the prosecutor to speak to their neighbors. "Please continue, Lady Thorson."

Finding the judge's manner surprisingly sympathetic, Anna smiled shyly. "I will try, sir. As I said, Charles told me our engagement was not one which

486

could be broken." She stopped then, licking her lips anxiously as she attempted to summon the courage to describe their conversation that afternoon when it sickened her so greatly to even think of it.

Phillip saw more than the others in that crowded room for he knew Anna better than any man on earth. The blush in her cheeks had grown too vivid and while her hands had lain quietly in her lap when she'd first taken the stand, she now twisted her handkerchief so nervously he could readily see she had no wish to continue. "Stop her, Bennett, she's destroying herself to save me. Stop her now!" he insisted in a low whisper which attracted no notice from the judge. The attorney ignored his pleas and made no move to keep Anna from finishing her story.

"He told me my father had owed him ten thousand pounds and when he was unable to pay that debt had offered me to him as a bride instead. Charles said either I could repay the money that afternoon or marry him. As I was quite penniless, and still am, I had no way to make good on my father's debt other than to marry him but I never intended to live as his wife."

Charles slumped back in his chair, his hand over his eyes as he realized Anna had managed to impugn his character without once speaking a cross word. Phillip, however, was on the edge of his chair, for he knew only too well how greatly Anna had admired her father and what agony learning the details of her engagement must have caused her. When Alexander Bennett placed his hand on his sleeve, he shoved it away, for he wanted so desperately to go to Anna and take her into his arms that he could not sit back and affect a calm detachment he no longer felt.

Judge Sanchez scowled deeply, his voice accusing as he asked, "You mean you planned all along to leave Jamaica with Captain Bradford?"

"No," Anna admitted softly. "Charles's overseer had recently drowned in the nearby river and I planned to seek the same fate. Since his slaves had been blamed for the man's death I intended to leave a note so all would know I'd taken my own life when my body was found." Once begun, Anna found herself describing that night with vivid detail. "I drank all the champagne I could at the reception, then went up to my room to write the note but I found Phillip there waiting for me. He said only that he wanted to tell me goodbye and wish me happiness but he could tell there was something dreadfully wrong in my manner and took me back to the *Angelina* rather than leaving me alone when he feared I might do myself some harm."

No amount of ferocious pounding with his gavel would restore order after that shocking revelation and Judge Sanchez made good on his threat to clear the room rather than put up with such a vulgar display of curiosity. Not happy about having to leave such an exciting trial, the throng was slow to disperse and more than fifteen minutes elapsed before a dignified calm was again restored to the room. Without excusing Anna from the witness stand the judge addressed those still present. "All we have here is a regrettable case of forced marriage which nearly resulted in the death of this lovely young woman. I find your actions beneath contempt, Clairbourne. You have treated Lady Thorson most rudely in every respect and that she has no desire to be your wife is very sensible in my view. Since he is to be congratulated for saving Lady Thorson's life with his quick action to take her from Jamaica, all charges against the defendant, Captain Phillip Bradford, are therefore dismissed." With that emphatic pronouncement the man went to his chambers, leaving the results of the brief trial to be recorded by the clerk while he had a stiff drink and did his best to forget it.

Chapter Twenty-seven

Charles was seething with a furious anger for he'd considered his plan to have the authorities of the Lousiana Territory take the responsibility for executing Phillip Bradford most clever. That the plot had not only failed, but had left him open to the most mortifying ridicule enraged him. He'd not tolerate such an affront and shoved the apologetic prosecutor out of his way as he moved swiftly to confront the handsome captain. Snarling a deadly challenge, he spoke in a threatening whisper none overheard in the confusion following Judge Sanchez's exit from the courtroom. "I care little what this court has decided, Bradford. You betrayed the trust I placed in you and I demand satisfaction!"

Phillip had been on his way to Anna but stepped back abruptly, repulsed by the arrogant lord's hostile greeting. That dueling was forbidden by law mattered as little to him as it did to Charles and he readily accepted. "Send your second with the time and place and I will be there." Hurrying on, he took Anna's hands to help her from the witness stand but she was trembling so badly he doubted she could walk across the room let alone out of the building the entrance of which was certain to be crowded by those who'd been forced to leave the courtroom in the final minutes of the trial and would naturally have tarried to hear the result. Not wishing to subject her to any further strain, he gathered her up into his arms and carried her through the door by which Etienne Sanchez had just left.

The judge had already downed one drink and was pouring himself another when Phillip and Anna entered. Since he had completed his judicial duties for the day he saw no reason to hide the crystal decanter of bourbon or the glass in his hand so his glance was not unfriendly.

"Excuse me for disturbing you, your honour, but Anna is in no condition to leave and I've no idea where else I might take her to rest." Phillip apologized hastily but his smile was a confident one.

"You may place her on that small sofa. I've no objection to her company nor to yours now that you are a free man," Etienne replied agreeably.

"Thank you." Phillip laid Anna down gently upon the couch then knelt by her side, his concern for her evident in his very gesture.

After watching the pair for no more than a few seconds, Etienne spoke. "You seem to be a far more devoted couple than your story led us to believe, Lady Thorson. You managed to praise the captain for his brave deeds without ever mentioning the fact you loved him. May I congratulate you upon a masterful piece of deception."

Insulted by that compliment Anna tried to sit up to

respond but Phillip pressed her shoulders back against the velvet cushions. " Every word she spoke was the truth, sir. Our relationship is a complex one neither of us need explain but that was not the question at issue."

"Oh, but indeed it was, Captain." Etienne sat down at his desk and leaned back in his chair to get more comfortable. "You may have satisfied the Lousiana courts but I do not believe Lord Clairbourne or his British friends will stop when the advantage is yours. I must warn you to be careful when you leave this building, not only for the lady's sake, but for your own."

Phillip shot the older man a warning glance before he returned his attention to providing for Anna's comfort. "I know better than to offer you whiskey, but perhaps I can find some water."

Anna shook her head emphatically. "Please, I am fine, just let me catch my breath, then we can go." She hesitated to say anything more in front of the judge but the terror she'd felt while testifying still filled her throat with a painful knot. She was afraid she might begin to cry and never be able to stop.

"As they'll surely be watching your ship, may I offer an alternative?" Etienne was quite charmed by the handsome couple. Their affection for each other was so clear in their manner, so honest in their gaze, he trusted them to behave well no matter what the circumstance.

Rising to his feet, Phillip turned to face him. "Of course, we are your guests momentarily. Say whatever you wish." But his glance was still a warning one for he did not want Anna frightened unnecessarily.

"I have an engagement this afternoon and a rather tiresome social obligation this evening. My home is not far. You could spend the day there without being troubled, remain there for the night as well then sail before dawn while the English are still asleep in their bunks. If you are not about today they will not expect so imminent a departure and you should gain a sufficient lead to escape their pursuit should they decide to give one."

"Oh, could we go to his home, Phillip, that would be wonderful," Anna asked hopefully, her smile bright as she looked up at him.

"I do not know what to say, sir. I had not expected such a generous offer. It is most certainly not why we followed you in here."

Etienne laughed with a good-natured chuckle. "I will take that as a yes then. I will summon my carriage. It will attract no notice from whatever curious souls are still remaining nearby and I can walk the short distance to my appointment." Getting up from his desk, he went to the door which opened out onto a small courtyard and waved to a waiting groom to send for his driver. "There, it will be but a moment. My decisions are not always so popular as this one was today and I often have to leave in a great hurry. My man will see you safely to my home, I can promise you that."

"The British have no right to anything here, do they, sir? I mean they can not seize Phillip's ship, or take me into custody?" Anna knew she would not be able to relax until Charles was gone but she did not trust him any more than the judge did to leave without trying some further bit of trickery to even the score.

Etienne never lied, nor did he usually make any attempt to soften the truth. But he had no intention of upsetting such a pretty young woman by a thoughtless word. "You already know Clairbourne is the devious sort, but he will never find you at my home so there is no need for you to concern yourself about him for the moment." When his driver knocked softly at the door, the judge stepped out first to be certain their exit would be unobserved, then beckoned them to come quickly. "Franz will take you to my home and see that you are received properly. Perhaps I will see you before you leave New Orleans, but if not I wish you both good luck with your travels."

Greatly encouraged by his generous offer of hospitality, Anna walked to the door with a confident step and reached up to kiss the startled jurist on the cheek before she gave him a warm hug. "Unpopular or not, I am certain your decisions are always correct. Thank you for everything, for offering your home and for—"

Laughing again Etienne shooed her out the door. "Dear lady, you must hurry and your smile is all the reward I require." He shook hands with Phillip, then sat back down at his desk to sip the remainder of his bourbon. He could not recall ever becoming so involved in a former defendant's life and hoped he would not soon regret it.

The judge's home was large and comfortable, immaculately clean and beautifully furnished. The happiness which shone on Anna's face as she climbed the stairs to their rooms convinced Phillip he had been right to accept the man's invitation but there were several things he needed to do before he spent any time there himself. The housekeeper, an ample-figured woman named Rose, showed them to adjoining rooms, then discreetly left them alone while she went to see what could be prepared for lunch.

Phillip stood in the doorway between their rooms as

he removed his coat and rolled up his sleeves. "I'm going back to the *Angelina* for a while. Jamie will have taken your things there and I want him to know where we are."

"Must you go?" Anna sat down on the edge of the wide bed, her fingertips lightly tracing the delicate design of the crocheted spread while she awaited his answer. She wanted him to stay with her. He'd said nothing in the carriage and she'd expected him to offer some opinion on her testimony. That he hadn't had confused her.

"Yes." He hesitated to leave when he had so much on his mind he did not even know where to begin, but he decided against speaking about things which might take hours to discuss. "I have a few errands, that's all. Try and rest and I'll be back by supper time and then we'll have all night to be together."

Anna's glance was curious but she did not press him to explain his unnamed errands more fully. "Just be careful. I would not put it past Charles to hire some bully to accost you in the street."

Phillip came forward to kiss her goodbye, his lips barely brushing her cheek. "It is time we forgot Charles and lived our own lives as we pleased for a change, Anna. If I wear neither a hat nor a coat I will attract no notice down at the docks and may come and go safely. You must simply rest for I want you to be in a fine mood when I return." With a sly wink he left her room and ran down the stairs. He went through the kitchen and out the back door just in case their whereabouts had been discovered.

Knowing Anna was now alone, Rose returned with a tray of tiny sandwiches and a pot of tea. Since Etienne was a bachelor she had scant opportunity to serve pretty young ladies and welcomed the chance. "Would you like something more, miss? I will be happy to prepare whatever you wish."

"Thank you, but this is more than enough for me." Anna sat down at the small table near the windows and placed her napkin in her lap. She could not remember when she'd last eaten but it must have been the previous evening when she'd been at Jean Paul's. "Oh, no!"

Rose responded anxiously, "Is something the matter with your lunch?"

"No, I am sorry, Rose. It is not your food which I am certain will be delicious, but there was a friend waiting for me at the courthouse and I completely forgot him until this very minute." After Jean Paul had been such a good friend to her she was terribly ashamed to have been so thoughtless.

"Would you like to send Franz with a message?"

"No, he probably went home and that's much too far to send Franz. I will have to go myself." She had no other choice really for if Phillip wanted to sail on the morning tide there'd be no opportunity for her to see the trapper before they left. "Do you think I might borrow a horse? I enjoy riding and know the way. Phillip won't be back for hours and I'm far too restless to take a nap."

Rose looked closely at the elegantly clad blonde, then shrugged her shoulders helplessly. "The judge has horses, but you'll need a riding habit and a groom to accompany you."

"No, that would attract too much notice and I don't want that. Could you find me something inconspicuous to wear, britches of some sort, a shirt and a hat? I really must go and I can't ruin this new suit."

While Judge Sanchez frequently entertained visitors, Rose could not recall him ever having so attractive a young woman stay there, nor one with such unconventional ideas. "What will the gentleman say when he returns and finds you gone?"

"He'll be furious with me, so I better be back before he is!" Anna laughed as she saw the woman's eyes widen but with a deep chuckle Rose left to find her something to wear and to arrange for a horse. She ate several of the little sandwiches and drank a cup of tea, her spirits rising since she had something to do which was worth doing that afternoon. "Oh, Phillip, why is it you always go off and leave me with nothing to do save worry?"

Jean Paul's cabin was not nearly so easy to find as Anna had thought it would be, but locate it she did. Much to her dismay, however, she found it deserted and after waiting awhile she wrote her friend a brief note telling him she was sorry she'd missed seeing him after the trial and left. It was nearly sunset when she got back to the judge's home and she handed the groom her mount's reins and hurried back into the house, dashing through the kitchen before running up the back stairs two at a time. She rushed into her room intent on having a bath, of being well dressed and beautifully groomed before Phillip returned but he was already back, seated upon her bed and scowling angrily.

"Just where have you been?"

"Well, I knew you'd be gone all afternoon and so—"

"Just where have you been, that's all I truly want to

know."

Anna turned back to close the bedroom door softly. The servants in the house appeared to be discreet ones but she'd no desire to let anyone overhear their argument if there were to be one. "I know Jean Paul must have been at the trial and I wanted to see him one last time, that's all."

"So you rode all the way out to his place?" Phillip asked incredulously.

"It's really not all that far. I would have been back before now but he wasn't home and I waited awhile hoping he might appear."

"He was with me all afternoon, but that's beside the point. I thought you knew better than to leave here, especially to run an errand so foolish as that one."

Offended by his hostile manner, Anna disagreed. "Are you forgetting that if it were not for Jean Paul you would not have found me after the hurricane? He is your friend now as well as mine and it was not foolish of me to want to bid him goodbye."

Phillip rose slowly, stretching to his full height, his pose as menacing as his words. "It is high time you learned to obey me when I tell you to do something, Anna. Come here."

Turning away, Anna walked to the windows and peered out at the gathering dusk. "Not when you speak to me so rudely, I won't."

"Now, Anna, come here to me this instant." Phillip had never been more serious. He counted to ten very slowly and when she still had not moved he went to her, scooping her up into his arms and carrying her back to the bed where he sat down and laid her across his knees ready to give her the spanking he'd always thought she deserved. But she started to giggle, distracting him so completely he couldn't carry out any threat when her sparkling laugh teased his senses so playfully. When he relaxed his hold upon her she pulled his shirt from his belt and, curving herself around him, nibbled his ribs with tiny bites, putting an end to all thought he'd had of punishing her. He'd not held her in his arms for days and lay back across the bed, all anger gone as he enjoyed her tickling kisses and light touch.

The day's excitement still filled Anna's amber eyes with a bright sparkle as she moved against Phillip, her mouth sliding smoothly across his bronze skin as she peeled away his shirt. With a quick toss he got rid of the garment and wound his fingers in her long hair to press her close as her tongue flicked across his stomach, sending waves of the most delightful anticipation up his spine. He could not resist her charming ways and pulled her into an easy embrace. That her clothes held the dusty scent of the trail she'd just traveled disturbed him not in the least for he didn't plan to leave her dressed for long. He unbuttoned her soft muslin shirt and was pleased to find she wore nothing underneath as it would save him a considerable amount of time in undressing her. He nuzzled the soft fullness of her breast with tender kisses as he asked curiously, "How do you always manage to find the clothing you need, Anna? Whether it's britches for riding, a stunning suit for the courtroom or the most lavish of wedding gowns, how are you able to continually produce your clothes as if by magic?"

Anna drew away hurriedly, sorry he'd reminded her of a wedding she'd not even wanted to attend, let alone be one of the principal participants. "Rose found these clothes for me, I don't really know whose they are.

Yvette's dressmaker provided the suit I wore this morning, and as for the wedding gown, Charles had seen it in the shop of a French seamstress in Port Royal and bought it for me hoping it would fit properly or could be altered for me to wear without too much difficulty." She pushed her hair back from her eyes as she moved off the bed, her affectionate mood destroyed by the grimness of her memories. "I would like to bathe before we have supper. Did you bring my things?"

Startled by her sudden aloofness, Phillip reached down to pick up his shirt from the floor as he rolled off the bed. "I thought the aroma of your horse rather appealing. It reminded me of when first we met and you'd been working in your stable, but if you'd be more comfortable by all means call Rose and bathe. I placed your things in the wardrobe."

The sharpness of his tone matched her mood but Anna didn't care. "Are we leaving here before dawn? If so I'll pack up everything now."

"No, I've something more which must be done before we leave. I'm sure the judge won't object to our presence for a day or two more." Crossing to the room he'd been given Phillip left her alone to dress for supper while he made his own preparations for the evening.

Phillip was so very charming during supper that Anna was reminded of the night on board the *Angelina* when he'd given her too much wine in hopes of making her reveal the whereabouts of her English relatives. That was the first time they'd made love and she found it difficult to swallow her food when the delightful memory warmed her blood to such a fevered level. She still found him so handsome she could not even glance in his direction without the beat of her heart quickening and she looked down

ow certain the desire which shown in her eyes was far
rom proper for a lady.

Phillip had no more interest in his supper than did
Anna and soon lay his knife and fork on the side of his
late, finished the last drop of his wine, then grinned
roadly. "I have so much to tell you, Anna, but talking is
he last thing I want to do tonight."

His smile was so enchanting, Anna could not help but
espond warmly. "I am finished also. Would you care to
it for a while on the veranda, or perhaps look through
he judge's library for something to read?"

"No." Phillip shook his head slowly, his voice teasing
s he continued. "I want to take you straight upstairs to
ny room, peel off each layer of clothing you've bothered
o put on, then lay you across my bed and begin at your
oes to—"

"Captain Bradford, I am shocked by what you suggest," Anna replied demurely, "Would my room not be
he more appropriate place for such an exciting diversion?"

"Wherever you wish to begin, my dearest." With a sly
wink he rose from his chair and came around the table to
assist her, taking her hand as they climbed the stairs at a
sedate pace, their intentions recognizable only in their
glance. But once inside her room, Phillip locked the door
securely behind them then ripped off his coat with surprising haste.

Anna backed away with an amused laugh. "I beg you
not to handle my gown as roughly as you treat your own
garments, sir, for I no longer have that many."

"A slight problem, for a woman of your beauty needs
little in the way of the dressmaker's art to be most attractive." Though he wished to take his time that evening, he

501

found exercising a calm restraint far too difficult an
reached out to catch her around the waist and pulled he
near, his kiss burning her creamy throat as his hand
moved rapidly down her back unfastening the tiny hook
which secured her dress to her shapely figure. "Hold still
Anna, do not make this impossible for me!"

Anna hugged him tightly, enjoying the nearness of hin
far too much to relax in his arms for any reason, but a
last he succeeded in freeing her from the confining ga
ment. She stepped back to remove it then tossed th
gown over a nearby chair. When he found the ribbon
which held her silk lingerie hopelessly knotted, Anna pu
her hands over his in a gentle caress. "You must not be s
impatient when we have the whole night to enjoy." In
deed she hoped they would have all their lives to spen
together. "Eternity if you wish, my darling. Now there
see, you need only pull the end of the bow and it come
loose."

Phillip laughed at her tender instruction. "I know how
to tie knots, Anna, you needn't teach me that skill to
night."

Coming easily into his arms Anna purred seductively
"Then what is there left to teach you?"

Phillip picked her up in his arms for the short trip to
the large bed and stretched out beside her, giving no re
sponse to her teasing question as his mouth covered her
to begin a slow, sensuous kiss which left her lying quite
languidly in his embrace. Her fingertips combed slowly
through his curls, drawing him near as she enjoyed hi
wine-flavored kiss. His touch was very gentle now
sweet, but she was entirely nude while he was still fully
clothed and she slipped from his grasp to help him dis
robe with a far steadier touch than he'd had. Her tan had

not yet begun to fade and her lissome figure glowed with a pale golden sheen in the soft light of the lamp and when she moved off the bed to put it out he caught her hand to bring her back to him.

"Leave it on, you are too pretty a sight to miss." His glance was so appreciative she did not argue but he knew she did not find him unattractive either. He had meant to make love to her slowly, to trail kisses up her slender limbs until she shivered with joy but now he wanted her too badly for such lengthy play. His hand moved over her smooth stomach but there was not the slightest swell to give him hope she'd bear his child and yet she'd not denied it and he prayed silently that it were true and even more fervently that he would be with her to raise their child. "I want to have a son, Anna, a blond one with your wonderful topaz eyes," he whispered softly as his lips caressed her sweetly scented skin. He wanted all of life's pleasures with her but those she'd give him that very night were all he could grasp with certainty.

Anna knew only that she loved Phillip too dearly to waste time in talk and began where she'd stopped that afternoon, her tongue slipping over the taut muscles of his stomach as her fingertips caressed the length of his well-muscled thigh. She felt his breath quicken and did not stop, her loving kiss driving him to the brink of rapture, but he forced her away then, his powerful body sliding over hers to pin her beneath him as he sought to finish her glorious loving with a smooth, deep thrust which joined them in an ageless pleasure. Being with Anna was always a marvelous delight for him, yet each time was more splendid than the last and he knew she had taught him far more than he'd ever admit, certainly far more than he'd ever taught her. The joy she gave him was unique, the possibilities for exploring the beauty of their love endless and many hours passed before they fell into an exhausted sleep, their hearts overflowing with the sweetness of their passion.

Before the first light of dawn cast a pink glow in the eastern sky Phillip eased Anna from his arms and slipped from her bed, dressing quickly to leave the house while the darkness of night still hid his exit. He waited in the shadows for Jamie and John who arrived silently leading another mount for him.

"You brought my pistols?" Phillip whispered hurriedly as he swung himself up into the saddle.

"Yes, I have them, now let us go quickly." Jamie turned his horse toward the road, anxious to be gone about their business.

The sound of the horse's hoofs striking the stones of the path awoke Anna with a sudden start. Finding Phillip gone from his place beside her, she rushed to the window in time to see him leaving with his two friends and knew instantly what mission took them out at such an unreasonably early hour. "Damn!" she hissed to herself and, pulling on the blouse and britches she'd worn for riding, she ran down the steps and out the back door. The mare she'd ridden was a gentle animal so she bothered with no more than a bridle. Urging the sleepy horse to pursue the men, she soon caught sight of them in the distance. A fine mist filled the air and she hung back, just out of sight for she knew Phillip would be displeased that she'd followed him. But if he were determined to meet Charles that morning she certainly wanted to be there. She kept a close check on the mare, following with a discretion that made her presence impossible to detect while she kept a sharp lookout to be certain no one was

504

trailing her.

The small clearing was well known as the frequent site of confrontations between gentlemen for it was close to the city and yet secluded enough to provide the necessary secrecy. It was a strangely attractive spot for the thick growth of cypress veiled the rising sun, the gnarled branches deflecting the light sending streaks of sunshine in wild patterns upon the soft dirt floor of the forest. The assembled group was small; Charles was flanked by two British officers, neither in uniform while Phillip was accompanied by the two men who'd come for him. Each side measured ten paces carefully, then the two men involved tossed a coin for selection of places.

Charles laughed gleefully as he won the toss. "A good omen, I'd say." He readily chose the eastern end of the clearing so Phillip would have to face the rising sun, then the coin was tossed again and his second won the right to give the call to present arms. "Since all is going my way, I'd like to complete this swiftly, Bradford." Taking his pistol in a firm grip he walked to the center of the clearing and waited for Phillip to take his place behind him.

With a nonchalant shrug, Phillip agreed. "I have no reason to delay this either." As he picked up his own pistol he wondered which Anna had used, for surely it would bring him luck but there was no way to tell one of the deadly weapons from the other. Both he and Clairbourne had produced the required set of pistols but since neither man trusted the other they'd used one of each rather than a pair but Phillip was confident his weapon was the equal of the earl's.

Anna slid from her horse's back and moved stealthily toward the small open space in the forest. She'd heard the men's voices and drew near enough to see the activity

505

from behind an uprooted tree where she was hidden from view. Killing a man in a duel was considered murder, she knew, but she had no idea how vigorously that crime might be prosecuted there in the Louisiana Territory. Her heart was pounding so loudly in her ears she could barely hear the man counting off the ten paces but he'd reached no more than nine when Charles spun around and took aim.

Anna screamed Phillip's name, giving him no more than a split second's warning. But Charles's bullet missed his shoulder by a hair's breadth as he wheeled about to face him. Charles stood in shocked silence. He'd fired early and all had seen him do it. He had no choice now but to stand in his place while Phillip fired his shot, but he was terrified and began to quiver noticeably for he knew he'd be a dead man within seconds unless he could think of some clever way to save himself.

Phillip had never thought Clairbourne's character worthy of admiration, but the man's unexpected display of cowardice sickened him. "How did you plan to explain I'd been shot in the back in a duel? That's a point I'd like to hear you justify. Well, go on, tell me how you planned to get away with such cold-blooded murder under the guise of dueling for sport?"

The British officers were so disgusted they walked back to their horses. Having no wish to be considered seconds for so despicable a man, they stopped only to argue about what should be done with his body and could not agree.

Seeing he had no one to help him, Charles began to plead for his life. "You may have the woman, I'll lay no further claim to her. She is yours, that's all you really want, isn't it? Just to have Anna for your own?"

Phillip shook his head slowly. "No, I want much more than that, Clairbourne."

"Is it money you want then? I will pay whatever you like if you will not kill me," Charles begged tearfully, praying aloud for Phillip to show him some mercy.

"Mercy is it? I am surprised you even know the word when you would stoop to forcing a man to sell his only child. The rats in the hold of the *Angelina* behave with more honor than you've shown recently and I'll be doing mankind a great service to rid the earth of your miserable presence."

Seeing Phillip's finger tighten upon the trigger, Clairbourne fell to his knees, a profusion of tears streaming down his face. "Please, I beg you to spare my life. I will give you anything you desire, gold in any amount!"

Phillip waited a long moment, the tension mounting to an unbearable level within Charles's breast as he continued to cry and plead for his life like the pathetic coward he was. When he could take no more of that pitiful display Phillip replied, "I want several things. First, the sum of ten thousand pounds; second, the note Eric Thorson signed giving Anna to you; and third a statement signed by you to be witnessed by Judge Sanchez that you are not Anna's legal husband and never have been. I will meet you in the judge's chambers at noon today if you agree, otherwise . . ." He looked down the sight of his pistol, his aim steady as he let his demands sink into Charles's frightened brain.

Leaping to his feet, the Englishman agreed joyfully. "Of course, I will be there!"

"Do not be late, Clairbourne. I do not want to have to come looking for you for I will not be so understanding when we next we meet if you have not complied with my demands."

"You may trust me. I will bring the money and the note and I'll write whatever you wish without argument!" When Phillip dropped his pistol, Clairbourne ran to his horse, climbed into the saddle with a shaky leap and rode off at a furious clip, so grateful to escape the fate he'd deserved he'd not tarry to press his luck.

Handing the still-loaded pistol to Jamie, Phillip surveyed their surroundings with a curious glance. The early morning mist played tricks with his eyes and he could see little outside the small clearing. "Where's Anna?"

"I dared not leave you to look for her but she must be nearby. See if you can find her, John, she can't have gone far."

"No, wait. You two go back to the ship, I'll find her myself." Phillip had to make no more than a hasty search to discover the blonde was nowhere to be found. Her footprints were visible in the soft damp earth behind the tree where she'd stood watching him but they led back to her horse and disappeared in the underbrush. "Damn it all, Anna!" Phillip shouted loudly. Would she not ever remain in one place long enough for him to catch her?

Chapter Twenty-eight

Etienne Sanchez yawned sleepily as he climbed the steps to his front porch. His evening had turned out far better than he'd dared hope. A woman he'd greatly admired in his youth had just returned to New Orleans, recently widowed and in great need of consoling. He laughed to himself as he thought how improbable it had been that Beatriz would return after an absence of twenty years and be invited to the home of a man whose invitation he had so vigorously sought to avoid. "Fate!" he proclaimed with a chuckle for Beatriz had been as thrilled to see him again as he'd been to see her and the evening had passed all too quickly for them. It had only been natural that he would see her home and then after a brandy or two remain for the night. Smiling at the warmth of their renewed friendship he had just fitted his key into the lock when he heard a rider approaching at a furious pace and to his astonishment saw it was the lovely Lady Thorson whom he knew could not possibly have been out riding at such an early hour unless she'd had a very good reason. Going on into the house he went up the stairs to the guest rooms and waited for her on the landing. "Good morning, my dear. I trust you found my mare an adequate mount for whatever race you were running just now."

Pausing to catch her breath, Anna greeted him briefly. "Yes, thank you, she is a fine horse, swift and sure footed. Will you excuse me please, I must get ready to leave."

"Is the captain up also? Perhaps he would take breakfast with me."

"Yes, Phillip is about someplace but he's probably already eaten breakfast so I wouldn't wait for him if I were you." Smiling in hopes of distracting him, Anna tried to slip by but the man reached out to stop her.

"Before I became a judge I was an attorney, and an astute one if I do say so myself. If Captain Bradford is in some danger I will be happy to render whatever assistance is necessary."

"No, Phillip is fine, I'm sure of it," Anna replied confidently but she was shaking so badly Etienne knew something was very wrong.

"My dear, I am not unsympathetic to the problems of young lovers." Or older ones, he thought slyly to himself. "If I can be of any help, you have only to ask."

"You have been most kind, sir, so helpful to us but I really must hurry." Anna rushed off then, leaving the puzzled man staring after her as she closed the door of her bedroom. She'd never expected to see him arriving home with the dawn but that was a small problem compared with the confusion which faced her now. She flung open the wardrobe and grabbed for her gowns, stuffing the first into her tapestry bag before she stopped to take a deep breath. Then knowing she'd have to take far better care of her garments, she withdrew the dress and folded it neatly upon the bed.

Before she had completed her packing, Phillip strode through the door and slammed it soundly behind him. "Don't tell me for once I've managed to arrive before you could make good on one of your incessant and totally unexpected departures!"

Anna did not even pause in her preparations to leave. "You needn't thank me for saving your life once again since it was entirely my fault it was in danger. Did you manage to kill Clairbourne or only wound him?"

Startled by her calm preoccupation with her wardrobe, Phillip asked pointedly, "Which would you prefer?"

"What difference does that make since I am never consulted about any matter of any importance? Had I not been there this morning you'd be a dead man. Not one of those fools there had the sense to call foul when Charles turned to fire early and yet you did not even tell me you were going to challenge him this morning." No, indeed, he'd given her another remarkable night. That he could have made love to her so tenderly while hiding a secret of such magnitude appalled her.

"He was the one who issued the challenge, not I. Since women are not usually included in the spectators at such an event, it did not occur to me you'd care to attend."

Anna had never been so angry with him and her fiery glance glowed with a fierce light as she responded. "Oh, of course not, you are merely the man I love more dearly than life itself. Why would I wish to attend such a spectacle when you might very well have been slain right before my eyes!"

"Exactly." Phillip leaned back against the door, turned the key in the lock and slipped it into his back pocket without her seeing what he'd done. Knowing the bitterness of her mood, he thought such a precaution a wise one. "That's not a sight I'd want you to witness, Anna, not today or ever."

"Good, then we agree, that's why I am leaving. I've brought you nothing but grief, Phillip. Time and again your life has been at risk because of me and I'll not be the cause of your death when you are so precious to me. You are a successful man and I think you were a contented one until I upset everything with my endless schemes to escape the life my father had planned for me."

"Now, Anna—" Phillip began soothingly but she would not listen.

"No! Clairbourne's dead, isn't he? Just because he was too proud to let me go, and there will be no doubt in anyone's mind who killed him. You've got to hurry, get back to the *Angelina* and get away before you're arrested for his murder!"

Phillip shook his head wearily. "This has been a long morning already and it's barely dawn but I'm not going anywhere until we have a long talk, Anna. There was no time yesterday to solve all the problems which still face us but I'd hoped to find you in a reasonable mood today."

"It is useless for us to talk! I won't let you risk your life again and again for me, now go. Hurry before it is too late!"

"Perhaps you are right, talking is a waste of time with a woman so willful as you. You understand one thing only it seems and I'll try that instead!"

Anna recognized the gleam in his eyes for the undisguised lust it clearly was and cried out indignantly, "You wouldn't dare!" She tried to get around him but he blocked her way, his defiant stance as proud as his deep blue glance and she knew she'd never be able to reach the door. She looked back over her shoulder wondering if she'd be killed if she leapt out the window and Phillip seized that instant of inattention to grab her tightly around the waist and half drag, half carry her over to the bed where he tossed her down and quickly stretched out beside her, his right leg covering both of hers so she couldn't roll away and elude him. He caught her wrists and held them firmly in his left hand while he used his right to turn her face toward him. She was furious with him again, as usual, he thought suddenly. Her golden eyes were filled with a raging hostility. He was thoroughly sick of their constant fights. He'd proved nothing again but that he was the stronger, a lesson she'd learned long ago which mattered little and he was disgusted with himself for not being more clever. But since she was in his arms he'd not waste that opportunity to further his cause.

In no great hurry now, Phillip lowered his mouth to Anna's throat, nuzzling her playfully with light kisses, enticing her to respond but she turned away, pretending to ignore his lavish affection until she could no longer catch her breath. He released her then, letting his hand glide slowly over her trembling body removing the borrowed garments which hindered his caress. He found her creamy skin flushed with excitement, her golden tan holding a delicate blush he thought most appealing and his kiss grew tender as his lips slid over

513

her lightly freckled cheek before seeking her lips, drawing her with enchanting sweetness into the passion he could no longer wait to express.

Giving up all pretense of composure, the pounding of her heart belying her forced calm, Anna lifted her arms to draw Phillip closer, her anger forgotten in the pleasure of his easy loving. His kiss delighted her now and she slipped her hands under his shirt to hold him more tightly. She wanted to touch him, to hold him near, to be certain he'd escaped all harm that morning and he responded readily to her affection by hastily casting aside his clothing so she might brush his warm skin with her lips as well as her fingertips. He strengthened his embrace then, nearly crushing her delicate body with the force of his devotion before he relaxed to enfold her in a delicious warmth, cradling her in his arms as he deepened his kiss, savoring the joy of her graceful surrender with a gladness that filled his heart with renewed hope. She was truly his woman now, only his and the tremor of excitement which shivered through her slender limbs flooded his senses with the same tantalizing spark. They had never been closer, their fiery spirits searing their tanned bodies with the heat of their passion until they were truly one being rather than two, their emotions blending desire with need into so perfect a match they rose to the heights of the shared ecstasy that is the most precious gift of love. Shaken to their very souls by the beauty of their love, they lay with their limbs entwined, each so comfortable in the other's embrace neither wanted to see that wonderful closeness end.

With Anna now lying so contentedly in his arms, Phillip hated to draw away. He covered her pretty face with light kisses before he whispered, "Do I have your full attention now?"

"Was that all you wanted?" Anna asked coyly. He had tricked her again, she realized, for she'd expected his most passionate anger and he'd overcome her resistance with the sweetest of affections. No matter what his mood, making love with him held a beauty she would always treasure and her smile widened to a delighted grin.

"To start, it will do." He kissed her again then with a slow caress of his lips before he asked the question that had plagued him for nearly a day. "I know how dearly you love me. Why would you have married Clairbourne and considered suicide preferable to coming to me for the ten thousand pounds he demanded? Did you not trust me to pay it?"

As Anna looked up, his finely drawn features blurred behind a veil of tears until only the shimmering blue of his eyes remained. "It was not a matter of trust, but of what would be best for you. Just as you wanted only the best for me when you thought you would always be blind and would no longer consider our marriage a possibility."

Shocked by the sincerity of her response, Phillip drew away and hastily pulled on his britches. "You are an amazing woman, Anna, truly unique, but that answer makes no sense whatsoever. Condemning you to spend your life with an invalid and troubling me for no more than money are two entirely different alternatives, but we've no more time to explore the error in your thinking now. I want you to wear the suit you wore to the trial yesterday. I'll send Rose so you can bathe and dress quickly as there is little time to lose."

515

Anna heard him unlock the door before he left but she continued to lie dejectedly upon the bed until she realized his life could well depend on the haste with which she dressed. When Rose arrived to prepare a bath, she spent no more than five minutes in the tub scrubbing her skin roughly with perfumed soap before climbing out to dry off and dress in the attractive beige suit she'd been told to wear. Her hair shone with the glow of health and she pinned the attractive hat atop her curls before bidding Rose a hasty goodbye and knocking on Phillip's door.

Phillip stood before a small mirror, a towel draped across his bare shoulder as he finished shaving. "Ready? I'll be with you in a minute. Just sit down and wait for me."

"Couldn't you do that later? There's no time to lose you said and—"

"Oh, sit down and hush, Anna. I won't keep you waiting much longer."

Perching primly on the edge of the closest chair, Anna regarded Phillip with a curious glance. He'd come dangerously close to being shot in the back that morning but his hand was steady as he drew his razor up his throat and she turned away, unable to watch him when her thoughts were so frightening. He was far too distracting a sight no matter what his activity. She fidgeted nervously until he finished and put on a clean shirt. "Now, may we go please? I don't want to remain for another minute here in New Orleans."

"That's understandable since the perils are nearly constant here. But the weather is clear, your health seems to be excellent, and after a brief stop at the courthouse I don't think we'll have any further legal worries."

"What?" Anna leapt to her feet. "Do you plan to just flaunt the fact you killed Charles this morning? Is your conceit so great that you think you can get away with that?"

"I'm not in the least bit conceited, Anna, but let's just see what happens, shall we?" Taking her bag he escorted her down the stairs and out to the judge's waiting carriage. He studied her expression silently as they rode along but explained nothing until they'd entered Judge Sanchez's chambers. The man rose to greet them, smiling warmly.

"Why don't you sit down, Lady Thorson. There is a document I believe I must witness before we proceed to the real reason for your visit."

Anna glanced furtively at Phillip, certain the judge had no idea what had happened to Charles that morning but his calm manner did not reassure her. The two men talked about the city's continuing efforts to recover from the hurricane while she did no more than count the passing of the minutes in her head, hoping they would still be able to escape the city before the most horrible of fates overtook them. When Charles walked through the door she gasped so sharply she nearly choked and coughed so violently Phillip had to come to her side to pat her back lightly. "Please excuse me, gentlemen, I had not expected to see Lord Clairbourne here. Perhaps you'll allow me to wait outside."

"There's no need for that, Anna. I promise to behave myself." Turning to the judge, Charles handed over an envelope containing a single sheet of his crested stationery with a few short sentences. "Will this be acceptable to you, sir? If so, I'll sign it."

Etienne read the note quickly. "Yes, this resolves the

question of your supposed marriage to Lady Thorson and you are free to take another bride should you so desire."

"Never!" Charles promised vehemently. He signed the brief statement, then turned to Phillip. "I have the money, the sum of ten thousand pounds, all my life is worth apparently." Withdrawing a second envelope from his coat pocket he placed it in the captain's hands, then stepped back. Having been humiliated so thoroughly that morning had left him a changed man. His manner was subdued, all trace of his former arrogance gone.

Handing the envelope back to him, Phillip explained, "This is for Anna, please give it to her instead."

When the earl gave her the envelope, Anna exclaimed in surprise, "What a remarkable coincidence, Charles, for I believe this is precisely the sum I owe to you. Please take it with my best wishes for your future." Anna thrust the envelope back into his hands without bothering to look inside but he turned to be certain Phillip would not object to her gesture.

"Anna is far more generous than I am, Clairbourne. I'd like that note her father signed as well. I'm certain you remembered to bring it." Phillip held out his hand, snapping his fingers impatiently as he did it.

A look of cold terror filled Charles's dark eyes as he fumbled through his pockets but at last he found the note and handed it over. "Surely you did not think that I would—"

"I think you're capable of any treachery and I'll not give you the means to embarrass Anna further. Should we ever meet again, which is an extremely unlikely possibility, I suggest you pretend we are strangers and I will do the same."

518

"With pleasure," Charles vowed firmly for if they never met again he would be greatly pleased. He hurried toward the door, fleeing with what was left of his dignity but Phillip called after him. "Yes?"

"I'd not have left your sons orphans, Charles. You're worth far more alive to them than you are dead to me. It's high time you stopped thinking solely of yourself and began to think of their welfare for a change."

Startled by that bit of advice, Charles only nodded curtly then left, closing the door softly behind himself as he went.

"I am going to pretend I have no idea what you two were discussing since I am an officer of the court and must report all cases of suspected wrongdoing," Etienne confided with a sly grin.

"Of course, I would not expect you to do otherwise," Phillip agreed amicably. "It is only a few minutes past noon but I expected my mate to meet us here. There may be a few others with him. They might have been stopped at the entrance of the building. I wonder if you would go and see if they've arrived."

"My pleasure, I will be no more than a moment." Nodding politely to Anna the judge left them alone to discuss whatever they desired in privacy.

As soon as the door closed behind the judge, Anna turned a fierce gaze upon Phillip, "That was cruel for you to let me believe Charles was dead. Why is it so impossible for you to confide in me?"

Phillip tapped her father's note upon his palm as he smiled. "We are both too proud, Anna, too proud by far but I want to name our first son after your father."

Anna looked away, too ashamed of the way the man had treated her to agree. "I'd rather not. I would prefer any name to his."

Slipping the note into his pocket, Phillip crossed quickly to her side and, taking her hands gently in his, pulled her up into his arms. "Had it not been for his passion for gambling, he would not have been able to arrange such a fine marriage for you. Charles can be very charming at times and doubtless your father was attracted to his wealth and thought him a fine prospect for you. It would not surprise me to learn he'd lost to him on purpose."

Anna's tawny eyes grew wide with surprise at that thought. "Really, Phillip, you didn't know him. His luck was usually dreadful but he never thought of quitting until he had no more to lose."

"Anna, had Charles not sent me to fetch you, how would we have ever met?" He raised his fingertips to the soft curls which brushed her cheek, then leaned down to give her a sweet kiss. "Your father was the cleverest of men in my opinion and I insist we name that baby you won't admit you're carrying after him."

A slow smile lit Anna's face with a radiant glow. "Oh, Phillip, if only I could remember him as fondly as I did instead of—"

"I am right, Anna, I know I am." He knew he could convince her of anything given enough time and he promised himself he'd restore her father's memory to its rightful place in her heart no matter what the truth of his character might have been.

When at last he released her, Anna lifted her hands to her flushed cheeks. Knowing how brightly she was blushing she was embarrassed to think others were coming. "Why is Jamie coming here, or any of the others?"

"I need someone to be my best man, and since we need

witnesses I told him to bring whomever would like to come."

"You mean we're getting married now, here?" Anna looked around the well-appointed office, trying to estimate how many sailors it would hold.

"The judge is willing to perform a civil ceremony. Do you have some objection? State it now so we can argue about it before he returns."

"No, he is a very sympathetic person. I do not object to him. It is only that I fear I shall make the very worst of wives for you."

Phillip laced his fingers behind her back to draw her near. "Jean Paul and I had a long conversation yesterday. The Louisiana Territory is enormous; it will surely prosper and those of us willing to work hard can not fail to be successful. I plan to sell the *Angelina* and—"

"What?" Anna was astonished he'd even consider such a thing. "But, Phillip, you can't sell your ship, you simply can't, not when you love sailing so!"

"That I do," Phillip admitted readily. "But I love you more, Anna. Boats are needed on the river and clever captains as well. We can have a real home, as large a farm as you want to manage and I will never have to be away for long."

Anna's shock was understandable and she tried to draw away as her eyes filled with tears but he wouldn't release her. "I don't want you to sell the *Angelina* for me, Phillip. I'd never ask that of you, please don't sell her for me."

"She is no more than an elegant barge, just wood and canvas, Anna. I do not love her nearly as well as I love you. Now what must I do to convince you of that?" The confusion in her gaze was easy to read and instantly he knew why she'd married Charles. He'd once told her the *Angelina* was all he'd ever loved and she'd obviously remembered that remark all too well. He'd not point out how greatly she had underestimated his devotion when he would have the rest of his life to win her trust. "I was wrong, Anna, I should not have been so wrapped up in my blindness that I refused your love, and you must never again allow any problem to overwhelm you so that you refuse mine. We must learn to depend upon one another from now on, to trust our love to survive any test. Well, answer me, what must I do to convince you I'll be the most devoted of husbands?"

When he glanced toward the door and then down at the small sofa Anna laughed and shook her head. "Oh, no, Phillip, I'll not begin our honeymoon before the wedding!"

"If the judge does not hurry you will have no choice, my beauty!" Phillip lowered his mouth to hers, remembering all the kisses they'd shared with the fondest of memories. He had waited years to make her his wife and a few more minutes wouldn't matter when he could spend them with her in his arms.

Anna relaxed against him, wanting so desperately to believe their future would be a happy and tranquil one, yet she dared not tempt fate with more than a plea for the next few minutes. Then suddenly they were surrounded by their friends; Jamie and John, Jean Paul and Michael, all the crew of the *Angelina* seemed to have crowded into the room and she had to shout as she reached up to speak to the man she loved. "We shouldn't sell the *Angelina*, Phillip, not ever. We simply can't for she is too much a part of us to ever let go."

Phillip sighed slowly as he waited for the judge to find

his book and begin. Anna was the most extraordinary woman ever born but he knew they were going to spend their entire lives entangled in endless debates. Yet that prospect did not trouble him in the slightest since he now knew there were no longer any secrets to keep them apart. He gave her a warm hug and winked slyly. "Just hush, Anna, hush."

When she looked up at him then, an impish smile lit her incredible amber eyes with the sweetness of honey and he thought himself the luckiest man ever born to have won such a beauty for his bride. He knew then she was right. He'd never sell the *Angelina* when their destinies were so firmly entwined with that of the magnificent ship. Someday soon they'd return to the paradise they'd found on the small island in the Caribbean. As he recalled the sun-filled days they'd spent in each other's arms, the scene in the crowded office disappeared from his view to be replaced in his mind with the memory of Anna's devoted loving, the vision of the sapphire blue sea's bright sparkle and the scent of the jasmine's seductive perfume on the warm Jamaican wind. That intoxicating fragrance seemed to swirl about them as they repeated their vows and Phillip could not suppress a satisfied grin, knowing the angel of his dreams was at long last his wife. He promised himself she would never escape him again, or ever want to try.

EXCITING BESTSELLERS FROM ZEBRA

STORM TIDE   **(1230, \$3.75)**
by Patricia Rae
In a time when it was unladylike to desire one man, defiant, flame-haired Elizabeth desired two! And while she longed to be held in the strong arms of a handsome sea captain, she yearned for the status and wealth that only the genteel doctor could provide—leaving her hopelessly torn amidst passion's raging STORM TIDE. . . .

PASSION'S REIGN   **(1177, \$3.95)**
by Karen Harper
Golden-haired Mary Bullen was wealthy, lovely and refined—and lusty King Henry VIII's prize gem! But her passion for the handsome Lord William Stafford put her at odds with the Royal Court. Mary and Stafford lived by a lovers' vow; one day they would be ruled by only the crown of PASSION'S REIGN.

HEIRLOOM   **(1200, \$3.95)**
by Eleanora Brownleigh
The surge of desire Thea felt for Charles was powerful enough to convince her that, even though they were strangers and their married was a fake, fate was playing a most subtle trick on them both: Were they on a mission for President Teddy Roosevelt—or on a crusade to realize their own passionate desire?

LOVESTONE   **(1202, \$3.50)**
by Deanna James
After just one night of torrid passion and tender need, the dark-haired, rugged lord could not deny that Moira, with her precious beauty, was born to be a princess. But how could he grant her freedom when he himself was a prisoner of her love?

Available wherever paperbacks are sold, or order direct from the Publisher. Send cover price plus 50¢ per copy for mailing and handling to Zebra Books, 475 Park Avenue South, New York, N.Y. 10016. DO NOT SEND CASH.

SENSATIONAL SAGAS!

WHITE NIGHTS, RED DAWN   (1277, $3.95)
by Frederick Nolan
Just as Tatiana was blossoming into womanhood, the Russian
Revolution was overtaking the land. How could the stunning
aristocrat sacrifice her life, her heart and her love for a cause she
had not chosen? Somehow, she would prevail over the red dawn
—and carve a destiny all her own!

IMPERIAL WINDS   (1324, $3.95)
by Priscilla Napier
From the icebound Moscow river to the misty towers of the
Kremlin, from the Bolshevick uprising to the fall of the
Romanovs, Daisy grew into a captivating woman who would
courageously fight to escape the turmoil of the raging IM-
PERIAL WINDS.

KEEPING SECRETS   (1291, $3.75)
by Suzanne Morris
It was 1914, the winds of war were sweeping the globe, and Elec-
tra was in the eye of the hurricane—rushing headlong into a marriage with the wealthy Emory Cabot. Her days became a carousel
of European dignitaries, rich investors, and worldly politicians.
And her nights were filled with mystery and passion . . . .